"Lori Benton has wr‌⁣ g the Revolutionary War period. The well-drawn characters leap off the pages and take up residence in readers' hearts, making history come alive. Her research is monumental, yielding a vibrant story that will keep you glued to the pages and eagerly awaiting her next novel."

— Lauraine Snelling, best-selling author of the Red River of the North saga

Praise for
The Wood's Edge

"Meticulously researched. Alive and engaging. *The Wood's Edge* is a journey through the footsteps of America's formative years, with characters so wonderfully complex and a story of redemption so deep, only Lori Benton could tell it. I was transfixed from the first absorbing page to the last."

— Kristy Cambron, author of *The Butterfly and the Violin* and *A Sparrow in Terezin*

"From the opening scene to the last line of the book, I was captivated by *The Wood's Edge*. Rich in history, with characters to weep for and to cheer for, this is a novel that will linger in my heart for a long time to come."

— Robin Lee Hatcher, best-selling author of *Love Without End* and *Whenever You Come Around*

"Open *The Wood's Edge* and see the secret. Then, hold it—page after page—breathless. Rich in history and lush in story, Lori Benton's novel brings to life a cast of characters in a tale that spans two generations, two cultures, two worlds. In an era underrepresented in Christian historical fiction, Benton takes on the challenge of presenting the message of faith in its purest form. Love, grace, rebirth."

— ALLISON PITTMAN, author of *On Shifting Sand*

SUMMERSET LIBRARY
BRENTWOOD 94513

A
FLIGHT
of
ARROWS

Books by Lori Benton

The Pursuit of Tamsen Littlejohn

Burning Sky

The Pathfinders Series

The Wood's Edge

A FLIGHT of ARROWS

THE PATH FINDERS
BOOK TWO

LORI BENTON

CHRISTY AWARD WINNER

WATERBROOK
PRESS

A Flight of Arrows
Published by WaterBrook Press
12265 Oracle Boulevard, Suite 200
Colorado Springs, Colorado 80921

All Scripture quotations and paraphrases are taken from the King James Version.

The characters and events in this book are fictional, and any resemblance to actual persons or events is coincidental.

Trade Paperback ISBN 978-1-60142-734-2
eBook ISBN 978-1-60142-735-9

Copyright © 2016 by Lori Benton

Cover design by Kristopher K. Orr

All rights reserved. No part of this book may be reproduced or transmitted in any form or by any means, electronic or mechanical, including photocopying and recording, or by any information storage and retrieval system, without permission in writing from the publisher.

Published in the United States by WaterBrook Multnomah, an imprint of the Crown Publishing Group, a division of Penguin Random House LLC, New York.

WaterBrook® and its deer colophon are registered trademarks of Penguin Random House LLC.

Library of Congress Cataloging-in-Publication Data
Names: Benton, Lori, author.
Title: A flight of arrows : a novel / Lori Benton.
Description: Colorado Springs, Colorado : WaterBrook Press, 2016. | Series: The pathfinders
Identifiers: LCCN 2015044917 | ISBN 9781601427342 (softcover) | ISBN 9781601427359
   (electronic)
Subjects: LCSH: Brothers—Fiction. | Frontier and pioneer life—Fiction. | BISAC: FICTION /
   Christian / Historical. | FICTION / Christian / Romance. | FICTION / Romance / Historical.
   | GSAFD: Christian fiction. | Historical fiction. | Love stories.
Classification: LCC PS3602.E6974 F58 2016 | DDC 813/.6—dc23 LC record available at
   http://lccn.loc.gov/2015044917

Printed in the United States of America
2016—First Edition

10 9 8 7 6 5 4 3 2 1

For all the warriors who stand between, in body
and in Spirit, through every generation.

And for Ashley, Tyler, and Graham,
Vladimir and Zarina,
Zac, Bruce, and Eli.
Bright arrows of my sisters.

As arrows are in the hand of a mighty man; so are children of the youth. Happy is the man that hath his quiver full of them: they shall not be ashamed, but they shall speak with the enemies in the gate.

— PSALM 127:4–5

Look and listen for the welfare of the whole people and have always in view not only the present but also the coming generations, even those whose faces are yet beneath the surface of the ground—the unborn of the future Nation.

— *Gayanashagowa Haudenosaunee,*
THE GREAT BINDING LAW OF THE
IROQUOIS CONFEDERACY

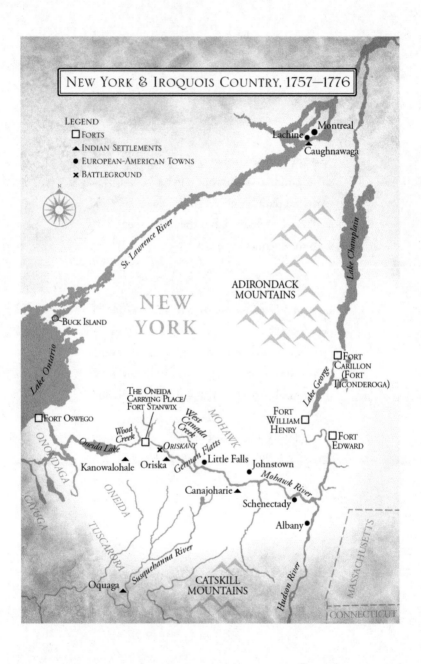

NEW YORK & IROQUOIS COUNTRY, 1757–1776

LEGEND
□ FORTS
▲ INDIAN SETTLEMENTS
● EUROPEAN-AMERICAN TOWNS
✗ BATTLEGROUND

N

Montreal
Lachine
Caughnawaga

St. Lawrence River

ADIRONDACK
MOUNTAINS

Lake Champlain

NEW
YORK

BUCK ISLAND

Lake Ontario

Fort
Carillon
(Fort
Ticonderoga)

Lake George

THE ONEIDA
CARRYING PLACE/
FORT STANWIX

West
Canada
Creek

MOHAWK

Fort
William
Henry

Fort
Edward

FORT OSWEGO

Wood
Creek

Oneida Lake

ORISKANY

German Flatts

Fort

ONONDAGA

Kanowalohale   Oriska

Little Falls   Johnstown

Mohawk River

ONEIDA

Canajoharie

Schenectady

CAYUGA

TUSCARORA

Susquehanna River

Albany

MASSACHUSETTS

Oquaga

CATSKILL
MOUNTAINS

Hudson River

CONNECTICUT

OCTOBER 1776–JULY 1777
THE MOHAWK VALLEY, NEW YORK
MONTREAL, QUEBEC
LAKE ONTARIO

Satahuhsíyost—Listen. Open your ears to a story I will tell you. It is the story of a warrior, and some of it you know. But you do not know the whole of it. Bear with me a while and you will.

Are you listening? *Iyo*—good. Here is a thing I have learned. It is not in a man's nature to forgive. A little wrong, the small ills of another's inflicting . . . maybe a man can bury that hatchet. Maybe that hatchet will stay buried and forgiveness will root itself in his soul and grow up tall and strong like the Great Tree of Peace. But forgiving is a hard thing, and even great trees topple.

The wrong done to the warrior of whom I speak was not a small thing. He had a son taken, on the day of that son's birth, as the child lay beside the one born-together with him. That son was taken up by the hands of a redcoat officer who left his dead child in place of the living. When the warrior learned of it, darkness entered his heart. He wanted his son back, but some believed he wanted more to kill the redcoat who took him—and all whom that redcoat loved. To hang their scalps over the door of his wife's lodge. To wipe all memory of that redcoat from the earth upon which they both went. He cherished his hatred as a tender shoot of corn coming up from the ground. He lusted for it to ripen into revenge, craved it like food for the belly.

What did that hate lead to? You may well ask it. It led to raging. It led to despair and much weeping. It led to jugs of trader's rum emptied *into that pit of pain. It led to a lonely son—that one not taken—who came to fear his father, to feel shame when that warrior failed to care for his family. It led to that warrior's wife being struck down in the field where she grew her family's corn by the hand of this one who could not forgive or forget the taking of his firstborn. When she could stand again on her feet, the woman put that warrior and his belongings out of her lodge. He lost everything. Not just the one son, but the other also. He lost his home. His wife. His heart. His manhood.*

It is a thing to think long about, the consequences of one act that follow many down the paths they take to escape it, driving them like the lashes of a gauntlet. But listen.

After that warrior's wife put him out of her lodge, he did a thing that raised the brows of all who knew him. He went to the missionary, the Jesus-sachem who lived among them, and he asked this man how to go back and undo the bad things he had done in the darkness of his rage against the redcoat. How to go back and reclaim the good things he had squandered. He hoped for a charm, a prayer to turn back the circle of time, but Creator has not given such power even to holy men. Only He is Master of Time, standing with one foot outside the circle and one in it. And so this warrior did not get the answer he sought. There was no changing what was done. The way to walk a right path from that point was to repent of sin—those were the missionary's words—and to ask for Creator Father's forgiveness through the blood of Jesus-on-the-cross. Those words sent the warrior away with a heart of stone, blind to his need for forgiveness and so unable to forgive. In his soul he was as weak as the newborn son who haunted him, giving him no peace, though that son was no more an infant but a boy living across an ocean, raised by a woman not his mother, among a people not his own.

Becoming a white man in his heart.

1

October 11, 1776
Aubrey farm, near Schenectady

*W*rapped in a shawl and drawn by the heartstrings, Anna Doyle let herself out of the white stone farmhouse before anyone else had awakened and strode briskly down a cart track past the harvested cornfields, headed for the strip of mist-draped woodland marking the creek near the farm's western boundary. It was her birthday, and the list of absent people she wished to share it with had lengthened, stretching those heartstrings to near unbearable strain.

North to her papa, Reginald Aubrey, gone from them these past two months. West to Two Hawks, the love of her heart, roaming forest paths for his Oneida people and for the garrison at Fort Stanwix.

Farthest of all to William, her brother, somewhere in Quebec—or so they thought. No one could yet be certain about William.

They weren't the only missing ones tugging at the cords of her heart that chill morning that sounded of geese calling and smelled of wood smoke and the earthy, sorrowing scent that was autumn in the Mohawk Valley. Anna crossed the creek on the new footlog Two Hawks had set in place and pressed on into the misty, golden wood beyond, thinking of a woman whose face she couldn't recall, whose name she didn't know.

The woman who'd been her mother for the first months of her life.

"Mama," she murmured, emerging into a clearing not far from the wood's edge. It was a name she'd never called another woman, though more than one had stood in a mother's place for her: Maura Doyle, housekeeper, surrogate grandmother; Lydia van Bergen, friend and mentor; and lately Two Hawks's extraordinary mother, Good Voice. But what of the woman who birthed her? How old had she been that August day Fort William Henry fell and she escaped the siege only to die at the hands of French-allied Indians on the road to Fort Edward? Anna's own twenty years? Younger?

Jerking her thoughts from the terror of her mother's last hours on earth, Anna crossed the clearing toward the hill that rose beyond. The creek tumbled from rocks and rhododendron at its crown, creating a little waterfall beside a stone shelf midway up.

She'd brought her basket from the house, but it wasn't for gleaning medicinal herbs that she'd crossed the creek. Two Hawks's absence had become too great an ache to bear, shut up in the house. Since the summer he'd come and gone, pinging like a shuttlecock between her world and his, scouting for his people, reporting what he learned along a chain of communication that began with Reverend Kirkland at their town of Kanowalohale and ended with General George Washington and General Philip Schuyler—and, she hoped, Brigadier General Benedict Arnold, with whom Papa was currently employed building a navy fleet at Skenesborough, on the southern shore of Lake Champlain.

Unless Papa was on his way home. He'd left them in early August, promising to return before her birthday. So had Two Hawks promised. He'd been gone a fortnight. As for William . . . three months had passed with no word from him at all.

She'd meant to stop at the waterfall. Instead she left her basket on the stone shelf and, gathering her petticoat, began the rocky climb to the little cave behind its rhododendron screen. Two Hawks had discovered the cave when they were still children, one of those times he'd waited days for her to cross the creek and find him.

So much waiting. Anna pushed aside the boughs shielding the cave's narrow mouth. Sweeping her heavy braid over her shoulder to prevent its snagging, she slipped inside, reminding herself that these weeks of waiting—for Two Hawks, Papa, news of William—paled before the years of waiting Two Hawks and his parents had endured.

Inside the chill cave, light filtered through rock fissures in a ceiling high enough for her to stand erect. Looking around, she felt a rush of disappointment at its emptiness. What had she expected? Two Hawks had never left behind evidence of occupation, save the blackened spot where over the years he'd built small fires. Not even his presence lingered.

"Jonathan." The cave's confines muffled the name Two Hawks had taken at his baptism, when he was just fifteen. She waited, hoping, but there was no comfort here. She was turning to leave the forsaken little cave when a clatter of pebbles without reached her ears.

"Bear's Heart?"

She sprang back from the cave's opening with a shriek, as startled as if the rattling stones had spoken her name—the name Two Hawks had given her. Then she tore her petticoat—and lost her cap—in the rush to get out into the chilly morning where Two Hawks crouched among the rocks, peering in at her. He stood as she launched herself into his arms—arm rather; the other held his rifle, the butt of which he planted among the rocks to brace himself. She leaned back in his embrace, taking in the sight of him: dark eyes alight with pleasure in her eagerness to greet him; long black hair shiny even in the dimming mist; skin bronzed from the sun; and his mouth, wide and supple and smiling down at her.

"How did you know I'd be here?"

He nodded toward the waterfall below. "I saw your basket. I knew it did not bring itself to this place."

"Clever." She cupped the back of his head, pulled his face down, and kissed him—too happy for restraint. She felt surprise jolt through him before he returned the kiss, his mouth warm and urgent. Her thoughts spun away in heady delight that he was there, holding her, until he pulled back from their embrace. In his eyes was a struggle.

"You know we cannot do this. We agreed we would not."

"Not under Papa's roof." She reached for him again, heart pounding with wanting. And warning. "We aren't under his roof. We're under God's sky."

"Anna Catherine . . ." Two Hawks's protest faltered when she smoothed her hand over his chest, warm under her palm even through his shirt. He closed his eyes, as though reaching for strength.

They'd had need of strength these past months, with Two Hawks's parents living at the farm while Stone Thrower's leg, broken by a musket ball, healed. The strain had been almost unbearable before Papa left to answer the call for carpenters at Skenesborough. Worse for Anna was his censure of her love for Two Hawks—unwisely voiced the night she confronted him about William's true identity. They'd steered clear of the subject since, but Papa's disapproval had been so thick before he left that Mrs. Doyle might have sliced it and served it up for supper.

She struggled to keep her voice light, teasing. "I've missed you so. Have you not missed me?"

Two Hawks took her hand in his, white and small against the fingers curled around it, pressing it against his chest.

"Not at all," he said.

She caught the echoing glint of teasing in his eyes before he captured her mouth again with his, giving her his true answer. Then there was nothing beyond the meeting of their lips, the desire building inside her, and the thought of the cave that lanced through her like a fiery arrow. It would be chilly, far from comfortable, but he'd a blanket tied at his back. Of course they mustn't, but . . .

Two Hawks stepped back, letting go her hand. "You are thinking of that cave. Stop."

"How did you . . . ?" Her face flamed as his eyes spoke to hers. He'd been thinking of it too. They should leave it, get far away.

Neither moved.

"You've been scouting?" she asked, because if she couldn't be in his arms, then she wanted to know everything he'd seen and done for the past fortnight. Because she wanted to put off going back to the farm, where many eyes would be upon them and they must go shy of each other for fear the merest telling glance would strain forbearance.

The Doyles had promised Papa to keep an eye on them.

"Much scouting," he said. "I was with Ahnyero—the blacksmith, Thomas Spencer. And with Skenandoah."

"Skenandoah. He's a war chief, yes? An old man?"

Two Hawks laughed, a soft sound in his throat. "Never let him hear you call him so, but yes, that one has seen seventy winters."

Despite their light words, Anna's insides had seized at his mention of "much scouting." So far Two Hawks had never crossed paths with violence on these missions into the wilds. None that he'd admitted to. "You didn't have to fight, did you?"

"Let us go and see my parents. I will tell all of it once." Two Hawks took her hand to lead her down from the rocks, then hesitated, gazing at her head. "Did you have a cap?" She retrieved it from the rhododendron that had snagged it off her head but didn't put it on. Two Hawks put a hand on her shoulder, his expression grave. "You must not come here again alone. Even here at the wood's edge is not safe now."

She blinked up at him, overwhelmed with loss. Of all the places on the farm, that clearing, that creek, that cave held her sweetest memories.

"I came here this morning to feel near you. I'm glad I did, because here you are, and we've had these moments together, stolen though they be."

Two Hawks drew her close, pressing a kiss to her forehead. "One day we will no more steal them," he told her, the words suffused with longing. "Father in Heaven—and yours on earth—willing."

2

*W*e picked up the trail of the spies near Cherry Valley and followed them back the way they came, into the west."

Two Hawks sat at the table in the Aubreys' kitchen, giving his account of the past half moon to those gathered to hear it, but inwardly he was agreeing with Anna Catherine. It was good they'd had those moments alone at their meeting. With her father's Irish servants, the Doyles, and his own parents watching him, listening closely to all he said, he was finding it hard to know where to put his gaze. It wanted to feast on Anna Catherine. He summoned the will to make it fast.

"We found them camped on our border," he said, casting his mind back to the morning he'd crouched on a ridge while a gray dawn teased color from the surrounding forest and rain pattered through yellow leaves with a noise like shaking gourd rattles. At the foot of the ridge, a clearing stretched, hummocky with grasses. Beyond was the camp of the spies they had tracked . . .

The icy rain had needled his face as he'd hunkered into his blanket and tried to mimic the indifference of his companions. Like Two Hawks they were *Onyota'a:ka*—Oneida—and scouts. They were also warriors, a title Two Hawks, at nineteen summers, couldn't claim in truth. One of them was Skenandoah, elderly war chief of the Wolf Clan, still hale enough to watch their western border for British spies. Those spies came to learn what the Americans were doing in their forts along the Mohawk River or in settlements dotting the wilderness around it. Settlements like Cherry Valley, the place the third scout called home. He was much younger than Skenandoah but older than Two Hawks. To his Oneida mother's Wolf Clan he was Ahnyero; to his white father he was Thomas Spencer.

During the previous moon had come word that the loyalist Sir John Johnson, who'd fled to Montreal that summer past, had landed in the west at the lake fort of Oswego with hundreds of Tories bent on wreaking vengeance against the rebel neighbors who drove them out. Ahnyero had traveled deep into neighboring Onondaga land to see if this was true. It was not. Then word came from Ahnyero's kin at Cherry Valley. Someone was spying there, lurking in the mountains. This rumor proved true, which was why they huddled on that ridge waiting for the spies—British-allied Mohawks—to break camp and continue their westward journey.

Two Hawks had grown impatient with their passive watching. Why not capture these spies, take them to Colonel Dayton at Fort Stanwix? Make them tell the whereabouts of Sir John Johnson and his Royal New York regiment, which wasn't at Oswego making ready to attack but *was* somewhere?

Make them tell where Two Hawks's brother could be found. The last anyone knew of William Aubrey, he'd fled north to join Johnson's regiment of angry, homeless Tories.

They were two-born-together, he and William, though William had been born looking as white as their mother, Two Hawks brown-skinned like their father. Stolen by a redcoat officer the day of their birth, Two Hawks's twin had remained lost to them for years, until a chance meeting alerted them to his whereabouts . . . only to find William gone out of reach again, taken across the great water to a place called Wales by the woman who thought herself his mother. A terrible loss to bear a second time. Until Creator gave someone to heal that pain. Anna Catherine . . .

Crouched in the chill and wet, Two Hawks set his teeth with longing. Anna Catherine had a way of filling up his mind, driving out other concerns. Even his concern for William, who had returned from Wales and learned at last who he was. Not the son of Reginald Aubrey, a Welshman, but the son of Good Voice of the Turtle Clan and the Bear Clan warrior Stone Thrower.

He-Is-Taken of the *Onyota'a:ka*.

Beside him Ahnyero stirred, the cloud of his breath thickening. Two Hawks's gaze flew sharp across the clearing. Movement was visible through the rain-darkened trees. The Mohawk spies were breaking camp. He leaned toward Ahnyero, blankets brushing. "Do we follow?"

Ahnyero's mouth tightened. "Wait."

The warriors across the clearing moved out in file, headed west into the forest of the Onondaga.

"Let them go," came the creaky voice of Skenandoah. "We have seen they watched the fort at Cherry Valley. We know it is of interest to them."

Two Hawks could not hold back protest. "Grandfather, they will tell what they saw in Cherry Valley."

"They will tell that whether or not we catch them," the old warrior replied, meeting Two Hawks's impatient gaze. "They are *Kanien'kehá:ka*. We will not raise weapons against brothers. The Council fire at Onondaga burns. The Great Peace holds."

The Great Law of Peace had bound the nations of the Haudenosaunee for many lives of grandfathers going back, even through the last war the whites waged with each other, French against English. All the nations—Mohawk, Oneida, Onondaga, Cayuga, Seneca, Tuscarora—hoped it would hold through this one between the Americans and their Great Father the King, though not all had the same vision for that hope. While the Oneidas and some Tuscaroras felt strong ties to the Americans, the Mohawks were for the British, who were doing their best to entice the western nations—Senecas, Cayugas, Onondagas—to side with them.

"We still stand to the side in this fight," Ahnyero reminded him. "It isn't the time for taking prisoners. Or for killing."

Not yet. The unspoken words hung in the chilling dawn, heavy as the dripping foliage.

"Pray to Creator not ever. But now we will be watching Cherry Valley too. These spies were not careful enough. We are warned." Skenandoah pushed back the blanket from his head, baring the white scalp-lock that hung feathered from his crown. He was first to rise. "The preacher will want to know these rumors are true."

Two Hawks stood, spirits sinking. They were going back to Kanowalohale to make their report to their minister, Reverend Samuel Kirkland, who would send it in a letter to General Schuyler in the east and Colonel Dayton at Stanwix, the fort at the Carrying Place between the Mohawk River and Wood Creek. Going without the one thing Two Hawks hoped to gain, word on the whereabouts of Sir John Johnson. And William.

"I ask you both to return and tell Kirkland that these rumors are true ones," Ahnyero said. "I will press on—to Oswego, if that is where these spies are bound. I will go among them and learn if I can why they pay attention to Cherry Valley." Dressed in the quilled leggings and breechclout of a warrior, Ahnyero could pass among any gathering of Indians without drawing suspicion. "But whatever their business, we will watch for it, as our elder has said." He met Two Hawks's frustrated frown and his mouth curved just a little. "Be easy, brother. It is more likely I will find out what we need to know if I go alone. But I will also learn what I can of Johnson's regiment."

As Skenandoah and Ahnyero exchanged words of parting, Two Hawks felt the sting of the scout's unspoken words: he was too inexperienced a spy himself to go among the British or their allies. He voiced no protest, but when the old chief stepped away, he drew near Ahnyero again. "Before we part, I wish to speak to you about a thing."

"Your brother?" Ahnyero asked.

"No. Other things." Things like . . . how did a man live in two worlds without being torn apart in his soul? How did he find a path to the heart of a white man whose daughter he loved and wanted to make his wife? Ahnyero had done the first—he used the blacksmithing trade learned from his father to serve both peoples, moving across borders with a seeming ease that made Two Hawks grasp at hope and glimpse a future he might share with Anna Catherine. Perhaps he had some knowledge of the other.

Ahnyero snaked a hand from his blanket and gripped Two Hawks's shoulder. "The scouting does not end today. When we meet again, we will talk. For now, see our grandfather safe home."

Swallowing disappointment, Two Hawks glanced toward the old warrior already trudging up the ridge at their backs. "I think that one means never to need a young man looking after him."

The scout grinned, then left to follow the spies westward. Two Hawks watched him slip around the clearing's edge, never breaking cover.

"*O-kee-wa'h,* brother. My prayers go with you."

Ahnyero was right. They had time yet to talk about what weighed on Two Hawks's heart, because another thing needed to happen before he had a hope of becoming a man of two worlds: Anna Catherine's father was going to have to permit him to try.

"Ahnyero followed them from there," Two Hawks said, coming to the end of his recounting, every word of which Anna had hung upon, trying not to stare too much at his moving lips since Two Hawks was doing an admirable job of not allowing their gazes to meet. "And for now that is all I know."

His father, Stone Thrower, sat across the table from Anna, crutches propped nearby. Earlier, watching him come up from the barn where he'd been helping Mr. Doyle with the stock, Anna had realized he was ready to discard the props he'd needed the past few weeks. She'd also noticed the ease with which the two men now worked together. An understanding between Mr. Doyle and Two Hawks's father had formed during Papa's absence. An amazing development, since it was Mr. Doyle who'd shot him—in a misguided attempt to protect Papa.

Two Hawks met her gaze for the first time since entering the house. "If they could get as far as Cherry Valley, those spies, then to cross the Schoharie River and reach this farm unseen is no hard thing."

"And that settles it," Mrs. Doyle announced, Irish accent thick as the porridge in the bowl she plunked on the boards under Anna's nose. She set another in front of Two Hawks and stood back, hands on ample hips. "You'll not go across that creek alone again, Anna—never mind scourin' the countryside for your bits of leaves and grasses."

"But those spies *were* seen," Anna protested. "And left without harming anyone."

"This time," Stone Thrower said.

Two Hawks started to reach across the table toward her, then pulled his hand back. Only his dark eyes reached. "Do not cross the creek alone. You will make my heart easier if you don't. All our hearts," he added.

Seated at the end of the table, Mr. Doyle cleared his throat. Stone Thrower's spoon scraped his bowl. Two Hawks was waiting for a response from her, too much of his heart in his eyes. Warmth flooded Anna's cheeks. Reluctantly she nodded. "And there's no word of Sir John's regiment?"

Two Hawks shook his head. "I have no news of William. Yet."

Silence fell as Mrs. Doyle moved the kettle from the heat. Into that silence dropped the unvoiced question: What if Johnson's regiment was part of the force said to be ready to attack on Lake Champlain? The force General Arnold was meant to repel with his hastily assembled navy.

"It is your day, yes?"

Anna looked at Good Voice, who'd taken a seat beside her with porridge and tea, wearing a short gown and petticoat Mrs. Doyle had altered to fit. Her blue eyes held the same troubled uncertainty that twisted Anna's heart; still she smiled at Anna, who replied, "I'm twenty today. That sounds old to me."

"It is the oldest *you* have been, so to you it seems so." Two Hawks's mother stared at the food before her. "My son's return makes you glad?"

"It does." Only with his mother—and with Lydia—did Anna need not pretend her feelings for Two Hawks, and his for her, were anything but consuming. Good Voice, it turned out, had known of their love long before Anna met her. She seemed accepting of it, but sometimes Anna saw a shadow in the woman's eyes when she caught her son looking at Anna. "Stone Thrower seems ready to cast off those crutches. You'll be anxious to return to Kanowalohale?"

She'd lowered her voice to ask the question, but Stone Thrower overheard. "I could not run the distance as does this son of mine," he said, with an amused glance at Two Hawks. "But I am ready to make the journey."

"You'll go before the major returns?" Mr. Doyle inquired.

Stone Thrower shared a look across the table with Good Voice. "We will wait for Aubrey's return. A little longer."

As if on cue there came a knock at the kitchen-yard door. Joy flared in Anna's chest before she realized Papa wouldn't knock. The latch sounded and the door opened a few inches. Lydia van Bergen's capped head came into view.

"Good morning," she greeted one and all cheerily. "Mind if I join you?"

Anna rose as Lydia entered and enveloped her in an embrace chilled from her ride from town. Anna had lost count of the births she and Lydia, as midwives, had attended together and the hours spent working in the kitchen of Lydia's house inside Schenectady's old stockade—a kitchen transformed into an apothecary workshop. Though Lydia, daughter and widow of apothecaries, didn't claim the title in an official capacity, people came to her for the treatment of ailments beyond the parturient.

"Happiest of birthdays, my girl." Lydia held her by the shoulders to gaze at her with warm affection. At nearly thirty-two, Lydia was strikingly lovely with her black hair and blue eyes set against pale skin, her smile so wide it lit a room.

"Hang your cloak," Mrs. Doyle said from the hearth. "I've a serving o' porridge left in the kettle. Come. Sit you down and eat it."

"You must have been away afore dawn," Mr. Doyle said, unfolding his long frame from the table to make room.

"Nearly so." Lydia hung her cloak on a peg by the door but lingered there. "I've my mare hitched outside."

Mr. Doyle said, "You'll find her down to the barn when you want her."

Anna was halfway to the table when she realized Lydia still hadn't followed. She'd caught Mr. Doyle by the sleeve as he made to pass. He bent his lofty head to hear something she whispered into his whiskered ear. The old man appeared to stifle a grin, then nodded and went out the kitchen door.

Stone Thrower followed, forgetting his crutches.

"Have you news of Papa?" Anna asked, as Mrs. Doyle set out the porridge.

Lydia hovered at the door. "I went down to the Binne Kill last evening to speak to Captain Lang. No word yet, I'm afraid." Ephraim Lang was Papa's partner in the trade he did with the forts, settlements, and Indian towns upriver, facilitated by the bateaux Papa built at his boatyard on the Binne Kill, the town's riverfront. Captain Lang had stayed in Schenectady to look after the business in Papa's absence. "I'd hoped more than anything to bring you such news today. But since that isn't to be . . ."

Lydia turned toward the opening door. A large parcel wrapped in canvas was handed in to her by Mr. Doyle, and the door shut. Lydia carried the parcel to the table and stepped back, face alight with expectancy. "For you, Anna. And high time."

Anna trailed her, awash with surprise. "What is it?"

"Open it." Mrs. Doyle wore a smile so broad Anna guessed she was privy to whatever the contents might be. Two Hawks, Good Voice, Lydia, and Mrs. Doyle all watched as Anna untied the string, unwrapped the careful layers of canvas, and gasped.

"My own medical case? Truly?" The large square case was constructed of polished mahogany. Anna opened the lid to find four rows of glass bottles capped in pewter. The front rows were part of a section that opened at the center on side hinges to reveal multiple sets of drawers for ligaments, instruments, pillboxes, and more, each with a tiny brass knob. "Lydia . . . where did you find this?"

"Captain Lang had it in a shipment from Albany. It wasn't bespoke, so he said it was mine if I wanted it. It isn't new . . ."

"It's *perfect*." Anna opened the drawers. "And you've stocked it. Lydia, *thank you*."

While Lydia ate her porridge, Good Voice and Two Hawks examined the case with Anna, fingering the glass bottles, asking after their contents, until Two Hawks stifled a yawn. With the excitement of his return abated and food inside him, he was beginning to look as though he'd journeyed the night through—which, he'd admitted, he had.

"Go on up and sleep," she bid him softly while Lydia and Good Voice chatted over the medicines and Mrs. Doyle busied herself scraping bowls. He did so, headed for the room that once was William's, leaving her with a sleepy smile that all but melted her into a puddle of longing.

Good Voice rose to help Mrs. Doyle with her work—they planned a special dinner to celebrate Anna's birthday—leaving Lydia and Anna alone at the table.

Lydia studied her fondly. "I'm glad you like it. I'd hoped to tuck in a letter from Reginald before I wrapped it, if only one had come." Lydia longed for Papa in the way Anna longed for Two Hawks. Now at last there might be a chance for them, if Papa could find his way back from decades of regret and guilt that had raised so many walls around his heart.

"The day isn't over yet," Lydia added, visibly brightening.

Though her well of hope seemed bottomless, the day wore on and there came no sound of horse's hooves on the lane. Even if he hadn't come to terms with Stone Thrower and Good Voice's forgiveness, and his tolerance for Two Hawks was as fragile as ice, and he'd have brought those tensions with him had he walked into the room, Anna longed to feel Papa's arms around her, to kiss the scar that crossed his cheekbone, the one he'd taken in rescuing her, that marked the joining of their lives as father and daughter.

But would his homecoming only serve to drive Two Hawks away? Was she going to have to choose between them?

3

October 11, 1776
Lake Champlain

*R*eginald Aubrey had long believed his death would be by violence—at the hand of a particular Oneida warrior. Though violence *had* swept him from the deck of the gondola *Philadel-phia* into the frigid waters of Lake Champlain, where he struggled now to stay afloat, the warrior had had nothing to do with it.

Reginald had meant to return to Schenectady and face the terrible wrong he'd done that warrior and his wife. What he'd done instead—when it was made clear General Arnold's need for experienced sailors had grown as desperate as his need for ships, with the British advancing up the lake from Canada to meet the newly fledged American navy—was to board the last rigged galley as a volunteer. Experience Reginald Aubrey possessed, having piloted bateaux on the Mohawk River for years. And he could swim—a fortuitous skill given that, after six hours' roaring exchange of gunfire, he'd been blown clean off the *Philadelphia* and that worthy craft he'd helped construct on the stocks at Skenesborough was fast going down to the lake bottom.

The battle had commenced before noon, off the shore of Valcour Island. Dusk was falling now, and the troubled water Reginald tread slammed a cold through his bones like the pounding of the guns still firing above his head. Smoke lay thick over the lake, obscuring what view the rough chop allowed of the battered American fleet: hulls and masts splintered by shot; sails and rigging in tatters aloft. The galleys, *Washington,*

Trumbull. Arnold's flagship, *Congress.* The gondolas, *New Haven, Providence, Spitfire, Connecticut, Boston, New Jersey.* Others not seen since the battle's commencement. The schooner, *Royal Savage,* run aground on the southern tip of Valcour, its crew fled into the island's woods to escape the British guns and the Indians in their swift canoes.

The *Philadelphia,* still going down.

Guns thundered. Grapeshot screamed overhead. Round shot cracked greenwood hulls. Splintered planks and bodies littered the waves.

Reginald knew himself wounded, though cold had numbed the pain within seconds of submersion. His left leg and arm felt weaker than they ought. His right leg, usually the weaker, barely compensated as he struggled to stay afloat. Where were the ships' boats he'd seen pulling through the chaos, collecting the wounded? Where was the hospital ship, *Enterprise?*

But no. He'd no wish to lose a limb to a surgeon's saw. Better to bleed out in the water . . .

Drifting smoke parted, giving him glimpse of a rescue boat. He called out, but a swell smacked him, pulling him under into suffocating dark. When his head broke the surface again, there was only smoke and debris and his lungs sucking in air. Gunfire stuttered in sporadic concussion, then ceased. Ringing silence brought a fusillade of questions. Were the British backing down? Had Arnold surrendered? He'd lost sight of the *Philadelphia.* Valcour Island was the nearest land, closer than the lake's western shore. He could swim for it . . . Did he know in which direction to swim?

He went under, clawed back to the surface, choking.

With the cessation of the guns, he heard the cries of wounded men, again thought he glimpsed a hull nosing among floating debris. He tried to shout and went under, chest swelling to bursting. Tight, airless agony.

It seemed a very long time he took going down, time enough to torment himself over those he was leaving behind—

Anna, his dear girl. That she should hear of this battle and know he'd died on her day.

Lydia, who'd loved him at his most unlovable, waiting years for him to love her in return.

William, driven into the arms of the enemy, tattered and hulled by the knowledge that his life was built on lies.

The warrior, on his knees and bleeding . . .

—until like a sack of drowning puppies he was yanked from the depths by his coat's nape and hauled against something hard. His chest seared as his lungs convulsed, greedy for air.

"I have him!" a voice barked. Hands grappled him. Then he was sprawled in the bottom of a boat, gagging, expelling water in a throat-burning gush.

"Aubrey!" the voice said. "Welcome aboard, sailor."

Then pain roared to life and he sank into blackness as drowning as lake water.

A blast shuddered through his bones, yanking him conscious, body convulsed in panic. Pain ripped through his flailing limbs before a steadying arm clamped across his chest.

"Easy," a voice hoarse with weariness admonished. "You're aboard the *Congress*—what's left of her."

Congress. Arnold's ship.

He began to get his bearings. A blanket covered him. Beneath it he was soaked. The breeze striking his exposed bits had an icy edge.

Memory surfaced, bobbing up like flotsam. He'd heard a blast. Not from a broadside gun. The shudder had gone through his bones but not the deck beneath him. That seemed intact. And crowded—with its own crew and those rescued brought aboard. Men spoke around him, but softly. The movement of the craft told him they lay at anchor. The cold air smelled of sulfur. It was near dark.

"Did I hear a blast?" he forced out, raw throated.

"That'll be the *Royal Savage,* what went aground on Valcour," said a sailor nursing a wounded shoulder. Reginald strained to hear him over the ringing in his ears. "The redcoats—or their Indians—set her aflame. Ye heard the magazine go."

Reginald absorbed the news as, in the relative quiet of snapping sheet and lapping swell and what sounded like hammers tapping, there arose in the distance a tumult of war cries.

He sat up, pushing back the blanket to assess his injuries. He was hatless, head wet and bared to the cold. His coat had been removed, dumped in a puddled heap on the deck beside him. His sodden shirt-sleeve, torn off at the elbow, bound his left forearm. Below the knee, his leg was wrapped in the remains of his stocking. Both bindings were bloodstained. The ringing in his head would be days in fading.

He was battered but whole. As for the fleet . . .

"Our losses? Besides the *Philadelphia* and *Royal Savage.*" He could make out the faces around him, features strained and powder blackened in the deepening twilight.

"Some as good as lost," said the wounded sailor. "*Washington* is barely afloat, taking on water. *Congress* here was hulled below the water line. Mainmast took damage. The British drew off and anchored out of range to the south. Patching their ships as we're doing, I expect."

"I can help with that." Reginald started to haul himself to his feet, but another sailor clamped a hand over his arm, keeping him down.

"Ye'll do no such thing. I kept you off the *Enterprise* as you insisted, but those splinters went deep. Yanked 'em out myself. Pray ye the wounds don't fester."

Reginald had no memory of the crude tending administered. All for the best, he thought, as a scream cut the air. It issued from the hospital ship. "My thanks you have, on both counts. But what is to be done? Wait we for morning?"

"Himself is deciding, yonder." The sailor canted his head toward the galley's stern, where three figures gathered close around a hooded lantern. Its feeble light revealed General Benedict Arnold, still in uniform—his only uniform; his belongings were aboard the burning *Royal Savage,* he having moved nothing but his flag over to the *Congress* before battle commenced—and the officers of his hastily assembled navy, General Waterbury and Colonel Wigglesworth.

"Sixty dead then?" Arnold was saying, turning to stare with narrowed intensity toward the leaping light on Valcour's distant shore, the lantern's faint glow limning his prominent nose.

"Yes sir," said Wigglesworth. "Best as we can count at present. Ammunition is nearly three-fourths spent across the fleet, the vessels themselves barely seaworthy. They'll not withstand a repeat of today."

"No question dawn shall see a resumption of the fight." Waterbury rubbed a hand along his bristled jaw. "The choice, as I see it, is retreat or surrender."

Silence fell while Arnold stared into the night. Reginald got haltingly to his feet. The shadowed forms of the fleet lay scattered at anchor. Beyond the light of the burning schooner, darkness hid the island's rocky southern shore, the Indians, the British fleet. And William, out there somewhere on that wind-swept lake?

Surely not. It would have taken him and Sam Reagan weeks to reach Canada afoot, find Johnson, join the Royal New Yorkers . . . if he'd carried through with that intention. Besides, it was British regulars and experienced sailors their ragtag navy had faced this day. Not raw colonial recruits.

Arnold, soot-blackened as a gunner, swept his gaze across the deck, giving Reginald a brief nod before addressing his officers. "We shall not surrender, but neither shall we engage them again in our present condition.

We retreat to Crown Point and preserve the remnants of our navy. Question being, which way?"

"They'll have us hemmed to the south. North around Valcour?"

"The wind is northerly," Waterbury countered Wigglesworth's suggestion. "We'd have to row against it, no sails."

Pulling at the braid of his battle-worn coat, drawn with weariness, Arnold weighed the options. The hazards of feeling their way around the north end of the island in the dark would be as unappealing to the general as it was to Reginald.

"Gentlemen," he said at last, and in the glow of the hooded lantern, Reginald thought he saw the general's mouth curve. "We shall not go north. We shall go south—but quiet-like—straight through the enemy's anchored fleet."

4

October 17, 1776
Aubrey farm

*I*t was done. A *fait accompli*. Reginald had survived it and was home, sitting in his favorite chair by the hearth and recounting the tale. *No sense being angry now,* Lydia admonished herself. But he'd said he was only going to *build* the boats.

"A risky move it was, but a bold one," Reginald said, addressing those gathered in the sitting room—Anna, Good Voice, Stone Thrower, Two Hawks, and Lydia, who, with three expectant mothers with imminent childbeds, had come meaning to entreat Anna to return to town. Thoughts of returning to Schenectady had fled upon Reginald's unheralded home-coming, a happy reunion sullied now as the truth of what he'd done sank in, filling her mind with the chop of dark water strewn with planking and the bodies of the dead . . .

"The British left us a gap near a mile wide between the flank of their anchored ships and the western lakeshore. Come midnight we rowed through it in file, sweeps muffled, lanterns hooded—praying British ears were still as deafened from the guns as were ours."

Stone Thrower and Good Voice, together on a settee, leaned forward, intent on the tale, but from her chair Anna broke in, "Were you wounded, Papa? When you went into the water?"

Earlier in the yard, as Reginald dismounted his horse, Lydia had known straightaway he'd taken hurt. She'd refrained from mentioning it thus far, but it didn't surprise her that Anna had noticed the subtle stiffness in his movements.

"Not but a few splinters," Reginald assured his daughter, waving away the horrific detail. "The British gave us not one gun as we passed. I came last aboard the *Congress* with General Arnold, and long could I see the *Royal Savage* burning behind us." As if feeling the keen edge of her gaze, Reginald paused. "Truly, Lydia, the wounds weren't grave."

His blue-gray eyes were warm yet wary. The water between them was as littered with debris as that of Lake Champlain. Memory of the kiss they'd shared months ago rose like an ache in Lydia's throat. Reginald fixed his stare on the hearth fire—avoiding the gaze of William's twin, who sat cross-legged beside it—as he picked up the thread of his tale.

"We'd hoped to make Crown Point and there be resupplied, but the wind turned against us, coming up from the south. It was all night rowing—and look you, Lydia, do not hiss in your breath," he added as she did exactly that. "'Twas hardly a man of us not wounded, see. All could lift an oar were needed."

Lydia shared a glance with Anna, then pressed her lips tight.

"We anchored in the night to mend as we could. By sunrise we saw the British sailing hard after us. We pushed through the day, rowing, strung out along the lake. The wind was yet strong from the south as we tacked, our bows smacking the chop, *Congress* shuddering as though her timbers would crack to kindling." Reginald leaned forward in his chair, his Welsh-lilted voice a gentler wave than those of which he spoke.

"Into another night we pressed, yet dawn showed the British fleet again come up with us, and we still twenty miles from Crown Point. Within hours the *Washington* surrendered, leaving *Congress* the nearest prey. We'd tacked toward the eastern shore with four of the gondolas. It settled then into a running chase, with Arnold keeping up a brisk return of fire. But we were taking losses . . ."

A glance at Lydia, and Reginald said no more of losses.

"By noon 'twas clear we were done for. Arnold ordered *Congress* and the gondolas run aground. We took what arms we could carry and fired the vessels. Arnold didn't strike our colors but let them fly above the flames."

"A good defiance," Stone Thrower murmured.

"That it was," Reginald agreed. "'Twas no winning that engagement, see. But the British didn't press us. I've heard they do not mean to. Not from that quarter. Not this year."

"*Iyo.*" It was Two Hawks who spoke, from the floor by the hearth. He and Anna shared a deep look before seeming to remember they were under Reginald's nose and broke the gaze.

Anna colored pink in the firelight. Reginald opened his mouth to address his daughter.

"How far was this from Crown Point?" Lydia asked, snagging his attention.

"About ten miles." Reginald shifted in his chair, pain tightening his mouth, and let whatever he'd thought to say to Anna pass. "We watched the fires take deck and sail. Then the magazines exploded, rolling flames into the air, scattering burning planks across the bay. Enough to break the heart, it was. Once Arnold saw the ships would make no prizes, we took to the wood and made our way to Crown Point."

Lydia gaped. "Ten miles afoot, after all that? I wouldn't think—"

"I had it in me?" Reginald's mouth twisted. "A near thing it was, and I'll pay a price for it yet awhile." He rubbed a hand at the base of his neck. "We reached Crown Point and warned the garrison the fort wouldn't hold, presuming then the British *would* press the attack. We put the place to the torch and proceeded to Ticonderoga, and here am I come home at last, who meant to be gone but a few weeks' time."

Anna had her arms crossed, her face a study in unhappiness. "And we never even knew this was happening to you."

Reginald's expression softened. "I suppose there is still that of the soldier in me, unable to refuse such pressing need."

Good Voice drew in a breath. With that one word—*soldier*—Lydia knew she'd been thrust back in memory to another war, another fort.

Seeking for something to say to cover the moment, Lydia glanced at Anna. Two Hawks had captured her focus again. It was wrenching to witness the depth of their longing, but . . . Lydia narrowed her gaze at the pair. There *was* longing in that shared gaze, but something else had supplanted it, at least in Anna's expression. *Pleading?* Two Hawks met it with a shake of his head.

Stone Thrower asked, "What of the other American ships?"

"They reached Ticonderoga," Reginald said. "Even the crew of the *Washington* taken prisoner was returned under flag of truce and the promise of parole."

The fire's snap was loud in the ensuing silence. Lydia felt tension gathering in the room. Again . . . there went Anna mutely pleading, as if she wanted Two Hawks to say something he didn't wish to say.

"We have waited for your return," his father said. "After one more sleep, we start our journey home to Kanowalohale. We have decided this."

Surprise, then dismay, chased across Anna's features. Whomever Stone Thrower meant by *we,* it hadn't included her.

Reginald too looked surprised. "You needn't leave so soon."

"We thank you for sharing your home this long while," Stone Thrower said, his handsome face burnished in the firelight. "But there is hunting to be done."

Reginald rubbed at his neck again. "Rowan has told me of your help with the harvest. I mean to send you home with a fair portion of the yield."

It was true. The Oneidas had been of great assistance to Rowan and Maura Doyle in Reginald's absence. Good Voice mostly, though Stone Thrower had done what he could, confined to crutches. It had been the first time he'd harvested corn—women's work among the Oneidas.

Good Voice said, "What you offer we accept. But still we go. Hunting will be hard, dangerous with spies going about the forest trails. But the furs will buy us many things needed. Not just food."

"It is not only for us we go," Stone Thrower added. "Some at Kanowalohale have none to provide. I am a warrior of my people. My place is with them."

Looking both regretful and relieved, Reginald cleared his throat. "What of Johnson's regiment? Is there news?"

"That is for my son to answer," Stone Thrower said.

Two Hawks sat straighter as he related the rumors that had circulated about Sir John Johnson and his regiment. "We put to rest each one until none remained to follow. We know where William is not—at the lake forts. We do not know where he is."

Reginald was silent, absorbing this, then said, "Too long have I been gone from my place on the Binne Kill. But once my business there is in order . . ." He met Stone Thrower's questioning gaze. "I've had time for thinking about what Arnold did on Lake Champlain. I thought of doing likewise—finding a break in the British lines in the north, slipping through to find William."

"No," Lydia said before she could think better of it. "Reginald, winter is nigh upon us."

Reginald ignored all but Stone Thrower, to whom he'd bound himself with a promise—that they would neither go after William alone.

"It is a bold plan," Stone Thrower said. "It stirs my heart to hear it. But we have taken hurt, you and I. To cross such distance in snow would take a man in his full strength to do. And I have reason to stay. For now."

"You don't know yet where to look for William," Lydia persisted. "You cannot even be certain he's joined Johnson's regiment."

"You do not let fly an arrow before you aim it," Good Voice added.

Stone Thrower said, "We do well to heed the wisdom of our women.

We wait. Pray. Trust our lost one to Heavenly Father. Until we have a target to aim at."

Reginald's jaw tightened. He closed his eyes, only to open them when Two Hawks stood abruptly. The young man's color deepened as all gazes turned his way, but it was Reginald's he held.

"I am glad you are safe from battle," he said. "We have been much worried for you, wishing you home. Now I am going down to the barn."

"The barn?" Anna asked in evident bewilderment.

Two Hawks jerked a nod. "Where I will sleep. I have moved my things to be ready for morning. Sleep well," he said to the room at large, though his gaze rested on Anna's upturned face with its own pleading. For what? Turning away too quickly for Lydia to be sure, he passed between her and Reginald and went out.

Anna stared after him. Only Lydia seemed to notice her hurt. Reginald was reaching inside his coat. He brought out something small, wrapped in faded cloth. He laid it on his thigh and removed the wrapping to reveal two framed oval faces. Lydia was near enough to see one was a tiny portrait of Heledd, his late wife, who had returned to Wales nine years ago with . . .

"William," she said, recognizing the face in the second frame.

"What is this?" Good Voice leaned forward, staring at what lay in Reginald's lap. Stone Thrower mirrored her movement.

"I found these among the things William left behind. Heledd must have had them commissioned soon before she passed. He looks to be nearly the age he is now. Here." Reginald held out the portrait that had captured their attention, his voice gone gruff with feeling. "See the face of your son."

As Good Voice's hands cradled the miniature, Anna wept openly, watching William's parents, hearing as did Lydia the involuntary sounds each made, eloquent of years of pain and loss and wondering.

"They are much alike," Good Voice whispered at last. "The brows, the mouth . . ."

"But the eyes . . ." Stone Thrower said. "He is like you."

Anna shot to her feet and all but ran from the room. Good Voice and Stone Thrower barely glanced up at her going, but Reginald raised his eyes to Lydia. Eyes still haunted by guilt.

5

*N*eed pulled Anna from the house, where Two Hawks's parents lingered over their first bittersweet sight of William's face. Forsaking shawl and propriety, she followed her heart's tether through the dark, down the wagon lane to the barn, ducking into shadow as Mr. Doyle, finished his chores, left the barn headed for the cottage he shared with Mrs. Doyle. Heart thumping, she laced her arms against the cold and waited for his boot scuffs to fade.

Papa would be angry if he knew she was doing this. But she had to know. Why hadn't Two Hawks spoken?

It had come to her on her birthday, the idea of Two Hawks working with Papa on the Binne Kill, crafting bateaux, learning the business. Becoming what she'd been for Lydia these past years. An apprentice. Made in a rush at the kitchen table, in a rare moment of privacy, the proposal had caught Two Hawks off guard. When he'd hesitated, she'd reminded him of something he said years ago, when they'd argued over what constituted a man's proper work. "*A man may build a canoe without shame.* You told me that, remember? A bateau is like a canoe."

"It is so," he'd conceded. "But why do you wish this?"

"Papa won't give us permission, much less his blessing, to marry if you remain a stranger to him. Papa needs to know you." Two Hawks's continued hesitation had made the pit of her stomach drop away. "Will you consider it, working with Papa?"

Mrs. Doyle had trundled in then, apron full of potatoes from the cellar. She stopped short, eyeing them. Two Hawks had stood.

"I will consider," he'd said, and left her hoping what she'd heard in his voice hadn't been reluctance but the constraint of Mrs. Doyle's watchful presence. But it *had* been reluctance. His refusal to speak to Papa proved it.

The barn door creaked as she pushed it open. Inside, by lantern light, Two Hawks was unrolling his blanket in an empty stall near the door. At her entry, he bolted to his feet in a fluid motion. Startlement fled his expression, replaced by a look she didn't want to see. Regret. "You should not be here."

She shut the door to keep light from spilling out. She'd reined in her tears. She would say her piece and not cry through it.

"Why?" She choked on the word as tears came. "Why did you say nothing? It would have worked. It still could. You could sleep in Papa's workshop. I'd be in town with Lydia and could see you every day. There are clothes you could wear. William didn't take all of his with him. They'd fit you perfectly until—"

Two Hawks crossed the space between them so swiftly, she broke off in surprise. He stopped near enough that she could feel his warmth, but he didn't raise a hand to touch her. "I never said I would ask your father this thing you wish. I said I would think about it. I have done so."

"And now you're leaving?"

"I must. For a time." His face was shadowed, the lantern behind him. He kept his arms at his sides. She curled her hands around them, beseeching. The linen of his shirt was soft beneath her fingers, his muscles firm, lean.

An ache lodged in her throat. "I want you to stay."

A tremor went through him, and he closed his eyes. "Others have need of me."

She stepped back, her shoes rustling straw. Somewhere in the darkened barn a horse ruckled. "For the hunting? Stone Thrower said he would hunt."

"He spoke the words of a father and husband," Two Hawks said, eyes opening to her, still shadowed. "But he is not ready to be the only provider for my mother. I must also provide. An apprentice is given no pay, and I cannot ask your father to hire me. I have no skill at his work. It would not be right."

"It would keep you safe!"

"At the expense of my people's safety? They need every warrior, now more than ever, to stand ready for whatever is coming."

"Two Hawks, you aren't a warrior. You don't have to fight."

He took her by the shoulders, dark eyes earnest and torn. "You must understand. I will not stand by and let my people suffer harm."

My people. She lowered her chin.

Cupping her face in his hand, he raised it. "Listen. Your father is no longer a warrior, yet when he was needed, he fought on that lake. I think him right for doing it. He held off the British from the north, he and that brave general, Arnold. How can I do less than this man whose blessing my heart craves?"

She searched his face, his words filling her with admiration—and fear. "Is there no hope for peace?"

"We must pray for peace but strengthen our arms for battle." That he was right only deepened her frustration. She tried to pull away. He didn't let her. "Why do you think your father did what he did on that lake?"

"Because he's a man. And men are stubborn, foolhardy creatures, too brave for their own good!"

To her annoyance, Two Hawks grinned. "That is maybe true, but he did it for you."

"Me? All I wanted was him home safe."

"What do you think he wanted? Because you are his treasure, he would see you protected." Two Hawks's thumb moved gently along her jaw. "When I say I am needed by my people, do you not know you are part of that? Here is something for which your father and I have one heart: I would make your world safe if I can. However I can."

Tears slid down her cheek, across his fingers. He was good. And brave. And selfless. When she was none of those things. *I love you*. It was all she wanted to say. As soon as she found breath.

"Leaving the rest aside," he went on, "I do not wish to see my father bring himself more harm. He is strong to travel but not to do all that needs to be done for winter. He will try to do it if I am not there to help."

I love you wasn't everything she wanted to say, after all. "Papa said you could stay. All of you."

What a child she sounded. Why couldn't she be brave for him? Let him do what he felt he must do? If he was disappointed in her, he hid it well.

"It was generous, but my parents wish to be home, among our people. They are needed. As am I."

I need you. She leaned her forehead against his chest, aching for his arms around her. Only his hands linked them, gripping her shoulders. If she pressed against him, moved but a little . . .

"I'm so selfish," she said.

His breath released, warm across the crown of her head. "Bear's Heart, do you think it easy for me to leave you? In my heart I am just as selfish."

Thrilling to the sound of the name he'd given her, she raised her face, saw the need in his eyes. He was on the edge of control. She'd pushed him there. Again. It was unfair of her, making him always be the strong one. She would show him she could be strong too. And as insufferably sacrificing.

Stepping back was a tearing inside her. "I shouldn't have come."

His gaze was so intense, she thought for an instant he would come after her; he didn't. "Our words needed to be said. I was wrong to walk away and leave them unsaid."

They stared at each other. Yearning. Hurting. Hoping.

"Go back to the house," he said. "I do not wish to anger your father or put another branch across the path between us."

Anger flared in Anna's chest, tightening her jaw. "After all he's done, I cannot understand why he doesn't see you as—"

"No." Two Hawks shook his head. "Do not close your heart to him in anger. Whatever else he has done, it is plain he loves you. I will honor that, and him, because he is your father."

The one pure thing, Papa once called her. The one pure thing in his life. She didn't feel pure. Nothing felt pure anymore. And yet . . . Good Voice and Stone Thrower, Two Hawks as well, had forgiven Papa. She'd had weeks to talk with them, to understand that though it had been wrenchingly hard to do, they truly had forgiven. And it had freed them.

"All right. I'll see you in the morning, before you go." Her lips felt numb over the words.

Two Hawks's gaze held sorrow. And tenderness. "Sleep well."

"And you." She put her back to him. Her hand was on the barn door when his voice stopped her.

"Bear's Heart. I would be in two places if I could. But *you* will have my heart. Tomorrow as I go, it will tear out of me and stay with you."

"And mine you will take with you," she said to the barn door, loud enough that he would hear.

"I will guard it well." Longing thickened his words. "Remember, and think about this . . . You and I would never know this love if not for what Aubrey did."

Lydia watched the figures diminishing along the track toward the creek and beyond, to the unknown paths that traced the wilderness between them and Kanowalohale. Good Voice led William's dappled mare, loaned by Reginald to carry the cornmeal her labor had earned. Stone Thrower, a limp in his stride though he'd cast off his crutches, carried on his person the miniature of William—a parting gift. Two Hawks took what he'd come with, weapons and blanket. But each of them was leaving without the one thing they'd most hoped to find, and for that Lydia's heart was grieved.

"I cannot say 'tis unhappy I am to see them go," said Maura Doyle, who'd left breakfast half-cleared to see their guests away. "Though I wish . . . But there it is. And those pots won't scrub themselves, will they?"

She sighed and went inside the house.

As Lydia stared after the departing Oneidas, Two Hawks, walking behind his parents, halted and looked back. Standing between her and Reginald, eyes red and puffy, Anna caught her breath. Lydia reached for her hand. The tension thrumming through the girl mounted until she feared Anna might bolt away and leave them.

Two Hawks turned his back and followed his parents. It had been but a last parting gaze.

With a muffled sob Anna pulled away, but instead of bolting down the lane, she hurried into the house.

"Anna," Reginald said as the door closed.

Lydia's heart ached for the man, staring after his daughter with all the guilt in the world pouring from his eyes. But she knew when next he met her gaze he'd have shut it away, as he had the evening before when he'd given Good Voice and Stone Thrower all of William he'd had to give. Not enough. He didn't seem to understand that it could never be enough. She'd hoped the act of condolence Stone Thrower had performed for Reginald—that astonishing ceremony that had taken place in the clearing, back in summer when they'd expected vengeance—would be the first step in Reginald's coming to terms with half a lifetime of guilt. In embracing a God he'd kept at arm's length because of that burden.

Instead he'd run away to build boats for General Arnold.

Lydia touched his arm. "Let her be for now. She needs—"

"Time," Reginald finished for her. "To forget about him. I understand."

But he didn't. Not if he thought Anna could simply put Two Hawks out of mind. Did he truly think they'd seen the end of that young man's involvement in their lives?

"I'd best speak to Rowan, see whether he needs me here today," he said, putting distance between them with the mundane. "Shall Anna ride in with you?"

The smile he gave her never touched his eyes, nor dispelled the shadow there. There was still William in his gaze. William wanted. William wounded. *William.*

Lydia ignored the question. "William is of great importance, Reginald, but he isn't the sun around which we all revolve. Do you expect all our hearts and hopes to hang in abeyance until he returns—or is dragged back—to reckon with what he's run from? There is life to be lived meantime. Will you live it?"

She'd been too blunt. Inwardly she cringed as Reginald's face began to close. Then something in his eyes broke open again, meeting hers with a bleeding need.

"Lydia." He took a step toward her. "When I was in the water, when I thought myself dying, you were—"

"Lydia? I'm ready."

Neither had heard Anna come out of the house. As they lurched apart, there she stood, a small bag and her new medical case gripped in either hand, looking at Lydia with a brittle determination. She wouldn't meet her father's gaze.

"I mean to stay with Lydia for a while, Papa. We've babies to deliver."

Reginald gazed at his daughter's bowed head. When he spoke, it was not of babies. "Anna, their leaving is for the best. They've their world, see, and we—"

"I should like to stay with Lydia for the winter, I think," Anna interrupted. "Keep busy in town, then maybe it won't be so . . ." Her chin quivered; she swallowed whatever she'd intended to say. "I'll be back another time for my things." She swung toward Lydia. "If that suits you."

"Of course," Lydia said. "Though perhaps you should ask your father if this arrangement is agreeable to him."

Pain lanced across Reginald's eyes as Anna met his gaze. He didn't wait for her to ask. "Aye. 'Tis fine. I'll drive the cart in with whatever else you need, when next I come in to town."

"Good," Anna said. "Thank you."

Heartache ravaged both their faces. Lydia couldn't bear it a moment longer. "I'll get my things then."

Reginald gave a stiff nod. "I'll help Rowan saddle the horses."

Lydia watched him stride away, his limp a disturbing echo of Stone Thrower's. What had he started to tell her, before Anna interrupted? Something about being in the lake, near to drowning—she shrank from imagining—and then he'd said, *"You were . . ."*

What had she been?

"It's going to be all right," she said, as much to reassure herself as the man limping away, or Anna, who stood staring toward the creek at the emptiness there. Waiting.

6

January 1777
Lachine, Montreal

*P*rivate William Llewellyn Aubrey—his name as he'd entered it in the rolls of the King's Royal Regiment of New York—was beginning to worry about his toes. He no longer felt them inside his cracked leather shoes. Nine years in England had dimmed his memories of New York's winters, but he judged the cold of Montreal more brutal still. Exposed skin ached after a moment's acquaintance. Every breath not muffled by layers of wool seared the lungs.

He'd meant to be warm in his billet by now, communing with a cannikin of mulled cider. Such succor wasn't to be. Between the termination of their guard duty at His Majesty's storehouse in the village of Lachine and making their report to Sergeant Campbell, William had lost track of Private Sam Reagan—*again,* blast his elusive hide. Distracted by the door of the officer's headquarters, which tended to stick fast in the cold, William had wrenched it open and glanced aside to find his fellow guard slipping off through the ranks of a passing company of Royal Highland Emigrants headed off to drill on snowshoes.

It was becoming habit with Sam, this cutting out early. One that left William to take the brunt of Sergeant Campbell's displeasure. News of recent rebel victories at Trenton and Princeton had every officer of the regiment going about grim faced and snappish, but Campbell, always a surly brute, had taken animosity to another level. He'd fixed upon William as his particular target, which struck William as prodigiously unfair, given it was Sam who played the truant.

Campbell was Scottish born, but unlike most of the Scots who made up Sir John's regiment, come over the mountains from the Mohawk Valley the previous summer, Campbell had been a Montreal merchant before joining. Somehow it had become known that William had spent the past few years reading law at Oxford's Queens College, an ambition Campbell had cherished in his younger years but never possessed the means— mayhap the brains as well—to fulfill. In his better moods, the man referred to William sneeringly as *Oxford,* a sobriquet that reminded William—with the subtlety of a prodding knife tip—that Queens was the last place he'd been certain of who he was, where he belonged, what sort of man he was destined to become.

A certainty built upon lies, even then. Every time he so much as looked at Campbell with his blunt nose, near-lipless mouth, and loathing gaze, William had to shield himself against the memories that still shredded his soul.

Casting about for an excuse not worn threadbare, William had covered for Sam's truancy once again, absorbed another verbal lash, and vowed as he stalked the frozen streets of Lachine risking important bits of himself to frostbite that it was the absolute last time. Reagan was up to his neck in *something.* Perhaps he'd found himself a willing maid among some merchant's staff and couldn't keep from her. William only hoped it was such a piece of foolishness. Regardless, he meant to have the truth. He'd no more tolerance for deceit in those who made claim to him, be it blood or friendship.

He spotted Sam on the wind-swept riverfront, down on the pebbled beach—knew him by the pale blond tail of his hair, for he'd already changed out of his regimentals. *Johnson's Greens* they'd been dubbed on account of their coats. Buff-faced, blue-trimmed, with a buckle depicting the Royal Crown, they weren't exactly objectionable, just not the scarlet

coat William had envisioned donning after their grueling mountain crossing last summer. Despite appealing to General Burgoyne for the bounty
other commanding officers received, Sir John had been told to foot the
bill himself for his regiment's raising. The King's Royal Regiment of New
York, regarded by army regulars as a motley provincial assemblage devoid
of discipline, must take what they could get.

Sam wasn't alone. He stood in conversation with what looked to
be . . . an Indian. The figure was wrapped in a wind-whipped trade blanket, quilled leggings and moccasins peeking out below. A small figure,
slightly bent—to the freezing wind if not with age. Likely one of the Indians from across the St. Lawrence. A Mohawk from Caughnawaga, a mission village on the river's southern shore. Longtime Catholic converts most
of them, they often passed through Lachine, where the Crown's Indian
gifts were stored and river trade for the western lakes began. William
avoided them. He hadn't known Sam to have truck with them either.
Until now. What business had he with this solitary Indian?

One possibility occurred, nearly halting William in his tracks. The
storehouses . . . the Indian goods . . . the truancies. Was Sam engaged in
illicit trading with the Caughnawagas, and appropriating the King's property for the purpose? Such temptation had overmastered more than one
soldier in weeks past. Those caught could expect the cat-o'-nine-tails. William had no trouble imagining Campbell volunteering to administer the
lash and gleefully dragging him into it as well. Guilt by association.

William was too far removed to catch their conversation over the
wind's buffeting whine, but his shout carried well enough.

"Reagan!"

Sam jerked round to face him. So did the Indian. A woman, boney
faced and wrinkled. The sight sent William's mind spiraling back to last
summer, to Anna's voice pleading. *"Then don't stay for Papa. Stay for
Good Voice, for Two Hawks . . ."*

"Shut up," he muttered. "Just shut up."

As he neared the pair, he forced himself to meet the wary gaze of the woman. Whoever she was, she took the seconds before William crossed the final stretch of beach to scurry off along the frozen riverside, retreating past a cluster of fishing shacks abandoned for the winter.

"William. Still loitering in this cold?" Sam's mouth crooked, hazel eyes behind drifting breath bright with the half-sheepish look of a man caught out. "You were talking of cider last I saw you."

Though a few years older than William, Sam could still display the reckless mischief of youth. It had been appealing back when William's most pressing concern had been convincing his father to let him return to his studies at Queens. "Figured you'd found yourself a sweetheart," he snapped through numbed lips. "But is that one not a bit old for you?"

Red-faced with cold, Sam smiled blandly as he took William's arm in a mittened hand, steering him away from the river. "Far too old and a savage to boot. Let's get indoors. This wind's vicious."

A savage . . .

"Her name is Good Voice," Anna had told him, there in the barn as his world shattered to pieces.

And he'd said, *"What sort of name is that?"*

"Onyota'a:ka—*Oneida,*" she'd said, on her face such hope resting, while he'd felt the shock of it like a lance thrust through his vitals.

"So that is what I am? An Indian. A half-breed."

"You are my son!" So said the man who'd committed the egregious act of his abduction and compounded it with a lifetime of lies. William's lifetime.

He'd swung onto his horse, unable to look Reginald Aubrey in the eye, emptiness raging where his heart had been. *"I am not though, am I? You've said as much. Wales, Oxford, this place—my* name. *None of it is mine."*

He yanked free of Sam's grip. "Next time wait till after you've seen your duties through before you run off chasing skirts—buckskin or otherwise."

He strode ahead of Sam toward the house they'd quartered in since November. The crunch of boots on gravel trailed him.

"William. What ails ye?" Keeping pace beside him, Sam shouldered past the few bundled figures braving the cold for the shops along Lachine's streets.

"Forget who the officer of the day is today?"

"Ah . . . sorry. Campbell doesn't like you overmuch, does he?"

"The sentiment is mutual. But I'm done covering for you, see. Next time I'll tell what you've been about, shall I?"

Sam halted. A pace more and William pivoted to face him, blowing breath like a winded horse. "What do you mean to say of me?" Sam demanded, no longer grinning.

"That depends. What business had you with that woman?"

Sam blinked, then visibly relaxed. "The Indian? She was soliciting me for business, if you must know. Not *that* sort," he added. "She wanted to tend our laundry. I told her we have that covered—and naught to pay her anyway."

William searched his friend's face, but Sam's features gave back nothing.

"You don't believe me?"

"Fine. Whatever. I'm getting indoors." He turned to go, but Sam grabbed his arm, detaining him before they turned a corner.

"It won't happen again." William's face was too frozen for expression, but there must have been a coldness in his eyes as well. Sam stepped back a pace. "You're truly cross with me?"

"Yes. No. I'm just . . ." Just so all-consuming angry. Still dislocated to the core of his being. He'd hoped to find his footing in the army, in his loyalty to the Crown, but even here he'd found scant common ground with the rank and file of Johnson's regiment, largely composed of the transplanted Highlanders Sir John's father, William Johnson, had settled on his landholdings north of the Mohawk River.

Like them, William was a Tory, but he wasn't hellbent on marching back into the valley he'd fled, wielding a fiery sword of vengeance against the rebel neighbors who'd driven him from his home. All he'd sought that summer night he galloped from Reginald Aubrey's barn was escape. A place to hole up, lick his wounds, regain his equilibrium. He'd been a branch uprooted, caught in a rushing stream, hurtled along its flow. Rashly he'd reached for the first mooring to hand—Sam Reagan, set to flee to Quebec to join the British in Montreal.

"Look," Sam said now. "It would have been hell getting here without you and I'm grateful you came with me, but you've never said why you were so keen for it. Whatever it is, it's been eating you inside out the winter long." When William merely glared at him, tight lipped, Sam pressed, "It's to do with your father, isn't it? You haven't so much as mentioned Reginald Aubrey since the night we left."

"That's because he's not my father!"

William instantly wished the words unsaid. He'd rebuffed Sam's attempts to uncover his reasons for journeying north until finally Sam had let the subject alone. They'd passed the weeks in Lachine working on local fortifications, doing rudimentary drill training, patrolling the river with orders to "seize all Rascals who may attempt to steal in or out of the Province, spreading lies." In other words, watching for rebel spies—the farthest thing from Sam's mind at present, to judge by the utter astonishment fallen like a sheet across his wind-chapped face.

"Aubrey isn't your father? But you bear his name. Did he . . . what? Adopt you, as he did with Anna?"

William ignored the question. "You want to know why I'm angry, do you?"

"If you're finally ready to tell me." People were passing on the street.

Sensing he'd no wish for an audience, Sam drew him closer to the stone wall of the corner building, another warehouse. "Come now. Getting it out will help."

Wishing it could, William bit the words through cracked lips. "Very little of what you know of me is true, Sam. I *was* born the day Fort William Henry surrendered, but not to the Aubreys. Not to my . . ." He swallowed past the painful knowledge that the woman who'd raised him, loved him—to her own distraction—had born no relation to him whatsoever. Heledd Aubrey had been deceived as well. "Another woman in the fort birthed me. When Reginald Aubrey's son died, he stole me from my mother's side. There were two of us. Twins. I suppose I looked white enough to pass for his son. He took me and left his dead babe in my place. I never knew any of it until the night I said I'd cross the mountains with you."

For the first time in William's recollection he'd rendered Sam Reagan speechless. He stared, eyes roving William's face, feature by feature, before finally he said, "You looked *white enough*? What does that mean?"

"Apparently I'm savage born. Indian."

Sam shook his head. "Not full blood. Your eyes."

"My mother was born white but raised Oneida. So I'm told."

His initial surprise spent, Sam was taking the news in customary stride. "I expect there's more to tell. In fact I'm sure of it, but save the details. Let's get inside."

"Agreed," said William, all but certain now his toes would never thaw again.

They turned the corner of the storehouse and stopped short to keep from running into the squat, burly form of Sergeant Campbell, who, judging by the look of satisfaction spreading across his blunt face, had overheard every word of William's confession.

7

Midwinter Moon
Fort Stanwix

*T*wo Hawks had barely outraced the coming storm. As he entered the fort at the Carrying Place, the snowfall that had pelted him since afternoon thickened to an angry blow, curtaining the log barracks and obscuring the blue-coated figures hurrying to put a door between themselves and the biting cold.

Two Hawks sheltered the horse he led—his brother's mare—catching glimpses through snow of the outer defenses, under repair by the new garrison from Connecticut, commanded by a colonel called Elmore. When he ducked into the trading post, hauling the bundled furs the horse had carried, warmth met him. And the stink of unwashed bodies. As his eyes adjusted to firelight, he picked out the owners of voices raised in conversation, more voices than the scant supplies stacked around the post could account for.

It had been General Schuyler's notion, this post for Oneidas to trade their winter furs for clothing and food. Hunger stalked the People. Warriors were often too busy spying on the British or watching their borders for those intent on mischief to hunt meat. Even when they had furs and skins to trade, the war in the east had disrupted the supply of goods. Two Hawks's mother wanted wool to make warm shirts and leggings. Little such met his gaze as he lowered his burden to the floor.

Around a brick hearth, men stood talking and warming themselves. Soldiers, scouts, Oneidas come for trade or news. Several broke away and headed for a cider barrel, revealing Ahnyero standing among the talkers, his hand around a cup. He flashed Two Hawks a look, nodding him over.

Two Hawks's spirits rose. Since his return from chasing the Cherry Valley spies, he'd seen the blacksmith-turned-scout only in passing, with no chance for the talk he wanted to have with the man.

Ahnyero made room for him in the fire's warmth. Two Hawks gave ear to the conversation while he began to thaw. Some of the talk was good—General Washington's victories at places called Trenton and Princeton. Some was not so good. Joseph Brant—Thayendanegea of the Mohawks, brother of Sir William Johnson's widow—had returned from a voyage to England where it was said he'd met the king.

"Brant's running hither and yon, boasting of being bosom friends with King Geordie," a Connecticut soldier complained. "Promising the Indians presents our side ain't able to spare—winning them over to the Crown. Can't one of you lot, some high-up chief, rein that stallion in?"

This was directed to the Oneidas present. Two Hawks knew his were not the only teeth it set on edge.

"The English king sent Brant to sway the People to his cause," Ahnyero told the soldier. "But when he came to Ganaghsaraga, he was scolded by the sachems who refused to side with the king." Ganaghsaraga was a village on the edge of Oneida land. Many living there were Tuscaroras. "The sachems told Brant they were standing apart and letting the whites fight their own battle. This is so. We only protect our lands from war parties crossing, as is right to do in any case."

Though *standing apart* was said when Oneidas were asked, the pressure to choose a side in the white man's war was partly what troubled those gathered in that fort.

When others took up the talk, Ahnyero leaned close to Two Hawks and said, "I still feel the cold coming off you, Brother," and led him to the cider barrel.

Two Hawks filled a cup. They returned to the hearth, squatting where a poker rested, its tip in the glowing embers. Ahnyero drew it forth and dipped it into Two Hawks's cider. The liquid steamed, its spicy fragrance clouding warm and pleasant between them. Ahnyero waited for Two Hawks to warm his hands around the cup, then his insides with a swallow.

"Your father . . . he will want to scout with us?"

"He has grumbled about it all winter." Two Hawks told how he and Stone Thrower had hunted together through the autumn. Though Two Hawks had left twice since to scout, his mother kept his father from following, doubting his leg was up to the challenge of trekking through heavy drifts. "My mother was right. The bone knit strong. He has no more limp now."

"*Iyo.*" Ahnyero dropped his voice though the others had gone on talking, some moving off to start a dice game. "Have you been east since the autumn?"

Two Hawks shook his head. "I hoped for word of William to bring." He fixed Ahnyero with a hopeful look. "Have you heard of Johnson's regiment?"

The Oneidas had cast a net of spies, strung out northward to the St. Lawrence River. Two Hawks was proud to be part of it but wished his part could be among those in Quebec gathering the war rumors from their spies among the British, that he might walk through some fort or encampment, turn a corner, and come face to face with his face—or one very like it—in the uniform of a Tory soldier. And he would say, *"Brother, since the day you were taken, you have lived in the hearts of our mother and father, and in my heart. Come now and know us so that we will be in your heart as well."*

Or he might say, *"Come now, forgive the man you called Father. Do this for my sake, so he will learn to think well of me . . ."*

Ahnyero told him, "The Royal Yorkers are said to winter in Montreal. Perhaps your brother is there?"

"It is what my brother told Anna Catherine he meant to do, join Johnson's regiment. Saying and doing are not the same." Speaking Anna Catherine's name drove other thoughts from Two Hawks's mind. He set the cider on the ashy hearth. "I have wanted to ask you a thing."

"Ask it then."

Two Hawks felt his face warm, not from the nearness of the fire. "How do you manage it, living among the whites and with the People, being at peace in both places?"

Ahnyero studied him, in no great hurry to reply. Two Hawks wondered what he was seeing. A foolish boy who'd lost his heart to an impossible love? Four moons had waned since he'd seen Anna Catherine. Two Hawks ached with missing her. Not that he'd thought time would change his heart. *For better, for worse*—words spoken when whites married, he'd learned. They warmed him, thinking of life with his Bear's Heart beside him. And they frightened him, considering the cost. He would need to remake himself after a pattern he couldn't clearly see. It ran before him like a deer through dappled thickets, giving only glimpses.

"You mean to marry that white woman then."

Two Hawks had never told the man that he loved Anna Catherine. It must show on his face, written like words on a page. "If I can persuade her father."

"It seems wrong to me," Ahnyero said.

Two Hawks's heart plummeted. "Wrong?"

"That you should seek her father's favor instead of the other way, after all that man has done. After all your parents have forgiven him. He is a difficult man, Aubrey?"

Two Hawks grunted. *Difficult* was a good word for that one. He was very tempted to say so, but he did not; he had told Anna Catherine he would honor her father. That did not mean only to his face. Or hers.

"I have tried to think how it would be," he said, "how I would see myself, had I done a thing I knew to be shameful. What would it take to restore me? What ways do whites have for cleansing a bad heart? All I understand are our traditions, and the ways of Heavenly Father, which I am learning. This man seems to have nothing for the purpose."

Ahnyero's brows lifted. "Nothing?"

"He has drawn himself apart. He is . . ." Inspired by their surroundings, Two Hawks said, "Like a man shut up inside a fort. Shut up where none can get to him. I think he believes even Creator cannot reach him there, where he hides. My parents tried to open that fort with forgiveness. Maybe they did. Maybe it is standing wide now. But he hasn't come out. I want this man to come out. I want him to be whole again. I want . . ."

He wanted Anna Catherine. Two Hawks stared into the fire, heart wrung with longing and helplessness. And conviction. He'd told Anna Catherine he was selfish. It was true. *Help me want Aubrey to be whole for his own sake, not just so my heart's desire might be granted me.*

"It is a tangled path you walk," Ahnyero said. "But maybe I can help you to clear it. My father taught me his blacksmith trade. A trade opens doors to places a man would otherwise be shut out of."

Two Hawks frowned. "You are saying I should become a blacksmith?"

Ahnyero started to smile, then suppressed it. "I am saying you should learn a trade that's needed by the whites *and* the People. It will help you live in both worlds, to be needed in both, if that is important to you."

"It is." He didn't want to stop being Oneida. Couldn't imagine such a thing. Neither could he imagine Anna Catherine living in his world. It was not their way for a woman to leave her mother's clan. "A man goes to live with his wife's clan," he murmured. It was the way it had always been. The right way, and good.

"True," Ahnyero agreed. "But this woman has no clan."

"She has people," Two Hawks said. "She has a place, a calling, and a woman she loves as a mother. She has a father. And *he* has a trade." Anna Catherine had had this idea. He'd been of two minds about it back in autumn, but now . . . his father no longer needed help to hunt.

"All those bateaux? I have seen that one who pilots his boats, Yankee Lang, with the white hair." The scout made a sound of interest—and approval, Two Hawks thought. "Maybe that is the way for you to Aubrey's heart, learning his—"

A sudden frigid gust had them breaking off their conversation and rising to their feet to see a group of Oneidas pushing into the crowded post, snow dusted, cheeks red with cold. One stepped forward and spoke, and because it wasn't in English, Ahnyero left the hearth to translate for those who needed it, but Two Hawks understood the news straight from the mouth of the warrior who brought it: "We come through this snow with dark news. There was a council at Onondaga, many sachems gathered there. During that council the spotting sickness came among them like a foul breath. Many are dead of it. Some of the dead are sachems."

As Ahnyero translated, a chill took hold of Two Hawks that had nothing to do with the wintery air let in.

"We come to tell Colonel Elmore, so he may pass the news downriver. There is mourning at Onondaga and condolence to be made. Because of this, the keepers of the Central Fire have stamped it out. It burns no more. Every man may choose as he will between the Americans and the British. That is what we have come to say."

Choose you this day whom ye will serve. The words sliced like a snow-snake groove through Two Hawks's mind as he led the gray mare along the drifted trail. His winter moccasins and the horse's hooves crunched the snow. Their breath billowed on stinging air. *Choose you this day . . .* Words of a war chief bidding his people to serve Creator or something else. No more standing apart.

The Oneidas were free to choose. To fight, if it came to it. Yet all Two Hawks wanted was to reach Kanowalohale, deliver the trade goods to his mother, then fly to Anna Catherine like an arrow loosed. There would be no fighting while snow lay thick. If he was to do this thing with Aubrey—this path clearing—it must begin now, before spring brought the season back around to war.

Such absorbing thoughts distracted him. He did not hear the party of travelers until the mare alerted him with a misstep in the snow. Two Hawks steadied her, then saw the figures clustered on the trail ahead beyond a snow-laden pine. The warrior leading them had an arrow to a bowstring, pointed at Two Hawks's chest.

With the heart in that chest kicking hard, Two Hawks held up the hand not holding the mare's lead and gave the warrior—bundled with a furred hood drawn close about his face, like the others in the party—a gesture of greeting, and the words to go with it. The warrior, slender even under thick clothing, eased the bowstring but didn't lower his arrow.

"You are *Onyota'a:ka*?" he asked in a high ringing voice. The voice of a woman.

Two Hawks advanced several steps with the horse. The woman drew taut the bowstring. He stopped. He could see now that the face framed in breeze-stirred fur was young and smooth, unquestionably female. Everything else—clothing, bearing, that pointing arrow—was that of a warrior.

"I asked a question," she said.

"And this is my answer: I am *Onyota'a:ka,* called Two Hawks."

If she was the one with the bow, then there were no men among them. He counted four others, all with white in the hair straggling from hoods. All carried large burdens, even the one with the bow. His heart slowed its beating and went out to them in pity.

"Where are you and these grandmothers going? Are you on your way to Oriska?" It was the village they would come to at the end of that trail, if they didn't turn north toward the fort.

"I am leading my mother and these others to Kanowalohale," she said, letting the bow down to rest against her thigh. "We come from Ganaghsaraga."

"You are Tuscarora?"

She nodded. "We seek a new home."

"In Kanowalohale? You have passed that place. Did you become confused in that snow last night?"

She had slanted brows like wings, slender and dark. They folded in at his question. Turning to the woman nearest her, she spoke words too low to hear, then handed over the bow and strode forward to meet Two Hawks where he stood, her moccasins breaking a path through the unblemished snow between them. She pushed back her hood. The sun came out of clouds to shine on her black hair. She was smaller than she'd appeared from a distance. Pretty. Or probably would be without that scowl pinching the skin between her brows.

"I come from the soldier fort at the Carrying Place," he told her. "I know what happened at Ganaghsaraga, with Thayendanegea and the sachems there. Why have you and these grandmothers left that place?"

"Because not all at Ganaghsaraga can agree on what to do. Most of my clan chose to move west to Niagara to be farther from the Americans. But my mother fears the British more than she fears that missionary at Kanowalohale. She could not be at peace until I moved her there. These with us are all who chose to come. All of our clan not gone over to the British."

Two Hawks peered past the young woman. Her elders looked cold, tired. Grief in their faces. "You set out yesterday? Into that blow?"

She tightened her lips, tilting her chin. "It had not begun when we left."

Anyone with eyes could have seen it coming. He nearly said so—then reconsidered. *He* had attempted to outrace the storm. Had a mishap befallen him on the trail, he'd have been caught out in it too. Mishaps were hard to avoid in winter. Harder traveling with grandmothers.

"I am going to Kanowalohale with these things of my mother's for which I've traded our furs."

The girl looked him over. "Your mother? What is her clan?"

For the first time it felt like he was talking to a female. "*A'no:wál*—Turtle Clan."

Interest brightened her eyes, letting Two Hawks know she wasn't Turtle Clan. He was accustomed to such looks from young women when they learned his clan, that instant assessment of a man as brother or potential mate. Usually it meant nothing.

"Could you have hit me with that arrow?" He smiled as he spoke, hoping to lighten the encounter.

The girl did not smile back. "Yes. I could kill you with my knife. If I had to."

His gaping at her did him no favors. Her eyes narrowed. "My father is dead. I have no uncles. For five years I have hunted. I taught myself to do it. I do well."

She certainly brandished a hunter's confidence. Two Hawks remembered trying to hunt for his mother during that time his father left them to live with the Senecas. Had she faced the same fears, doubts, dangers? A *girl*.

"Will your missionary forbid me to hunt?" she demanded now. "Will he make me plant corn instead? I will not stay where I cannot freely hunt."

"Reverend Kirkland?" Two Hawks raised his brows. "I think you would not listen even if he tried to tell you such a thing. But you need not worry for that. He has *o'sluni'kéha'*—his white ways—but he is a friend to the People, good in his heart."

Her gaze weighed his words, and him. In her eyes, interest sparked again, bolder this time. Two Hawks looked away. She *was* pretty, and there was spirit in her. But she wasn't Anna Catherine.

A breeze kicked up, stinging his face. It blew powdery snow off the pine, sending it across the huddled women like a veil. One called in a querulous tone, asking how long they would stand on the trail talking while old toes were freezing and old bones going stiff.

Her back to them, the girl grimaced. "Since you go to Kanowalohale, we may travel together . . . if you wish."

She had her pride, this one. Hiding his amusement, he said, "I do wish it. But first, Little Sister, *Náhte' yesa:yáts*—what is your name?"

For the first time, the girl seemed aware of her rudeness. The color in her face deepened as she replied, "I am She-Strikes-The-Water, daughter of the Deer Clan."

8

February 1777
Schenectady

All right, Anna. The Ten Broecks are an hour's ride down the Albany Road, so I'm away."

Lost in thought, Anna straightened from the hearth in Lydia's kitchen, where she'd been stirring syrups set to brew. She'd the vague impression Lydia had spoken but was caught off guard by the sight of her cloaked and standing at the door to the snowy back garden. "Oh . . . you're going?"

"Yes," Lydia said with slow exaggeration. "I am."

"All right. I'll visit Charlotte Stuhler later, see whether she's resting as you prescribed." Anna heard the dullness in her voice—like February, cold and desperate for spring. Mentioning Charlotte Stuhler hadn't helped. Charlotte was Anna's age, contentedly married and expecting her second child before the month was out.

It was quiet in the kitchen crowded with jars and bundled herbs, pungent with the brewing syrups. Lydia hesitated in the doorway, studying her with concern.

"You can go, Lydia. I'm fine."

"How I wish that were so," Lydia said but didn't press. "Expect me home by supper."

Anna nodded, then widened her eyes when Lydia still didn't budge. "*Go.*"

Though it seemed by conscious effort, Lydia smiled and swept out the door, leaving Anna to push along against the tide of loneliness that waited each morning to engulf her. Loneliness and worry.

Two Hawks. She'd relived their last moments together in the barn until the memories were polished as beads. Was he safe? Warm? Thinking of her?

She asked herself those same questions of William, though from a different frame of heart.

She knew Papa was safe and warm. What he thought about these days—besides the bateaux he was crafting for General Schuyler's northern army—was anyone's guess. Anna grieved over the distance grown between them that winter, a chasm of hurt, frustration, and thus far fruitless hoping on her part. Though she'd seen Papa in town, and at Lydia's, on many occasions, all her efforts to engage him in conversation about Two Hawks had been stubbornly thwarted. Papa seemed determined to forget William's twin existed, much less that they desired to marry. If only Two Hawks had done as she'd hoped he would back in autumn and asked Papa to be his apprentice . . .

She was still chasing that thought, and dipping out one of the syrups into a clay jar, when a thud at the back door made her drop the vessel. It shattered on the hearth, spattering syrup across the bricks and the hem of her petticoat.

Leaving the mess, she went to the door. "Lydia? Did you forget—"

The door swung inward. Two Hawks stood before her, clad in a long winter shirt, breath ghosting on the air. "Anna Catherine, I've come to—"

"I know!" she all but shouted, and with her heart unfolding like a flower in her chest—spring at last—drew him into the house and shut the door.

He laughed as he touched her with hands chilled from the cold. "What do you know?"

"You're going to try." She grabbed his hands and pressed them between hers, trying to warm them. She felt the smile straining her face, felt her whole being ablaze with joy. "With Papa, on the Binne Kill. Aren't you?"

His smile for her was blinding as the sun. "If he will have me. Yes."

She gave up trying to warm his hands and threw her arms around him. His thick woolen shirt was cold enough to make her shiver. She pulled back to drink in his face. "Stone Thrower? How is he?"

"Strong now. Well mended."

"And Good Voice?"

"She is also well." Two Hawks touched a fingertip to her cheek, then leaned down and kissed her. His lips warmed as she melted her mouth against his. Abruptly he pulled back. "Lydia?"

"Gone. Until supper."

Awareness of their solitude rose between them, delicious and terrifying. Almost tentatively he kissed her again. Then with growing urgency. The longing of the past months wrapped her like cords. She didn't want him ever to let her go, but too soon he wrenched from the embrace.

"Bear's Heart, I must not be here." He turned toward the door. Leaving her.

"No!" She caught his arm and clung. "We'll be all right. I won't even touch you." She released him and backed away. "Two Hawks, I promise. Just don't go."

His head was bent. He lifted it and looked at her. "I do not know, now I see you again, if *I* can promise."

She was shaking. "I ached so badly to see you. Now here you are—and I'm aching even worse."

"And I," he said.

Such raw and honest words. The moment held them suspended—until their gazes caught and something about it all struck them as funny and they both fell to laughing. It shattered the tension.

"Please stay," she said.

They sat at the table—on opposite sides. Two Hawks for the first time looked around the kitchen and spotted the broken jar. "Did I startle you, make you do that?"

"The syrups!" She jumped up to move them from the heat, found a linen pad to collect the pottery shards, then scrubbed up the spill. She needed to bottle the syrups but could hardly think straight with Two Hawks sitting there watching her.

"Are you hungry?" She turned toward the back of the kitchen, to the alcove where they kept their food stores. "Let me feed you. Then you can tell me everything."

The crooked grin he gave her threatened to melt *her* into a puddle of syrup. "Everything? That will take time."

She laughed again—how long since she'd laughed? It felt glorious. "Just all you've seen and done since I saw you last, and especially . . . what made you decide to come back? Let's start with that."

Lydia thought it odd, what could trigger memories. On her return from the Ten Broecks, a doe had bounded across the snow-patched road ahead and vanished into the pines. It caused her placid horse no more than an ear twitch but sent her back in time with such clarity she might have sworn Jacob rode beside her, red hair blazing in the winter sun. The very thing had happened the second year of their marriage, on that stretch of road. Another doe. Another lifetime.

She was still thinking of her late husband when she reached her gabled house inside Schenectady's stockade, with its stable in back.

At twenty-one she'd married her father's longtime apprentice, though she hadn't felt for Jacob van Bergen the love he'd had for her. He'd understood that. For her, theirs was a marriage of friendship and convenience. He'd offered her a continued presence in her father's apothecary shop, until such time as children were born, children that never came. She'd spoken her vows with eyes open, aware she was making a commitment of the will, but to Lydia's surprise, her heart had followed. She'd grown to care deeply for Jacob. He'd known that, too, before his death.

As she dismounted and opened the stable, Lydia was grateful to harbor no regrets concerning Jacob, save that his promising life had been cut short. But his death had made it possible for her, after a true and proper mourning, to at last open her heart to a longing she'd denied herself since a girl: her love for Reginald Aubrey, who was free now to love her back.

Or should be.

She led the horse inside the stable, startled to find William's gray mare occupying the extra stall. *William*. Then she remembered in whose possession she'd last seen the horse.

It wasn't William who had come.

She tended her mare and hurried to the house.

In the kitchen the hearth blazed. Bottled syrups lined the bricks. At the table Anna and Two Hawks sat, hands clasped over the boards, brown fingers and white entwined. Their hands sprang apart as she shut the door, pushing out the cold.

"Lydia." Anna stood, rocking the bench on the flagstones. "I haven't started supper. Two Hawks arrived . . . We've been talking."

"I see." Lydia set her medical case on the table and greeted the young man with a smile. He'd stood with Anna, tall and sleekly muscled in his Indian garb, disconcerting her still with his face so like—and *un*like—William's, as if the same bold features had been twice sculpted, one hewn in marble, the other cast in bronze.

As Anna wrangled supper from their pantry, Lydia asked, "Have you just arrived?"

"In the morning," he said. "I wanted to come into the town when the streets were quiet."

Had he and Anna been together the day long? Lydia turned to look at Anna. "How is Charlotte Stuhler?"

Anna halted, clutching a round of bread. "Oh no. I forgot about Charlotte."

"Who is this one forgotten?" Two Hawks asked.

Anna put the bread on the table, a knife beside it. "She's expecting a babe soon. I meant to check on her today. I'll go first thing in the morning." She chewed her lip in indecision before blurting, "We had so much to talk about, Lydia. Two Hawks has come to ask Papa to apprentice him at the Binne Kill. He wants to learn the boat-building craft."

Joy and uncertainty vied on Anna's face. Two Hawks gave a small nod of affirmation, though his features were unreadable. "If Aubrey will have me, that is what I want to do."

His expression might have been inscrutable, but his eyes were eloquent, gazing at Anna with such unshielded longing that it pricked Lydia's eyes with tears. Without their saying a word, she knew they were about to place their hearts in her hands. "Let me guess. You wish *me* to put the question to him?"

"We were going to ask you at supper," Anna admitted. "Will you help us? With you on our side, there's a chance Papa will agree."

Lydia took leave to doubt the efficacy of her influence, but since when had she been able to deny Anna anything so badly wanted?

"Of course I'll help you. Both of you," she added, as her gaze slid down the length of Two Hawks's frame, stopping short of those lean thighs scandalously bared by leggings and breechclout—the long woolen shirt he'd worn outside was draped across a kitchen bench. "But, Anna . . . might you have brought anything of William's from the farm over the past months? A pair of breeches, perhaps?"

With all the good intention in the world, their timing might have been better. Lydia halted at the doorway of Reginald's workshop, mindful of

Anna and Two Hawks—Jonathan, they'd agreed he would be called—waiting down the passage in the sitting room. Praying their hearts out, no doubt. Lydia stood in need of prayer.

Reginald wasn't alone in the spacious, wood-scented shop. His partner in business, white-haired, trim-muscled Ephraim Lang, had interrupted work on the long bateau set on the stocks to air a grievance concerning the finished vessels lining the bank of the iced-over Binne Kill.

"The side's hulled sure as if a six-pounder hit it square. A mallet was used, I'd say—and a deal of mean spirit. We'll have to haul it back onto the stocks for repair."

Visible in profile, Reginald's jaw was stiff, his brow tight. "Were you not here last night then?"

"For a time," Lang replied. "But I've my own bed and a wife in danger of forgetting the look of me, I've spent so many nights here of late."

Lydia's stomach tensed beneath her stays. She'd never heard the two so near an argument. She waited, breathing in motes of wood dust hanging in the air. She caught the wearied stoop of Reginald's shoulders as he said, "All right, Ephraim. I'll be the one to sleep here from today. That's what you're after, is it?"

Hope surged. Perhaps her timing wasn't so unfortunate. Surely there would come no better opening than this.

Lydia tapped the doorframe. "Reginald? Captain?"

Both men started, turning toward her.

"Lydia," Reginald said. "What do you here?"

Ignoring the less than cordial greeting, she stepped within and rounded the bateau, the hem of her petticoat sweeping a path through wood shavings. "I'm sorry to interrupt, and overhear, but as it happens, I may have another solution to the problem you appear to be facing . . . should you care to hear it."

"I'd like to hear it," Ephraim Lang said.

Lydia beamed, grateful. Reginald waved a hand for her to continue, then folded his arms as if already set to refuse her suggestion.

"I hadn't known you were suffering the depredations of vandalism, Reginald. It's only that lately"—*how* lately, she refrained from elucidating—"with the increased demand for bateaux from the northern department, it occurred to me you could use another set of hands at work here. It sounds as though you could use another set of eyes as well. An apprentice, perhaps?"

Captain Lang slapped his thigh in approval. "There now. The very thing I've been attempting to persuade him of since he returned from Skenesborough."

Reginald had the look of a man cornered. "'Tis the pair of you ganging up on me, is it?"

Captain Lang grinned, showing strong, yellowed teeth through his white beard. "I like the way this woman thinks. Get yourself an apprentice. Give him this shop for a billet. Save our old bones the discomfort."

"Mind who it is you're calling old." Reginald held his defensive posture a moment longer, then the corner of his mouth twitched. "All right. I'll look about town for a likely lad I can train—once I get a bit caught up. In a day or two—"

"Today, Major," said Lang. "Else there'll never be any catching up."

"Actually, about that likely lad . . ."

Reginald peered at her, suspicion gathering in his gaze. "This conversation hasn't been wholly theoretical, has it? You'd someone in mind before you came through the door."

"That a fact?" Captain Lang asked, interest in his gaze.

Lydia's face warmed. "Was I that transparent?"

Reginald all but rolled his eyes in resignation. "Who is he? Where shall I find him? I see I'll have no peace until I do."

Lydia smiled with a brightness she hoped wasn't overdone. "You needn't go looking. I've brought him with me."

Reginald's face stilled. "Have you?"

Knowing she'd seconds before he guessed for himself, Lydia turned toward the doorway and called, "Anna? Will the two of you come in now?"

"Anna?" Reginald repeated. "What has she to do with this?"

Lydia's heart gave a skip as Two Hawks stepped from the shadowed passage into the window-lit shop. Anna had thought ahead, in hope, and brought to town weeks ago not only a pair of breeches William had abandoned in his flight but two shirts, as well as a hat—no longer stiffened into corners but still presentable. To this Lydia had added a neckcloth once belonging to Jacob and a pair of dark stockings she'd yet to turn into rags. Jacob's coats would need altering to fit Two Hawks's leaner frame, but a pair of buckled shoes had been of a suitable size. With his hair clubbed, the hat covering its shiny blackness . . .

Reginald stared at William's twin, his face registering shock, then an instant's joy, replaced almost at once by recognition and disappointment as Anna moved to stand beside Two Hawks, the pair of them tense, visibly nervous, but radiating hope.

"Papa, will you have Jonathan for your apprentice?"

9

Half-Day Moon
Kanowalohale

On her way back from the lodge of the Tuscarora women, Good Voice spied the girl, Strikes-The-Water, skulking at the forest's snowy edge. Catching her gaze, the girl stepped back into the pines, knocking a bough-full of snow onto her head.

Good Voice pressed back a laugh as Strikes-The-Water's mutterings carried on the winter air. She called to the girl, drawing the attention of those working nearby. Strikes-The-Water emerged reluctantly from the trees. Across her shoulders rode the meat of a deer wrapped in its hide. Snow dusted her head.

"*Shekoli.* You have had success with your bow." Good Voice had heard much of this girl while visiting her mother, two aunts, and another elderly Deer Clan woman, having gone to their lodge bearing gifts of provisions from the Turtle Clan. One thing Good Voice had learned: though she'd told Two Hawks her name was Strikes-The-Water, the girl had been known for some years by another name. Girl-Who-Hunts.

It wasn't unheard of for a woman to hunt like a man, but this girl seemed not to want to draw attention to herself. For the hunting maybe, though Good Voice knew another reason.

"If you are trying to avoid Reverend Kirkland, you need not bother. He has gone away east. Some warriors and sachems went with him." One of them was Stone Thrower's uncle, Clear Day. "Kirkland is taking them to see whether what Thayendanegea says is true, that the Americans have no guns big enough to win this fight against their king. Maybe they will meet the chief, Washington."

The girl looked unimpressed but relieved.

"I am come from your mother's lodge with gifts of welcome from my clan sisters," Good Voice said. "But she will be happy to see that venison. You are a good daughter to her."

Strikes-The-Water looked embarrassed by the praise, yet Good Voice spoke only truth. Those Tuscarora women had little meat in their lodge. No one had overmuch these days with the extra demands on the men. At least Two Hawks had done well for her, finding a soldier at the fort willing to trade cloth for furs. Some soldiers were trading from their own possessions. He'd found the wool she wanted, two blankets, and cloth for making warm leggings and shirts.

Strikes-The-Water was frowning. "You are Two Hawks's mother. Turtle Clan. Yet you serve my old mother as if she was your grandmother."

Good Voice thought it sad that those dark eyes with their lovely tilt should look out at the world with such mistrust. "Heavenly Father bids us love our neighbors and do for them what we would want done for us. Whatever their clan."

Strikes-The-Water's sculpted face reflected wariness but also a hint of gratitude. "You are alone now. This is so?"

Good Voice swallowed back a shard of sorrow. "My son and husband are away, to different places."

Stone Thrower had been at Fort Stanwix for six sleeps. Two Hawks was gone to Anna Catherine and Aubrey. It was a hard thing, seeing her son in love with that girl. She liked Anna Catherine. Had she been born Haudenosaunee, Good Voice couldn't have been happier with her son's choice. As it was she'd let him go, clinging to the possibility—she couldn't call what would bring him heartache a *hope*—that Aubrey would refuse him. But had that happened, Two Hawks would have already returned. He'd been gone twice as long as his father. She'd asked Clear Day, on his way through Schenectady with Kirkland, to find Two Hawks or get word of him. Clear Day knew to go to the Aubrey farm or the home of Lydia van Bergen, who would know where to find Two Hawks in the white's town.

"I see now what you have told me is true," Clear Day had said before his going, when she had placed in his rope-veined hands the tiny image of her firstborn, given by the man who stole him. "He is like his brother, yet not."

The old man had been unable to tear his gaze from the small face, just as she and Stone Thrower had been unable to do that night they sat in Aubrey's house and stared and stared, trying to fill up nineteen summers of longing, half afraid of the thing they held, as if it might somehow hold William's spirit.

Finally her husband's uncle had raised his netted gaze. "My nephew has not spoken much about your time spent in that house."

"You returned to Kanowalohale before Aubrey left to build those boats," Good Voice said. "He stayed away long. When he returned, Stone Thrower was ready to walk home. It was not the parting I hoped for. I am not certain what I hoped."

Their going had left a hollow place in her heart, a certainty that something had been left unfinished. Unspoken. Undone.

Clear Day grunted, as if he guessed as much. "I have thought many times about you and my nephew sleeping under that man's roof. That could not have been an easy thing. What did you say to him about those long years without your son?"

Good Voice admitted they'd shared little. "I do not know everything Stone Thrower said to Aubrey when I was not there to hear, but I do not think it was much more than I said. Why do you ask?"

Clear Day dropped his gaze to the face of her firstborn. "It is in my mind to wonder whether Aubrey understands how great a grief he brought to you by what he did."

She remembered Aubrey's head bowed as she told him of his dead infant, left beside her in that fort called William Henry. She remembered his tears as she spoke of burying that child at the fort the French had called Carillon. Had they been tears for his own son, dead and abandoned, or for her son, stolen and lost? Had they been tears for himself?

"The white beads my nephew gave to that one may have opened his ears to hear your words—he let you into his home and gave you this," he said, lifting his palm on which her son's face rested. "It is something. But that wampum did not clear his throat to speak to you."

"True," Good Voice said. "My husband does not know what is in that man's heart. It is why he made him promise not to go after William without him."

"Ah. I had wondered about that." Clear Day had said no more about Aubrey, or William, though Good Voice had seen much thinking in his gaze as he gave back the image of her son.

Soon after that conversation, Stone Thrower took her son's image with him to the fort to show the scouts there or anyone who had been among the redcoats wintering in Quebec. With all her men gone away to different places, Good Voice had gone about living, often wondering what the rest of her years would hold. She'd begun to see herself—forty summers, best she knew—as a woman getting old. Getting old without children at her fire. There would never be another child at her fire, with no daughter to give her grandchildren to carry on her clan line. That line would end with her.

"Both are away?" Strikes-The-Water asked, recalling Good Voice from her sad thoughts. "Then maybe you need some of this deer?"

Good Voice decided she liked this girl, no matter if she prickled when one tried to come close. Like nettles that were good to eat but could sting you in the picking.

"I would take it gladly," she said, adding, "There is something more I would give your mother. Come to my lodge. You may take it to her with this meat you've brought her."

The girl hesitated but nodded and fell into step with Good Voice, who passed through lodges to the bend in the creek where the Turtle Clan dwelled, certain she'd have thought of something to give the girl before they arrived.

Strikes-The-Water collided with someone as she was leaving Good Voice's lodge, toting her venison and one of the blankets Two Hawks had traded for at the fort. Good Voice rose from tidying the things she'd moved to get at the blanket, recognizing Stone Thrower's startled apology as the girl ducked past him and hurried away.

"*Shekoli,* Husband." Good Voice crossed to where he stood with the door open, looking after the girl. He turned, snowshoes in hand, taking in the sight of her with a smile that made her heart glad. "Come in and be warm. I have food."

Stone Thrower made a sound of pleasure. "You always do. For that I am thankful."

While Good Voice warmed the corn soup she'd fixed earlier for herself, Stone Thrower crossed to the place he kept his belongings. He removed his blanket and haversack, then sat on their sleeping bench.

"That girl," he said with a nod at the door. "She is the one our son guided here?"

"She is that one." Good Voice told him about meeting Strikes-The-Water and exchanging a blanket for the venison, which needed to go into a kettle to boil. "I noticed a thing about that girl," she said, adding water to the thickened soup as it warmed, then setting about cutting the venison and adding it to another kettle simmering over the fire. "How she looked at our son, before he left."

It had happened the day Two Hawks and the girl had arrived together, before the Tuscarora women were taken away by a Deer Clan matron who would see them settled. A brief glance, but telling. She caught Stone Thrower's gaze, making sure he understood what sort of look she meant.

"Did she look at him like that? I did not notice. But it is you women who see such things before men do."

Good Voice smiled, her attention on the knife in her hands.

"She is pretty, that girl," he added.

"That is a thing a man notices." Good Voice's thoughts from earlier flooded back, and she couldn't keep a light heart, no matter how glad she was at Stone Thrower's return. "So is Anna Catherine . . . a pretty girl."

Stone Thrower grunted agreement. "I think our son has eyes for only that one."

Good Voice ladled soup into a bowl. "I have been thinking about that. About our son marrying a white woman." She brought the bowl to Stone Thrower where he sat. "We would lose him."

Lose another son.

Stone Thrower took the bowl but held her gaze. The pain in her heart was matched in his eyes. She went to the fire to stir the simmering meat. When she looked up, her husband was looking around at their snug home, at the log walls hung with their possessions. The benches below. The place where Two Hawks slept, empty now.

"Whenever our son marries," he said, "he will leave us. Even if she is Haudenosaunee, he will go to her people. As I came to yours."

"True. But their children would have a clan."

Stone Thrower took a mouthful of soup and swallowed. He didn't take another. Good Voice knew he carried the same struggle over letting Two Hawks follow his heart, even if it led away from them. Away from the People. "I should not have said these things with you just come through the door," she told him.

Stone Thrower set aside the bowl. Despite his sober look, her heart leapt. "What is it? You bring news?"

"It is to do with William. Before I left the fort, a party of scouts was leaving for the east, to go up the Hudson to Quebec to speak with the Caughnawagas. I asked them to listen for news of Johnson's regiment and to look for a young man with the face of Two Hawks."

"You showed them the little painting?"

"I did."

"May I . . . ?" But he was already taking out the likeness from the pouch he wore on a cord around his neck. Good Voice looked with longing on the face of her firstborn. "Do you think—" She swallowed and began again. "Do you think they will find him?"

She searched her husband's face for hope.

"It is much ground they will cover, and our son is one among many. Still I had to ask it."

Tears threatened, but Good Voice blinked them back. "I have long feared our firstborn will never be Oneida, never think of himself as an Indian person. But I never expected Two Hawks . . ."

"To cleave to a white woman in his heart?" Stone Thrower asked.

Good Voice nodded. "I did not take it seriously enough when he was young and spoke to me all the time of Anna Catherine. I am sorry for letting him go so many times to her, when you did not know about it."

Stone Thrower raised a hand, beckoning. "Sit with me."

They sat on the bench together, and he put his arms around her. She leaned into him, thankful for his broad chest, his familiar scent, all of it wrapping around her now.

"You were making the best choices you knew to make at a time I was no good to you." His hand stroked down her long braid. "If I had been the husband you needed, it might be different for us. But what good is thinking these things? Creator allowed it."

This was true. And if they believed that the God Kirkland preached, the Creator in whose name they had been baptized, desired their good, surely they could trust Him to work out these hopes of theirs for the best.

She felt the tug of fingers in her hair. Stone Thrower had worked loose the leather strip that tied her braid and was running his fingers through the sections, loosening them. But absently, she saw, when she leaned back enough to see his features, strong and brown in the fire's light. There was more on her husband's mind.

"*Satahuhsíyost,*" he said. "Listen carefully, my wife, for I want to try to tell you a thing."

"I am listening." She watched his face, seeing the struggle there to find the words he sought.

"It has been a thing hard to understand, though I have thought about it since the summer when I knelt bleeding in front of the man who stole our son, when I gave him my forgiveness."

It was a sight that would never be wiped from Good Voice's memory. The only other memory of her life as powerful was when she stood looking back at a fallen fort, knowing her firstborn was lost to her.

"I want to tell you what happened to me, in my heart, when I did that hard thing." Stone Thrower had been watching the fire while he spoke. Now he met her gaze. "Did you know until that moment I had not decided which I would use, the white beads or the hatchet?"

She didn't flinch from his steady, searching gaze. "I knew."

"Yes. You and my son, going to that place without me." One side of his mouth turned up as he spoke; he understood the choice she'd made to go to William without telling him and did not hold it against her. "Creator won that battle in me. And He gave me spoils. Not a scalp. Not a life." There was wonder in her husband's face as he spoke. "He took the chains of my hate and bitterness and in their place gave me compassion. Gave me a heart to pray for that man, who I believe is still bound by his own chains because of what he did against our son, against us."

Good Voice felt the shudder in her husband's breath, the beat of his heart so precious to her. He was a different man from the man she married. One who could grieve and yet be whole. Praise be to Creator. She took his face between her hands, catching a glimpse of his startled eyes before she kissed his mouth soundly.

She pulled back, smiling.

"What is this for?" he asked.

"For those good words you spoke. For your good heart."

He kissed the tip of her nose. "I could do better. I could . . ." He leaned back, his expression strangely shy. "Prayer is a thing we do alone. That is not a bad thing, but I would pray with you now, for the ones our hearts are aching for."

They prayed first for Two Hawks and Anna Catherine, then for William. When they finished, Good Voice smiled and touched her husband's face. "I have missed you, my Caleb."

She didn't often call him by the name he received at his baptism. The surprise on his face at her doing it now melted into a smile . . . one with mischief in it. His arm tightened around her, and he pulled her across his lap. When she would have exclaimed, he silenced her with a kiss.

She pulled back breathless from it. "What is *this*?"

"I am living up to that name you called me. Caleb was a warrior, as strong at eighty as he was at forty. He went into the land Creator gave him and fought the giants living there."

Good Voice raised a brow. "Is this true?"

Stone Thrower matched her look, his long mouth smug at its corners. "It is written in Kirkland's Bible. He read it to me."

Before he could move to stop her, she slipped from his grasp and was on her feet, backing toward the fire as the hair he'd loosened swung across her shoulders in a golden shawl, falling in braid-waves to her waist.

"You are not yet eighty, my Caleb. And I am not a giant for you to conquer."

Surprise at her playfulness passed swiftly into delight and hunger— but not for food. "I am forty-four summers. Though just now I feel like twenty-two."

She could sense his body coiling to spring. She balanced on the balls of her feet, ready for flight. "I still am not a giant."

"You are my wife, who has said she missed me. Did you mean it?" He waggled his eyebrows at her, suggestive of ways she might prove it to him.

Good Voice giggled—*giggled,* as she had not done since a girl. She backed away another step, holding up her hands. "I misspoke. I did not mean—"

He sprang for her, coming off the sleeping bench with astonishing speed. With a screech, Good Voice dodged around the fire as if she meant to make for the door.

She didn't get that far. After only a step or two her foot caught—or seemed to catch—on the frayed edge of a mat and she stumbled—or seemed to stumble—so that Stone Thrower caught her easily around the waist, swept her up against his chest, and carried her back to their bench piled with furs. Only now she was too busy kissing him to remember to resist.

10

Late March 1777
Schenectady

*O*utside the tiny house tucked near the eastern stockade, all was cold and scattered snow. Inside its single bedroom a fire blazed, water steamed, and Charlotte Stuhler sweated to bring forth her second babe.

"'Tis well—you're sure?" the laboring woman asked, abed still though a birthing stool awaited the babe's arrival.

"As I can be," Lydia said, examining Charlotte between pains. "The babe is positioned. 'Tis only a matter of time."

Charlotte's reply was strained with the next building pain. "This one's . . . in no hurry . . . to join us."

The birth had already lasted much longer than Charlotte's first. Anna and Lydia had been called before midnight. Dawn was approaching, with possibly hours yet to wait.

Charlotte gripped Anna's hand through the pain, as Lydia crossed the room to check the water on the hearth. Anna wiped Charlotte's perspiring brow, then her own, and removed her cap. She caught Lydia's amused gaze; as a girl she hadn't been able to keep a cap on her head to save herself. How William had teased . . .

William. Worry for him harried her thoughts fleetingly before the sound of voices arose beyond the room, where Charlotte's husband waited with their sleeping son. A knock sounded on the bedroom door. It pushed inward, revealing a stout middle-aged woman, face half-shrouded in a hood. She pushed it back. Still it took Anna a moment to place the woman in this setting—Mrs. Baird, housekeeper for the Kennedys, a wealthy merchant and his expectant wife who lived across town.

"'Tis my mistress," the woman announced, no beating round bushes. "Brought to bed with the latest. Can one of ye come, or shall I see to it meself?"

"Would you?" Lydia asked, straightening at the hearth. Mrs. Baird's mouth sagged, revealing several missing teeth. Lydia laughed. "I'm not in earnest—though it's likely to be a quick birth."

It was Mrs. Kennedy's fifth.

Lydia beckoned Anna from Charlotte's side. "Will you go? I should like to remain with Charlotte." Her eyes conveyed more than her words. She wasn't as sanguine about Charlotte's long-progressing labor as she'd tried to appear.

Though they'd discussed her doing so in the near future, Anna had yet to be the sole attending midwife at a birth. "Are you sure? Sure you wouldn't rather I stay with Charlotte?"

"I'm sure. You've your case, yes? Everything you need? I'll come as soon as I may." Lydia all but pushed Anna toward Mrs. Baird, hovering in the doorway. "Anna Doyle will attend your mistress."

Anna donned her cloak, took up her medical case, and followed Mrs. Baird's broad figure out into the cold, through the waking streets to the Kennedys' large brick home, where the courage she'd gathered during the brisk walk crumbled at the back garden gate, met with the sound of Mrs. Kennedy's screams.

Three hours later Anna left through that gate more stunned than when she'd entered. She hardly knew the direction her feet carried her from the Kennedy home until she'd arrived—not at her bed, where Lydia had sent her upon hastening from the Stuhlers', where Charlotte had at last presented her husband with their first daughter. Anna's brain abuzz with wonder and fatigue, her feet had taken her to the Binne Kill. To Two Hawks.

She found him on the quay, where activity was afoot near the warehouse. Papa conversed nearby with several merchants while Captain Lang oversaw the unloading of three bateaux. The river had opened—barely. The bateaux and a few canoes had hazarded the passage from points upstream. Merchants and townsfolk and river men milled about, giving and receiving news from the western settlements and Fort Stanwix. It was all a blur to Anna. Figures, voices, the cold river. All except Two Hawks, leaving Papa's side to return to the office.

"Two Hawks!" His name was out, flying ahead of her, before she remembered she ought to have addressed him as Jonathan. Just shy of the office he halted, turning to spot her. Other faces turned as she parted the crowd. At the last moment, she stumbled over a foot in her path and fell against Two Hawks, who caught her and held her upright, strong hands gripping her arms. For an instant she clung to him, then straightened hurriedly, but already she felt the narrowed stares of those nearest them. "I've something wonderful to tell you! I'd no idea it would be today, but—"

"We will talk inside, yes?" His voice was strained as, with a hand on her arm, he ushered her into the office, shutting the door behind them. In the silence her ears rang. They both peered through the front office window. Several of the men on the quay were still staring after them, some with distaste, one or two with indignation. She watched Papa catch their attention, drawing them back into conversation. Forcing a smile.

"I tripped. I didn't mean to—"

"I know."

"Do they?" she asked, nodding toward the merchants on the quay.

"It will be all right." It wasn't an answer, but Two Hawks's shoulders eased and his gaze warmed, focusing on her. "Look at you, my Bear's Heart. I cannot say whether you look more in want of sleep or dancing."

She smiled, putting out of mind what had passed. She reached a hand to her head, realizing she'd left her cap at the Stuhlers'. "Both at once, could I manage it. I must tell you what's happened."

"So I left Lydia with Charlotte and went to Mrs. Kennedy and . . . Oh, she was in such difficulty, I thought I was going to lose them both, mother and babe. It wasn't her first—her fifth! And never a complication before. But this time the babe was crosswise. I tried to turn it."

Anna hadn't stopped talking since they reached the green-paneled sitting room behind the office. Beside Two Hawks on the settee, her words were coming jumbled. She couldn't stop them, even when Two Hawks, listening wide eyed, attempted to respond.

"*Turn* it?"

"I've helped Lydia do it. But it wouldn't work. For hours I tried, with the poor woman screaming—"

"Screaming—"

"*I* wanted to scream. There was nothing more I could do. I'd sent Mrs. Baird for Lydia, but she hadn't come. Mrs. Kennedy had swooned. I put my hands on her belly and prayed. I don't know what I prayed. Maybe just *God, help* because He did! The babe inside her turned. Perfectly."

"It turned when you prayed?" Two Hawks asked.

"Yes! I felt the baby shift. Then Mrs. Kennedy's eyes popped open. She raised up and gave this horrible groan and pushed and there was the baby's head." Anna laughed, remembering the shout of relief she'd been unable to restrain. "Then it was out of her and crying, and Mrs. Kennedy was crying, and Lydia came in but it was done. It's a *girl*—"

She choked suddenly and burst into tears. Then she felt at last what she'd been longing for—Two Hawks's arms drawing her to his chest, to the strong beat of his heart—and everything was right and perfect as he stroked her back and said, "Bear's Heart, you have done well."

She sniffed, blotting tears against his shirt. "God did it. Not me."

"Would He have done it if you had not called to Him?"

"I don't know. I'm just so relieved." She heaved a sigh and sat up, smiling through the tears. "And I'm no longer an apprentice, Lydia says. I'm a midwife."

He touched her face, sharing her joy. But fresh memory was seeping back in, dimming its radiance.

"I hope I didn't cause trouble on the quay—between you and Papa." Nearly four weeks had passed since Two Hawks became Papa's apprentice. Anna felt as if she'd held her breath the entire stretch, waiting to see how Two Hawks would fare. He was sleeping at the boatyard, doubling as guard, spending his days learning the boat-building craft. There had been no more destruction of Papa's property. Papa thought the troubling incidents must have been the work of disgruntled Tories. His wasn't the only Patriot property targeted.

Two Hawks flicked a glance at the doorway. "Maybe not just with him."

Anna's bubble of peace burst, leaving her with a dizzying, sinking feeling. She closed her eyes, trying to order her thoughts, but her mind swirled with exhaustion. "You're William's twin. And you're Oneida. Your people are friends to . . ." When she opened her eyes, Two Hawks was shaking his head, what looked like amusement tugging at his mouth. "You laugh at me? Why?"

He put a hand over her lips to silence her. "I am not laughing. I am pleased because that is your heart for me talking and I like what it says. But listen. What do you think most whites see when they look at me? An Oneida? A friend? No, the first thing they see is *Indian*. Even with these clothes that is what they see. And they are afraid or angry. Bear's Heart, this is a thing we will face for the rest of our days."

For the rest of our days. His words sent her thoughts spiraling in too many directions to grasp them all. She caught the trailing edge of the one that held her hope. "Does that mean Papa's pleased with your work? That you'll be staying?"

"He has not said, but I think so. And there is something I did not expect."

"What is that?"

"I did not know how much *I* would like this work with wood." He hesitated, his expression awash in a shy pride. "I am good at it."

Was he telling her the truth or only what she wanted to hear? But Two Hawks had never done that. He was honest, even when it hurt to be.

"Mmm," Anna replied, too happy now for words. Too tired for them. She lay her head against the settee's back and was startled when her chin jerked upright. She opened her eyes to find Two Hawks sitting quietly, watching her with a look so tender she longed for him to take her in his arms.

"Even asleep you glow like a flame," he said. "It is good to see you happy."

Two Hawks brushed his fingertips against her cheek, then grasped her hand and pulled her to her feet. "You should go to your bed." He drew her close, though their bodies didn't touch, and kissed her forehead gently.

"All right," she said. "But will you come for supper this evening? I'll ask Papa too."

"I will come if your father allows. Now go. I must work, and you sleep."

Neither had so much as uttered Anna's name the past few hours, yet the tension in the workshop was as thick as if she stood between them. Reginald couldn't banish the sight of his daughter embracing the young man now planing a steering sweep on the other side of the half-planked bateau set up on the stocks. She'd stumbled and fallen against him, but not everyone had seen that. Nor could *he* forget the cold blade that sliced through his vitals at the looks cast at the pair on the quay.

At least the lad had possessed the sense to lead her indoors. While that had served to help Reginald distract the attention of the men to whom he'd been speaking, he was finding no comfort in the memory now. How long had it been, those moments between their vanishing into the office together and Anna emerging alone? Ten minutes? Fifteen? When she'd appeared at his side, he'd broken off a conversation to hear her happy news and supper invitation. Pride in her still suffused him, though it was tainted with suspicion. Dread. Did she know what she was doing to her reputation? Not with the midwifery, but with her patent attachment to William's brother, who looked too Indian for anyone's good.

Reginald stood back from the plank he'd been shaping, bringing that dark head into view between the curving frames of the bateau's sides. The young man's aptitude for the work had surprised Reginald. Already he was moving beyond basic carpentry skills, grasping the finer aspects of the craft with a readiness that betrayed the spark of passion Reginald had hoped to strike in William.

He is the same blood as William.

Reginald clenched his teeth against the conviction that he'd no right to tell the lad what he should or shouldn't hope for, with Anna or anything else. He'd come to Reginald, placed himself under his authority of his own free will. *That* gave him some right, did it not? Besides, whatever else Reginald had forfeited, he was still the only father Anna had. He had every right to concern himself with her well-being. Her behavior. Her attachments.

He broke the silence. "So Anna is a midwife proper now, and we are celebrating this evening. I suppose she told you?"

The scraping ceased. Jonathan turned, regarding him through the bateau's frame. No defiance marked him—unlike Reginald's last sight of features so eerily similar.

"She was full with her joy. Creator did a wonder for her. For the mother and babe."

"A wonder? Nothing she hasn't done with Lydia for years now."

"She did not tell you how Heavenly Father turned the babe in the belly of that mother, when it seemed they both would die?"

Anna hadn't told him that. Granted he'd been distracted when she approached him, his attention demanded by work. Perhaps she'd meant to tell him over supper. "That's what the pair of you were doing? Speaking of such things?" Doubt laced his tone.

"I will tell Anna Catherine she must take more care in front of others."

The unexpected words, in answer to the question he hadn't asked, lanced to the heart of what was troubling Reginald. He met the dark gaze fronting him across the bateau. There was no challenge in it. Neither was there flinching.

"Only for watching eyes?"

The lad set the sweep aside and stood. "I have made my promise to her, and to Creator, not to take what is not mine for taking. I make it now to you as well. But on that day I have your blessing, I wish to make Anna Catherine my wife."

Reginald felt the blood leave his face. His next words ground out of him. "Is she worth it to you? Have you counted the cost?"

Two Hawks did not look away. "I have counted what we would face from the people of this place. Not all of them. But some. I have counted what I would leave behind—my place as a warrior and protector of the People. I have counted that my children will be of no clan down all the generations that come after me. These things I have counted, but still my heart is full with Anna Catherine."

Reginald felt sick. "And has Anna made a like accounting?"

A flash in the dark eyes. If it was anger, the lad spoke with unshaken calm. "Should you accept me as her husband, still I would not take Anna Catherine as wife unless she had done this counting for herself. For us to have a life together will take much courage, for her as well as for me. This," he made a motion of his hand at the bateau, the tools, the wood scattered about, "is the time of counting for her. And for you."

The lad put Reginald in mind of Lydia, who often disconcerted him with her honesty. And he was right about one thing. Should Two Hawks do everything possible to live as Jonathan, a white man, he would never be accepted as such by some. Reginald had heard him called *half-breed* in the town. And worse. Fear and hatred of Indians ran deep in the valley. He once knew it himself, though he'd learned to see past it, at least in his dealings upriver with the Six Nations and those Indians who came through Schenectady to do their trading.

But this was Anna. Her life. Her heart. Was she prepared to live with the costs this young man envisioned?

He rounded the bateau, leaving no barrier between them. He halted a pace too close, but William's twin didn't step back.

"Enough of this," he snapped. "There is work needing done."

Jonathan's jaw hardened, but he nodded and made to return to his work on the sweep.

Reginald didn't think he could bear the sight of him just now. "Fetch Captain Lang for me. I need to speak with him."

William's twin brushed at the wood shavings on his borrowed shirt and went to do Reginald's bidding, leaving him smarting at his own craven longing for the impossible. That it could be William working beside him, never knowing what manner of man he called *father*. He wished he'd never agreed to Stone Thrower's demand of sharing the burden of finding William. The lad's defection was a constant, condemning lash across his heart.

Reginald went back to setting planks for a time before realizing his apprentice hadn't returned from the quay. He'd made up his mind to go in search of Lang himself when he heard the office door bang open and the captain's voice shouting down the passage.

"Major, you had better get out here!"

11

Groggy from her nap, Anna halted in surprise at the pantry alcove at the back of the kitchen. Occupying half the space was an astonishing sight—a bathing tub, wood framed and copper lined. Occupying the tub, submerged to her neck, was Lydia, head lolling back against the tub's curved head.

"Lydia? Where on earth did *that* come from?"

Cheeks flushed a rosy shade, Lydia peered through the steam rising from the water's placid surface. "This, my girl, is all your doing."

"What do you mean *my* doing?"

Though her hair was pinned high, steam had curled tendrils about Lydia's face, making her look nearer Anna's age than a woman in her early thirties. "A certain Mr. Kennedy insisted on showing his gratitude for the life of his newest daughter *and* his wife by passing along this glorious contraption. I suppose I should have let you try it first, but you slept through its delivery and I hadn't the heart to wake you." Grinning impishly she added, "So I told myself."

Water sloshed as Lydia made to rise. Anna snatched up a waiting towel and held it wide, doubling as a curtain.

"I suppose we'll need to hang a drape." Lydia wrapped herself as she exited the tub.

Anna busied herself scanning pantry shelves, debating what to fix for supper. When she turned, Lydia had donned a wrapper. "Perhaps a rug would be a welcome addition," she said, as Lydia's feet did a little dance on the chilly stones.

"That's the spirit." Still damp around the edges and warm from the bath, Lydia reached to embrace Anna. "Congratulations—and thank you for this," she added, with a rap of knuckles on the tub's edge. "Though it did take a prodigious lot of hauling and heating water to fill it."

"Then it shan't be a daily affair," Anna said.

"Lovely for a treat, though. If you'd like, I'll see to supper while you—" A banging on the front door silenced Lydia, who gestured at the shift, stays, and petticoat draped over the bench, brows arching in half-apologetic amusement.

"I'll see who it is." Anna hurried through the house to the front door, which banged open as she reached it, causing her to leap back in surprise, even as she saw that it was Papa and Captain Lang, supporting a sagging figure between them. A man, dark haired and lean, drenched and reeking of mud as though he'd been in the river. His head drooped, presenting her only its sodden, muddy crown.

Papa's voice was strained. "Where is Lydia?"

"I . . . She . . . Bring him in, Papa. Who is it? What happened?"

Rousing to her voice, the man Papa and Captain Lang supported lifted his head, showing her a face so bruised and swollen, it took her a span of clutching heartbeats to recognize Two Hawks.

A fire warmed the room at the foot of the stairs where years ago Reginald Aubrey had convalesced in the McClarens' spare bed. In that bed Two Hawks now lay, drifting in and out of awareness. Anna occupied a chair at his bedside, clearly with no intention of budging from the spot should the rest of Schenectady come pounding on the door in need.

With a basin to empty, Lydia left the door ajar and stepped into the passage. She found Reginald sitting alone in the kitchen. Lydia set the basin with its red-stained contents on the table. "He's patched as well as can be," she said in answer to Reginald's querying look. "Anna's with him. Now—what on earth happened to your apprentice?"

Reginald winced at her words. "That is a story only he can tell."

"Obviously someone—several someones—gave him a thrashing and tossed him into the river like a sack of kittens. What I want to know is *why?*"

Lydia was nearly as angry as Anna had been since her first sight of Two Hawks being dragged, battered and dripping, into the house. With lips clenched and bloodless, Anna had ministered to her beloved's abused flesh, jealous for the task of stripping off the sopping clothes, washing away the blood and mud, while Lydia had assessed his injuries.

His beautiful face. Though a shocking sight presently, Lydia had assured Anna he'd probably heal without disfigurement. There were no deep lacerations. No broken teeth or facial bones. Perhaps a cracked rib beneath the welter of bruising on his torso. Fists had done the work, not weapons, except for the nasty scalp wound that had required stitches to close.

Now she'd time to think beyond the immediate crisis, the implication of that wound sent a chill down Lydia's spine. "Did someone mean to *scalp* him?"

"No. Surely . . ." Reginald rubbed a hand over his face. "Honestly, Lydia, I don't know. We'd had words over Anna, see, and I wanted him out of my sight. I sent him to the quay to fetch Ephraim. He was overlong at it. I was about to go looking when Ephraim came shouting for me. He'd found Jonathan lying half in the Binne Kill—beaten as you've seen. And that is all I know."

Reginald shuddered; despite his words there *was* more. Lydia sat across from him, the languor of that glorious bath long vanished.

"What is it?"

"Something happened on the quay outside my office. Anna came to us after that birthing this morn. She called him by his Oneida name, in front of listening ears."

"Well? 'Tis no secret he's Oneida."

"Let me finish," Reginald said. "She called to him and then . . . it seemed she stumbled, tripped I suppose, but she landed square in his arms—with all the quayside looking on. If only she had taken more care."

Lydia felt a sinking of heart, a stirring of unease. "She loves him, Reginald. She wanted to share her happiness. And no doubt she was exhausted. It was an accident."

Reginald's fists clenched on the table. "Accident or no, it will not do. Can you not see? She is blind to the shade of his skin, but I cannot be. Not when there are those around us who will never be so blind."

Lydia pressed her fingertips to her throbbing temples, hating this.

"The lad had the sense to put her from him," Reginald went on. "Or perhaps it was Anna's doing. 'Twas over in an instant, and I hoped nothing would come of it. But what else could have provoked such an attack? The lad has kept to himself, done his work, made no enemies in this—"

Reginald's gaze shot past Lydia, sharpening before Anna's voice cut in, as hard and cold as Lydia had ever heard it.

"They weren't *his* enemies, Papa. They were yours!"

Turning to see her—tall and slender in the doorway, hair mussed, face white and set—Lydia rose to her feet, placing herself between the two. "Reginald's enemies? What do you mean?"

"I mean that what happened to Two Hawks had nothing to do with us. He's told me." Anna didn't take her gaze from Reginald, an accusing look Lydia knew must be breaking his heart. It was breaking hers. "He went as you sent him, Papa, to fetch Captain Lang. As he was passing your bateau on the stocks outside, he heard noises. He found three men setting fire to your boats. More Tory sympathizers, no doubt, trying to stop you building bateaux for the Continentals. Two Hawks stopped the fire's catching, but instead of fleeing, they caught him—and beat him!" Tears flowed, choking her voice. "Why did no one stop them? Didn't anyone see?"

Reginald was on his feet, expression pained. "Someone may have seen."

"And gave no aid? Why?"

Reginald took a step toward his daughter and stopped. Lydia hadn't seen such vulnerability on his face since the summer past, when he knelt before Stone Thrower in a clearing at sunset, expecting to die. "You know full well it is because he is an Indian."

Anna's nostrils flared. "He's William's *twin*. Hasn't anyone eyes to see that? They'd never have done such a thing to William."

"They thought William my son. There is no knowing what would happen now the truth—"

"Then never mind William. If you would just accept Jonathan, accept *us,* others would follow your lead. Your resentment is making it harder. *You* make it harder."

Reginald's mouth firmed. "No one said this arrangement would be easy, or safe. Anna, look you . . ." He started toward her again, but her rigid stance held him off.

Reginald, Lydia silently pleaded, *tell her what she needs to hear. Even if you cannot promise to soften your heart, at least be sorry for it.*

Reginald stood there unbending, inscrutable, and so Lydia did what was probably the worst thing she could have done—blindly wielded the scalpel of her own words, hoping nothing vital would be nicked. "Anna, 'tis more complicated than that. That's what your father is trying to say. Choosing Two Hawks, marrying him . . . It won't be an easy path for either of you."

Anna turned wounded eyes to her. Her slender throat convulsed as she raised her chin. "I wanted to tell you both what happened. I'm going back to him now."

She pivoted on her heel and left them without another word.

Reginald didn't go after her.

Lydia hugged her arms to her chest, as if to hold together the pieces breaking inside her. Disappointment wrapped her tighter—disappointment in Anna, in Reginald, in the whole of mankind. Most of all in herself. How often in the past had she found a path through tangled hurts with her words? Blunt, honest, brave words. They had deserted her.

Reginald stood there in his misery, cut off from his daughter, from her. As he'd always been in the deep places of his heart. She'd never seen that as clearly as she did now.

"Reginald, there will be no supper tonight, and it will be some days before your apprentice can resume work. I suggest you go back to the shop or home. Leave us—him—to heal."

They'd stripped him to his chilled skin while he lay unconscious, needing to assess his injuries as quickly as they could. Anna grieved over the sight of him. *She* had wanted Two Hawks in her world. *She* had pressed for the apprenticeship. *She* had drawn unwanted attention on the quay. What if Papa was right? What if her carelessness had caused some of those men to devise this hurt? How could God, in the span of a few hours, answer a desperate prayer with a miracle, then allow her to do something so unforgivably stupid?

Two Hawks had refused more than a bark tea for his ease, still he slept again, brows pinched, pain etched on his battered face. The quilt was pulled to his waist now. Sitting in a chair drawn close, Anna studied every uncovered inch of him, imagining the fists that had struck him—eyes, mouth, arms, belly. Then, as he'd fought back with strength and skill, someone had produced a knife . . .

She winced at the gash across the front of his scalp, running from just below the crown of his head nearly to his left ear. The hair surrounding it was shaved away, the red line of the wound bisected by Lydia's neat stitches.

They hadn't thrown him in the Binne Kill. He'd gone in to escape his attackers, swimming underwater and hiding in thick cattail growth until the men left him for drowned. Shivering and bleeding, he'd tried to get ashore. It was all he remembered until looking up into her horrified face.

He'd taken long to warm. The room was verging on hot now, but she would keep that fire going. Whatever it took for him to heal. She started to touch his face, but there was no place that didn't look too tender. Instead she slipped her fingers beneath his hand, resting at his side. His knuckles were badly scored.

The touch awakened him. His eyes opened, mere slits in swollen, discolored flesh, yet the pain in them went so deep, she felt she was falling down a well into his soul. Afraid to cause him more harm by raising his hand, she bent and pressed her lips to the back of it, tasting tears. "I'm sorry. So sorry." Besides the snap of the fire, silence was the only reply. She raised her head, wondering if he'd fallen unconscious again. He was looking at her.

"Anna Catherine." His cut, swollen lips barely moved over her name. "Do you still want me?"

She blinked. "What do you mean?"

"Are you certain this is the life you want?"

Her stomach gave a lurch of dismay. "Two Hawks . . . what happened today, surely it won't happen again. Maybe Papa's right. Maybe this *was* my fault. I'll be more careful. I promise I will. I'm so sorry."

That steady gaze was hard to bear, harder still to read.

"It is bad . . . how I look?"

"Yes." She wouldn't lie to him. "But nothing that won't heal in time. Lydia's sure of it, and so am I. You've some broken ribs. You'll be in this bed for a time. But I'll be right here all the while."

He shifted on the bed, sucked in a breath, and went still. "Aubrey will let you care for me?"

"He hasn't a say in it!"

"Anna," Two Hawks began. She could see he was growing weary, expending precious energy in speaking. "He is finding his way. Be patient. It is you and me . . ."

Her throat ached. "What about us?"

"No clothes, or work, or name will change my skin."

Anna let go his hand and sat back. She didn't want to hear these words of Papa's coming out of Two Hawks's mouth, giving them the weight of validity. She leaned close again, fingers spread across his chest where the bruising was lightest. "If it's going to be this hard for us here, then take me to *your* people. Where and how we live doesn't matter. Only that we're together."

Her heart beat wildly at what she'd heard herself offer.

Two Hawks reached for her hand but only brushed it with his. Instead of the pleasure she'd hoped to see, a distance came into his eyes. "A man goes to live with his wife's people. That is part of being *Onyota'a:ka*. I will need to change much, and I am willing. But not everything. Not that."

"All right." She thought desperately, seeking a way. The image of his mother, Good Voice, sprang to mind. "Then help me get a new family. Is there someone who would adopt me, someone of a different clan, so we can marry? Clear Day—he's not Turtle Clan, is he?"

"He is Bear Clan." Two Hawks's eyebrows twitched. "You would do this?"

"To be with you? *Yes.*" She laughed through her tears, but Two Hawks didn't even smile. He only looked at her, dark eyes searching her face. "Did you hear me? I said I would."

Still he didn't answer. He closed his slitted eyes and turned his battered face away, as if sleep had claimed him. But she was almost certain it hadn't.

12

Early April 1777
Schenectady

*S*o, Major. You mean for the lad to resume his work, or will you send him hightailing it back to his people?"

Bent over office ledgers, Reginald raised his head to find Ephraim Lang leaning in the inner doorway. He'd heard the question but pretended otherwise. Lang wasn't fooled.

"See him today, did you?"

Reginald took up a quill, jotted a note. "He was asleep."

Anna had been away in town. She and Reginald hadn't spoken since their angry exchange the day of the beating—a tearing to his soul—still he'd been glad to find her gone from the house and only Lydia watching over his apprentice. It did not bear much thinking on, Anna and the lad under the same roof, even though it was the rest of the world he most mistrusted to treat his daughter well, given the path down which her heart was leading her.

Lang's voice intruded again. "I see you're perusing Schuyler's orders for bateaux. Seems another pair of hands is still needful. And I'm limited in my hiring by the number of bateaux you're able to crew. So I ask again, Major—will it be Jonathan, or will you start over with another apprentice who likely cannot tell a plane from a pitchfork?"

"He's barely on his feet," Reginald countered, "sooner than Lydia would have it so. He rose from bed the day after the attack and moved his blankets to the floor."

Lang chuckled at that. "No surprise there. Most Oneidas don't sleep on feather ticks. But you haven't answered my question."

"I don't know—and there is honesty for you, Ephraim. What think you? Should I keep him on despite what happened?"

"What happened is the lad saved your boats and took a beating for it."

"Well do I know it." And well had he examined his heart, the guilt he felt over it, the pain of Anna's condemning gaze. "If only it was so simple a matter."

Lang studied him, blue eyes piercing. "You want simple? How does this suffice: 'We hold these truths to be self-evident, that all men are created equal, that they are endowed by their Creator with certain un-alienable Rights, that among these are Life, Liberty and the pursuit of Happiness.' Recognize those words, Major? Would you surmise that Jefferson, Franklin, Adams, and the rest meant them?"

"Doubtful they'd have put their names to the declaration—or their necks in the Crown's collective noose—did they not believe them."

Lang nodded. "And does 'all men' include William?"

"Of course it does. Or will. You know I hope it will."

"I know it," Lang said. "But what of his brother, whose skin isn't as white? And while I'm being blunt, I might as well say that to my mind you've less right to hope anything for William's sake than you do his twin's, who's come to you of his own free will."

Reginald felt his face stiffen. Lang knew the truth about William, to whom he was born and how he came to be an Aubrey, but in his gruff, forbearing way had never openly judged Reginald for it. Was he doing so now?

"Because he wants something of me. He wants Anna."

"He wants you to know him and to know you in return. Given everything you've told me of what happened before we met in the wood between Fort William Henry and Fort Edward, that says a lot about that young man's character." Reginald started to speak, but Lang held up a hand. "Would it surprise you to know you aren't the only one with secrets in his past—or present? I'm fixing to divest myself of one, so hear me."

Reginald waited, attention and curiosity captured.

"The woman you know as my wife," Lang said, "isn't my first. My first was a Mohawk woman from Canajoharie. I married her about the time you stopped your trips upriver so you never knew of it, but she bore me two children before she died. Boy and girl. Three and five years they be now, living with their people. I see them every time I pass on the river."

Lang crossed the office to the outer door, wrenching it open when it stuck. "Whatever Jefferson and his lot may truly believe, *I* hold those truths to be self-evident for my children. For their aunties, their uncles, and their old grannie too, should they want them. And that's all I aim to say on the matter."

He stepped out onto the quay, shutting the door behind him.

It was five sleeps since they brought him to Lydia's house, though Two Hawks had done his sleeping during the day. Awake now on his pallet, he knew by the room's slanting light that the sun wasn't long for setting. He expected to spend the coming night as he had the others, awake before the hearth fire, staring into flames he fed through the long dark that wasn't truly cold enough to need a fire. Its presence helped him to pray, to think—and being awake at night made it less likely he would find himself alone with Anna Catherine.

Not that he didn't want to be alone with her. Nor did he regret her seeing him wounded. Among his things brought up from the boatyard was a looking glass he used to shave the beard that was coming in thicker than his father's now. In it he had seen his bruised eyes, the egg-sized knot on his cheekbone, his scabbed-over lip, the stitched gash across his scalp. Though it hurt Anna Catherine to see him so, she bore it with courage.

That wasn't why he wished to avoid her. She'd given him much thinking to do, and her nearness made it harder to think about some things.

On his feet, he reached for his brother's shirt, draped on the too-soft bed beside the other garments he'd worn the past weeks. Careful of his healing ribs, he pulled it over his head.

Anna Catherine's offer to come and live with the People had filled him with such painful joy, he'd been unable to answer her. He was glad now he hadn't. The answer he'd wanted to give went against what he believed was right for a man to ask of his wife. To leave her people? Join his? Despite what had happened, he knew in his bones he was meant to cross that line. Not his Bear's Heart. But he needed help to do it. Aubrey's help. Not only his permission but his blessing and support. His heart.

Two Hawks eased his arms through the shirt-sleeves. He hadn't yet grown used to the breeches but pulled them on, then sat on the floor and stuck his feet into stockings, fastened the garters, buttoned the breeches over them at the knee. He buckled the shoes that had belonged to the man who had been Lydia's husband.

He hadn't spoken to Aubrey since the attack. Nor had Anna Catherine. That was not good. Two Hawks needed to make her see that she would have to find it in her heart to forgive. To honor. Not an easy thing to ask, or do, but he had the example of his own father to follow. His father and the white beads.

Now he had come to an end of thinking and it was time for speaking. A bad thing had happened, but he would heal. They would be strong in Creator's grace and not let it cause their hearts to grow afraid or bitter. They would set the pattern to follow in future years, whenever such things happened.

He was no such fool to think they never would again.

Two Hawks hadn't ventured often from his room, not wanting to alarm Lydia by prowling her house at night, but he knew his way to the kitchen. If Anna Catherine was home, she would be there, where the women worked and ate their meals. But the kitchen was empty. A fire in the hearth looked tended, but he saw no sign of either woman.

Were they outside, behind the house where they had a garden? It was too early for planting, but he decided to check and was heading for the door when he heard a splash. It came from behind a curtain hung across a portion of the kitchen used for storage. Thinking one of the women was back there pouring water, he went to the curtain and moved it aside, starting to speak Anna Catherine's name.

The name caught in his throat. She wasn't pouring water. She was immersed in it, sunk inside a basin with legs and wheels on the legs, with her head above the water at one end, bare knees poking up near the other. Her eyes were closed, her hair spilling over the back of the basin onto the floor, a river of honey glinting in a candle's light.

His heart beat strong and fast. It led his mind straight over the present uncertainties to a day when he and she were one in the eyes of Creator and he could fill his gaze with her like this and never have to stop looking.

Then he remembered. That was not now. *Turn away. Stop looking.*

Surely he would have done so had Anna Catherine not opened her eyes and seen him there.

"Two Hawks!" Water sloshed from the basin as she gripped its sides, pushing up out of the water so her knees went down and her shoulders came up, slender, graceful, and bare. Her eyes were startled but unafraid. They held him, drew him.

He gripped the curtain, heat building in his face. He had only come looking to speak with her, but now he was gazing on what he had no right yet to see. He looked away, putting the curtain back in place, turning to retreat to his room.

His retreat was blocked. Behind him in the kitchen stood Reginald Aubrey, disbelief and outrage on his face.

13

*I*t was smashing to bits. Everything she'd tried to build. Anna heard it breaking through the curtain—Papa accusing Two Hawks of dishonoring her, betraying his trust. And in his defense, Two Hawks said nothing. Not one word.

Neither of them heeded her protests as she bolted from the tub and scrambled to dress. She'd been startled to find Two Hawks watching her bathe, but it was clear he'd been as startled to find her so. Only a second had passed before he drew back. A *second*.

"I'd come here to speak of your returning to work," Papa was saying, voice tight with fury. "But I tell you now I'm done with you. I want you gone from this house. And my daughter's life."

A thump. The clatter of an overturned bench. Was he *forcing* Two Hawks from the house? With battered face and broken ribs?

"Papa, no! Don't hurt him!" She'd yanked on her shift. Trembling fingers fumbled the lacing of her stays. "Two Hawks? Don't leave!"

Two Hawks spoke at last, but not to her. "I will go," he said, the words heavy, anguished. "I ask only to take my brother's horse as far as your farm. From there I will go on foot."

Papa agreed, grudgingly. "I'll not be long behind you. The horse had best be in my stable when I reach it."

"It will be," Two Hawks said.

"No!" Anna cried, fighting the wretched stays. She heard footsteps, then Papa's voice beyond the curtain, hard and clipped.

"There is no need for you to speak to him, Anna."

"Papa, call him back. Don't do this—"

He spoke over her as though he hadn't heard. "I was wrong to let you put yourself at risk for him. Dress yourself and we'll speak."

Cold flooded Anna's bones, though the warmth of the bath still clung to her skin. "No. We won't. I've nothing more to say to you."

"Anna! You will not address me so. I'm still your father."

With her hair down loose, clutching her gown, Anna snatched the curtain aside. Papa blocked her passage from the pantry alcove.

"You are no more my father than you are William's. Let me pass!"

Papa's face drained of color. For an instant she thought he might lay his hand to her. "Anna . . ."

She saw it was shock that blanched him, not anger. The harshness of her own words pierced her, but she didn't take them back. When she said nothing more, he finally stood aside and she hurried past, holding back her sobs until she reached Two Hawks's room and found she was too late.

He was already gone.

Papa had gone too, and twilight had fallen by the time she was dressed, hair pinned beneath a cap, cloak fastened. Lydia was exiting the stable as Anna reached it and of course wouldn't let her rush off without knowing why she needed the horse.

"Is it a childbed? Whose? Where is your case?"

Too distraught to elaborate on the subterfuge Lydia had unwittingly offered, Anna spilled the truth. Next thing she knew, Lydia was marching her back to the kitchen, sitting her down at the table, facing her with hands on hips, features tight with apprehension.

"Where is Reginald now?"

"I don't know or care."

"Anna." Lydia shook her head but must have decided to leave Papa out of it. For now. "You cannot ride to the farm in the dark. Wait for—"

"Tomorrow? Lydia, he'll be long gone—and he didn't even say *good-bye*." That cut the deepest. Deeper than Papa's rejection. Since the attack, Two Hawks had seemed closed off to her, almost always asleep when she was nearby. At first she thought it due to his wounds. Then she began to suspect he was sleeping during the day to avoid her. If the beating had changed his mind about living in her world, then why hadn't he answered her about living in his? Had he changed his mind about marrying her? Was that why he gave in to Papa without a fight?

"If he didn't say good-bye," Lydia reasoned, "maybe it's not good-bye. Maybe he was simply trying to keep the peace and doing as Reginald insisted was the only—"

"I mean to go to the farm tomorrow regardless," Anna cut in. "I want to bring all my things to town. I want to live with you, permanently, if you'll allow it." Before Lydia could draw breath to answer, she added in an angry rush, "And if you won't, I intend to follow Two Hawks to Kanowalohale and ask Good Voice if I can live with her. Surely they need midwives too."

Lydia's gaze widened with alarm. "Anna, of course you can live with me. For goodness' sake, I'd never turn you away." Tears filled her eyes as she spoke, drawing an answering flood from Anna.

"Oh, Lydia. I think I've lost him."

"Never," Lydia said. "Reginald loves you. Whatever he's done—if he overreacted—it was out of concern for you. Of that I have no . . . But you weren't speaking of him, were you?"

"No."

Lydia pressed a hand to her eyes. "Anna, I'm sorry this has happened. More than I can say. But can you try to see it as Reginald must have done? He came into the kitchen and found Two Hawks watching you bathe."

Anna stood, cold again. Tearless. "He ought to have trusted me, if not

Two Hawks. He oughtn't to have assumed the worst. I suppose when one's own heart is full of deceit, that's what one sees in everyone."

She went to her room, both proud and miserable that she'd rendered Lydia speechless.

She had the horse saddled and was halfway to the farm before the rising sun struck her back, too feeble to warm it. Lydia had pleaded to accompany her, but Anna had refused.

Skirting the farm, she kept to the trees until she crossed the creek, then rode through the beeches to the clearing. She'd rarely come there so early in the day that time of year. The shadows were cold and watery. Around her, plants she knew intimately were starting their cautious push through the thawing soil, but she paid them no heed as she dismounted and wrapped the horse's reins round a budded sapling at the hill's base. Her breath came short, white on the air, as she hurried up the path her feet and William's feet had worn. The smell of wet earth hung around her, rich with the promise of spring, while in her heart it was winter. Would be until she saw Two Hawks again. She prayed as she had through the night, in agony for dawn to break.

Let him be here. Let him have waited . . .

Above, among the jumble of stones half-choked with rhododendron, all was still.

Near the little waterfall, her shoe sent a pebble skittering down slope, a sound louder than the stream's chatter and the trills of awakening birds. She was among the rocks, one hand gathering up her petticoat, the other grasping stone, when she caught the movement above. Relief exploded inside her, until she saw the figure staring down at her. Almost she screamed but clamped a stifling hand across her mouth even as she recognized him. By the bruised eyes and cheek, the broken mouth. The stitched gash that carved its ugly line across his scalp. A scalp that now lay bare. He'd shaved or plucked his hair away to behind his ears, only the strip from crown to nape left to fall, feather tied, down his back. Despite the morning's chill, he wore only breechclout and leggings. His chest gleamed like copper in the sun's rising light.

"Two Hawks," she said, as though naming him would banish this startling vision, return the man she'd known. Her voice was too small, powerless to recall anything that was lost. She was left staring up at this stranger. A warrior, fearsome and formidable. In that moment she knew; he'd made his choice: his people over her. And he'd done this thing to himself to assure he wouldn't be persuaded to change his mind.

But he'd lingered. Long enough for her to find him. It was a tiny thread of hope, but she clutched it tight, forcing her limbs to carry her up to the cave's entrance.

Not a muscle twitched in Two Hawks's face as he watched her climb, as if he were a statue rather than flesh. As she stood before him, she saw at his feet lay his bow and quiver, his knapsack, rifle, and old blue shirt. The stone that had lodged in her chest at his leaving swelled to an unbearable ache.

"Why?" It was all she could say, though she knew the answer.

"I must. You heard your father's words. He was right to tell me to go."

Her face tingled at the sound of his voice, knife edged as it used to be when he spoke of Papa, as though the bladed words had struck her. "No, he wasn't. I should have waited until Lydia was home to have a bath. She could have warned you."

Her words had no effect. Not a ripple of feeling touched Two Hawks's face. "It was not your fault."

"Then it's Papa's," she said, desperate to elicit some response from him, some sign he cared that everything they'd worked for, everything he'd said he wanted, had unraveled. "Come with me to the house. We'll make him understand."

"Anna Catherine. It is not your fault, or your father's." At last there was the smallest break in his voice. "It is mine. I have been awake this night through, praying. I know what I say is true. I have dishonored you. There is no undoing that by sitting down and talking like sachems at a peace treaty."

"Two Hawks, you haven't—"

"Listen to me." She gasped as he took her by the arms. "I have prayed. Heavenly Father has shown me the way forward."

She searched his eyes, looking for confirmation of what she thought he meant. *The way forward.*

"Then you still want to be with me?" She tried to melt against him, needing to hold him. His arms were like iron, unbending at his sides, but there was struggle on his face. She raised her hands to his arms. "Take me with you. If you cannot be part of my world, let me be part of yours. Let your people be my people."

"You are not meant for that world."

Tears burned. She raised her head, willing them away. "How do you know? I've never even seen it."

Longing came into his eyes, but he mastered it. "A man joins his wife's clan. I wanted to do this, to become part of your world. Instead I broke it in pieces. You are angry with your father, and he with you. I cannot now take you from him, only leave you to mend what is broken."

"Two Hawks, I'm not going to live with Papa anymore. I've already settled it with Lydia. I'd rather live with her, and she'll have me, but . . ." She shook her head to banish everything that wasn't to the point. "I *want* to be with you. Please . . ."

Two Hawks looked dismayed. "If I took you with me, we would only drag harm behind us. Harm to my people. My parents. What kind of life would we have there with a dark cloud of shame over—"

"There's nothing *shameful* between us!"

Two Hawks closed his eyes, drawing breath. "I feel no shame in loving you. But in defying your father would be much shame. Aubrey did not start you in the womb of your mother, but he gave you life, risking his own for yours. Even if Creator did not bid us honor our parents, for that alone I would honor him in my heart. Taking you from him without his blessing is not the path I am to walk."

"What then?" she said, hating in that moment that he was so good, even as her heart rejoiced over it. "What path do you mean?"

"There is one thing I can do. I must find my brother. Return him to Aubrey. To my parents. To you." He'd gushed the words like blood from a wound, as if he feared he'd never get them out otherwise, then clamped his lips tight. But he couldn't mask the anguish rippling over his face. "Bear's Heart . . ." With a groan, he reached for her, wrapping her in his arms. At last.

She clung to him, speaking against his chest. "You're going to find William to redeem yourself in his eyes—Papa's eyes—aren't you?"

"What other way is there for me to clear the path to his heart? It is all Creator has shown me to do. I do not want to leave you, but I must if I am to find my brother." He took her by the shoulders and put her from him. But he was flesh now. No more stone.

"What about what William wants? Has anyone thought of that?"

She saw in his eyes that he had.

"I cannot know what my brother wants until I find him. But I will do it. Only then will you see me again."

The comfort she'd felt in his arms chilled. "How are you going to find him? Scouting? Spying?"

"If I must, I will do those things." His jaw firmed. "I will also do what my people need of me. Maybe what those soldiers in the fort need doing."

She'd begun to think she'd been mistaken about why he'd shaved his head, but now she saw her initial interpretation was correct. He was going into danger, prepared for battle. He'd set his mind, and there would be no pleading him out of it. She would get no more than he'd promised. *"Only then will you see me again.*" He needed her to understand that and to let him go.

She couldn't stop her hands shaking, but she raised them and cupped his bruised face. She gazed into his eyes, memorizing him, this warrior looking down at her, features set, eyes pools of anguish. "I love you. I believe in you. Always. *Remember.*"

Relief flooded his gaze. "I will. You remember to trust in Heavenly Father. Life is blessing, but it is also testing. Take the one as you do the other and trust Him who allows all. Trust what Creator is doing, though we cannot understand it or see the full path. Honor your father."

Her throat was too thick for speaking. She nodded.

"Let me hear you say you will do this," he said, his breath warm across her brow.

"I'll try," she choked out. "God be your shield and give you wisdom and bring you back to me safe. That's all I want." *With or without William,* she added silently, though she hoped for all their sakes it would be *with.*

He took her hands in his and kissed them. Then he kissed her lips. She felt the roughness of his healing wound. "Bear's Heart," he whispered against her mouth. "Let whatever come, my heart is in your keeping."

"And mine you take with you."

They'd said such words last autumn, in the barn the night before he left with his parents. She'd hoped they would never need say them again.

Eyes closed, she clung to his hands, knowing she would have to be the one to let go. She forced herself to do it and felt him step away. The morning's chill enveloped her, bereft of comfort. She heard him take up his kit and weapons, heard his moccasins on the stones. But she didn't open her eyes to watch his going.

14

Early April 1777
Lachine, Montreal

*S*t wasn't snowing, sleeting, or raining, which was the best that could be said. Muddied to his gaiters, Private William Aubrey stood with his assembled regiment while one Corporal Dewitt, charged with stealing Crown provisions and trading them to the King's Indian allies, received a reduction to the ranks and the first one hundred of five hundred lashes laid upon his bare back. They were up to thirty-nine.

The heads in front of William rose short of his own, save for a lanky private in front who topped his height by an inch. Shifting to the right, William could block sight of the metal-tipped lash falling across Dewitt's pasty flesh, the jerk of his bony frame with each blow.

He couldn't shut his ears. Half-muffled screams broke over the otherwise silent parade, relentless as an ocean tide. *Forty-one . . .*

Unpleasant as it was, William wished Sam Reagan were witnessing the spectacle. Sam was gone—back to the Mohawk Valley on an intelligence-gathering mission organized by Major James Gray, who commanded the Royal Greens while Sir John Johnson was away in British-held New York City. William hoped Sam had the sense to stay clear of Schenectady. *If* he'd any sense at all.

Maybe what Sam had was the luck of angels; had he not gone a'spying, he'd likely be sharing the lash with Dewitt. Though William had yet to catch him in the act, his suspicions of Sam's involvement in illicit trading had never been completely squelched.

Forty-seven . . .

He leaned left, perversely granting himself a peek at Dewitt, shackled arms raised, head pressed to the post . . . and leaned back again, mind seared. The administering sergeant wasn't showing mercy. Campbell never did.

Fifty-one . . .

Leaning left had brought him into close proximity to Private Robbie MacKay—near enough to have heard the lad's labored breathing. He cast a sidelong glance and was alarmed by Robbie's pallor. The lad was barely old enough to have enlisted. His father, Angus MacKay, had come north over the mountains with Sir John, bringing his entire family into exile. While all the former tenants of the Johnsons shared a bond of hatred for their rebel neighbors, William had seen nothing to match the rage that seethed in the heart of Angus MacKay over the loss of his estate. His eldest son, Archie, harbored a matching lust for revenge. Robbie did his best to make his father believe his rage burned as hot, but William found the younger MacKay's efforts lacking in conviction.

Just now, the Royal Green's newest recruit looked ready to slump into the mud at their feet. "Bend your knees a bit," William said under his breath.

Robbie uttered a faint groan but stayed upright.

Positioned on the right flank of his company, William had a view across the grounds. Over by the headquarters building, behind the doors of which Major Gray was ensconced, William spotted his new commanding officer, Captain Stephen Watts, grim gaze fixed on the whipping post and its hapless prisoner.

William's transfer into Watts's light infantry company had happened a week ago at firing drill, thanks to his having hit his target six reloads in sequence while Captain Watts, seeking to fill the ranks of his company of sharpshooters, had paused to observe.

William suspected his being plucked from the ranks might have had something to do with the vitriolic abuse Sergeant Campbell had been breathing down his neck while he took those six shots—surely being pinned under enemy fire couldn't prove as rattling—yet he still felt the mixture of smugness and relief that had engulfed him at the look of fury and disappointment on Campbell's face when Watts stepped forward and recruited William.

Sixty-two . . .

He hoped Campbell wasn't venting his displeasure on Dewitt.

The suspicion vanished like his clouding breath as another contingent of the proceedings' audience snagged his gaze—a cluster of Dewitt's illicit customers; Indians, a dozen of them, congregated around a stack of barrels at the parade's edge. Warriors all, most of them young. Canadian Six Nations come in answer to the call to fight in the spring campaign.

Eyeing them sidelong, William recognized a few he'd seen about the drill square, remote and alien in their garish trade-cloth shirts and breech-clouts, leggings and moccasins decorated in beads and quills, heads shaven into a variety of scalp-locks, silver in their mutilated ears. A shudder ran through William at sight of one warrior's slit and stretched lobes hanging in fleshly loops nearly to his shoulders. To think that might have been him standing among their ranks tricked out like a peacock, had Reginald Aubrey not—

He bit off the thought, spat it from his mind like rancid meat.

The Indians were intent on the whipping, brown faces set in disapproval . . . all but one, who appeared to be watching *him* with equal interest. He'd never seen the warrior—he'd have remembered that one. The Indian towered over his companions. Biggest Indian William had ever seen. Or tallest. Length of bone lent him his size; no spare flesh clung to that lean frame. Dark eyes burned into William like tiny fierce suns. William looked away. Counted a few more cries from Dewitt—whimpers now rather than screams. Looked back.

The Indian watched him still.

His scalp prickled as if a horde of ants had crawled up under his hat.

At last Dewitt was dragged away. The regiment was dismissed, Corporal Cameron's command, to which William belonged, to a wood-cutting detail. Robbie MacKay was part of the company, his one proficiency being a deadeye for target shooting, a skill learned hunting squirrel along the Mohawk. Visibly relieved to have the flogging over, he trailed William to the axes.

"I thank ye," he said softly, as they each hefted a blade. He didn't look at William as he spoke.

"Not a pretty sight, flogging." It wouldn't be the last the lad would be forced to watch.

They prepared to head out with the rest, pausing to let pass the troop of gaily bedecked Indians William had seen watching Dewitt's lashing. Off to watch one of the companies at drill? It seemed a favorite pastime among them, ogling the troops.

The tall warrior was last to file by, giving William that intense stare from his lofty vantage. Though his head was shaved to a scalp-lock, his ears bore only a simple piercing. He was younger than he'd appeared from a distance. Not many years past William's age.

Gripping the ax, he returned the Indian's scrutiny until the imposing warrior passed him by, making to continue on into the village with his fellows.

Robbie gave a low whistle and said something in the Gaelic, needing no interpretation. "Aye," William agreed. "Glad I am he's on our side."

He'd just relaxed his grip on the ax when behind his back a voice spoke another stream of words he didn't comprehend but knew for Mohawk. Both tone and speaker he recognized.

Campbell, giving insult.

The tall Indian pivoted, crow-wing brows lofted high at whatever Campbell had said. For an instant William thought the sergeant had lost his mind and maligned the savage, until those dark eyes locked on William. The Indian voiced a question at him. Pure gibberish.

William shook his head.

The Indian's gaze shot past William as Campbell spat out, "Half-breed."

A word the Indian apparently knew. Surprise washed over his face, then a look of enlightenment that left William grinding his teeth in baffled anger. Without further glance at William, the warrior strode away.

"Get a move on, soldiers," Campbell barked. "Wood isna goin' to chop itself now, is it?"

Amid muttered "Aye sirs" from the rest of the men, William turned to troop down to the riverside to which felled trees had been dragged, ready for the ax.

A rough hand grasped his shoulder and spun him round. Campbell's blunt face tilted up at him, inches from his own, as the man strained his spine to minimize their disparity in height. "What was that ye muttered then, Breed?"

With a cringe at the man's breath as well as at the sobriquet—despite loathing it at the time, he much preferred *Oxford*—William stood at attention and though he hadn't muttered a word said, "'Twas my agreement I was stating, sir—about the wood. Right enough it won't chop itself. A thing we learned at Queens."

Expression fixed in innocence, William inwardly cursed himself for goading the man. He expected a scathing dressing down or to be sent off to some more menial detail than woodcutting—emptying privy pans in the hospital or the like. But Campbell merely nodded him off to the riverside.

William went, wishing he hadn't seen the calculating twist of the sergeant's mouth as he turned to go.

They were nearly done the task when William next saw the Indians. Stripped to his shirt-sleeves as he tossed the split hardwood faggots into carts waiting to be trundled off, he ignored them for a time, focusing on the burn of his arms and shoulders, the prick of splinters in his palms . . . until he felt his neck hairs rise.

Ax clenched, he turned in the direction he knew the Indians loitered, yards down the pebbled beach noisy with wheeling gulls and the river's lap and rush. A few warriors lounged against a rise in the bank. The rest stood in a knot around a short, burly figure.

It was Sergeant Campbell, and he was speaking to the Indians in some earnest. Among them stood the tall warrior. William was turning away and so nearly missed it when Campbell waved in his direction. Like mules hitched to a single trace, every Indian's gaze swung to follow the gesture to where William stood with the wind whipping across his bared head, drying the sweat on his face and forearms.

"Private!" Campbell shouted at him. The man had in hand a long, slender stick of driftwood, or so William thought it until he squinted and realized . . .

Blast the man, he'd been to William's billet—likely with the excuse of routine inspection—and filched the Welsh bow.

Before he knew his own intention, William was striding down the beach toward Campbell, while the rest of his detail left with the wood carts. How did Campbell even know of Grandfather Aubrey's bow? He'd kept it wrapped and concealed the winter long, never once taking it out.

Not his grandfather. Not even his bow. He'd as good as stolen it when he took it from the farm. Smarting nevertheless at the violation, he halted before Campbell, doing his best to ignore the brown faces staring at him, the split ears, the dark, expectant eyes.

"Yes sir. What is this about, sir?" But he knew. His blood. Campbell had decided it was a good day to rub his nose in it.

"They've seen how bonnily ye shoot a Brown Bess." The sergeant tilted a nod at the assembled warriors. "Now they've a mind to see can ye shoot as well with your wee *Welsh* bow. I suggested a demonstration . . . in the interest of keeping friendly with our allies, aye?"

William didn't bother inquiring what might follow should he refuse the *suggestion*. Like as not he'd rue it, but he was furious enough to try the man.

Campbell read the thought and smiled. "Dinna make me order it, Private."

"Very well, sir." As Campbell handed over the bow, William added, "I'll be needing arrows."

Marking this development, the Indians began jabbering among themselves. William faced them as one of their number, a sinewy fellow with a crested scalp-lock, stepped forward with a quiver and bow of his own. "We have game?"

It was a competition they wanted, not a demonstration.

"All right," William said, whereupon the Indian yanked three arrows from the quiver at his back and thrust them at William, who took them with a nod. Voices again rose in a babble. The loungers on the ground stood to join in.

William knew the laying of a wager when he saw one.

Campbell had drawn off to watch the scene he'd set in motion, legs planted wide, beefy arms crossed, enjoying William's discomfort. Hoping for humiliation?

Ignoring the man now, William moved to stand beside his challenger. "The shed, yonder? That do for a target?"

This being accepted, another Indian produced a piece of charcoal and loped off down the beach to one of the abandoned sheds—near where he'd found Sam talking to the old woman, months ago. The warrior drew a series of circles on the weathered timbers, then came loping back.

While the Indians wrangled over who would shoot first, William's gaze was drawn to the tall one who'd watched him on the parade ground.

He caught William staring and raised his chin in acknowledgment. Or had it been a signal? Was this one of Sam's acquaintances?

William thrust the arrows through his belt and strung the bow that belonged to a lineage he could no longer claim. It was an old bow, well kept, made of a single elm stave. No match for the great medieval bows he'd seen, reaching six feet in length, this bow had been crafted as an ambush weapon, meant for close quarters among Welsh woods and hills, not the distance shooting of the longbow. Drawing and testing it now, William felt the imposter, yet couldn't quell his attachment to the weapon. It was one thing knowing the bow, and the old man who'd looked down his patrician nose from the portrait in the hall of the Aubrey estate, bore no true relation to him. Try telling his heart that connection was a lie.

The heart could be deaf as a stone and twice as stubborn.

It was decided. William would shoot first. He wasted no time getting on with it. There was a stir when he took his stance, fit an arrow, and drew—not to the ear but to the chest, as he'd been taught by his father's factor, Mr. Davies.

Not his father . . . The thought slammed him in the gut, robbing him of breath. He shut his eyes until his heartbeat slowed, then opened them. There was nothing now but the bow, the arrow, the cloud-bright sky. The target waiting down the beach. He let the arrow fly.

It hit the target, though not its center.

The wiry Indian took his first shot. It hit nearer the center than William's, to the warriors' delighted hoots and jeers.

William took his second shot, forcing back a tide of sickness surging up from his belly. He despised this limbo in which he was caught, wanting to cling like a drowning man to who he'd been, terrified of letting go and sinking . . . into what? Savagery, like that surrounding him now, egging him on to his third shot? He'd missed his challenger's second. It was good, he saw. Better than either of their firsts.

Ought he to let the Indian win or try to best him?

Be a white man. Be an Indian. *Oxford. Breed.*

He took his stance and let it flow through him, the black despair, the bleeding betrayal, and loosed the third arrow with a shout of rage as if Reginald Aubrey stood before the target. For a moment after the string's twang he saw nothing but a haze of red. Heard nothing but the blood rushing in his ears. Felt nothing but an oily wave of self-loathing and confusion. Then a thump on his shoulder roused him to the excitement swelling around him.

It hadn't to do with the shooting. Campbell had disappeared. Another Indian, out of breath from running, was gasping out news of some import to his fellows.

William snatched up his discarded regimentals and hurried with his bow toward headquarters, where the news was abuzz. Weeks ago they'd received word that Brigadier General Barry St. Leger would command the forces gathered at Montreal, but exactly when and where they'd be campaigning remained obscured in a fog of speculation, until now. They had their orders at last: a three-pronged British attack meant to divide the colonies, with St. Leger's command to muster in the west at Oswego with Colonel John Butler's loyalist rangers and Indians. They would then march east to Albany, through the Mohawk Valley, sweeping all rebels before them with fire and sword.

And between Oswego and Albany, defenseless against such onslaught, lay the farm owned by Reginald Aubrey.

Anna . . . Lydia . . . the Doyles. Their faces rose before him as he made his way to his billet, intent upon putting the bow out of sight. He didn't want to think of Reginald Aubrey as well but did so. Most of all he didn't wish to think of those other hazy figures, a mother, father, brother, also in the path of destruction. Would any of them survive the coming campaign? Would they despise him forever for taking part in it if they did?

The thought had barely formed before a mountain of brown flesh and flashing silver loomed across his path. Clutching his bow like a stave, William drew up. The tall Indian was alone this time. They were in a populous place, near a market that reeked of fish sellers. He mastered his alarm.

"What do you want of me?" He'd spoken overloud, drawing the attention of several around them, most who took one look at the towering Indian and drew off. But the warrior gazed at him with eyes that reflected no hostility.

"You are William Aubrey."

It wasn't a question. "You know my name? Did Campbell tell it you?"

"Your officer said nothing of your name." The Indian's English was surprisingly good.

"How then do you know me?" They were standing in the way of customers attempting to buy fish. The Indian nodded his head, started to move off. After a brief hesitation, William followed.

Sam. He must know this warrior. Since Sam wasn't here, was the man attempting to make contact with him, hoping William had goods to sell?

He stopped the Indian with a hand to a lean, powerful arm, a hand he snatched away when the Indian halted to face him. William took an involuntary step back. "Listen. I don't know what arrangement you and Private Reagan have, but I've nothing to do with . . ."

He let the words trail off as incomprehension crossed the Indian's high-boned face, feeling a chill creeping out from his innards. This hadn't to do with Sam.

"Had I not heard your name," the Indian said, "I would know you by your face. I know your mother, your father. When I lived at Kanowalohale, I was friend to the brother you were born with."

They were standing at the corner of a stone-built structure. Against the wall a hogshead stood. William groped for its rim, feeling himself blanch. "My brother?"

"He and I went under the water on the same day. Made our hearts clean in Jesus."

William blinked, struggling to make sense of the words. "You're Oneida?"

The Indian shook his head. "No, but my father is Oneida. Years ago he sent me to Kanowalohale, where I came to know your kin. Your brother spoke of you—you and that Welsh bow." The Indian nodded at the bow William had forgotten he clutched. "He wanted much to see it for himself."

William couldn't get his breath. His brother knew of his bow? How?

Anna. For a mortifying instant, William thought he was going to be sick with the tide of regret and longing that crashed over him, the fruitless longing for home—one he could never return to, had never truly existed. The Welsh had a word for such impossible yearning. *Hiraeth.*

He avoided the dark eyes studying him. "And what are you called?" he asked the Indian, having no idea what else to say.

"I have been called Tames-His-Horse since I was young," the warrior replied. "But the name I favor now is Joseph."

15

Thundering Moon
Kanowalohale

While warriors kept watch along the great north river called St. Lawrence, from Lake Ontario to Montreal, spying on the British to learn their plans for war in the coming season, sachems had journeyed west to Niagara to treat with Colonel John Butler, head of the British forces there. When they returned, they carried news of substance. Daniel Clear Day, scarcely home from seeing the American army with Kirkland, had traveled to Niagara with the sachems. While the fire popped beneath a kettle of boiling hominy, Good Voice, Stone Thrower, and Two Hawks listened to what happened there.

"That Butler is one who speaks with two tongues," Clear Day told them. "In the hearing of all, he told the *Onyota'a:ka* not to meddle in this war but to go on standing to the side. After we departed, we learned from one who heard it that Butler spoke to the Haudenosaunee out of our hearing. He told the Mohawks, Senecas, Cayugas—Onondagas too—that they could take American scalps and much plunder if they fought for the British. He promised to liberate the Mohawks surrounded by the whites at Canajoharie and Fort Hunter."

Stone Thrower grunted at this. Butler's false face to them was no surprise, even if it was unwelcome news. "Butler is no friend to the Oneidas, keeping his true heart from us."

At mention of true hearts, Good Voice glanced at her son, still finding it jarring to see his head bared and that scar running down nearly to his ear. As always when she saw it, she forced down a throat-full of anger and confusion, nearly as choking now as on that day he returned to them. Though his bruises had faded, in his eyes as he caught her gaze was a brokenness unhealed.

"Another thing we learned," Clear Day said, capturing their attention again, even Two Hawks, who'd left the fire to sort through the provisions he'd been preparing before Clear Day arrived. "The warriors out hunting around Niagara and Oswego have been ordered to return by the Planting Moon, the moon the whites call May."

Good Voice knew what that meant. Whatever attack the British were planning, it would come soon after the Planting Moon.

"I will go to Fort Stanwix and look for Ahnyero," Two Hawks said. "I was going anyway, but this news makes me want to go with more urgency. It may be I will find . . ."

He didn't finish the statement. Good Voice didn't need him to. Two Hawks wanted to find his brother before fighting began, to convince him to leave the British and return south.

Good Voice made no argument against what her son proposed. Neither did Stone Thrower. They'd said all they had to say about it. Their words had fallen on deaf ears.

Clear Day read this in their faces, for when he spoke, he only gave counsel to be careful, to listen to Ahnyero, as Two Hawks rolled up his bedding and gathered his rifle and bow for the journey to the fort, where the army would supply him for any scouting he might do. He appeared to listen, but Good Voice doubted he was thinking of anything but Anna Catherine. All the while, she'd been putting dried venison and parched corn into a sack. She gave it to her son as they met in the doorway of the lodge.

They had a door of wood now, hung on stiff leather hinges. Two Hawks pushed it open. In the light of afternoon that showed his scar no mercy, he took what she offered and held her briefly in farewell. She gripped him with care, knowing he'd taken hurt in his ribs and it was still not fully healed. She knew of the beating, what sort of men had done it and why. He'd told them that much. What she didn't know was why Aubrey sent him away after he'd done such a good thing for the man, saving his boats from being burned. What happened to make her son leave the woman he claimed to love and wish to make his wife? What words were said? What was done to him, or what did he do, that there was such pain in his eyes?

Those were the questions her son wouldn't answer. It took much restraint not to ask them again but to take his face between her hands and pray for his safety, for his skill and wisdom in what he was setting out to do. Then she lingered in the doorway, watching him walk away through the town toward the trail to the fort, already feeling the wrench of his absence in her chest and thinking how hard it was to be the mother of a warrior, to let go when the heart yearned to clutch.

Before his path took him from sight, Two Hawks was intercepted by a smaller, slender figure. Strikes-The-Water. Good Voice couldn't hear what words they exchanged, but what their bodies spoke needed no ears to interpret:

The Tuscarora girl questioned where her son was bound.

Two Hawks told her.

She put a hand to his arm, asking to go with him.

He shook off her hand, refusing her.

Though Strikes-The-Water's shapely mouth opened to argue, Good Voice could see it was no use. Two Hawks stood unmovable as a stone that a river sweeps past. Still he let Strikes-The-Water say all she had to say. Good Voice couldn't see her son's face, only the girl's. Frustration, anger, and hope moved like currents across her features. When she stopped talking, Two Hawks shook his head and made a cutting motion with his hand, meant to end the talk. He sidestepped her and strode away.

Good Voice's heart went out to Strikes-The-Water, whose face showed a crush of disappointment. There'd been more to her request than that proclivity to do the things men did. Strikes-The-Water wanted to go scouting, but maybe more she wanted to be with Two Hawks, wherever he was going.

As she watched the girl slip away between the lodges of the Turtle Clan, Good Voice ached to know the true heart of her son concerning Anna Catherine. He'd come home from whatever bad thing had happened looking gaunt as a wolf in winter, one that had tangled with another too strong for it. Had her son said more to Clear Day in that brief time the old man had been in Kanowalohale, between his trips? Those two had grown close in the time Stone Thrower wasn't present to be a father. That closeness hadn't ended, though much was healed now between her son and husband.

Good Voice went inside her lodge to find the men discussing Reginald Aubrey. She hurried to her kettle and settled there to mind it and their talk.

"No," Clear Day was saying. "He said nothing to me. I wish that he had, for I am much troubled in my mind about that man."

"We are all troubled," Stone Thrower said. "It has been in my mind that when he did that thing that harmed us so and still hurts our hearts and the heart of our firstborn, he may have done a worse thing to himself. He has lived all this time with it beating his soul like a club. I know what that does to a man, to walk the earth with the burden of his sin on his back. It poisons all he touches."

He met Good Voice's gaze, eyes speaking to her gently of the sorrow he still felt over those years of neglect and abuse but also joy that they were past and he was forgiven by Creator. And by her. She smiled, reassuring him, as he sometimes needed to be, that it was so.

"I wish now I had gone into that place on my journey back from the American army," Clear Day said. "I wish I had known how badly things had gone. I might have learned more."

Clear Day had returned to Kanowalohale sooner than some of the warriors and sachems Kirkland had escorted east. Kirkland himself hadn't returned. They didn't know whether he would. It seemed the generals wanted him elsewhere, ministering to soldiers. She wished he were with them still, and his wife, Jerusha, who had become her friend.

"Do you think I should go back to him?" Stone Thrower asked.

Clear Day sat forward, gray braids swinging from his chest. "Go back?"

"To Aubrey. Maybe I can speak to him about Two Hawks, discover what went bad between them."

Good Voice expected her husband's uncle to approve this idea. Instead he stood to his feet, more slowly than a year ago he might have done, and looked down on the nephew she knew he considered a son.

"Maybe that is a thing to do, but I do not know. Many have done this and done that, said this and said that, still Aubrey's heart is shut to Creator. And, it would seem, to your second-born." The old man shook his head, staring into Good Voice's fire, face creased with troubled musings. "Let an old man think on it and be sure."

"Kawʌniyó, Uncle," Stone Thrower said, rising to his feet as his uncle made to leave. "A good word. We will be sure of what we do."

On her knees, Good Voice stirred the boiling corn, staring through the steam as the ashes she'd added worked loose the outer hulls, leaving behind the soft inner kernels. She was grieved for her son and Anna Catherine, sorry for their pain, yet how much easier it would be if her son would choose a wife among the Haudenosaunee.

"I suppose you also will be leaving me soon?"

She looked up at Stone Thrower's words. "Leaving you?"

There was teasing in his eyes. "You have not been to the women's hut for your moon time yet."

Even as he spoke, his strong brows drew in. Good Voice blinked at him, thinking about the women's hut and how long it had been since she'd needed to go there.

"True . . . I did not go this moon," she said, thinking maybe soon she would be counted among the grandmothers. Then she thought further back. Stone Thrower knew of only this moon. He was away at the fort during the time she should have gone last moon but didn't. Because there had been no need. And the moon before that was when . . .

The thought dawned in their minds at the same instant. Good Voice knew it because their gazes were locked, while the steam and the smoke of her food cooking rose up to the roof. She stood to her feet so hastily it dizzied her. She put a hand to her mouth, took two steps, and sat down hard on her sleeping bench. She felt Stone Thrower's strong hands on her shoulders, steadying her.

"When?" he asked, kneeling before her.

Not *When did you last go to the women's hut?* That wasn't the *when* he meant.

"I know when." She raised her eyes to his. "The very day . . . my Caleb."

His Christian name was all the reminder he needed of that day. Understanding lit his eyes. Then he was grinning like a warrior half his age, and she thought he might loose a jubilant cry, but he sat beside her and said, "Come here," and reached to pull her onto his lap. "Both of you."

Both of you.

"But . . . I must be *forty* summers now."

"What is forty? A number!" Stone Thrower glowed as if a torch burned inside him. His hand spread across her belly, tender and possessive. She placed hers over it. She'd been so certain her body would never again try to grow a child, not after the one lost when Two Hawks was six summers. Shock and wonder resonated through her as she recalled now other signs she'd ignored: the tiredness, the weight coming on around her middle, the illness she felt some mornings. She'd been distracted by Two Hawks's heartache, against which she felt helpless, thinking her body was responding to that. And now . . .

. . . even God, who quickeneth the dead, and calleth those things which be not as though they were. Words out of the Book—she knew not when she might have heard them—came to her, she whose womb had been long barren, as if Creator were speaking to her, flooding her with trust that this child would thrive inside her, that she would see it, hold its life in her arms come . . .

"Autumn," she said and pressed her face into Stone Thrower's smoke-scented hair, threaded now with gray. "She will be with us in the last moon of autumn."

16

Planting Moon

A day's journey north of Fort Stanwix, with a moonless night closed round, Two Hawks and Ahnyero settled in the lee of a ridge. They lit no fire. Even within sight of the fort, it was possible to be ambushed by Mississauga or even Mohawk scouts.

Ahnyero took first watch, but Two Hawks found his mind yet running its trails. The other man stood some paces off, a pillar against the stars, alert for disturbances beyond the rustlings of night creatures. Two Hawks sat up, hooding his blanket, and just loud enough for Ahnyero to hear said, "That new commander at the fort, he is a friend of yours?"

Ahnyero stood silent a moment, then came and settled on his haunches near Two Hawks, rifle resting in the crook of his arm. "Peter Gansevoort is a friend to the People. It is good he is come to command. He will lead well when attack comes."

When. Not *if.*

The new fort commander was an imposing white man, tall and thick chested, not yet thirty. He and the first of his New York regiment had arrived before Two Hawks and Ahnyero set out to scout northward. Gansevoort had taken swift charge of the fort's repairs and planned to improve the road running east to Fort Dayton at German Flatts. Something was also happening west of the fort, which occupied the Carrying Place between Wood Creek, passage to Fort Oswego on Lake Ontario, and the Mohawk River, passage to Albany and the Hudson.

"As we were leaving," Two Hawks said, "I saw the party he sent to Wood Creek. Why does he risk men out that way?"

"He has them felling trees across the water. The British will need to move all those trees from their path to bring their cannon and supplies to the fort, if they try to come that way. Like the path you wish to clear, eh?" Ahnyero wasn't referring now to the clearing of a creek. "Tell me what weighs on you, brother. Then maybe you can sleep."

Though his belly churned with the bad feelings he'd carried away from Anna Catherine, Two Hawks was glad to be prodded to speak of it.

"I did a shameful thing. Her father caught me." He told Ahnyero how Aubrey found him watching his daughter bathe, though he'd done so only for the time it takes to draw a startled breath. A breath too long. He told how Aubrey ordered him, not yet healed from saving his boats, to leave. "I went to that place wanting to remove every branch from the path between my heart and his," he said, hearing the bitter current in his voice. "Instead I felled a great tree between us."

He was glad no one but Ahnyero heard these words. He'd held them inside, unable to tell even his mother, afraid to see relief in her eyes. She liked Anna Catherine, but he knew in her heart she wished him to marry a woman of the People. He thought of Strikes-The-Water but shook the image of her away.

"What have your parents said about this thing that happened?"

"I did not tell them."

Ahnyero let his silence speak to that. After a moment, he said, "It seems to me it was not a thing you meant to do, nor a thing for which you should feel shame. You did what a white father would want you to do. You looked away. He was too harsh about it, I think."

"Her father did not know what was in my heart." Two Hawks surprised himself by defending the man. "But if I could find my brother, maybe I could convince him to come back and that would clear a whole forest between Aubrey and me. If Creator wills it," he hastened to add.

Beside him in the darkness, Ahnyero made a low sound. Laughter. "That is why you are with me now? To help Creator's will along?"

Two Hawks frowned, unsure whether he'd been reproached. Out in the dark, a branch cracked. Ahnyero stiffened, then relaxed when a raccoon trundled into starlight, chittered at them, then hurried on its way.

Ahnyero squeezed his arm. "Sleep, brother. Or if you cannot for thinking, talk to the Almighty about it." Concern warmed the blacksmith's voice, mingling with wryness as he added, "Only do your praying in your heart. I would like some quiet."

Next morning they met scouts coming south. Two were Oneidas from Oriska Town, known to Two Hawks. The third was known to him by reputation alone.

Born to an African father and an Abenaki mother, adopted by Caughnawagas, Louis Cook had fought against the British in their war with the French. Two Hawks watched the dark-skinned man with his head shaved to a feathered crest and ears heavily pierced as he spoke of what he'd seen in Montreal, a place he could enter with safety, being fluent in French and known as a Caughnawaga.

"The British are at Lachine, preparing to push up the St. Lawrence from that place. They will gather at Oswego, on the lake."

It was momentous news, no matter how long expected.

"When will it begin?" Ahnyero asked.

"Before summer is much advanced. That is all we three know at present."

They spoke a little longer before Two Hawks dared interject, "What of Johnson's regiment? Are those soldiers at Lachine?"

Louis turned dark eyes on Two Hawks. "They are. Have you business with them, young brother?"

"It is a brother I have with them. The brother born with me that I have never seen."

Recognition lit the warrior's gaze. "You are the son of that woman captured and held at the British fort, who gave birth to two but brought away only one?"

"I am that one she brought away."

Louis regarded him. "I am heading south now and cannot turn aside, nor say where my path will take me in coming days, but if it takes me again among the ranks of Johnson's Greens, would you have me look for him, this one who wears your face?"

Two Hawks stiffened his knees, weakened with a wash of gratitude. He hadn't looked for such a thing from this great warrior. "I would. He is called William Aubrey. I am told he does wear my face, but as a white man wears it. His eyes are blue."

"If ever I am among those Royal Yorkers, I will look for him. If I find him, what would you have me say?"

"Tell him of me, of our parents, that we want him to return to us. Tell him so, and if he will come away with you . . ."

Louis Cook gripped Two Hawks's arm in farewell. "If he will come, then I will lead him home."

At midday they paused to eat a handful of parched corn and drink from a burbling stream. They continued north, bearing a little west on a path that cut back and forth across the stream, skirting stretches of swamp. Beside them ran a series of ridges. Ahead rose higher peaks, patches of late snow clinging in their shadows.

Behind them someone followed.

It took no more than a shared glance to confirm what both had sensed. Moments later, when Ahnyero veered off the path at a place where the ground was moist but passable, Two Hawks guessed what he intended. With a fierce surging of his blood, he followed. Skirting the marshy place, they made a wide, staggered turn, following the terrain of a hillside, weaving through downed timbers, heedless of tracks left in the wet ground. Thus they circled back until they reached their own tracks on the trail they'd abandoned.

There were three sets of footprints now.

They set their ambush simply, each sheltering behind a tree, one to either side of the trail. There they crouched, rifles primed, and waited. Perhaps they would watch and let the tracker pass. It was only one enemy and they were two. Maybe killing wouldn't be—

The arrow thunked into the tree inches from Two Hawks's face. He felt his bowels seize, then caught Ahnyero's gaze and knew their trap was prematurely sprung. Two Hawks hesitated, waiting to let Ahnyero be the first to fire.

In that moment a voice called out in a tone that hinted of humor, "*Shekoli*. It is one you know who follows you!"

Two Hawks knew the voice well. Motioning Ahnyero to hold his fire, he stepped out from behind the tree to see Strikes-The-Water stepping from behind another tree, a second arrow fitted to her bowstring. In the time it took Two Hawks to reach her, astonishment worked itself into vexation so hot it clogged his throat.

"What are you doing here? Did I not make it clear when you asked that I did not want you?"

Hurt flashed across her features like a sheet of summer lightning before thunderclouds of indignation gathered. "Am I a child to be told where I can and cannot go? And I am not *with* you. We happen to be traveling the same path at the same time."

Speechless at this twisting of the situation, Two Hawks shot a look of appeal at Ahnyero, who seemed amused, and a little impressed, by this unwanted tagalong. "This girl is known to you then?"

"Yes." Two Hawks turned back to her with his anger still hot, though not so hot as to make him ask why she wasn't busy planting corn in the women's fields. "Why are you not hunting for your mother and those Deer Clan women, as you like to do? Why are you wasting your time and ours following where you have no business going?"

The girl showed not the slightest sign of chagrin. "I did hunt for them. I got a good deer that will last many days. I got it quickly and so came fast to the fort. I learned you had left only that morning. I found your trail and followed. Did you know your right foot turns inward more than does your left?"

At that, Ahnyero laughed out loud. Strikes-The-Water looked at him and smiled. It was a dazzling smile. Even Two Hawks, who wanted to shake the girl, had to admit it.

"Never mind about my feet. You should go back home and stop following us and . . . you shot an arrow at me!"

That detail had sunk in at last.

Her smiled vanished. "I shot the arrow at the tree behind which you skulked. Had I meant to hit *you*, I would have aimed for you."

Two Hawks made a derisive noise.

Her eyes flashed with ruffled pride. "Kanowalohale is my home too, threatened by this war. I have every right to protect it as do you."

"I have never said you did not have that right. But you do not have to claim it by my side!"

Something moved in the girl's eyes when he said those words, something that struck Two Hawks deep enough to let in a bit of light to his thinking. *By his side.* Was that where this girl thought she wanted to be?

He was aware of Ahnyero watching, listening to their words. The humor on his face had faded. "Come, brother. Step aside with me. Sister, will you let us have this moment to speak?"

Strikes-The-Water glanced between them, wary, clearly hoping to get her way even if they begrudged her presence. Two Hawks felt a stab of pity. Was this the way the girl had lived her life, fighting to be included where she was not wanted?

Not waiting for them to draw away, she took herself off to the trail they'd followed before they set their ambush and sat down on a stone beside it, pointedly not looking at them. Two Hawks put his back to her and waited for Ahnyero to speak.

"Brother, I am sorry, but you need to take this girl back to the fort." The blacksmith raised a hand, silencing Two Hawks even as he started to protest. "Will she stop following if we bid her do so?"

"She will only be more careful not to be caught at it."

Ahnyero looked past him to the girl waiting on the rock. "It is you she wishes to be with. She will go back if you go with her. Not happily. But she will go."

Two Hawks stiffened his jaw, his every fiber in rebellion.

"Listen," Ahnyero said. "I will go on and come as close to Montreal as I can. Maybe even go into that place called Lachine. Maybe I will see your brother's regiment."

Two Hawks frowned. "That regiment is made up of Tories. Some could be your neighbors from Cherry Valley. You might be known there."

"As you would not be?" A corner of Ahnyero's mouth rose. "Do not look at me so startled. I know this is what you hoped to do. Go into that place, among those soldiers, and find your brother."

The weight in Two Hawks's chest felt like a stone, but he knew he was going to give way and do as Ahnyero bid. "Do not risk your life. Mine I would risk, but not—"

A commotion of branch breaking and a shout—of challenge, not fear—ended the conversation. Two Hawks whirled to see Strikes-The-Water on her feet, knife drawn, about to attack a half-naked white man staggering out of the wood. He was pale haired, coated in sweat-streaked grime, and bore the bruised swellings of a beating about the face; the small, deliberate burns and cuts of torture on chest and arms. Blood crusted where it had flowed.

Two Hawks and Ahnyero reached Strikes-The-Water before she could further injure the man. Putting themselves between, they gave her the moments she needed to see the stranger was no threat to her, weaponless and outnumbered. Clothed in tattered breeches, the white man fell to his knees.

"You've a woman with you," he said in the English of one born Yankee. "I heard you arguing. I didn't think you a war party, not with a woman . . ."

The man's eyes rolled toward Strikes-The-Water, still brandishing her knife.

Ahnyero took the man by the arm and hauled him to his feet. "Tell us who you are and what you do on Oneida land, and we will keep that one from getting near you again." He jerked his chin at Strikes-The-Water, who pulled back her lips in a grin as fierce as it was lovely.

"You're Oneida? Thank every angel . . ." The man swayed on his feet.

Ahnyero gripped hard, keeping him upright. "We will ask the questions."

The man winced at the grip on his damaged arm. Two Hawks took him by his other arm, equally bruised and spotted with burns. They lowered him to the rock Strikes-The-Water had vacated. She drew back a pace, wary and watchful. Silent for once.

"Have you water?" The man sounded parched. Two Hawks realized he was young, a few years older than him. Younger than Ahnyero, who put a hand to the ax at his belt.

"Talk first."

The man licked cracked lips. "I'm on a mission—for your side. I went north to the British last summer, joined up with Johnson's Greens—as a spy, see? For the Americans."

Two Hawks's heart leapt, a hard and eager beat that hurt his ribs. It was with great effort that he restrained himself from speaking as the man spilled his secrets, desperation in his voice.

"I volunteered to spy for the British, back to the Mohawk Valley, only so I could get to . . ." The man at last hesitated. "What's important is I managed to slip away from my party and made my report. I'd planned to make my way back to Lachine, give out as I'd been captured, only that's precisely what happened. Six of them caught me—Mississaugas, I think. Crown Indians, anyway. They tortured me before I escaped. Just north of . . ."

"The fort at the Carrying Place?" Ahnyero asked.

The man stilled, even in his distress seeming to weigh their faces, though there was little to be read on Ahnyero's. The man looked last at Two Hawks, blond brows drawn over narrowed eyes that filled with question. He shook it away and said, "Yes. Fort Stanwix."

"We come and go from there. I have never seen you." Ahnyero glanced at Two Hawks, brows raised.

"I have not seen this one before."

The man sat straighter on the rock. "On account I never let myself be seen."

"He ask name." Strikes-The-Water came closer, slender fingers gripping the handle of her knife. "You not say."

The man's eyes flashed to her, then with seeming reluctance, he said, "Sam Reagan. Out of Schenectady."

Two Hawks's breath came sharp into his lungs. He knew this man, though he'd never seen him. This was the one who piloted bateaux for Aubrey until last summer, when he revealed his Tory sentiments then led William away over the mountains. Lunging for Sam Reagan, he shoved him to the ground, a hand to his throat, a knee to his chest. "You are a spy—for the British. You are telling lies!"

The chest beneath his knee heaved. The throat made a gurgling beneath Two Hawks's fingers. "I was sent north to Canada—a spy— enlisted—better to—troop movements—"

"You are choking him, brother," Ahnyero observed calmly. "We will learn little from a dead man."

Two Hawks released Reagan, who scrambled to his knees, coughing and gagging. When the retching passed, his bewildered gaze settled on Two Hawks, who saw questions flare again in the hazel eyes. Knowing he'd little time before Reagan saw past the shaved head and darker skin to the resemblance he bore William, Two Hawks thought quickly, scouring his memory for everything Anna Catherine had said about his brother's leaving.

"I am going to ask you a question. I will know by your answer whether what else you have told us can be trusted."

Reagan's brows shot high. "Ask. Then whatever else you do, for pity's sake, give me water."

"My question is about that one you led away to the British last summer."

Reagan's gaze went momentarily blank. Sounding dazed he said, "You mean Aubrey? William Aubrey?"

Heart beating hard at the hearing of his brother's name, Two Hawks held up a hand for silence. The question he'd meant to pose was unneeded now to verify the man's identity. Still he asked it. "The bow that one has in his possession, where did he get it?"

"His *bow*?" The man gaped at him, long enough for Two Hawks's confidence to be shaken, to fear the man had been lying about everything, that this thread to his brother he was trying to grasp would slither from his fingers like pond weed.

Then the man said, "William brought it with him from Crickhowell—in Wales."

Flooded with equal measures of relief and anger toward this troublemaker turned up in their midst, Two Hawks shared a nod with Ahnyero. The latter unfastened the water skin he carried and offered it to the man, who took it and drank, long and deep. When he surfaced, chin streaming, water tracking grime and blood, Two Hawks asked, "That one who claims the Welsh bow, he is at Lachine? He is part of Johnson's regiment?"

"Aye. He is." Sam Reagan stared hard at Two Hawks, the question on his battered face shifting, beginning to resolve into comprehension. "And just who is William Aubrey to *you*?"

17

May 21, 1777
Schenectady

R eginald stepped onto the quay, where Lieutenant Colonel Marinus Willett, with the help of recruited river pilots, oversaw the loading of his 3rd New York regiment and their provisions into every bateau the Binne Kill could spare. Eager to commence the journey upriver to Fort Stanwix, where he would serve as second-in-command to Colonel Gansevoort, Willett adroitly sidestepped the men shouldering supplies across the quay to fetch up at Reginald's side, blue regimentals fresh despite the morning's sticky warmth.

"We'll be snug as barreled beef, but we'll make do. My thanks for the loan of your crewmen. Him especially." Willett nodded toward Ephraim Lang, whose white head appeared briefly in a gap between boarding soldiers. "An old campaigner, I judge."

"That he is," Reginald confirmed. "We both saw the surrender of Fort William Henry."

"A harrowing," Willett said. "I'm grateful for an able pilot, but will you not reconsider making the journey as well?"

"Lang is glad for the going," Reginald said, feeling suddenly older than the six or seven years that lay between him and this officer still visibly in his prime. He laid a hand to the hip that pained him continuously and could, if overtaxed, make rising of a morn a gritted act of will. Yet he couldn't deny a stir of longing. Willett's vitality, the sense of untainted purpose and untarnished honor he exuded, put Reginald in mind of the officer—the man—he might have been if . . .

He shook away such thoughts. "Here is my place now."

Willett nodded, scanning the ranks of waiting soldiers hugging what shade the warehouses afforded, then turned back to Reginald with a grin that belied his next words. "Moving the regiment and its kit is no light undertaking. Not with the terrain we'll face—as I'm sure you're aware." A shout from a loaded bateau distracted Willett. A private flailed precariously over the vessel's side, saved a dunking by the quick reflexes of a comrade. Willett cupped his mouth and shouted, "Too late to swim for shore, soldier!"

Willett took his leave, bidding Reginald jovially to build more boats and be quick about it. As the first bateau pushed off from the quay, Ephraim Lang came to bid farewell, blue gaze fixing Reginald squarely.

"Wager you're wishing now you didn't run the lad off."

Lang had made it clear he thought Reginald's judgment of Two Hawks hasty, its execution severe. But what should he have done? Pretend he hadn't seen what he saw? Yet Anna's misery was a noose about his neck, tightening as the days slipped past and the distance between them grew.

"We managed," he said, indicating the emptying quay.

"You could do a deal better than manage, Major."

Reginald watched Lang board the craft he would pilot. He'd see them off, then return to his work . . . though he could easily fall down where he stood and sleep for a week.

In the end he did neither, for Lang looked back at him, nodding at a point over Reginald's shoulder even as he gave the order to push off. As the fleet crowded the river, beginning the laborious journey westward, Reginald rounded to scan the thinning crowd. At its edge Lydia stood, clad in the blue gown that made her eyes appear the most vivid hue he'd ever seen in a woman's face. Though half that face was shielded by a broad-crowned hat, he knew by the set of her mouth she wasn't there to see the regiment away.

Pain like a fist squeezed his chest.

"You haven't lost all. Anna loves you, else she wouldn't be so distraught—nor would she still be under my roof. She'd have gone with Two Hawks when you sent him away. She went after him, did you know? He refused to take her from you. Even so, Reginald—believe me in this—she'd have found a means of convincing him were it not for loving you . . . a love that's hanging by the merest thread, which you will snap if you do not take the utmost care now in its handling."

There on the quay Lydia had spilled her heart in what felt like a final bid to heal the relationship that had been the cornerstone of her world since she was twelve; Reginald and Anna, her dearest friends. Her loves. The wound between them had festered with Reginald holed up in his workshop, Anna going about like one half-dead, miserable and much too thin.

"It isn't the family of your making that you now stand to lose but the family the Almighty has been making in spite of you. Stop resisting and let Him make it."

The Almighty was weaving something beautiful out of Reginald's tangled mess. In the hearts of Anna and Two Hawks, uniting in love two families long embittered enemies. She could see it. She was fairly certain Good Voice and Stone Thrower had seen it, were at least open to the possibility of it. Why couldn't Reginald see?

"Is it that for so long you expected to die at Stone Thrower's hands, felt you deserved to die thus? Are you unable to face what their forgiveness granted you—life, and the living of it?"

She'd waited until the regiment departed to do this desperate thing.

She didn't know if her timing was inspired or her words were right. At least she'd convinced Reginald to abandon his shop and come to the house, sit down with Anna and talk. Now if only Anna, unaware of Lydia's errand to the Binne Kill, could summon the courage and grace to do the same.

Lydia let Reginald into the house. With his tired footsteps behind her advancing toward the kitchen where Anna worked, she was still imploring in her heart: *You've let one decision define you for too long. Here now is a new choice you can make. For Anna's sake, for your own, make the right one.*

At the last, she turned and whispered, "Perhaps it would be best to wait here, let me speak to Anna first."

"Does she not expect me?" He clenched the hat he'd removed, running its brim through callused fingers. "Lydia, what are you about?"

"Please, Reginald. I'm sure she'll want to talk to you."

He looked monumentally less certain than she'd managed to sound but did as she bid.

"You've brought him *here*?" Already pale, with sleepless bruises beneath her eyes, Anna's face went bloodless as she gripped the worktable where she'd been grinding fragrant rosemary in a mortar. "How could you, with things as they are?"

"With things as they are, how could I not?" Lydia raised her hands in helplessness. "You are miserable. Reginald is miserable. *I* am miserable for you both." Her heart twisted at the brokenness in Anna's face, the stubbornness, the pride—more like Reginald than she knew. "Please, if only for my sake, will you go into the parlor and speak to your father?"

Tears glazed Anna's eyes. She put down the pestle, wiped her rosemary-scented hands on the apron covering the gown that hung loosely from her wasting frame, drew herself straight, and strode from the kitchen. Tense with hope, Lydia followed into the parlor, where Reginald sat in a stiff-backed chair. At sight of his daughter, he rose, a clench of pain in his face that made Lydia wince. *Let me have done rightly . . .*

No sooner had she lifted the prayer than it was evident she hadn't.

"Why, Papa?" Anna demanded, striding into the room with fists clenched at her sides. "Answer me that at last. Why did you send him away so shamefully?"

Reginald flinched. "Shamefully? Do you tell me 'tis no shame *you* felt for his gawping at you in that tub yonder?"

Lydia reached for the doorframe. *No,* she wanted to shout. *Not this.* But it was Anna doing the shouting, or near to it.

"He barely caught sight of me before he looked away. If you were standing behind him as you said, you'd have seen that. I think you came upon him already turning away and assumed the worst. Of us both!"

Reginald took a step toward his daughter. "Anna. Look you, that is not how—"

"I tried to go with him! He turned me back. He said starting our marriage by betraying your trust was unworthy of us. Are those the words of a shameful man?"

Like an ebbing tide, there went the color draining from Reginald's face. "Your *marriage*? What consent have I given to such a thing?"

"None, of course. But here is a thing you should know, Papa. William tried to convince me to go with him to Canada. He was willing to take me from you—but not Two Hawks. Now tell me, which of them has behaved with more honor?"

Reginald looked to Lydia, rooted in the dining room doorway. "Did you know of this as well?"

Anna took a step, putting herself squarely in his sights. "Don't accuse Lydia. This is between us. And I want your answer. If William and I never knew the truth of his blood, would you have gone on treating him like a son, an heir?"

It was a trap, of course. Yet nothing for Reginald to do now but walk straight into it. "I would have, yes."

Anna hovered on the verge of tears, then pressed them back and said in a voice flat with pain, "Why then do you close your heart to his twin? Why drive him away when he tried so hard to please you? What makes him different from William? Besides the color of his skin."

Reginald snatched up his hat from the chair on which he'd left it, then hurled it down again. "'Tis what you wish me to admit? That the color of his skin matters? Well, Anna, I'm sorry for it, but it matters and 'tis unrealistic to pretend otherwise. It matters in how he will be treated. How *you* will be treated, did you marry him. But that is not the only difference. There is the raising they both have had, see. Jonathan is Oneida. He'll have different expectations of a wife than someone raised among us, all else aside."

"True, Papa. But those expectations aren't the evil you seem to think them to be. Women of the Haudenosaunee have rights that I, or Lydia, could never have. Oneida women aren't property. They *own* property. Fields, crops, homes—all of it is theirs. They have a voice in who leads them and whether their warriors make war or peace. It seems to me I'd have a better life as a woman if I went and begged them to make me Oneida—which is what I tried to do."

Lydia judged it the worst thing Anna could have possibly said. Reginald had seen Indian women aplenty, back in the days when he made his trading trips upriver. He'd know how they were respected . . . until the warriors got a taste of liquor. Then would come the howling savagery, the brutality, and woe betide any woman who didn't hide herself then.

The appalling thought of Anna living in such conditions had rendered him speechless. Into that suspended moment came an urgent rapping at the door.

Anna wouldn't hear of Lydia answering the untimely call for a midwife. She gathered her case and all but hurtled out the door on the heels of the worried young father who had come knocking. Reginald didn't go after her. Perhaps, Lydia reasoned, collapsing into a parlor chair, stunned by the utter failure of her plan, it was best he let her go this time.

A scalpel. That was what was needed. A scalpel that could excise the bitter infection of Reginald's soul, a purulence that had spread now to Anna. She'd saved him once—in body—but clearly that wasn't to be her role again. She simply hadn't the necessary tool to hand.

When she could speak, she raised her gaze to Reginald, standing where Anna had left him.

"I am done with it, Reginald. I remove my hands. I will pray for you, for Anna. She is welcome to remain with me—indeed I hope she will. But I shall do nothing to prevent her making her own choices now. I am done."

Until, or unless, the Almighty gave her an indisputable sign that there was something more she could do. Until, or unless, He put the scalpel in her hand. She looked away from Reginald, unable to bear the breaking in his face.

"Do you think she's in earnest, about going to . . . them?"

"*Them?* Can you not even say their names?" She was bruised. Battered. She'd dashed herself one too many times against the fortress he'd built around his heart. "I've done the very thing of which I accused you, forced my will upon what God was doing and made a snarl of it. *Mea culpa.*"

She waited, knowing that if Reginald stood there and said nothing now she was going to weep. And maybe never stop.

"Lydia." His voice was graveled. "I'm sorry—"

"Don't." Wanting his apology less than his silence, she held up her hand. "Please. Leave my house. Now."

Reginald did so. Most willingly, it seemed.

"I feel no shame in loving you . . ." Anna could hear Two Hawks speaking, clear as if he stood beside her in the low-ceilinged, soot-smudged bedroom, while she encouraged the laboring woman in the bed, checked the progress of the babe's passage, prepared the twine and the shears and the soft swaddling ready to receive the infant. *"But in defying your father would be much shame . . ."*

She had defied Papa, addressed him in a manner she never would have dreamed herself capable of weeks ago. She didn't know what she felt about it. Aggrieved. Shaken. Yet at the same time filled with a sense of triumph she shied from examining for fear it was rooted in anger, pride, bitterness.

"Aubrey did not start you in the womb of your mother, but he gave you life, risking his own for yours . . ." That was indisputable. If not for Papa, she would never have had a life. Never known all these many years with their blessings. And their travails.

"Soon now," she said, comforting the sweating, suffering young woman by rote, lost inside her own writhing soul, where a different battle waged.

"Even if Creator did not bid us honor our parents, for that alone I would honor him in my heart . . ." Two Hawks would honor Papa for that one heroic act, saving her life that Two Hawks might know her, love her. But how could she honor Papa when he was wrong about so many things? Unfair. Unyielding. Unforgiving. He who had been forgiven so much.

"Taking you from him without his blessing is not the path I am to walk."

She should have left with Two Hawks. If she was going to be the wife of an Oneida man, why couldn't she also be Oneida? She'd been taken in once by those not of her blood. Why not again?

"You are not meant for that world."

But it was only his tradition preventing her from trying. He was willing to break other traditions for her. Why not that one?

The babe was coming, the young mother straining, tendons standing like ropes in her neck, face suffused with red. Anna reached to cradle the emerging head. "One more push. Good . . . good."

Was this rebellion in her heart, or might it be God's leading?

Her soul was a welter of confusion, a careening of emotions that sprayed like sparks from a smith's anvil. Blow after blow. She'd hurt Papa and Lydia with her words, yet she couldn't shake the notion that going after Two Hawks was what she needed to do. Instead of diminishing, it had been building in her over the weeks since the chill spring morning he'd left her. There was only one glaring problem. She didn't know the path to Kanowalohale.

The newborn—a girl—was out of her mother now, alive and perfect. Anna cut the cord and placed the squalling baby into the woman's reaching hands, smiling, saying words she'd heard Lydia speak over and again . . . meanwhile scouring her mind for a face, a name, anyone who'd be able and willing to help her.

She had to find Two Hawks. Or Good Voice, who would know where he was. But who would be her guide?

18

Green Bean Moon
Fort Stanwix

*D*uring the past moon, Two Hawks had helped his father hunt for meat and deerskins, but they made sure their hunting took them often to the fort at the Carrying Place. With midsummer past, they were come to Stanwix again to learn what the scouts ranging north and west and winging back home like crows to the nest had to say. They hoped to find Ahnyero. Two Hawks hadn't seen him since their parting on the trail where Strikes-The-Water found them and ruined everything.

He'd never been nearer to losing his self-possession than when he'd been forced to watch Ahnyero continue north with the rebel spy, Sam Reagan, knowing he'd lost his best chance of finding his brother before the redcoats began their campaign.

"And just who is William Aubrey to you?" Reagan had asked him, the marks of torture angry on his flesh.

"He is my brother, born with me at Fort William Henry, as I think you have already guessed. And you are the one who led him away just when he learned of me and our parents."

"His twin!" Reagan had said, no longer questioning what his eyes confirmed. "But you have it wrong. He was determined to leave Schenectady—doubt he cared for where, he was so furious. I said I was going over to the British and he was welcome to come."

Two Hawks had narrowed his eyes, trying to stitch the man's words together with what Anna Catherine and Lydia and Aubrey had said of that terrible night his brother learned the truth. "As a spy for the Americans, you have said—to us. But does my brother know you are a spy?"

Reagan shook his matted head. "He's been in no frame of mind to hear it. This—you—the truth coming out . . . he's still reeling from it. Took me months to get it out of him."

Two Hawks wanted to believe he was hearing a true thing about his brother's heart, hard as it was to accept. Reeling still, after so much time? How could that be?

Because he ran from every hand that might have steadied him.

As the thought sank like a stone into Two Hawks's heart, Ahnyero and Strikes-The-Water standing by silent, their prisoner's wary hazel eyes flicked between them. He wet his cracked lips. "Listen . . . Help me return to my regiment—with a story that'll prevent my being flogged for desertion—and I'll speak to William. Before this expedition gets too far underway, I mean to break from it, come over to my rightful place. I'll bring William with me . . . if he'll come."

Switching to Oneida, Two Hawks and Ahnyero had discussed the matter. Ahnyero proposed guiding Reagan north, pretending to be an Indian sympathetic to the British who'd rescued a hapless spy from his tormenters. If it proved safe enough and chance provided, Ahnyero would speak to William himself. Meanwhile, Two Hawks would return to the fort with Strikes-The-Water.

Two Hawks had seen the wisdom in it. That didn't mean he'd liked it.

Now, as he and his father entered the fort through the main gateway, they passed soldiers with saws and hammers, barrows and shovels, busy strengthening the walls and buildings within. New chimneys smoked in the day's early cool. They'd heard Ahnyero had returned from Lachine and been sent out on other missions, but neither Two Hawks nor Stone Thrower knew whether he'd spoken to William or even set eyes on him.

"Look." With his chin, Stone Thrower pointed toward the commander's headquarters, a log building across the open parade ground. Men were issuing from its door. Among them was Ahnyero, deep in talk with an officer Two Hawks recognized as Gansevoort's second-in-command, Marinus Willett. The scout saw them coming and ended his talk with Willett as they reached him.

"It is good at last to see you both," Ahnyero said as Willett strode away. "I know you will want to hear what happened with me and that one who found us on the trail." This he said to Two Hawks, gripping his arm in greeting.

"Did you see my brother?" Two Hawks interjected, impatience getting the better of his manners. "Did you speak to him?"

Stone Thrower thinned his lips to show he noticed his son's rudeness but also lifted a hand to the leather bag strung around his neck. His father had made the little bag; his mother stitched it with white beads. It held the painted face of their firstborn.

Ahnyero's gaze followed the gesture. "I never saw him. It is a long tale, and I would not make you wait to hear that part."

Two Hawks's hope, taken wing at sight of the scout, plummeted back to earth.

"I went with that spy all the way to his post at Lachine," Ahnyero said. "I saw the regiment—Johnson's Greens. I spoke to one who is captain over the one you seek. That man, Watts, took the spy back and accepted the story we gave. But the one you seek had been sent away on an errand to Montreal. I found a place to wait, but before he returned, I was seen by an Indian who knew me. A Mohawk from the Seven Nations who lived for a time at Kanowalohale—a tall one, his father's people are Oneida."

"Tames-His-Horse?" Two Hawks turned to his father. "He was at the river that day you returned from the Senecas. He went under the water as well and took the name of Joseph."

"That one is not easy to forget," Stone Thrower said. "What did he say to you, up there in Lachine?" he asked Ahnyero.

"He wanted to know what I was doing there. He tried to get me to come with him and speak to other warriors who are hanging about, waiting to fight. I knew then I could not stay, so I spoke to our spy and told him to remember his promise to give your lost one word of you. Then I left to return."

Two Hawks saw his disappointment and frustration mirrored in his father's face. "Does even Creator wish to keep him from us?"

Stone Thrower's face cleared. "I do not know. I pray not, but Creator is working this out in His way and time. Do not lose hope."

Ahnyero cleared his throat. "Listen—I do not know if this will be of help to you, but I have just spoken with Gansevoort and Willett. I am sent to Oswego."

"Oswego?" Two Hawks said. "Where we hear the British will gather?"

"It is so. I am to go among them, talk to the Indians there—present myself as one whose sympathies have changed if I am again known. But here is a thing that will make you glad, brother. I need runners to go with me, to carry news back to this fort. Yours was the face that came first into my mind when these plans were told to me, and here I step into the sunlight and who do I see?"

The scout smiled at the eagerness Two Hawks knew his face must show. "I will be a runner for you. Do you think Johnson's regiment has already come to Oswego?"

"It will be soon, in any case. I must find other warriors to be runners," Ahnyero said. "Once that is done, we can make ready to leave. Do you wish to be one along with your son?" he asked Stone Thrower.

"I will be needed for the hunting, now that this one flies from me again like an arrow." Stone Thrower turned to Two Hawks, half his mouth pulling into a smile, somehow proud, sad, amused, all at once.

With reluctance Two Hawks said, "If you need me . . ."

Stone Thrower put a hand to his son's shoulder. "No. Do this thing for our people and theirs," he added, with a nod toward Gansevoort and other officers ducking out through the headquarters entry. "And may Creator at last give you word or even sight of your brother. I will tell your mother what it is you do. We will send our prayers up for you."

Turning, he gave Ahnyero a look, steady and speaking. Two Hawks in his eagerness caught only its tail but knew his father was asking the scout to guard the son he had always had with him, as well as to find the one in the portrait he carried against his heart.

19

July 1777
Buck Island, St. Lawrence River

*A*s Private William Aubrey understood it, the Crown's campaign had lost one of its three vital prongs. General Burgoyne was descending south from Chambly, in Quebec, along the lake passage to the Hudson, while Brigadier General St. Leger would lead his 34th Regiment and the rest of his loyalist forces east from Oswego, joined by a detachment of the 8th, Butler's rangers, and whatever forces Joseph Brant had collected. Their initial objective was the investment of Fort Stanwix. Once that reportedly thin-garrisoned fort surrendered, they would pour into the Mohawk Valley, sweep the back-country militia before them, and converge with Burgoyne at Albany, severing New England from the rest of the rebelling colonies. But the third prong, General Howe—still in New York City—intended to focus his energies on hunting Washington's rebels in and around Philadelphia and refused to alter his plans to join Burgoyne and St. Leger.

The latter's brigade was well underway toward Oswego. They'd put in at Buck Island, near the point where the St. Lawrence broadened into Lake Ontario, for a temporary halt. It had needed a fortnight to travel upriver from Lachine with the seemingly endless series of rapids and cataracts, unnavigable to bateaux, requiring the soldiers to manhandle baggage and equipment over each portage; tedious, disheartening work, often watched by Indians lining the riverbank like spectators at a cricket match.

They were no sooner ashore at Buck Island than William, along with

Angus MacKay, Robbie, and some twenty others, were set to clearing ground for an exercise field, St. Leger being of the opinion Johnson's Greens stood in need of more drill practice.

"Aye, weel," MacKay grumbled under his breath. "We're a step closer to home and justice done. We ken a neck or twa we'll be that glad to see in a hangman's noose. Aye, Robbie?"

The lad's reply was dutiful. "Aye, Da. That we will."

A mile long and heavily forested, Buck Island boasted a ship-building operation. The bateaux on stocks, some of them massive transports set to ferry soldiers down the lake to Oswego, stirred memories William would rather have banished, but as he shouldered an ax and trooped away from the milling encampment and set to work grubbing brush, those memories felt more solid than the existence he was living now.

Anna, forgive me. The words chased through his thoughts a dozen times a day. As did a plea directed at the man she called Papa. Rage and hatred had at last simmered down, letting grief and regret rise to the surface. And the burning need to know . . . *why?*

He was awash in such thoughts when Sam appeared at his side, ax in hand. William caught his glance, then pretended he hadn't. He raised the ax to sever a pine sapling near the ground, then set about grubbing the stump, the scent of sap and crushed needles sharp in his nose. Sweat dripped down his face in the heat.

Sam worked beside him, his silence a reproach.

William wanted to say something to alleviate the strain between them since Sam's return to Lachine, which had occurred in William's absence. An Indian had come in from the wilds with Sam, a warrior whose corroboration helped him wriggle out of the desertion charges awaiting him, returning a week behind the party with which he'd been sent out. Sam had given William the tale he'd presumably told Major Gray and Sir John—one of capture and torture. He'd the wounds to prove it. Only one thing Sam confessed to him that he'd kept from their commanding officers: he'd encountered William's brother, Two Hawks, during his misadventure.

"I didn't know him for your twin right off. He's got his head shaved as they do and a wicked scar just here." Sam, who had just removed his shirt, sniffed it, and tossed it aside with a grimace, touched a spot above his ear. "He's darker, but in feature very like you."

Alone in their Lachine billet, William had stared in renewed horror at the healing wounds on his friend's chest. "Do you tell me my *brother* did that to you?"

"No." Sam pulled a freshly laundered shirt over his head.

"But they were Oneidas?" If his brother had been among those who captured Sam, might that warrior—his father—have had a hand in administering the torture? He grasped Sam's arm. "'Tis truth you tell me, Sam? My father and brother didn't do this to you?"

For a suspended moment, Sam searched his face, indecision warring in his eyes. "I never saw your father."

William let go his arm. "You're not being honest with me. I don't think you have been since we came over the mountains. You disappear for hours at a time without explanation—save I've seen you talking to Indians. Now you get yourself captured by Oneidas, *happen* to meet my twin, and I'm to think it coincidence?"

Sam's indecision vanished in a thrust of his jaw. "If you're accusing me of something, William, come out with it straight."

William had backed down, at the time uncertain he wanted to know the truth. *Were* those marks of torture the work of his brother's hands? Anna claimed to have befriended his twin. What exactly had she said of this Two Hawks? Having so long suppressed the memories of that terrible night, they proved too fragmented to recall now with certainty.

If only he'd waited, learned a little more . . . maybe he'd never have gone north with the man clearing ground beside him now.

Bone-weary, bug-bitten, and sweat-drenched, William was returning to camp with the rest of the detail when the Mohawk found him again. Looming out of the dusk, he stepped across William's path, blocking his progress toward the beckoning aromas of cookery beyond a thicket of spruce. Above leggings and breechclout, the Mohawk wore a calico shirt belted with a colorful sash, through which was thrust a hunting knife and tomahawk. A neck sheath with a buck-horn knife hung at his chest. Slung at his shoulder was a rifle.

Last among the stragglers from the field, William halted, letting the others trudge on without him. Weary and spent, not a one looked back. He clenched the ax until the handle bit into his palm. His first encounter with Joseph Tames-His-Horse on the streets of Lachine had been curtailed once he'd realized the warrior's connection to his Oneida kin. Twice before the regiment departed the village, the Mohawk had attempted to speak to him. William had managed to elude the man each time. He'd hoped the Indian had gotten it through his lofty head that he'd no wish to deepen their acquaintance.

Apparently he hadn't.

"The King's army works you hard?" the Indian inquired. When William turned a hand palm upward, revealing its raw state, Joseph's face showed disbelief, as if he couldn't credit a man letting himself be worked like an ox. Then he shrugged. "You come to my fire now. There is food," he added as William's stomach gave an impatient rumble.

Joseph Tames-His-Horse was one determined Indian. Worse than the mosquitoes whining round their ears.

"Look you," William said. "I'll eat what's provided yonder if I don't fall asleep first, so say whatever you've been wanting to say to me and get it over."

There was light enough to see the lift of the Indian's sweeping brows, the dark gaze tilted down at him. "Listen then. There was a party of scouts sent south to Fort Stanwix, most of them Mohawk. They were sent to take prisoners and learn from them how many are in that fort, how much is its strength, for when you and those with you come that way." Joseph jerked his chin toward the trees and the encampment beyond and the ship-building site where masts bristled dark against a sky still tinged orange with sunset.

Despite hunger and exhaustion, William was suddenly interested in what this Indian was saying. "Did you go with them? Where are the prisoners? Have they talked?"

"Five prisoners we carried to that one who is over the things to do with Indians."

Daniel Claus, British Superintendent of Indian Affairs, he meant.

"Are they still being questioned?"

"We did our own questioning. Here is what we learned: the garrison at Stanwix is strong. Much soldiers. The fort is built up—this I saw. Already they know you come and the number of your warriors."

William frowned, uncertain whether to credit a report at stark variance with the army's intelligence—Sam's included—that Fort Stanwix was thinly manned and still under repair. But he pretended to believe the Indian. "Will this intelligence alter St. Leger's plans?"

A shrug. "If he trusts the words of captives."

"Already they know you come and the number of your warriors."

Fatigue fell away like a blanket discarded. "The rebels at Fort Stanwix know Johnson's regiment is coming?" He didn't need the Indian's grunt of assent to know it was so. Had word gone beyond the fort? Gone as far as Schenectady? Did Anna know he was part of the invasion force set to descend upon her?

What else Joseph Tames-His-Horse had said belatedly sank in. He'd said they know *you* come. Not *we*. "Are you no longer in this fight?"

Before Joseph could reply, a familiar growl rose behind him. "Since ye dinna seem interested in your grub, Private Breed, ye'll take first guard duty down at the boats."

William turned as Sergeant Campbell stalked past the spruces and stood with feet planted wide, reaching out a broad hand. "Collect your arms. I'll be takin' that ax."

"Aye sir." Clenching his teeth as his stomach clamored in protest, William handed over the ax.

Campbell stood back, waiting for him to proceed. William cast a glance back to where Joseph Tames-His-Horse stood, wondering how the sergeant could ignore such a presence, to find naught but a spruce bough waving as if in a passing breeze.

Sam Reagan rose from the fire as William emerged from his tent, smothered in full regimentals, accoutered for sentry. Around them in the falling summer dark, men's voices murmured, laughed, quarreled as they downed the evening's rum ration. Somewhere a knife blade was being scraped against stone. A fifer struggled over a tune too broken to recognize. The faces at the near fire hung in haggard lines. Most were too tired from the work detail to do more than gripe and yawn.

Sam thrust a linen-wrapped parcel at him. "I set aside your ration and grease for your face—have you seen the like of these mosquitoes? I itch from scalp to soles." His gaze held steady, offering more than food.

"They're appalling." William took the parcel, hesitated, then added, "I appreciate it."

Sam's long-absent grin flashed in the firelight. "Manage not to land on me when you fall into your bedroll later and we'll call it square."

20

July 1777
Lake Ontario

William wasn't rowing, poling, or otherwise engaged with propelling the massive bateau in the vanguard of the advancing army. He was leaning against the vessel's side, gazing westward into shrouding mist, when the bark canoe appeared out of the drifting vapor. It was one of many such small craft surrounding them in the veiled, watery dawn, moons to the vanguard's planet. St. Leger, discounting the intelligence obtained from the Mohawk's captives, had ordered an advance—the Royal Yorkers among them—to proceed down the lake to Fort Oswego to join Butler, Brant, Claus, and their assembled forces.

They'd left Buck Island in darkness, amid the splash of oars and sweeps, the terse bark of orders. By the time they reached the lake—little more than a sense of the river's islanded channel widening into something far more sweeping in size—dawn had flushed the enclosing mist the delicate hue of a ripened peach. Somewhere a loon gave its eerie call. Ahead, a flotilla of waterfowl, disturbed by the bateaux's passage, burst into raucous motion and scattered before them on indignant wings.

By contrast, the canoe, and the Indians in it, emerged from the mist in silence, as if the vapors themselves had coalesced into form off the bateau's side. The warrior at the bow sat a head higher in the craft than his fellows, long bronzed arms gripping a paddle that sliced the lake's dark waters. Slowing the canoe to glide in tandem with the bateau, Joseph Tames-His-Horse looked at William. No surprise lit the dark gaze—

never a chance meeting with this Indian—but a measured intensity that drilled like a lance, as if the Mohawk meant to underscore the words spoken by firelight the evening before.

More than a week after their first encounter on Buck Island, Watts's company had been ordered to draw their firing allotment of fifty rounds per man. William had been on his way back to his tent, cartridge box full, when once again the Indian cut him from his fellows with the skill of a collie among sheep.

"Come," he'd said. "I dreamed of you. We must talk."

Bemused by the invitation—or command—William nonetheless followed the Indian past outlying tents and sentries, past stumps of trees felled for boat building, to a faint trail leading through untouched forest. In moments they reached a fire and a brush shelter. The warrior motioned William to sit while he went about pouring coffee from a pot steaming at the fire's edge. Joseph Tames-His-Horse handed him a cup, then seated himself and unearthed a clay pipe, which he packed with a mixture of dried bark, leaf, and tobacco. Its fragrance mingled with the coffee's, a brew surprisingly rich. When he got it drawing well, the Indian raised the pipe to the four directions, then offered it to William, who accepted, thinking that aside from the forest ringed about and the stars accumulating above, he might have been in some gentleman's parlor on a summer's eve, such were the unhurried manners of his host. He passed the pipe back and waited.

After topping off William's coffee with the last in the pot, Joseph sat back and said, "Here is the thing about why I am in this fight."

Having all but forgotten the question he'd put to the Indian days ago, William listened, sensing an urgency to communicate simmering beneath the outward calm.

"I have a sister, back along this river a distance." Joseph nodded toward the rushing chatter that reached them through the wood, the St. Lawrence flowing east toward Montreal. "A thing happened with her that I did not like. She took a husband. That is why I left. Why *I* am here."

William's brows bunched in an attempt to understand why a sister marrying would have driven this Indian from his home. Had he disapproved her choice? Seeing how that powerful jaw was clenched, he hadn't the nerve to ask.

"I also have a sister," he surprised himself by saying. "Or one I thought of as a sister, though she isn't in truth. Anna." As her name hovered on air thick with smoke and the drone of mosquitoes, the rhythmic croak of frogs and the fire's fluttering, he was blindsided by memory of Anna standing at the top of the stairs at Lydia's house, bathed in candlelight, clutching her forgotten cap. "I left her when I came north to join Johnson's regiment."

A year gone. Did she think of him still, pray for him? He felt the Indian's gaze.

"She is your sister . . . but not?"

"You know of me," William said, "that I was taken—stolen—at Fort William Henry. That's when Anna came to be my sister. She was rescued by . . ." He cleared his throat. "By the man who raised me. His wife had birthed a son the same night we—my twin and I—were born. That son died. Reginald Aubrey took me to replace him. He and my . . ."

Who is my mother and my brethren? He'd lashed the question at Anna, wanting no response. Now it gnawed at his soul, demanding answer.

"The Aubreys were attacked with his regiment on the wilderness road. That's where he found Anna, her parents dead beside her. We were together on the farm until I left for Wales, still a boy. I saw Anna no more until I returned last summer." He stopped, overwhelmed by the recital of these bare facts, though oddly grateful for the chance to voice them.

"You regret leaving her," Joseph said, as if he knew.

"We didn't part well, see. And it troubles me now, thinking of her in the path of . . . this." William waved a hand at the dark wood, in the direction of the army encampment. "Terrifies me, if I'm honest."

Unlike the MacKays, he'd come north seeking refuge, not revenge. The regiment had offered him a place between what he'd been and . . . whatever he would be. Or so he'd thought. How had he not foreseen it would come to this?

"You parted with her in anger?"

William looked at the Indian, catching in his eyes a glint of pain.

A breeze off the river met the fire, ruffling the flames. William took a sip of coffee and, finding it cold, set the cup on the ground.

"I wanted her to come with me. She'd suffered nearly as great a shock as I, discovering the truth about me, about my brother she'd befriended years ago. She guessed it, see, the moment she set eyes on me again."

"She is that girl?" Joseph asked, a light in his eyes. "I remember now, your brother spoke of seeing her. All these years she has been between you, a bridge to each other, though she did not know it?"

William stared at the Indian. "I suppose that's true."

A bridge. One he'd recklessly burned?

So much they hadn't known. *Anna, I'm sorry.* He flung the plea southward yet again, but for the first time sensed its echo coming back to him across the mountain wilderness, though not from Anna. *William, I tell you I am sorry . . .*

Joseph leaned toward him, his intensity disconcerting. "Listen. You must go back to this sister who is not a sister."

A mosquito buzzed at William's eye. He swiped it away, covering the shock of the Indian's words and those others he must have imagined. "I cannot. And if I could, it would mean going back to . . ."

"Your father?"

"That's not what he is," William bit out, more harshly than he'd meant to because the word was wrapping itself around his heart and making him sick with longing. Regret. "My father's an Oneida called Stone Thrower. You know him."

The Mohawk drew on his pipe, found it had gone out, set it aside. The breeze shifted the fire's smoke across their faces—relief from the mosquitoes. "It has been how long since you learned the truth of who you are?"

"A year."

"And still you hold such hate?"

"Not hate." He heard the defensiveness in his tone, even as honesty spilled forth. "Not anymore. I might still have left in the end, but I regret doing so without understanding why he did it. I thought him a good man."

Joseph Tames-His-Horse gazed at him. "I have not lived long enough to get much wisdom. But it is my thinking that men do most of what they do for two reasons: for love or for pride. For which of these did the man who made himself your father do what he did?"

William opened his mouth, then shut it. He'd nearly told a boldfaced lie. "For love," he said through a tightened throat. "For my . . . for his wife. He did love her. Once."

"You can admit he maybe did this thing unthinking, or thinking only of his pain in that moment, or the pain of the woman he loved? Maybe as you felt when you left your sister, a thing you now regret?"

The words were said without condemnation, yet William's face burned. He nearly rose to bolt back through the trees to the safety of his tent, to men who asked nothing of him but obedience and duty and the keeping of the oath he swore. Instead he blurted, "What of you and your sister? Do you regret leaving her?"

Anguish rippled over the Indian's features before it was suppressed. "I cannot be with her as I would wish."

"*Be* with her?"

Joseph Tames-His-Horse hurried to say, "You must understand how the Haudenosaunee reckon kinship. My sisters are not only those born to my mother but every woman in my mother's clan. Burning Sky was not born to my mother or any woman of the Wolf Clan, but she was adopted by one. That makes her my sister, no matter her blood."

"Your sister is adopted?" William asked, startled by the revelation.

Joseph nodded. "Born white but taken, like you. Only she was made Indian where you were made white."

William gaped at the man seated cross-legged beside him, the planes of his face shining in the firelight, the tail of his scalp-lock tied with feathers—aside from wearing no war paint, as wild an Indian as William could picture. And his sister, this Burning Sky, was a white woman.

"At what age was she captured?"

"Fourteen summers."

No infant. A girl near grown who would remember—her name, her life, her family.

"You wish to ask of her?" The Indian watched him closely. "Ask. I will answer, if it will help."

William heard his breath coming loud through his nostrils, breathing in the smoke from the fire. "Has she found peace? Has she forgotten? Or . . . forgiven?"

The questions might have been poised on his tongue, waiting to be called forth.

Joseph briefly closed his eyes, opening them to stare into the flames, as if in them he could see the sister called Burning Sky. "It was hard for her, at first. I left Kanowalohale and returned to our village soon after she came to be there. I'd had a dream of her and thought that meant . . ." He paused, shook his head. "Dream paths do not always lead where it seems they will."

The Indian didn't explain the statement.

"I did all I could to be a brother to her, reminding her that Creator is over all, and in all, and with her always. She learned to be content. I believe in her heart there is peace. But there is also grief. Maybe soon there will be children to fill her heart."

The man wouldn't look at William now. "Dream a lot, do you?"

Joseph took up a stick and pushed at the fire's embers. "Too much."

A coldness opened in the pit of William's belly. "You said you dreamed of me."

"I did." The Indian shoved the stick into the flames, sending sparks toward the shadowy branches above. "In my dream you turned your coat," he said. "You turned your coat inside out and went another way."

William felt as if he'd been slapped. Heat flared in his face, beading sweat across his lip and brow. "You speak of desertion?"

"What I said is what I saw." Joseph Tames-His-Horse met his gaze square but said no more about the dream. "Those Oneidas who are your family, to them you are known as He-Is-Taken of the Turtle Clan. Your place among them has been long empty, but you are not forgotten. That place is waiting for you. Think about that. And there is this about that man who took you—this Aubrey. You cannot see his heart. You did not stay to let him speak it to you. There is no going forward for you until you first go back and clear that path between you. But there is hope."

William glanced into the dark. *Hope?* "Not if I invade with this army."

The Indian raised his brows. "Maybe that is not a thing you should be doing."

"I haven't a choice. I'm not free to leave, and I'm no turncoat."

Wasn't he though? He'd deserted Anna. And those Oneidas who'd grieved his absence for nineteen years without even looking upon their faces. His father, mother, brother.

William stood to his feet. "What of you? Will you ever go back to your *sister*?"

He hadn't meant to ask it in such a mocking tone, but Joseph didn't flinch. "One day I will go back. Unless Creator calls me to Himself first." He looked up then, bronzed face reflecting sorrow. "I am still her brother."

Joseph Tames-His-Horse held the canoe alongside the bateau a moment more, then dipped his paddle with his companions'. The bark vessel veered off, vanishing back into the mist with no more than a cutting wake to show it was ever there.

"See that?" said a soldier behind him. "Fair made my skin crawl."

A hand nudged William's shoulder. "That big one looked straight at ye, Aubrey—like he fancied your scalp. Glad he's on our side, aye?"

William glanced aside at Sam, silent beside him on the bench. Sam had seen the Indian, no doubt, but was gazing now at William, a question in his hazel eyes.

"Glad enough," he said to satisfy whoever had asked but wondered if, out in the mist in his canoe, Joseph Tames-His-Horse felt the same screaming dread building inside him, or the growing conviction that he was advancing toward the worst mistake he would ever make and no way out of it with his honor intact.

"You turned your coat."

"Creator is over all, and in all . . ." Maybe so. For even on the edge of the wilderness, the Almighty had found him—sent a praying Indian, of all things, one who knew both his names.

William Llewellyn Aubrey. He-Is-Taken of the Turtle Clan.

Neither name seemed claimable as his own. Nor did he know what manner of man he was becoming, only that there was no path forward from that shadowy place between without his betraying someone.

21

Green Bean Moon
Fort Oswego, Lake Ontario

*T*he day the ravens darkened the sky over Oswego was the day Two Hawks saw his brother for the first time.

He witnessed what happened with those birds from the forest where he waited, watching the fort and the field encampment outside it busy with the comings and goings of warriors. Mississaugas were coming in over the lake in canoes. From the south came Senecas—two hundred at least. From the east, passing near the rock outcrop where Two Hawks hid, had come Thayendanegea leading some whites willing to follow him and over three hundred warriors from Oquaga and other towns loyal to the British.

Earlier that morning, down from the north along the lake, had come the first of St. Leger's army. With leaping heart Two Hawks had seen the great bateaux disgorge soldiers in green coats onto the shore, seen them march into the fort behind its earthen rampart. More warriors came with them, Caughnawagas in their canoes. These didn't go into the fort but joined their brethren on the field outside, an impressive number—nearing a thousand, Two Hawks guessed. Down among them were Louis Cook and Ahnyero, pretending to be like minded, learning all they could of what the British leaders meant next to do.

Though too far away to hear what the warriors outside the fort were saying, Two Hawks knew they weren't happy. Supplies promised at Niagara were nowhere to be found at Oswego. Some had come without muskets or with no powder and ball. Many needed clothing, food, hatchets, blankets, things they'd come to expect from armies that invaded their lands and enticed them to fight. Thayendanegea and Colonel Butler and the one called Daniel Claus had assured the warriors that soon their needs would be met. Wait for St. Leger to come with the bulk of his army and its supplies, they said. Then they would see British promises kept. Then they would see British might.

Maybe such talking went on still as evening came down again. Two Hawks couldn't know. It was while he stewed on it with unraveling patience that he saw the ravens.

They came out of nowhere it seemed, thousands of them darkening the sky above the fort, their grating calls and thrumming wings a cacophony that made Two Hawks clap his hands over his ears. The ravens didn't pass over the fort and fly away. They circled back, covering the summer sky. Masses of them bulged and dipped like black smoke billowing, blotting out the sunlight, casting false dusk. Never had Two Hawks seen ravens behave so, or so many come together in one place. That it should be here above this fort, with all these warriors gathering . . .

With a prayer on his lips to drive back the horror raising every hair of his body on end, Two Hawks ducked from behind the rock and stood looking, listening. Some of the ravens alighted in the trees above him, cawing to each other. Fighting unreasoning panic, he asked Creator if this was a sign and if so what it meant, but the birds or their noise seemed to block his prayer.

When true dusk threatened and still the ravens circled and Ahnyero didn't come, Two Hawks's patience failed. Their supplies and extra weapons he pushed inside a hollow stump. Gathering only his rifle and his courage, he stepped out under an orange sky banded with shifting black, headed for the fort.

As he wove through the fires that edged the field like a scattering of stars, most of the warriors around him were too intent on watching the sky to notice one more Indian passing by. Though overall the camp was eerily silent, except for the swelling grate of bird voices, he heard mutterings of bad omens and premonitions and death. Unease weighed like the pressure before a storm breaks. Two Hawks moved among them, pretending he had a place to go and was going there. His breath came hard. William would be inside the fort. Probably staring at the sky like those outside.

Looking ahead through the warriors standing in clutches by their fires or arrested in their passage to stop and stare, he spotted a few green-coats and soldier hats among the shaved heads and painted faces clustered near the fort gate. His heart was a drum beating, his grip on the rifle a clench. Should he find Ahnyero, or dared he go inside the fort and look for William?

Brother, I am close. I am here, coming to you. Sending his thoughts ahead, he strode toward the gate. No one stopped him. Other Indians were going into the fort, some coming out. He could do this. He could find—

"Go no farther!"

The hard grip on his arm, the hissing in his ear, shattered his focus so abruptly he yelped in surprise. Ahnyero had him by the arm. Beside him was Louis, his darker face radiating censure.

The scouts propelled him toward a stack of casks waiting to be hauled away to somewhere, out of the path of those passing through the gate in the falling twilight. There Ahnyero released him. "It is too much risk, going in there. Go back to the wood and wait."

Two Hawks put his back to the gate and stood straight, taller than Ahnyero if not Louis. "My brother is here, unless not all Johnson's regiment have come?"

"They are come," said Louis. "If your brother is part of that regiment, he is here."

"I can find him. I will be careful." He thought Ahnyero began to shake his head, but whether or not the scout would have relented, Two Hawks never found out.

"Spencer?" a voice said behind him. Ahnyero's English name.

The scout's gaze flew past Two Hawks, recognition lighting his eyes. He thrust Two Hawks aside and stepped past him. Two Hawks turned to see the pale-haired rebel spy, Sam Reagan.

Much recovered from his ordeal back in spring, Reagan was clothed in the green of his regiment but nearly as desperate looking in the eyes as he'd been then. So intent was he on Ahnyero, he didn't notice Two Hawks standing silent by the casks, a pace or two removed and partly blocked by Louis Cook's large frame.

"I didn't think to find you again. I've news . . ." Reagan dropped his voice. "There's to be an advance column sent out. Word's come from St. Leger, back at the Little Salmon River. Thinks he can take Stanwix without artillery, based on his presumption the fort isn't fully manned." He grinned crookedly at that, having been one of those to give him that misinformation. "I'm ready to take this news myself to Gansevoort—I've but moments to make my break before I'm looked for."

"You are sure of this advance?" Louis asked in English, stepping in closer to the pair. Two Hawks leaned sideways to see Reagan look with suspicion at this new face.

"He is a friend," Ahnyero said.

Two Hawks kept his shoulder partly turned, his gaze on a group of Butler's rangers straggling past into the fort. Twilight was thickening, the air still filled with bird noise, drifting feathers, droppings, though the ravens had thinned, leaving gaps of deepening blue.

Reagan gestured at the sky filled with ravens. "Butler and Brant just got the Indians settled over not having supplies enough to go round and now this. Captain Watts is about to call assembly, but I can slip away if I don't go back for anything. Is there a guide can take me to Stanwix?"

Two Hawks at last drew near enough in the deepening twilight for Reagan to recognize him. "I will take him, after I find my brother."

"You." Reagan took a half step back, gaze darting over Two Hawks's features. "Does William know you're here?"

"No," Ahnyero said, addressing Two Hawks. "You will not do it. I am sorry, brother. As for you," he added, turning back to Reagan, "better you stay for now. Do not alert your officers by deserting. I will stay and attach myself to the Indians here for as long as I can safely do so. I will be your guide."

He turned, questioning, to Louis, who nodded. "I will remain until St. Leger comes or I see with my own eyes men marching to meet him, know their number, the way they take."

"There will be another time," Ahnyero said to Two Hawks. "For now, return to Gansevoort with the words this man has told us. It is more than the other runners knew, and you are the last until we come."

Two Hawks fought down the impulse to argue. While he struggled, Reagan said, "I'll stay—for now. And I'll persuade William to go with me when the time comes. It'll be soon."

Two Hawks's disappointment was like the sky full of ravens crashing down to bury him. If only he could have looked upon his brother's face, even a glance . . .

No sooner had he wished it than a crowd of warriors and rangers at the gate parted, leaving clear an aisle like a gauntlet. Down its center strode one tall figure in green. Two Hawks had seen his own face in a mirror often enough to know the cast of his features. And he'd seen that portrait. It was William.

He thought his brother saw him too. William's head lifted. His stride lengthened. His mouth opened.

"Reagan!" Sound of his brother's voice froze Two Hawks. Then the crowd shifted. Bodies came between them. "Sam!"

Either his brother hadn't seen him, or he hadn't known who it was he looked upon. He'd spotted his friend and was coming for him, pushing through those now blocking his path.

Ahnyero turned to him, urgent, and said, "Go. Quickly."

Two Hawks turned and walked on unfeeling feet into the dark where the fires of a thousand warriors burned, no more than orange smudges in his blurring vision.

Kanowalohale

Still catching his breath after running the last miles from Fort Stanwix, where he'd made his report to Colonel Gansevoort, Two Hawks sat on the edge of his sleeping bench in his mother's lodge and told his other news— that which he'd been thrumming with since he slipped back through the grim-faced warriors on the field at Oswego, beneath the ravens' ominous shadow.

"I have seen my brother. With my own eyes—I have seen him!"

Clear Day sat by the fire, pipe suspended halfway to his lips, but his parents had risen upon his arrival. They stood near enough to each other that when his mother reached out blindly with a hand, she found his father's reaching for hers.

"Tell us of it," his father said, as his mother's free hand came up to cup her rounding belly.

Two Hawks had known for over a moon about his mother's pregnancy. At nearly twenty summers, he felt toward this child to come more like an uncle than a brother, but he was happy for it. Happy his parents were in a good place, following the path of Creator and Savior Jesus. But now his mother's eyes were all for him. She was likely thinking not of the coming child but of long ago when she carried him and his brother together beneath her heart.

"I saw him," he said again. "In his green coat, coming toward me through the gate at Oswego."

"You went into the fort?" This from his father, the words gruff with surprise. "That is not a thing Ahnyero meant for you to do, I think."

"Ahnyero stopped me at the gate. But I saw William in the crowd. I heard his voice calling. I thought . . ." Two Hawks felt a thickness in his throat every time he recalled the sound of his twin's voice. "I thought at first it was to me he called, but it was to that one called Reagan, who stood with us." Before his father could ask, he said, "I have not told you all there is to know about that one."

Good Voice, her face golden from days in the cornfield, wiped a tear from the corner of her eye. "Did he see you? Did your brother know you? Did you speak with him?"

"I did not. Ahnyero thought it unwise to reveal myself. He needed me to carry news of St. Leger to Gansevoort. So that is what I did. I turned and walked away before William could come near."

He'd tried to speak without emotion but heard the edge in his voice.

So did his father. "It is good you did as Ahnyero said, but it must have been hard to do. I would have found it so."

His father was looking at him as a man looks at another he respects. Two Hawks sat up straight on the bench. He would put aside disappointment and behave himself as a man. Creator, who saw everything, made everything, would also make a way for them to find William again. If He willed it.

Good Voice sat beside him and encircled him with her arm. "I am happy, my son, that you have seen your brother at last."

Even as she spoke, his father was pulling out that tiny portrait of William from the pouch he carried against his heart.

"May I see it?" he asked his father. Stone Thrower gazed at it a moment, then handed it over. Two Hawks had looked upon it only twice but saw now that the likeness was true.

"Anna Catherine," his mother said as her arm slipped from his shoulders. "And Aubrey. Should we take word to them?" She looked first at Two Hawks, as if thinking he might already plan to go to them, but he knew all she would read on his face was indecision.

"They must be told," Stone Thrower said.

"I wish to be the one to tell them," Two Hawks hurried to say. There was nothing he wanted more than to stand before Anna Catherine and tell her he had seen William. "But how can I leave when this army is coming into our lands? How can I go running to Anna Catherine and not stand between her and what is coming? Would I not also be abandoning my brother, who comes with this army?"

He shook his head, torn in two directions even after days of thinking it through, praying for his path to be clear.

"That is also my heart," Stone Thrower said, sitting heavily beside Good Voice. "I wish to go to Aubrey but feel I must stay."

Clear Day, who had been silent so long at the fire that Two Hawks had almost forgotten he was listening, made a rumble of throat clearing and stood. "Aubrey and his daughter need to know of this news, to know we have not forgotten the words spoken between us. You made a promise to that man, to help him find your son."

Stone Thrower looked grave and a little chagrined as he confessed, "It was not a promise made without some guile. I did not wish for Aubrey to go off alone, against the will of Creator."

"That is also in my heart," Clear Day said. "So *I* will go to him with this news while you young men, you warriors, stay and guard the People."

The silence that dropped into his mother's lodge was so complete, Two Hawks heard nothing but the crackle of the fire that had burned in the background of all their days.

"Uncle," Good Voice said, "that is a long journey to make, and you have traveled far already these moons past."

Though she did not say he was an old, tired man who should stay awhile by his fire, the creases of Clear Day's face deepened with amusement. "It is true I have journeyed far and seen much, but I have yet the strength for this."

"But there was no army coming down upon us when you made those journeys," Stone Thrower pointed out. "Who can say what a man might meet on those paths now. More likely an enemy than a friend, and you would be alone."

"He will not be alone," said a high, bright voice. The door of the lodge pushed open, and in came Strikes-The-Water, unashamed to let them see she'd been skulking outside, listening to their talk. "I will go with you, Grandfather. I can use a bow—or a rifle if one was given to me. I am not afraid of meeting an enemy on the path."

Good Voice rose off the bench, crossed to the girl, and, to Two Hawks's surprise, welcomed her with an embrace, approving her offer. It wasn't gratitude stirring in Two Hawks's chest but annoyance. Even a tinge of jealousy. He started to object to this girl's interference in matters that were none of her business—a habit she couldn't seem to break—but shut his mouth when his father stood also and approached the girl. His parents' relief was palpable. Clear Day put his wrinkled hand to Strikes-The-Water's arm, speaking words of thanks. Sitting to the side, looking on at the group standing close at the fire, Two Hawks saw the Tuscarora girl with new eyes. Yes, this was a good thing she was doing, not beyond her ability. She would be almost as good as a warrior going with their uncle. And they couldn't spare a warrior.

Contrition filled Two Hawks's heart. The girl was trying to help. Trying to be good to people who'd been good to her. He had no right to resent that.

While his father was saying, "You must travel fast, there and back. I will find someone to lend a horse to carry you," and making for the doorway, Two Hawks stood. He thanked his uncle for being willing to take

word to Aubrey and Anna Catherine. Then he turned for the door to follow Stone Thrower—and caught the gaze of Strikes-The-Water as she
flicked up guarded eyes. He paused before her, putting a hand to her
shoulder.

"Thank you, Sister, for what you are doing. You are brave and good to
do it."

Sister. It was all of his heart he had to give to her, but he gave it now
without reservation and saw by the sad acceptance in her lovely eyes that
at last she understood what it was she had from him, and what she never
would.

22

July 25, 1777
Fort Oswego

*A*n assembly was called for the evening, at which General St. Leger would address his gathered forces. Just now, however, Private William Aubrey was behind his tent puking up his guts.

It was the waiting getting to him, he'd told himself. Two days of utter boredom had followed two heart-pounding hours when they'd looked to be marching straight into battle. Refusing to believe the captured rebels' report, trusting rather to his earlier intelligence about Stanwix's garrison, St. Leger had paused with the bulk of his army at the mouth of Little Salmon River, intending to send an advance force ahead to invest the fort. But as Colonel Butler and Sir John began to comply with the absent St. Leger's order, the war chief, Brant, objected to the plan. Given the Indians' disgruntlement over the supply debacle, he'd insisted St. Leger bring his main force to Oswego. Impress the warriors with their numbers, placate them with the promised gifts — or risk them decamping for home.

It didn't need Brant to elucidate how disillusioned the warriors were over conditions at Oswego. The ravens, and the ominous sign so many had taken them to be, had made a bad situation worse, leaving behind an army nearly as dispirited as its native allies. St. Leger, who'd arrived at last that morning—fuming over the ruination of his plan of attack—had his work cut out for him if he meant to rekindle a fighting spirit in his brigade.

Joseph Tames-His-Horse was still among their ranks. More than once

William had seen that lofty head moving through the gathering in time to avoid the man. The one person he wished to find was proving as elusive as he'd been at Lachine. The evening of their arrival—as the ravens first darkened the sky—William was certain he'd seen Sam Reagan talking with a group of Indians outside the gate. By the time he'd cut his way through the press of men gawking skyward at the avian spectacle, Sam had vanished. So had the Indians.

William wiped his mouth on a grimy shirt-sleeve, wincing at the continued cramping of his midsection. A muttered curse on the other side of the canvas came as welcome distraction. He ducked inside and found a messmate therein, tugging off a shirt. No mistaking that scarred back.

"Sam, I've been looking for you."

Sam freed himself of the garment. "Will you look at this?" He held up the shirt, spattered in bird excrement, then tossed it aside with a grimace and unearthed a fresh garment. "Leastwise the ravens are finally flocking off to bedevil someone else now. Damage done though. Indians are calling it a bad omen."

"Been taking survey of our allies about it, have you?"

"No need. That lot's all but hit the trail for home. Maybe they've the right idea."

Sam's look as he spoke that last was direct and humorless. William came deeper into the tent, letting the flap fall closed.

"Heathen superstition getting under your skin?"

Sam settled his shirt into place and reached for his stock, which had escaped the ravens' attentions. "Tell me you aren't having second thoughts."

"You turned your coat."

"Look you, Sam," William said, silencing the mental echo. "Stanwix isn't heavily manned. It'll surrender with little fight. That is what you said, isn't it?"

Though he didn't flinch at William's words or his doubting tone, Sam's fingers stilled on his stock. "It is. But, William, I lied."

Outside the tent, a company of soldiers had passed as Sam spoke, regaling one another, half-drunk out of boredom. "You what?"

"You heard me. I said I—"

"Lied? About Fort Stanwix?"

"Aye."

"Why would you? Unless you were . . ."

"A spy?" Sam's mouth drew up crooked. "Got it at last, have you?"

William attempted a laugh, though his heart was pounding as if already it knew where this conversation was going. "I know you're a spy. A poor one. Got yourself captured, remember?"

"Of course I remember, and that's not what I meant." Taking a step nearer, Sam lowered his voice. "I'm a spy for General Schuyler. And Gansevoort at Stanwix. The *Americans,*" he added when William merely stared. "And it wasn't Oneidas who did *this* to me." He yanked up his shirt front, baring his scars. "It was Oneidas saved me, helped me back to Lachine. Your brother among them. I should tell you too that I'm fixing to go to them. This time I'll not be back."

"You're going to them?" William wagged his head, trying to sort through words that refused to line up straight and make any sort of sense. His brother had helped. And Sam was leaving. Leaving the regiment? Leaving *him*? Though his brain was balking, the flush of heat in his face and his racing heart belied denial. "You cannot mean to *desert*?"

"I do," Sam stated, adding even more outrageously, "and I want you to come with me."

William had no words. None fitting. He could only shake his head again.

Sam grasped his arm. "Do it, William. You belong on the other side of this fight more so than I. You've two families there, and I've naught but my convictions—I support the colonies' break with the Crown."

The words assaulted him, as others had a year past, kicking out the foundation of his world. His thoughts spun back over the months of shared billet, Sam's absences, the thin excuses. Right under his nose, his one friend in the whole of that army—the world—had all the while had his heart pledged to the people they'd left behind. The people *he* had left behind.

Like a painted canvas dropped before him, he saw again Anna's wounded gaze, Reginald Aubrey's guilt-haunted eyes, felt the gutting truth take hold as they faced him in the barn. His father wasn't his father; the name he'd worn wasn't his to claim; the life he'd lived . . . a lie.

It didn't feel like a lie now. He yanked free of Sam's grip.

"How far back does this go? All those tavern brawls out of which I wrangled you—or helped you fight. That talk of politics in the streets of Schenectady. Was all of it a lie?"

"Most of it," Sam admitted. "I'd already volunteered to follow Sir John to Quebec when we met. I was making myself a believable loyalist."

"Then why bring *me* into it? Why, if you intended *this*?"

"William, our friendship was no sham." Sam's infuriating calm was but a twisting of the knife. "I didn't want you haring off alone to who knew where, to do who knew what. But I had my mission before me. I'd hoped you'd come to your senses before all was said and done."

William glared, seething at this fresh betrayal. "So now what? You'll just go? Break your oath to the Crown?"

"My pledge is to the Continentals," Sam said. "In my heart it was never broken, no matter what was signed. I think it's so for you if you're honest with yourself."

"Oh, it's honesty you want now, is it?" William's head was throbbing, his belly threatening to purge itself again. "If our friendship was no sham, why didn't you admit any of this sooner?"

A muscle in Sam's jaw clenched. "Talk of honesty—for all love, William, it was *months* before you'd even tell me why you left home and abandoned Anna."

"Leave Anna out of it!" He stepped nearer Sam, surging with the need to do him violence.

Sam didn't back down. "What do you think she'd have to say to you now, poised to come down upon her at the head of this army? To destroy all she knows and loves. She loved *you*—"

He'd no idea he truly meant to hit Sam until the pain exploded through his hand. Sam took the blow without striking back, as he'd done on the Binne Kill the day their friendship began.

Their supposed friendship.

William shook his smarting knuckles.

"You'd think you'd learn to pick a softer spot." Rubbing his jaw, Sam took up his knapsack. "I thought by now you'd have seen reason, realized you never should have left. Obviously I was wrong."

Sam wasn't wearing his regimentals, only shirt-sleeves and breeches, both white. He'd stand out like snow in summer in the wood unless he covered himself with forest loam. William opened his mouth to say so, then clamped it shut, realizing the nature of the stray thought that had floated up through the shock of this defection: worry for a friend.

Blast it all. Sam wasn't wrong about one thing. Neither of them belonged in that green coat. But the oath Sam so lightly sidestepped felt insurmountable to William. He'd signed it full willing, with no previous hold on his heart. None he'd been willing to acknowledge at the time.

Sam searched his face, hazel eyes wary. "What do you mean to do?"

"I cannot go with you."

"Idiot," Sam said, regret in his voice. "That's plain enough. I meant about me. Will you turn me in or let me go?"

Eyes stinging with sweat and—but no, not tears—William stiffened his face and stepped aside, clearing the way to the tent flap.

Sam hesitated.

William stared forward. "Get out, Sam. Go. Before I change my mind."

Sam ducked past him and was gone. William's breathing was loud in the empty tent. He stood rooted, fighting to keep from running heedlessly after the traitor, down a path that led straight through dishonor, to home.

The sky still held a greenish glow along its western rim, though overhead stars clustered. Dotting the edges of the grounds adjacent to the fort, the fires of Indian, ranger, and regimental camps burned, snapping sparks into the night, conflagrant eyes gazing inward at a wildly various assemblage from across oceans, lakes, and vast frontiers, come to meld themselves into a consolidated force. So their leaders hoped.

William stood near enough one of those fires to feel its heat radiating down his face and limbs. It was second nature now to seek out smoke at night—blast all mosquitoes to some bloodless wasteland.

Though attendance at the assembly was compulsory, they weren't made to stand in rank. Even so, William stood immobile as the talk went on. St. Leger had spoken briefly, then Colonel Claus, officially in command of the Indians. The latter had also been given their chance to speak. Sachems and war chiefs, Senecas, Mohawks, Cayugas, Onondagas. Surrounded on all sides by soldiers and Indians standing, sitting, wandering in search of liquor, William watched as men ascended the makeshift stage erected for the evening and proclaimed their grievances against the rebels, what it was they meant to do in the coming days, how King George would reward his faithful subjects.

After Sam's defection, William had grasped one final hope—that the campaign would unravel. That St. Leger would prove unequal to the task of holding on to his native auxiliaries, on whom the campaign depended. Instead he'd sensed the Indians' mood rising with each speaker, mounting like a gathering storm, until now there came a breaking tumult of howls that jarred like a thunderclap, prickling his scalp. St. Leger had presented the Indians with their long-awaited gifts. The delighted screams were bolstered by the crack of muskets firing skyward in celebration—and relief, William sensed, catching sight of Angus and Archie MacKay among a knot of fellow Scots, eyes shining with exhilaration as they took in the hair-raising ferocity of their allies.

But among the crowd, William spotted a countenance that reflected no pleasure. Joseph Tames-His-Horse stood a stone's throw away, beside him a Negro nearly as tall. Or was he also Indian? William blinked as firelight tossed shadows with abandon, then realized he was looking at another mixed blood, a man both African and Indian. Another Indian joined the pair, slipping out of shadow to put a hand to the darker man's arm.

William caught his breath, recognizing the warrior he'd seen with Sam the night of their arrival. None of the three joined the shouting or rushed forward to receive St. Leger's gifts. Joseph stood tall in the firelight, arms crossed. William stared, minded of their last conversation. *"Creator is over all, and in all . . ."* Did Joseph still believe it, standing so grim while all around him celebrated? How did one know such a thing?

When, he wondered, was the last time he'd prayed? Not by rote but honestly from his heart. He'd no prescribed words, only raw need. *Are You in this? Because I don't see it if You are.*

Before he'd even finished the prayer, a cold blade lanced down his spine. Colonel Butler had taken the stage to address the Indians, reaffirmed in their purpose by St. Leger's gifts. Bronzed faces lifted, shining in the firelight. The screaming died away.

"This army you see gathered here, my brothers," Butler called to them, gesturing expansively, "will soon be marching upon Fort Stanwix. With it you will go. There, if it please you, you may stand and watch as that fort falls to us. Then the valley it protects will be open to you, and I tell you now that upon its inhabitants you may make war however you desire!"

Scattered ululations rent the air, but Butler wasn't finished. "For every rebel scalp taken, you may expect to receive from your Father, King George, twenty pounds worth of gifts, such as you have received this day!"

The bedlam that shattered the night in response to this pledge nearly struck William to his knees. Had any of these warriors still harbored reservations over committing themselves to St. Leger's campaign, those reservations were just obliterated. *For every rebel scalp . . .*

Butler couldn't mean to let the Indians make war upon women and children. Would the people of the Mohawk Valley stand against such brutality?

Sam had lied about the garrison. It was stronger than St. Leger believed. Could the army still be halted at Fort Stanwix?

Around William the air crackled and seethed, a cauldron of bloodlust on the boil. Butler stoked the fire with his martial words. Indians yelped. Drums beat. A few danced their war dances. Soldiers in green and red began to draw together, made uneasy yet held in thrall by their allies' fierce display.

"Anna," William whispered, her name drowned in the tumult. And he was about to be swept along in its tide, used as an instrument of destruction against those he ached to protect. Unless he could swim free of it. Unless he threw honor to the wind and did whatever he had to do to see them brought through the coming storm safely.

Anna. Lydia, Rowan, Maura. Even *him*. Aubrey. Had he once stood in such a place as this, contemplating the doing of a thing he never thought within his scope? Because he loved?

He looked for Joseph Tames-His-Horse and found him standing alone, his companions gone into the night. He was staring at William—also thinking of that conversation back on Buck Island? Compelled as though a fist had shoved the small of his back, he took a stride toward the Indian.

"Private Aubrey!"

He nearly tripped, so quickly did he turn. Sergeant Campbell wore his grinning sneer.

"Feelin' at home, are ye? Here among your kind."

William clamped down on the urge to send the sergeant reeling into the nearest fire. He hadn't kept the wanting from his face. A pitiless glee lit the Scot's eyes.

"Your captain requests the pleasure o' your attendance, Private. Now."

Finding Captain Watts in his tent as ordered, he learned he would be part of an advance guard finally heading out in the morning for Fort Stanwix, as would nearly sixty other handpicked marksmen from Johnson's regiment. Their mission was to prevent the blockage of Wood Creek, to seize the lower landing on the Mohawk River and capture any supplies or reinforcements attempting to reach the rebels.

"Find Private Reagan," Watts told him. "No one's spotted him in the crowd this evening. Tell him, will you, Aubrey?"

William saluted his commanding officer, came within a breath of telling the captain there was no point in looking for Sam, then cleared his throat and asked, "Sir. Are they—we—certain the fort is thinly manned?"

Watts looked up from his camp desk, upon which he was scribbling in a ledger, brows raised in inquiry.

"Those prisoners taken from the fort, sir," William hurried to add. "What if they spoke truth?"

Sweat ran down the side of the captain's face, the trickle white with hair powder. "The general thinks otherwise, Private. Whatever awaits, I've no doubt my men—including you—are the equal to it. You've your orders. Now get some sleep."

23

July 27, 1777
Schenectady

War and rumors of war. Such was the refrain in the background of their days. While war raged in the east, rumors of war came downriver from the west with the increasing regularity of birth pangs, mounting with intensity. They marched into Lydia's kitchen on the lips of the wives of merchants and river men. Quiet alarm pinched the faces she passed on the street, sharp reminder of the last war when French-allied Indians ravaged the frontier and folk as far east as Albany trembled in their beds.

"And where are we to go then?" asked a cooper's wife, come for tending of a suppurating gash on her fleshy upper arm. The woman blew a frazzled breath, puffing out strands of equally frazzled hair fallen from their pins. "Albany's no safer, now Burgoyne's taken Ticonderoga and those forts up the Hudson. The British have The City. Now more redcoats gather westward, 'tis said. Wolves got us circled, *I* say."

"There is no safety," Lydia said, thinking aloud as she applied honey to a linen pad. "Only under the wings of the Almighty."

"Hmph," the woman said, patently uncomforted.

Lydia understood. Trusting in unseen Providence when a very visible enemy threatened required more than a little faith and yet . . . she had to trust. For Anna—away since dawn, delivering a babe most like since it was past noon and she hadn't returned—still going about mired in bitterness and grief. For Reginald, who seemed to have cut her from his life for her meddling. For Two Hawks and his parents, longing for their lost one. For William, lost. It was a torment to see loved ones in pain and be unable to do anything about it for lack of knowledge or medicine. Or a suitable scalpel.

"And there went those bateaux upriver yesterday," her patient was saying. "Stuffed to the gills with provender for the forts up that way. Dayton, I suppose. Or no—must be Stanwix, at the Carry. Pray they hold back whatever's coming, for where are we to go if the redcoats and their savages get past them?"

It was the second time the woman had voiced the query. Lydia gave no answer, too busy absorbing this news so casually dropped. There'd been high activity on the Binne Kill for weeks, reinforcements sent upriver, regular companies, militia, supplies and arms, but she hadn't heard of this latest flotilla's departure. She asked, but the woman couldn't say whether Reginald Aubrey had gone along.

Even so, a shadow fell across Lydia's soul.

She was tidying up after the woman's departure, the urge to go down to the Binne Kill all but yanking her out onto the street, when there came a knock at the door. The fourth of the day. Busy days were good days. They gave her something to occupy her thoughts and divert her from fretting. And the temptation to go and plead yet again with Reginald.

Turning her thoughts to who it might be, what the need, she opened the door and gave a yelp of startlement.

On the threshold stood an Indian.

Lydia's heartbeat was still going at a trot but no longer out of surprise. Daniel Clear Day occupied a bench at her table, sipping at garden-leaf tea served in her best china cup. Lydia sat across from him, waiting for the man to explain this unexpected visit.

Clear Day's pockmarked face had aged in the years since their first encounter in her father's apothecary shop. Sun-weathered creases bracketed his mouth; careworn furrows tracked his brow. Thin gray braids lay against the yellowed linen of his shirt. His eyes, when they lifted and caught her staring, were so grave in their appraisal that Lydia's stomach clenched. *Not more grief to bear,* she was thinking when Clear Day set down his cup.

"Is that one who called himself the father of my nephew's firstborn still on the river, making his boats? It is with him I must speak."

Lydia struggled to keep her voice steady. "Have you looked for Reginald at the Binne Kill? I've only just heard—more bateaux are gone upriver with supplies for Fort Stanwix. Did he go with them?"

Clear Day frowned. "I do not know this. It was in my mind *you* would know where to find him."

Warmth climbed Lydia's face. Clear Day had visited her home on his way east with Samuel Kirkland to see General Washington's army, back when Two Hawks was still Reginald's apprentice. She debated concealing how badly her relationship with Reginald had deteriorated since then, but what was there to be gained by hiding the truth?

"Anna and her father have barely spoken since Two Hawks left us," she blurted before she'd quite made up her mind. "That's partly my fault because I tried to bring them together—meddling, I suppose. I so wanted to *fix* everything—" She clapped a hand over her mouth to stifle the rush of words, mortified as tears spilled.

Silence reined in the kitchen. When she could bear to raise her gaze to check his reaction, Clear Day looked neither surprised nor dismayed by her outburst.

"You are one whose heart is for healing," he said. "It is how Creator made you to be, what He made you to do. Will you go now with me to the place on the river where Aubrey builds his bateaux? We will see if he is to be found, and I can give him the words I bring."

Lydia was on her feet, heart beating hard now with hope. "Of course. What do you mean to say to Reginald? Is it to do with William?" And if so, was it good news or . . . ?

"It is." Clear Day rose from her table. "He was seen by his brother. At Oswego, far in the west. He is there with the army that will be coming into our land. He wears the green coat of Johnson's regiment, as we have learned."

And feared. William was in the enemy's ranks.

"Was he alone?" Lydia asked. "I mean was Sam Reagan—the man he left with—was he part of Johnson's regiment as well? Oh, but I suppose Two Hawks wouldn't know him even if he'd seen him. Or . . . would he?" Lydia amended, catching the sharpness that had come into Clear Day's gaze at mention of Sam.

Clear Day hesitated but at last said evasively, "Of that one I cannot speak."

Could not, or would not, Lydia wanted to ask, but the old man continued too quickly.

"My nephew and his son are needed by the soldiers at Stanwix fort, to come and go as scouts, and by the People to be ready to fight. That is why I am the one come to tell Aubrey this news." He looked at her searchingly, seeing her own sudden indecision no doubt, for he asked yet again, "Will you show me where it is Aubrey has his boats, or shall I find my way alone?"

"No, I . . ." Lydia began. "It's only . . ." She had no idea how Reginald would react, what he might do, once he heard this news. She remembered how eager he'd been back in autumn to strike out recklessly after William, not even knowing where in all of Quebec to find him. What would he do with the certain knowledge of Oswego?

But he had to be told. As did Anna. She'd no right to keep this knowledge from them, and she didn't wish to. What if this news was the very thing that banished all else and reconciled their hearts?

Lydia gazed across the table between them, praying that she was looking upon what for years she'd sought to grasp and wield, though she'd never expected it to take the form of an aging Oneida warrior—her scalpel.

"Come," she said. "I'll take you now."

Was it possible for the threads of a heart to wear so thin they could fray apart? Just disintegrate into scattered filaments and cease to be?

The July sun beat down, causing sweat to gather beneath Anna's cap and trickle in rivulets down her neck as she pushed through the stifling air. She'd paid scant attention to her wandering since leaving the Brouwers' home . . . ten minutes ago? An hour? She didn't register the faces of those she passed in and out of meager shade thrown by shops and trees. Didn't hear the voices bidding her good day.

It was unbearable. All of it. The streets, the faces, the sticky heat dragging her down—limp in spirit, parched in soul. Days of waiting and yearning and fearing that looked like stretching on forever. The relentless ache of longing. The bitterness.

That last was a black root inside her, thickened and twisted, choking off each seed of hope that dared to sprout. It coiled round every thought of Papa. Entangled her prayers. Pulled her down like petticoats in deep water. She'd just helped bring a healthy baby into the world and placed him pink and squalling into the arms of a woman who'd prayed ten years for a living child . . . and Anna felt nothing. Nothing she ought to feel.

With her midwifery case and her hot, dragging feet, she wandered the streets of Schenectady, lacking the will to go home. There was nowhere now that painful memories didn't linger, waiting to pounce. Lydia's house. The Binne Kill. The farm.

Home had vanished at the wood's edge, with Two Hawks.

Hearing a sob, Anna halted and looked around, only to realize the sound had slipped from her throat. She'd drawn the attention of two matrons outside the chandler's shop, faces crimson with the heat. Anna turned from their solicitous stares, got her bearings, and made a beeline for Lydia's, still lugging the case Lydia had presented her on her last birthday. She had prayed for a guide, someone willing and able to lead her to Two Hawks's village, but now she was desperate enough to drop her case in the street and keep on walking all the miles to the farm, to saddle William's mare and ride it west along the river until she found someone who could point her to Kanowalohale.

Did Two Hawks still want her? Did he hope for a future with her? Or was all hope and wanting obliterated, silenced forever by some enemy's arrow or musket ball? Would she ever know?

She'd reached the house and the alley to the stable in back when footsteps sounded behind her.

"Anna!" Lydia reached her, flushed as if she'd been running up and down the streets in the heat, blue eyes animated, bright. "Come into the house. I've something to tell you."

Without curiosity or care, she let Lydia push her into the house, pluck her case from her grasp, and place it on the table. Without reminding her to restock it immediately, as was her unswerving practice, Lydia grasped her hands. "Daniel Clear Day is down at the Binne Kill, with Reginald."

It needed a moment to absorb that. Clear Day was *here*. Come to see Papa. The blood drained from her heated face, leaving her dizzy. "Is it William? Two Hawks? Lydia, *tell* me."

"Anna, sit down." Lydia caught her as she swayed and walked her to a bench. "Two Hawks is well, or was when Clear Day left to come here. And, Anna . . . so was William. Two Hawks has seen him."

"Seen him?" Anna echoed, the blood now pounding in her temples. "William? You mean they found him? He's at Kanowalohale?"

Lydia sat beside her. "Not there. And no, they haven't found him exactly."

"But you just said . . ." Anna shook her head. "Lydia, what *did* you say?"

"Let me start at the beginning." Anna refrained from interrupting—barely—as Lydia told her the tale of Two Hawks scouting and the fort at Oswego and the ravens in the sky and his going down to the fort gate and getting that fleeting glimpse of William in his green coat. "I took Clear Day down to the Binne Kill, and thankfully Reginald was there. I left them together and came to find you—are you all right now?"

The bench beneath her was solid, but Anna felt insubstantial, a feather that might float away on the merest breeze. "Oh, William . . . and Two Hawks wasn't able to speak to him? How wrenching hard that must have been." It wrenched *her* heart.

"Yes," Lydia said, though her smile blazed wide. "And there's more. Two Hawks told Clear Day to tell you he hasn't forgotten the words you spoke at your parting." Lydia searched her face, as if those words might be readable there. "He said he'll find the way to Reginald's heart if he must fight through a hundred redcoats to do so. He'll find William again."

Almost Anna felt joy. Two Hawks lived. He remembered. But he still wanted to please Papa. To make *him* happy. *"I cannot now take you from him, only leave you to mend what is broken."* Those were some of the parting words Two Hawks professed to remember. *Mend what is broken.*

Her face felt cold, stiff as clay. "I want to see Clear Day. Talk to him myself. Now."

Lydia's smile faltered at her bitten-off tone. "I knew you would. That's why I've been looking for you, so we can go to him together."

"No, Lydia. I'll go alone. I've waited, you see. For a guide." Anna rose, steadied herself with a grip on the table's edge, and headed for the dining room. "Someone to take me to Kanowalohale. Clear Day can do it."

She needn't pack much. Kanowalohale wasn't too long a journey. A couple of days afoot was the impression she'd had from Two Hawks. But he was swift and could run for miles. Perhaps if she took William's horse . . .

She was halfway through the dining room when Lydia caught her up. "Anna, wait."

She whirled, fury spitting from her like sparks. "No! I'm beyond sick of *waiting*. I want William found, and I'm relieved he's alive, but I don't want him back at the cost of Two Hawks's life. I must find him, tell him he doesn't need to risk his neck finding William in order to have me. I'm giving *myself* away—without a by-your-leave from Papa or anyone else."

She made for the stairs. Lydia's footsteps dogged her. "Anna, no. Don't do that to your father. He—"

Anna turned on her at the bottom stair. "I don't care! Don't you understand that?"

Lydia flinched back. "Don't care?"

"I don't care about pleasing Papa, or clearing the path to his heart, or whatever it is everyone thinks *he* needs." She heard her voice, brittle, full of rage. From a distance, it seemed, she watched herself spew up the darkness that had long filled her. A spurting wound. "He doesn't deserve to have it cleared. He's the cause of it, all the grief and pain we've endured. Let him stew in it if that's what he wants!"

"Anna Catherine Doyle, do you even hear yourself?" Lydia's face grew stern in a way Anna had never seen. A fire lit her eyes as she drew her small person up straight. "You need to forgive your father."

"Forgive him? He's the one who stole a baby. He's the one who lied and deceived and destroyed William. He's the one who couldn't bring himself to treat Two Hawks like the son he tried to force William to be. He's the one who—"

"Aubrey did not start you in the womb of your mother, but he gave you life, risking his own for yours." Two Hawks's words echoed like a crack of thunder in her bones. *"Even if Creator did not bid us honor our parents, for that alone I would honor him in my heart."*

Anna nearly choked as her voice broke. "He's the one who didn't let me die on that wilderness road!"

Lydia had gone as pale as bleached linen. "Oh no," she said, reaching for her. "No, no, no. Don't *ever* say that."

But it was true. It would have been better had she died a baby. Never known such pain. Anna drew back, opening her mouth to say so, but all that came out was a wail. She covered her face with her hands, unable to bear the sight of Lydia's devastated gaze. Still she could see another pair of eyes, dark and beautiful and piercing her with their disappointment. She groaned, stricken and convicted.

"What will Two Hawks say to me? He bade me mend what was broken between us, me and Papa. Oh, what will he say?"

"Life is blessing, but it is also testing. Take the one as you do the other and trust Him who allows all." She'd promised to do so and utterly failed.

"Oh, my girl." Lydia's arms were around her, hot and pressing. "More importantly, what is God saying to you about it?"

She stood stiff in Lydia's embrace, gutted by the sudden absence of anger, the withering of the root within. Desolate without it. Its strength had kept her going, even as it devoured her from inside.

"That I need to repent," she got out at last, the barest whisper.

Lydia held her tight. "Then do so. It's never too late to be obedient to the Almighty, not while you still draw breath. You're breathing, aren't you?"

Anna sucked in a shuddering lungful of air, then wilted onto the stairs, hands over her face. "I wanted Papa to be first. I've waited and waited. But it's going to have to be me, isn't it? I have to forgive him. I have to *honor* him."

Two Hawks had understood. Papa's failings didn't exempt her from doing what she knew was right. She lifted her head. Lydia was on the stair beside her, face streaked with tears, eyes alive again with hope. "There's my girl . . . my beautiful, brave girl. Oh, how I've missed you!"

It was too warm in the house to cling to one another in anything resembling comfort, but Anna needed a different sort of comfort, that of a mother, which Lydia had always been to her.

She also needed her father. Needed to restore him to his rightful place in her heart, for him to know he was restored. She pulled herself up straight, knowing she had to act, and fast. "I still want to talk to Clear Day, but can we go and see Papa. Right now?"

Lydia bit her lip, then gave her the unreserved smile Anna adored.

"Clear Day doesn't strike me as one to beat around bushes. We'd best hurry. Let's wash our faces and go."

July—August 1777
The Mohawk Valley, New York
Oneida Lands

*T*hese things I have said are hard things to hear—but listen, I am going to say more. I am going to tell you another story about that warrior whose son was taken, which is the same story told from the other side. It is like a basket, these two stories that weave together to make a whole, seen and unseen. I am going to tell you the unseen story now.

Through all the bad that came of what the redcoat did to that warrior and his wife, and the son not taken, Creator was not looking aside as though He did not see. He was busy in it, all the while weaving good things out of it. For when that warrior left his home and went away, he went to a People the missionary had known before—the Senecas—a few of whom had chosen to follow a Jesus path through life. Among them this warrior finally stopped running from his Father in Heaven. He let his heart be caught and broken by the crushing of sin. Not the sin of that redcoat. His own sin. That warrior cried out for forgiveness, and at last in his heart the Great Healing began.

Had all these bad things not come to him, to wound and to rob, would he have softened his heart to the missionary's God? Who can say? I am only telling you the story of what happened, how that warrior became a man again, one whose wife could without shame claim him as her husband. A man a son could respect and follow.

Even so, while they waited for their lost son to return from that far land where he had gone for white man's learning, the warrior struggled *with a hard thing Creator asked of him—forgiving the redcoat for the thing he had done. But now the warrior had weapons to fight that battle, which he had come to see was not against the redcoat after all but against his own sinful nature, and against the one who is enemy to us all. Those weapons were these: truth like a girding sash; righteousness like leather across the chest; peace like moccasins for feet to walk in; faith like a shield to protect a family; eternal saving a covering for the head.*

Word came at last that the lost son had returned to the land of his birth. It was time to face the redcoat, to show everyone who worried about it whether that warrior had given his whole heart to Creator or had held some of it back. But he held nothing back. Though wounded and bleeding, he gave the white shell beads to the redcoat, along with his pledge of peace.

Now here is a thing worth thinking on. That warrior believed he was setting the redcoat free in forgiving him the great wrong done his family, but it was himself he set free. Where once in him was hatred, leading him like a rope around the neck, now there was compassion, even though the lost son, when he learned the truth of who he was, ran from them all in despair and anger at this great betrayal. This has been a sorrow in many hearts, but Creator is still watching. Still working. He is still telling that warrior's story, and the story of all of us.

24

July 27, 1777
Schenectady

From house to quay, Anna in tow, Lydia prayed. With the Indian in her kitchen, so earnest with purpose, she'd been certain his arrival and the news he carried to Reginald was of the Almighty's orchestration. About to face its result, she was reaching for trust and hurrying her steps.

A breeze wafted off the river to meet them. On the quay the usual figures milled—bateau pilots and crew, merchants' apprentices shifting cargo into storehouses or away into town. There was the usual barrels, goods, and coiled rope to navigate. She and Anna wove a path through it all, and there at last was Reginald's office . . . and Reginald, shutting the door. He took up a knapsack lying at his feet and made for a canoe moored nearby.

Of Clear Day there was no sign.

With a steadiness she didn't feel, Lydia raised her voice. "Reginald? Where are you going?"

He'd dropped the knapsack into the canoe but pivoted at his name to see them coming.

"Papa!" Anna ran the last few yards and threw herself into her father's arms. The impact rocked him backward, nearly sending both off the quay into the river before they caught their balance. Lydia could hear the girl's words muffled against the shoulder of Reginald's summer coat. "Papa, I'm sorry. I've been so—"

"There, my girl. I was going to come find you—"

Anna pulled back, slender waist encircled by her father's arms, gazing tearfully into his face. "You were?"

Reginald tucked his chin to smile at her even as emotions contrary to joy played over his face. Sorrow. Regret. Contrition. Lydia's heart leapt with renewed hope. Perhaps he was only headed to the farm . . .

"I was coming to tell you," Reginald said. "I must leave the pair of you to one another's care."

"What?" Hope dashed, Lydia drew near.

Anna stepped back from her father's grasp, tear-stained face bewildered. "Where are you going? After William?"

"You've had the news then?" he asked, fixing Lydia with blue-gray eyes that burned with purpose. With need.

"Two Hawks saw him at Oswego. Clear Day told me, and I've told Anna, but Reginald—"

He held up a hand to stop her. "Lydia, you and the others dissuaded me from seeking William last autumn, but not again. Not this time. I'm going upriver, see, and there is nothing you can say to prevent me."

The words, though spoken without rancor, struck Lydia silent.

Not so Anna. "Alone, Papa? But you promised Stone Thrower you wouldn't."

"I did, and I'll make good on my promise if I can. Stone Thrower is scouting out of Fort Stanwix, so that is where I'm bound, in hope of finding him there. But with you, Anna, I must make peace ere I go. For I mean also to look for Two Hawks, should you wish me to do so."

At the mention of her beloved's name, light infused Anna's countenance. "Papa, yes. Please! But what will you say if you find him?"

Reginald raised his hand to her face, brushing away a tear with his thumb. "That I judged him too harshly. That he is welcome back as my apprentice. Will you forgive me, my girl, for the way I treated him, and you, these past months?"

With a wondering glance at Lydia, Anna said, "I was coming to tell you that very thing. That I forgive you. And to ask the same of you. When Two Hawks left, he bid me mend what was broken between us, and I didn't do it. I didn't even try. I'm sorry."

"There, 'tis all right now. But . . . it is a grave disservice I've done that young man." Reginald drew Anna to him, kissed her brow, murmured words too soft for Lydia to hear. Against his shoulder Anna's capped head nodded.

They stood thus—her loves—reconciled at last as she had so long prayed, and a warmth of relief encompassed the ache of confusion forming round this precipitous departure. Confusion and . . . something darker. That shadow again.

Then Reginald put Anna from him and looked at Lydia.

Which of them took the final steps, Lydia would never remember, only that suddenly they stood touching, hands to arms, and there was none in the world but they two. No voices on the quay. No crew unloading that solitary bateau. Not even Anna.

"There is . . . I mean to say . . . Lydia—" An expression of almost comical helplessness overcame him, then a longing as raw as it was old. Abandoning words, Reginald kissed her.

Lydia was left dazed, flushed from more than heat. Their gazes held, his tender and questioning.

"Reginald," she finally managed, voice coming breathless. "What, exactly, did Clear Day *say* to you?"

Indecision warred with the tenderness in Reginald's gaze. "He told me about William."

"That is all?"

"He . . . No, that is not all. But there is no time to tell you of it now. Only, Lydia, I could not leave things between us as they have been." His gaze found Anna again. "With either of you. But now we've spoken and I must go. I intend to overtake the bateaux brigade that left yesterday, so I'll not travel the river alone."

Lydia's mind felt sluggish in the heat, her heart beating hard with . . . *dread*. "Reginald, if you find Stone Thrower, what then? Do you plan to take on the British army, the two of you, to get to William?"

This was what she'd feared to find when she reached the Binne Kill. But could this driving need to find Stone Thrower be of the Almighty's leading? Or was it born of that same stubborn need to set right twenty years of wrong? What had the old Indian said to Reginald, apart from the news about William?

"Reginald, where *is* Clear Day?"

"On his way to the farm. I asked him to travel with me on the river. He said he didn't come alone."

"He told me he did—come alone, I mean."

"Into Schenectady, yes. Someone awaits him in the woods near the farm."

"Two Hawks?" Anna broke in eagerly.

Reginald shook his head. "He didn't say it was Two Hawks. I sent Clear Day with a letter for Rowan to provision him with anything needed for the journey home, including another horse."

Anna stepped closer, her hand to her father's sleeve. "Papa . . . what about us, Two Hawks and me? He's set on risking his life to find William so he—so you . . ."

Reginald covered her hand with his. "Let it be enough to know that if he will give our former arrangement—and me—another chance, then he has my blessing to court you. Only be sure, my heart. Is this what you truly want?"

"It is. But Two Hawks needs to know we've your blessing." Anna clasped his arm. "Let me come with you."

Lydia nearly heeded the unbidden need to grab his other arm and underscore the plea but saw it would be useless.

Reginald firmed his mouth. "No, Anna. I cannot go without knowing you are safe out of whatever trouble is building in the west." He turned to Lydia, his gaze direct, tender still, beseeching. "You will keep her with you?"

She could no more deny him than deny the sun its right to rise; even so the words came dry as husks. "She'll not leave my side."

Anna's eyes were eloquent with dismay. "Papa, *please.*"

"Hush, my girl," Reginald said, his hand rising to cup Anna's cheek. "You shall stay, and I shall go, and that is settled."

Anna nodded, but in her eyes Lydia saw her own thoughts reflected. Nothing about this situation was settled.

Reginald didn't see what Lydia saw, or else he chose not to see it. "Now I must away. Watch over each other. Send to Rowan if you've need."

They stood and watched him climb into the canoe. With a paddle he pushed off from the quay and began the journey upriver against the sluggish summer current. Lydia didn't look away, unable to quell the thought that it might be the last sight of him she'd ever—

No. A chill was creeping up from her hands, spreading inward toward her heart. Beside her Anna cried—she could hear her sniffling—but not until Reginald was no longer in view did Lydia turn.

When Anna glimpsed her face, her expression sharpened in fresh concern. "Lydia? What is it?"

"I don't know." Lydia gave her head a shake but failed to dislodge that sense of foreboding. "Honestly, I don't. A feeling, is all."

"Not a good one." Anna clasped her wrist. "And I see you want to go after Papa. Well, let's do so."

"Go after him?" Lydia replied.

"Not *after* him, exactly. Clear Day cannot be far ahead of us. Let's catch him up, go with him to Kanowalohale. What if Two Hawks is there with Good Voice, not at the fort? Papa won't be going to their town. *We* can."

Urgency vibrated from Anna's slender frame, catching like contagion. A giddy sense of *hurry* stirred beneath Lydia's ribs. They wouldn't be venturing alone, not if they found Clear Day in time, and she could see that Anna was determined to try, with or without her.

She drew a steadying breath beneath her stays. "I just promised Reginald to keep you safe."

"You promised to keep me by your side," Anna countered. "If we do this together, then I'll *be* beside you. The whole way."

"Anna . . . the British aren't gathered at Oswego to enjoy a summer by the lake. We'd be headed straight for them."

"Not necessarily. They'll have to get past Fort Stanwix, and Kanowalohale is miles from Stanwix—or that's the impression Two Hawks has given." A distance an army could cross in a matter of hours, should the fort surrender, or fall.

"And I'm not trying to be disobedient to Papa," Anna hurried on. "I think God's been prompting me all along to go to Two Hawks. At least to Good Voice. Now Papa's given his blessing and Clear Day has come and—"

"There's going to be a battle." Lydia knew it beyond doubt. She didn't know where it would be fought—Stanwix or elsewhere—or on what scale; it was part of that shadow, premonition—whatever it was.

Anna paled but remained resolute. "If there *is* a battle, you and I could be useful. There'll be wounded."

A grim certainty, but Lydia couldn't deny what the prospect kindled, a flicker of that calling to heal she'd felt since childhood.

More than a flicker. A leaping flame.

Weakening before it, she began to reason . . . The Oneidas had scouts. If danger threatened, they'd bring warning. They'd have plans to keep their women and children safe. Good Voice would know where to go if it came to that. And meanwhile, it was true, they might be of use.

Anna sensed her wavering and started to speak again, but Lydia held up a hand. "All right. You've convinced me—nearly. I mean to take Gideon's lead on this."

"Gideon?" Anna's frown gave way to enlightenment. "Oh. A fleece?"

"Figuratively speaking. If we reach the farm and catch Clear Day before he leaves—*and* he agrees to take us without our forcing him at gunpoint or anything else so drastic—then I'll believe this is the Almighty's leading."

At least, she thought, *not a preposterous mistake.*

Anna was already tugging her along the quay. "We must pack swiftly. We'll need food and—oh, I left my box without resupplying."

"Mine's ready. I'll saddle the horse while you ready yours. Gather up extra bandages and lint. We can share a blanket."

Lydia pushed through the heat, heart thumping beneath clammy stays, knowing it impossible to anticipate everything they might need or for her horse to carry it if she could. They would take themselves, provisions, their medical cases, and their prayers.

They'd paused on their way out of Schenectady to inform another midwife of their departure so the women presently under their care wouldn't find themselves untended. Riding double, uncomfortably close in the heat, they reached the farm as the sun was beginning its westward dip.

"Dare we go to the house, see whether Clear Day is there?" Lydia voiced the question as they approached the lane to the farm. Anna, holding to her waist, freed a hand to shield her eyes against the sun's glare, strong even with the shielding brim of her straw hat.

"What if the Doyles take against our plan?" She'd worried over that likelihood for the past mile. Obviously so had Lydia; Anna felt a shudder pass through her trim frame and realized it was rueful laughter.

"You needn't twist my arm. I haven't the courage to face Maura, let alone Rowan, given what we mean to do."

"Let's go straight to the clearing." Anna pointed farther down the track. "Beyond the fields, that clump of trees where the land starts to rise. Make for that."

Though more farms had sprung up in the vicinity over the years, great patches of forest still spread between, heavy and green now with summer's fullness. No one met them before Lydia guided the mare into the enclosing shade, picking a way forward until they encountered the creek that bounded Papa's farm, winding down through impenetrable thickets from the spring.

Clear Day hadn't come alone, Papa had said. Someone would be waiting for him. Two Hawks? Papa thought not, yet it could be. If he hadn't found William, he mightn't want to see Papa and so have stayed behind, waiting in the place they'd so often met.

The horse's hooves splashed across the creek at the first point the brushy bank allowed. They jolted up the steep bank opposite, Anna clinging to Lydia, and rode along the creek until the foliage along its course thinned again at the beginning of the beech grove. Before they passed into the beeches, Anna looked back, past the wood's edge, gaze flinging across rows of corn standing hot and listless to the farmhouse and cottage tucked close by, both looking small and remote.

A figure was crossing the yard. Maura Doyle, going about her endless chores. Somewhere there was Rowan Doyle too, probably down at the barn. What did they think of Daniel Clear Day's visit? And Papa bound away upriver, headed into danger?

Godspeed, she thought. *To us all.*

It wasn't one Indian they found at the base of the hill where the creek tumbled down from its rock-bound spring, but two. And two horses. One was William's mare. Daniel Clear Day knelt near it, sorting through supplies on the ground—sacks, canvas-wrapped parcels, rolled blankets. The other horse was strange to Anna. So was the slender Indian boy straddling it in leggings and long linen shirt, sleeves rolled high off skinny arms. His hair wasn't shaved but fell long—nearly to his waist. Not Two Hawks.

The boy saw them first. His posture stiffened, causing the horse he sat to snort.

"Clear Day!" In her relief, Anna didn't spare another thought for the boy until they drew to a halt and she realized Clear Day's companion wasn't a boy but a girl, near her own age. A very pretty girl with the proud stare and supple grace of a warrior.

Clear Day stood as Anna dismounted, dragging her petticoat across the awkward burden of their supplies, tied on the horse's rump. Lydia slid down after her. Clear Day stared at the horse's burden, then looked from Lydia to Anna, his gaze questioning. Not disapproving. Not yet. Unless he hid it well. *Please,* Anna thought but left it to Lydia to explain their purpose and their request.

While Lydia did so, Anna glanced at the girl on the horse and found her staring back, looking down her small nose, her face a mask of stillness. Anna offered a smile, but the girl's features remained immobile. Unnervingly so.

At a clearing of throat, Anna dragged her gaze away.

"That one is called Strikes-The-Water," the old man said, pointing with his chin at the girl. "She is of the Tuscarora people, Deer Clan. She is a girl who hunts."

"Ah," said Lydia, as if uncertain what else to say, but turned to address the girl. "I'm Lydia van Bergen and this," she added, placing a hand on Anna's taller shoulder, "is Anna Doyle."

The girl looked at Clear Day, a pinch between her slender brows, and uttered a string of indecipherable words in a tone that might have indicated resentment or only boredom.

Clear Day said, "She knows who you are. She speaks English not well," he added, with a small frown at Strikes-The-Water.

"I see." Lydia seemed momentarily disconcerted but, to Anna's relief, undeterred. "Will the pair of you allow us to accompany you back to Kanowalohale?"

Clear Day stood in silence with a hand to his chin, as though sorting his thoughts as he'd done the supplies from the farm. It seemed an eternity before the old man sighed. "It is a long way. You have food?"

Strikes-The-Water spoke again. Anna had thought she'd learned enough Oneida over the years from Two Hawks to understand their speech but could make out nothing of the girl's words until she recognized Two Hawks's name.

Clear Day interrupted the speculation by saying sternly to the girl, in English, "Enough. They will come. We should take their burdens onto our horses because they ride together."

The girl understood enough English to grasp his meaning. She swung lithely off the horse and, pointedly ignoring Anna, helped Clear Day distribute the extra burdens between their mounts. In the end, Lydia's horse bore nothing but the two of them and the saddle bags containing their food and personal items. They mounted up, watered the horses at the creek, then followed Clear Day into the forest westward.

It had fallen out with astonishing ease, as if the old warrior, once over his initial surprise, had deemed it perfectly natural they would show up asking to go along. Not so the girl who hunted, last in the procession. As the horses plodded along, picking their way through the wood, Anna felt the young woman's gaze burning a spot between her shoulders, where the sweat gathered and trickled down beneath her stays.

Strikes-The-Water wasn't pleased at all.

25

August 1–2, 1777
Oneida lands, western frontier

*T*hey were six days out from Oswego and already one of their objectives had met with failure. After struggling through thicket, morass, and gullied wood, bug bitten and drenched in sweat or rain, then a night and day of rowing by water, William's advance patrol had reached the mouth of Wood Creek—to find that Stanwix's garrison had anticipated them. As though a regiment of beavers had been loosed upon its banks, the final fifteen-mile water passage to the fort was choked with fresh-hewn timber. Now the sun was setting, time was pressing, and Lieutenant Henry Bird, commanding the patrol, was fast losing his composure.

The Indians were balking again.

Two days into this trek, they'd been forced to halt and wait for a contingent of Senecas and Mohawks to join them. Shortly after had come another pause to await arrival of a larger party of Mississaugas. While their numbers when they materialized were heartening, they'd had in their possession two stolen army beeves—and had it in their minds to roast them on the spot. Failing to dissuade them, Lieutenant Bird had gathered up his green-coated troops and pushed on through the everlasting trees and oppressive heat. Nineteen miles later they'd feasted on stale bread and salted ration.

Over the long march, William had thought of Sam Reagan, wondering whether he'd made it alive to wherever he meant to go. Likely Fort Stanwix, with William's luck.

He'd thought of Anna. Feared for her. Longed to defend her from the very army he was helping lead her way.

He'd thought of his mother—with growing wonder to think he *had* a mother still. With each passing day, his desire to see her, to know her, seemed to grow. She was white, but in her heart he knew she was Oneida. *She must have blue eyes . . .*

He'd thought of his father. Fathers. What sort of man was the one whose blood he shared—the warrior? Would he ever know? He'd thought he'd known the other . . .

He'd thought of his brother. Longed to ask his twin a thousand questions. But longing was of no profit. His course was set, that of serving king and country. He did his best to ignore the voice within insisting that it wasn't *his* king, *his* country. Not anymore.

When the Indians failed to appear post-feasting, Lieutenant Bird had lost patience and set off without them. When finally they'd reached Wood Creek—in company with at least part of their Indian contingent—the warriors again found reason to delay the final push to the fort.

Along with most of the patrol, William sat on the ground several yards from the obstructed creek, knees bent, head cradled on folded arms, while Lieutenant Bird wrangled—it wasn't yet an argument—with a warrior called Captain John Hare, whom, in the absence of Joseph Brant, behind them with the main force, the Indians looked to as leader. The Senecas were concerned over pushing on en masse to the fort, across Oneida lands.

"Rest your men." Captain John gestured at the sprawl of green-coats littering the piney clearing. "You have worn them out getting this far. Let warriors go ahead to the fort, see its strength and what we walk into."

A reasonable plan, William thought it. He removed his hat and wiped his streaming brow with a grubby sleeve facing. He wanted out of the coat. Off with the pack. Water, most of all.

He reached for his canteen and found it empty.

Lieutenant Bird expostulated about the need to strike swiftly since their numbers were few. Too few, if they lost the cooperation of the warriors. Bird was at the Indians' mercy. Surely he saw that? He was young. Not much older than William, who'd be turning twenty in . . . eight days' time?

Perhaps he'd mark the day inside the walls of Fort Stanwix.

Blearily he gazed across the clearing at the Mississaugas standing aloof, awaiting the outcome of the debate. Bird was red faced and sweating: "I'll not be content unless you accompany me, but should you refuse, I shall take my patrol and proceed without you!"

A fool you'd be to do it, William thought. But Bird didn't know what William had done in letting Sam walk out of that tent with his knowledge of St. Leger's plan of attack, when any loyal soldier would have taken him into custody and marched him straight to Captain Watts. Would it make the slightest difference if he confessed to it now? St. Leger hadn't believed the captives the Mohawks brought him. Was the whole western prong of the campaign going to turn on his word?

Was he a loyal soldier?

His attention returned to the warriors. They wore little in the heat: breechclouts, moccasins, leggings—some minus the latter. Their sleek bodies were painted for war, greased against biting insects. One, a lanky fellow William had heard called Ki, purportedly a crack shot with the rifle he carried, was casting impatient looks eastward as if he wished to be sighting down the gun's long barrel, picking sentries off the fort walls. Captain John was arguing, unconvinced by Lieutenant Bird, who by now ought to know the warriors would do as they pleased. Free to question their leaders, they felt no call to unswerving obedience—a mind-set William chose to emulate.

He bestirred himself off the ground. Still hung about with all his gear, knowing better than to shed it, he picked his way down through the pines to the creek. Canteen uncorked, he knelt and dipped it into the flow, looking around him at soaring trees, the raw stumps of those felled by the fort's garrison, the tangled underbrush that might hide a company of rebels.

While not thinking of his equally tangled familial situation, William's mind had hovered over memories, ones he kept returning to as they'd marched through that raw land, seeing another in his mind.

During the years he'd been tutored at Crickhowell, and between terms at Queens, he and the factor, Davies, had tramped the Breconshire hills, often coming across the remains of older times. Cairns—graves of heaped stone, their entrances gaping black. Or the grass-grown embankments of hill forts where the Celtic folk had lived. He'd poked about such places, finding bits of iron or potsherd, or stood taking in the view those ancient people had known. He'd wondered how many of his ancestors had tramped those places before him, gazed upon those vistas. The Aubreys had settled in Wales at a later time, but along the way since, older blood had married in. Bloodlines going back to those pre-Roman times . . .

Now he knew. Wales wasn't his homeland, though he spoke as one born to it. Still he missed those open hillsides, largely treeless though once—it was said—they'd been as thickly wooded as this land of the Oneidas. How many of his ancestors had roamed *these* woods, not blue-eyed Celts but dark-eyed Indians?

In the distance thunder rolled, bringing his head erect, still down on one knee in the mud of the bank. The light, which had slanted golden through the trees, vanished behind clouds piling up to block the setting sun.

He took a drink, corked the canteen, and was dipping his hands into the burbling flow to douse his heated face when he caught movement at vision's edge. He grabbed for his musket as his gaze darted across the creek, heart slamming in his chest.

Like a panther he was, so still in the thicket. A shadow against the fading light. Then he shifted—deliberately, of course—and William discerned his features. Paying no heed to the soldiers and warriors disputing in the clearing, the Indian stared at William.

Sweat sprang up on William's brow and trickled down, stinging his

eyes. He blinked them clear. When he looked again only a tiny glow—
evening's first firefly—pulsed where Joseph Tames-His-Horse had stood.

Lieutenant Henry Bird, furious but resigned, told the warriors he was
prepared to wait the night for them to send their scouts. He ordered camp
pitched, guard mounted, and dashed off a message to St. Leger, dispatched
by a runner, while a party of Senecas left to scout the fort.

Having one more night to spend before he could reasonably expect to
engage in battle—or siege—William settled in the clearing and, a blanket covering all but his eyes, watched the stars between passing clouds that
troubled the air with rumbling but offered no rain. No relief from heat.

Snatches of conversation reached him; Scots-burred declarations of
bloody revenge, often directed toward specific persons. Indians came and
went, moccasins thudding the pine duff. None was Joseph Tames-His-
Horse. There had been farewell in that look leveled at him from across the
creek. Joseph had made his decision about the campaign and wanted William to know it.

"You turned your coat inside out and went another way."

Had he already done so? Had he, in letting Sam go free, played the
traitor and sealed his own death? And that of these men around him? If so,
perhaps he'd also made it safer for Anna, Lydia, all those standing helpless
in the path of St. Leger's forces eager for revenge, scalps, and glory. He
could live with that, he decided. If he lived beyond tomorrow.

William lay, sore in every muscle, needing sleep but unable to yield to
it. He listened instead to a sudden breeze thresh the pines, pushing off the
aggravating swarms of insects. And he watched hazy stars wheel overhead
as the sky cleared, clouded, cleared again, dozing at last to the chirping,
croaking night chorus of his native land.

Thunder had rumbled around them for days, at times so distant as to be barely noted, other times hard on their heels like the worrying of wolves, unnerving the horses and prickling the hairs on Anna's nape, making her glance over her shoulder—only to meet the uninviting gaze of Strikes-The-Water, riding behind Lydia's mare.

Anna wished for a deluge, willing to endure sodden garments for a blessed break in the heat, but the rain that threatened rarely fell, save in restless spatters. Halted at sunset, she'd yearned toward the distant rumbling, but once again the storm rolled past over the mountains, leaving the valley sweltering in its juices.

She lay now beside Lydia under the stars, clasping hands for comfort. It was alarming in the forest at night, no shelter between them and whatever rustled and prowled out in the blackness, save an aging warrior and a brooding girl with a musket across her thighs.

"Our last night thus."

Anna turned at Lydia's whisper to see she'd also risked the top half of her face to the whining mosquitoes and was staring up at the stars, what could be seen of them through the tree canopy.

The journey had taken longer than anticipated. Anna suspected Clear Day of coddling them—stopping early, deliberately slow to rise come mornings. In some ways she was grateful. Sleeping on the ground had lost whatever novelty it initially held. Every joint ached. She'd lost count of the number of mosquito bites tormenting her or the wood ticks she and Lydia daily removed from their clothes and persons.

They would reach Kanowalohale tomorrow.

The thought stirred eagerness and apprehension. At long last she was entering Two Hawks's world. She would see where he'd returned to each time he'd left her at the border of her world. Know what he was choosing to leave for her, better understand the man she would call *husband*.

"Are you afraid?" Lydia asked, voice muffled.

It was stifling under the blanket. Worse to be bitten by the mosquitoes that swarmed in the dark. At first they'd resisted smearing on the grease Clear Day and Strikes-The-Water used to keep the insects at bay, but at last had given in—on their faces and hands. It helped, though it didn't prevent the needle pricks that pierced through clothing.

"A little. Mostly I just want to *see* him." Anna was careful not to say Two Hawks's name aloud; Strikes-The-Water was doubtless awake. Anna had yet to discern how much English the girl understood.

"He may not be there," Lydia cautioned.

"He and Stone Thrower might have returned," Anna whispered back.

Clear Day hoped so. He wanted to give Stone Thrower warning that Papa was coming to find him. Clear Day wasn't happy about how his talk with Papa had gone. At least that was the impression Anna had. The old man would say little of it. But Clear Day's words—whatever they had been—had propelled Papa on his present journey to find Stone Thrower, and they had moved his heart to stop impeding her and Two Hawks building a life together. For this Anna was thankful beyond words. There would be impediments enough. *But not from Papa.*

So complete was her happiness that for a while even the shadow of war, and William's part in it, had receded to the back of her mind. Now, on the eve of reaching Kanowalohale, worry for William rose like a root pressing into her back, keeping her wakeful. She lay in the insect-buzzing dark, looking up through looming branches, wondering if William watched the same stars. Still clutching Lydia's hand, she prayed for William to come through this trouble and back to them, to find a way to forgive Papa, to see he was part of their family and always would be, no matter the circumstances that began it. He was her brother, and he was loved. Then she gave him into God's hands and fastened her thoughts on Two Hawks.

He was looking at the stars with her. She knew it as though he lay beside her instead of Lydia, who, to judge by her slackened grip, had fallen asleep.

Anna smiled into the dark and watched the stars wheel across the breaks between the trees.

The sky along the eastern rim of the world was graying as dawn approached. Two Hawks gave it a glance, then faced westward to watch the stars fade.

The old war chief, Skenandoah, was with him again. They were north of the Carrying Place, part of the ring of scouts Gansevoort had placed more thickly around the fort after a bad thing happened—three girls had been attacked while picking berries outside its walls. Only one made it back alive. Since then Gansevoort had sent the garrison mothers and children away east to Fort Dayton, at German Flatts. He had stationed militia soldiers outside the fort to protect the bateaux expected to come with supplies and more soldiers to strengthen the garrison. These would be a target of attack unless they arrived very soon.

Praise Creator Anna Catherine was safe, farther away than German Flatts. Even so, she had felt strangely near to him this night, part of which he'd sat wakeful while Skenandoah slept. Perched below the crest of a ridge—as they'd done back in autumn when he and Skenandoah and Ahnyero tracked the spies from Cherry Valley—he'd watched the wheel of heaven turn. Sometimes clouds rolled up to beat their drums, drop a little rain, then move on. Other times the stars shone hazily through the thick, damp air.

With his father he'd arrived at Fort Stanwix to find the men there furiously at work in the summer heat, strengthening the fort. Wood Creek was made impassable. It would take days to clear that creek, up which the British must bring their cannon and supplies or else spend days cutting a road for it. But enemies on foot could emerge from the forest at any moment. Rangers, loyalists, warriors. Some of these had been spotted camped at the place where Wood Creek entered Oneida Lake. A small patrol coming ahead.

Was William part of that patrol, or was he back with the main force coming with St. Leger? Two Hawks hoped he'd come with this first wave of soldiers and warriors. He prayed he could find his brother, cut him from those others like a wolf its prey from a herd, get him away to their father and safety. It would be like that, he feared—the taking of prey that did not wish to be taken. He doubted William would come willingly, even if he knew it was his twin who sought to bring him away.

Two Hawks ran a hand over the dome of his head, plucked clean save for the swath from crown to nape. He hoped when at last they faced each other his brother would know him. His fingers traced the wound Lydia had stitched, healed now. One day it would be covered again. For now it lent him the look of what he needed to be. A warrior.

We are each what our lives have made us, but we are still one blood, Brother. I mean you to know it. Be ready for me.

The old warrior near him stirred out of sleep. As Skenandoah rose in silence to pray in the coming dawn, Two Hawks found himself remembering that the man's daughters had been married, each in turn, to Thayendanegea, who now led their brethren into Oneida land against the fort the Oneidas had sworn to protect. Those daughters had passed from this life, but Two Hawks wondered how Skenandoah felt to be facing the father of his grandchildren as an enemy. For all he was assured in his convictions, sorrow clung to the venerable warrior as he knelt in prayer. It was the sorrow Two Hawks felt about his brother being over on that side of things. A knot in the chest that wouldn't unravel. He was seeking words to speak of it when he saw the Mississaugas—three of them—skulking through the wood across a gully opposite the ridge on which they camped.

Two Hawks put a hand to Skenandoah's wiry arm, interrupting his prayers. Wordless, the old warrior turned and saw their enemy.

26

August 2, 1777
Oneida lands, western frontier

The Mississaugas looked to be going away west, toward that patrol likely on the move now toward Stanwix. Two Hawks's heart beat like a drum. "Do we follow?"

Skenandoah pressed his lips downward. "Let them go. Only at the threat of my own, or yours if you are with me, will I take a life again."

"My brother may be among those coming."

"If so, how will you get to him without throwing away your life in trying?"

"I must try, Grandfather."

Skenandoah's eyes, half-hidden in wrinkles, grew softer, but his mind on the matter held firm. "Creator will unfold it as He intends. Do not force it to come too soon. Await your time and you will know what to do. For now . . ." He nodded toward the vanished Mississaugas. "We do as those ones have done. Go tell what we have seen. And quickly."

When it came to finding his brother, Two Hawks had spent his whole life awaiting his time. How much longer must he wait?

As he ran behind Skenandoah with the sun already hot on his face, memory of a dream he'd had in the night returned. A dream of William. He'd seen his brother's face—the face in the portrait their father carried next to his heart. That face had grown man-size and spoken to him under the stars, as a friend might sit and speak. *Be careful, Brother,* the face that was William's had said—in Oneida! *Be careful. Keep my father safe.*

That was all Two Hawks remembered. Was it a message from his brother's heart? If so, what had he meant by it? More than awaiting the chance to get him back, was Two Hawks meant to *do* something for William? And which father had he meant?

Dreams. His own had never made sense to him, not like that young Mohawk who lived awhile with them at Kanowalohale. Not like the dreams that one used to have. Tames-His-Horse. That Mohawk had been kind to Two Hawks, like a brother, that year Stone Thrower left them. He went under the water the same day Two Hawks and his parents professed faith in Savior Jesus, that day of his father's dramatic return from the Senecas. What had been that Mohawk's new name, given then?

Joseph. A fitting name for an Indian so dream plagued. A dream took him back north to his people, Two Hawks recalled. A dream about a white girl waiting for him there. A girl whose eyes did not match. Two Hawks wondered how that turned out, if he'd found such a girl. He hoped so. But more, he hoped Joseph Tames-His-Horse wouldn't be among the Mohawks he might have to fight his way through to get at William.

They heard the stuttering cough of gunshots before they reached the edge of the cut-back forest surrounding the fort. Shouts followed. White men's shouts and the shrill cries of warriors. More sporadic shots.

They skirted northward, sweating as they ran, hoping to get round to the fort's sally port. When they did, Two Hawks grabbed Skenandoah's arm, turning the old man to view the fleet figures of Oneidas, one, two, more, slipping from cover, making for that small gate. Scouts and pickets like themselves, dodging fire from south of the fort, where powder smoke plumed from the trees. The British advance patrol was come.

"I will not be shut up in there." Skenandoah held himself tense. "What good would that do anyone?"

Two Hawks agreed but didn't say so for just then a ball, shot high from the distant wood to the south, whirred past his ear and went rattling through the trees behind him, snapping leaves and twigs. He ducked behind a holly bush, pulling Skenandoah down with him. Crawling forward, nose to the earth, he got a look along the river to the landing there. The long-expected bateaux had arrived. They were empty, supplies and soldiers gotten into the fort without a moment to spare.

Not so all their crew. The last of those were running hard up the track from the landing, beset by warriors. A hurled hatchet halted one man's flight in an arch of agony. In seconds a warrior was on him, taking his scalp with a victorious cry. Another two boatmen were captured and dragged away struggling. Others were still making for the fort, among them one who moved with a limp in his stride, though Two Hawks hadn't seen him hit. That limp was from an old wound, taken in another war. Two Hawks's eyes knew it well. It belonged to Anna Catherine's father.

William was trembling and trying to hide it. Lieutenant Bird was taking visible pains to master his own reaction at seeing the second goal of their mission fail before his eyes. They'd taken the lower river landing but arrived too late to capture the supplies and reinforcements sent upriver to the rebel garrison. If he mentally cursed the Indians for the delays they'd caused, Lieutenant Bird wasted no time voicing such resentment.

"Take whomever you need and go after Captain John and his warriors," he ordered two nearby Yorkers in the forest south of the fort, where they'd regrouped. "Bring back those captive boatmen—while they can yet speak."

Brant's warriors, sent ahead by St. Leger, just starting his advance up the timber-choked creek, were trickling in through forest paths. Brant himself, formidable in paint and feathers, carried a message from the general. Lieutenant Bird read it through, ordered camp pitched on the spot, then those not needed for the purpose stationed round the fort. "Shoot anything that moves on those walls," Bird told his marksmen, Indian and loyalist. "Keep them pinned inside until General St. Leger arrives."

William fell in with those pitching camp and saw to the raising of tents, the gathering of wood, the laying of fires, the gradual steadying of his hands and knees. Reconciling himself to what he'd seen down his rifle's barrel was another thing. With the rest of the Yorkers under Bird's command, he'd stationed himself behind a brushy stump and taken aim at the fleeing rebels, only to send his shot winging high over the last of the stragglers attempting to outrace their attackers—for the appalling realization that among them was Reginald Aubrey.

Sick with dread yet a telling relief, William had pulled himself together and was still helping with the camp setup amid the rising smoke of fires and the *chunk* of axes felling trees to fuel them, when his fellow Yorkers returned with the warriors and their prisoners, the latter white faced as they were marched toward Lieutenant Bird's newly erected tent.

Frozen in their path, William waited for the inevitable as the oldest prisoner, blood drying down his face, locked gazes with him as they passed. He knew the man by sight—a bateau captain called Martin. And the man, to judge by his sharpened gaze, knew William.

Spittle flew. Though too far away for that manifestation of contempt to touch him, William's face went tight with heat as if in the wake of a slap.

Anna Catherine's father was inside the fort. And that captain who'd been friendly to him, white-haired Lang, he was also among those trapped within. Two Hawks could understand about Lang. That man was often up and down the river. But what was Reginald Aubrey doing there when Clear Day had traveled far to speak to him? Had Clear Day never reached him? Who was watching over Anna Catherine, Lydia?

Questions swarmed like hornets in Two Hawks's skull. Should he stay and seek William, surrounded by enemies who would be streaming in from the forest now, or find his father, praying he wasn't already closed up inside the fort too?

"Oriska," said the old warrior beside him. "That is where I go. Word must be taken to the Americans to send men fast before more British get here." Skenandoah didn't wait for Two Hawks to agree but set out through the forest.

Two Hawks followed, still making up his mind what to do.

They'd gone less than a mile when steps sounded on the path behind. Slipping off the trace into the wood, they waited in the still heat, rifles ready.

It was a woman, running fast. Skenandoah called out, "Sister, bide and speak to us."

Two-Kettles-Together, wife of the warrior Honyery Doxtater of Oriska, drew up startled but unafraid, having recognized Skenandoah's voice. She'd news to share of interest to Two Hawks, beyond the word she meant to bring eastward about the siege.

"Ahnyero goes ahead," she told them, still catching her breath, her face gleaming. "To send word—though he did not know about the siege when he went."

"Ahnyero?" Two Hawks asked, surprised and pleased.

Two-Kettles-Together nodded. "He arrived at the fort before the sun and spoke to Gansevoort of all he knew of the British coming. He left before those bateaux arrived. He will be at Oriska if you wish to find him. I am going farther, all the way to that soldier-trader at the Little Falls Carry."

Nicholas Herkimer, she meant. A militia general. Skenandoah nodded, approving. "He will send word on and come himself to help his brothers in the fort. We will go with you as far as Oriska."

The pair started off down the forest trail.

Two Hawks hesitated, still undecided. He could do nothing for Aubrey inside the fort. His chances of slipping into a camp filling up fast with enemies to drag his brother away were slim. Skenandoah was right about that. Maybe nothing more would happen until St. Leger arrived with his big guns, which were still far down Wood Creek. Maybe the Americans would stay shut up in their fort, which last he'd seen was well advanced in repairs. It couldn't be taken without those big guns. Two Hawks doubted Gansevoort would surrender. Why should he?

Maybe William and Aubrey would keep in peace a little longer. Long enough for him to find Stone Thrower.

Keep my father safe.

"I am trying, Brother." Choking down frustration, he ran after Honyery's wife and Skenandoah, hoping Stone Thrower was making his way to Oriska as well, and not behind him trapped inside that fort.

Kanowalohale proved a surprise. There were no straight streets or avenues but paths that wandered among clusters of homes strung along a lively creek. In other ways it looked remarkably familiar. The homes were mostly squared log cabins with shaded arbors, though several, glimpsed as Clear Day led them out of the forest, were more elaborate frame houses one could have set down in the middle of Schenectady without raising an eyebrow among its denizens.

Surprise greeted her even before she saw the town, as they threaded their horses past swaths of cleared acres planted in corn, beans, squash, and sunflowers, all on the verge of summer ripeness.

And the orchards! Apples, peaches, nut trees.

Then there were the people, turning from work to watch them pass. Wrinkled old men sitting in their arbor shade, tattooed and fierce. Women with long black or gray or white hair uncovered. Children of all ages. Skirts and tunics and billowy shirts made of trade cloth or calico or deerskin, sewn with beads and silver and feathers and copper and quills.

She'd known Kanowalohale would be full of Oneida people, but to be suddenly among them, a stranger, was disconcerting. Anna smiled and, despite the disapproving glare of Strikes-The-Water, offered a *shekoli* to a group of grinning children who called out to them, *"A'sluni."* White people.

They dismounted, sore and weary, at a cabin from which Good Voice shortly emerged, blond hair braided, blue eyes wide and wondering. *"You* have come?" she said, sun-brown hands spreading over a belly that poked out round beneath her calico tunic.

Anna, first to see her, looked with astonishment at the handsome face of Two Hawks's mother, marked with approaching middle age, then at her slender wrists and hands cupping that protruding belly.

"You're with child," she blurted, before a word of greeting passed her lips. "Good Voice . . . how? I mean—that is to say—" She stammered to a halt, blood mounting in her face as Good Voice's brows rose.

"You are happy for this?" she asked.

"Yes—just all astonishment." A child on the way, and her twins nearly twenty! Did Two Hawks know? Of course he knew. He'd eyes. Anna looked past his mother, eager for sight of him coming out to greet her.

The cabin doorway stood empty.

"I am also happy," Good Voice was saying. "I thought never again to bear a child, but Heavenly Father gives beyond all I could expect."

Anna opened her mouth to ask about Two Hawks, but Lydia was suddenly there, exclaiming in her turn over Good Voice's pregnancy. The two fell to talking about its advancement, Lydia's guess of nearly six months proving accurate.

"Are you come because of William?" Good Voice finally had space to ask. "There is news of my son?"

"Not beyond what Clear Day brought," Lydia replied.

Despite their lack of news, Good Voice's face lit. "Two Hawks has seen his brother. Maybe soon *I* will see my son. You also, now you are come."

Anna glanced at the people going about their work at nearby cabins— or pretending to while watching their reunion—still expecting to see Two

Hawks. It took a moment to realize there were no young men about. Few men at all save those of Clear Day's generation. Grandfathers. She turned back to Good Voice, unable to hold back asking any longer, but Strikes-The-Water called from over by the horses, capturing Good Voice's attention. Anna only realized the girl had asked about Two Hawks when Good Voice replied in English, "My son has been gone many days. My husband . . . him you have just missed. He set out for Oriska, taking news of the council."

Clear Day stepped away from the horses. "There has been a council?"

Good Voice told them of the sachems and chief warriors who'd gathered at Kanowalohale several days past—an attempt to appeal to the Mohawks and the rest of their brethren for peace. "But there will be no peace. It is known that the British, and Thayendanegea with his warriors, and all those whites who are for the Crown are coming now from Oswego. All the warriors have gone away up to the fort, or to Oriska."

Lydia had warned her, still the disappointment was crushing.

Clear Day went away with the horses tied in a string. Strikes-The-Water gazed after him, shoulders stiff.

As they gathered their medical kits and what provisions remained and piled them beneath the arbor, the sound of distant shouting arose. Under the arbor they turned, craning to see the cause of the disturbance. Whoever was shouting was doing so in Oneida. Then the shouter came into view—a warrior coming up a main path of the town, his pace swift.

"What is he saying?" Lydia asked.

Anna felt a clutch of alarm as the faces of those the crier passed turned anxious and grim, even before Strikes-The-Water answered in startlingly clear English, "Soldiers surround the Carry fort. Guns fired. Some dead. That he say."

Without another word, the girl ran to intercept the bringer of news.

27

August 3, 1777
Fort Stanwix

*T*he morning air trapped within the fort's turf-and-timber walls hung as heavy as a battle's aftermath. The smell of powder smoke wasn't the predominant fug assaulting his nose upon rising, still Reginald suffered a brief lurch of displacement, as if he'd slipped backward in time to another August dawn, another fort.

Heledd. He wished for even a moment in his late wife's presence, to tell her he was sorry. To tell her he had loved her, however imperfectly. Did the dead have such knowledge? Did they remember? Or forgive?

He rose in the oppressive dawn to the torments of the present. There'd been fleas in the straw pallet he'd been provided. He shook out his clothing and searched his person, ridding himself of the pests as best he could, but as he left the barracks where he'd billeted, he imagined his sweating scalp still crawled with them.

Such annoyance paled before his chief disappointment; he'd discovered that Stone Thrower wasn't at the fort as he'd hoped. A blind hope, as it turned out. Had the warrior been there and seen the approaching British patrol and made his escape, even as Reginald was being chased inside Stanwix's walls? Was he out in the wilds somewhere scouting with no knowledge of the siege? He'd found no one who could say for certain, and his frustration was mounting. He was trapped, unless he wanted to try his luck getting through the enemy that ringed them. He'd been so certain the journey upriver, unplanned and rash as it was, had been an urgent necessity. In fact, he'd almost dared believe he'd heard the voice of the Almighty again at last . . .

Even as the thought formed, the distant bark of a rifle had him dropping in a painful crouch—before his brain told him he wasn't a target. He scanned the ramparts and embrasures, seeking a body tumbling. Whatever enemy marksman had taken a shot at a guard or at a work detail had missed.

Heart-heavy for the boatmen killed or captured in yesterday's harried dash, Reginald headed toward the smell of cookery. Turning the corner of the barracks, he ran headlong into someone rounding it from the opposite direction.

"Sorry, sir!" said a familiar voice as Reginald bent for his hat, knocked into the dirt at his feet. A hand reached down and gripped his arm, as though he needed steadying.

Shaking off the hand, Reginald straightened and found himself fixed by the startled hazel eyes of the traitor, Sam Reagan.

Who wasn't a traitor at all—so Reagan hastened to explain in a fervent burst of chatter—but a Patriot spy who'd infiltrated Sir John Johnson's regiment to gain intelligence about the British plans for war in the north and then secret that intelligence south to Generals Schuyler and Washington. Dumbstruck, Reginald let the lad talk until finally he came to the salient point that lay between them. "And as for William, sir, I—"

The name put iron into Reginald's bones. He grasped the sleeve of Sam's coat. "Where is William?"

Surprise, then guilt, rippled over Sam's face. "More'n likely out there now." He bent a nod toward the southeast bastion, beyond which St. Leger's advance force haunted the wood's edge, sniping at Stanwix's walls. "Before I left Oswego, I learned Captain Watts's company—mine and William's—was to accompany the forward patrol, ahead of St. Leger's main force."

Reginald thrust Sam's arm away. "Before you . . . you *left* William? Abandoned him?"

"Not abandoned, sir. I tried to bring him away with me, but he wouldn't desert."

William had chosen to stay. It was a worse blow even than the thought of him abandoned among the enemy forces.

"I gave him a choice," Sam went on. "Let me walk away or turn me in for the spy I'd confessed myself to be. He chose the former, though I think it was a near thing."

Reginald let the words sink in, sifting them for meaning. *A near thing.* Were William's loyalist sentiments less entrenched than Reginald had long feared? Was there still a chance, if Reginald could but get to the lad, he could be persuaded to see reason?

As for Sam Reagan—traitor or no—Reginald couldn't fathom what passed for reason inside the murky depths of his brain. "It was you led William away. Why do so, why let him enlist, knowing all the while you were never in earnest?"

Sam hesitated, as if to gather words long rehearsed for such a moment as this. "My course was set that night last summer when William found me. He never told me the truth about his birth. Not till months later. But I could judge the state he was in—like he'd taken a blow to the head. I feared letting him go off alone," Sam went on hastily, when Reginald flinched. "Not in everything have I been false, sir. Not where William is concerned. He was my friend. Still is, for my part."

As the words hung between them, Reginald thought, *More truly your friend than ever my son, but oh, William, it must seem the whole world has played you false.*

He stepped back. "Look you. William had you all these months. He wasn't alone. For that I'm grateful."

Sam blinked, clearly taken back. Awkward silence lanced between them before a familiar voice said, "Major . . . Reagan. I see you've found each other."

Ephraim Lang joined them, one callused, big-jointed hand cradling a bowl of what looked like congealing porridge. "Breakfast." The captain thrust the bowl at Reginald, who took it, though his appetite had fled.

Lang's gaze shifted to Sam. "I'd expected to find this one beaten to a pulp should the two of you cross paths. I commend your restraint, Major."

Sam had the grace to redden. "Thank you, sir," he said to Reginald. "And not just for now. For everything."

Bowing briefly, he took leave of them. Reginald watched the lad make his way across the drill ground until Lang's laconic voice recalled him.

"I'd tell you to save your breath to cool your porridge, Major, but I think it's bordering on cold."

Reginald dipped his fingers in and took a bite. Cold and tasteless. He nodded toward the distant rifle cracks outside the fort, which had sporadically followed the first. "You know then . . . about William?"

"That he's likely out there with a rifle trained in our general direction? I do. You've my prayers on the matter, for what they're worth to you."

A pressure bloomed at the base of Reginald's throat.

Lang gave him a curious glance. "When you caught us up at Herkimer's Carry, you said you meant to find the Indian—Stone Thrower. And Two Hawks. Neither are here, and as you know we're likely looking at a decent stretch of time inside these walls. What mean you now to do?"

"What can any of us do?" Reginald replied, but he wasn't seeking an answer. In that moment he dared to do a thing that terrified him more than being trapped within the walls of another besieged fort. He addressed himself to heaven. *Was it You sent me here? Had You a purpose in it? Is there atonement for me to make after all?*

There was no reply from the Almighty.

Reginald gave no better answer to Lang's question, though he had one in mind: before St. Leger's main forces arrived, before William managed to get himself killed, Reginald had to get free of those walls.

When the sun was high, Colonel Peter Gansevoort assembled the garrison. Still a young man to Reginald's eyes—not yet thirty—Stanwix's commanding officer was tall and thick chested, with a voice that carried over the parade ground to the soldiers manning the ramparts, gazes trained westward for the first sign of St. Leger.

The fort was as ready as it could be, given the hasty state of repairs. The garrison itself stood somewhere short of eight hundred, comprising Continentals from the 3rd New York and the 9th Massachusetts, three dozen artillerymen, various Oneida and civilian scouts, and eight women who hadn't evacuated to German Flatts. Though small arms cartridges were plentiful, artillery ammunition remained in distressingly short supply.

With his back to a barracks wall at the parade's edge, the straps of musket and shot bag crossing his chest, Reginald listened as Gansevoort made no effort to sweeten the situation. While the fort boasted fourteen artillery pieces, he'd received intelligence of more powerful field pieces among St. Leger's retinue. "But should our enemy attempt to storm the fort," Gansevoort said, addressing the assemblage, "we shall see the value of those fourteen guns!"

There followed a general exhortation to the troops standing in ranks before him, their sweating faces lifted—reflecting dread, anticipation, exhaustion—to continue as they had begun, with courage, fortitude, and faith in a delivering Providence . . .

Now, Reginald thought, while Gansevoort encouraged his troops to make every rifle shot count, every target sure—now was his time to slip away out of the fort. His chances of getting free of every obstacle, of finding Stone Thrower, or Two Hawks, or William, were overwhelmingly slender, but with a final glance around to be sure no one was intent upon him, he took the two strides needed to reach the corner of the barracks, turned it, and made for the sally port. There a guard challenged him, as he knew would be the case.

"No sir." Thin-faced and flushed, the soldier stood in his path, rifle held crosswise. "I cannot let you pass. Not 'less you've permission from the colonel, or one of the officers?" The soldier's gaze fell to Reginald's coat, as if anticipating his producing written evidence of such orders.

"I haven't any, nor do I require it. I'm under no one's command here."

The soldier's gaze shifted to his fellow guards; then he set his narrow jaw. "Begging your pardon but *I* am, and I've orders to let none without—"

"By the grace of God we are going to defend this place!"

Gansevoort's sudden shout, commanding the troops to attention, captured the guard's as well. In unison they turned toward the parade. Reginald thought wildly of slipping past and making his escape—surely they wouldn't *shoot* him—but Gansevoort's last exhortation caught him before he could act, resurrecting a similar incitement from the depths of memory. Colonel Monro had shouted such words as the French and their Indians surrounded Fort William Henry, twenty years ago . . . *to the day.*

The third of August.

Past and present clashed in a frisson of dread that tightened the sweating scalp beneath his hat, as from the parade a roar of cheers erupted—a roar that faltered prematurely, dying by degrees, until breathless silence overhung the fort.

Reginald's gut knew its purport before his ears, trained like those of every man within the walls, detected a stir—too faint yet to be called sound—beyond its tensely listening bounds. His gut knew and turned over in dismay before the distant *rat-tat-tat* of drums swelled on the humid air and rolled across his nerves like approaching thunder.

28

August 3, 1777
Fort Stanwix

*R*eginald watched from the southwest rampart, Ephraim Lang beside him, two among those lining the embrasures, thrumming with tension, reeking of sweat and fear. Most watched in silence as St. Leger's forces emerged from the forest to the west and marched toward the fort, drums rattling, bugles blaring, banners fluttering in the breeze sprung up with morning's passing. British regulars in their scarlet and white. Sir John's Royal New Yorkers in their green and white. Hessians and Tory rangers in varying shades of green. Ranged alongside the regular forces were the Indians in war paint, bristling with feathers, armed with clubs, spears, bows, tomahawks, and guns—a sight intended to shatter whatever confidence Gansevoort had instilled in the garrison.

After the last of St. Leger's army emerged into the open, the columns deployed, fanning into lines that swung around as if to encompass the fort. But for all their pageantry, they were few.

"That the lot of 'em?" a voice along the rampart queried.

Ephraim Lang leaned back from the embrasure he and Reginald shared. "See any field pieces? I'll wager half this brigade's still inching up Wood Creek—forgotten the mess you lads made of it?"

A rueful laugh. "With these blisters? Still—"

An abrupt cessation of bugles and drums had them back at the embrasures, gaping. Save for the piercing cry of a hawk circling high above the field, stillness had fallen outside the fort.

The blood-pounding silence stretched out long, until with no apparent prompting, a tall warrior in a breechclout took a dozen strides toward the invested fort, raised a hatchet, and with blackened face thrown back unleashed a scream. The rest of the enemy ranks, white and red, loosed their shouts in unison. While the combined roar of hundreds assaulted the fort, Reginald exchanged a look with Lang.

"Twenty years, Major," the captain said above the clamor. "Had ye thought of it?"

Reginald had, almost continually, and said so.

Beyond the fort the roar was fading. Officers shouted. Columns reformed. Drums beat a marching cadence. The Indians, many still yipping like wolves, melted into the woods to the south.

There was a siege to plan.

Aware of a rising murmur at his back, Reginald turned to see several of the officers of the 3rd New York talking in earnest with three of the women who had remained, below the rampart where he perched. The women, petticoats hitched, left at a run toward a barracks. An officer hurried off in another direction.

"What's to do?"

"It's to do with a flag," Lang said.

Reginald glanced around the fort's interior, only now realizing that Stanwix flew no flag. More men were running about. One joined the group below, carrying strips of white cloth. A woman returned, red petticoat and sewing kit in hand.

Reginald descended the rampart and made his way through the press of bodies gathered round a pole laid on the ground. A ring of women hunkered round a large rectangle of cloth taking shape under their stitching fingers, rough cobbled amid the sense of defiance rippling through the garrison. Reginald had never seen this flag's configuration. Before he'd more than a glimpse, he felt a presence at his side: Lieutenant Colonel Willett, grinning down at the work of the women's hands. "The white bits were cut from a shirt, the red stripes from her spare petticoat." He nodded toward the pretty blond stitching down one of those red stripes to the white on either side. "But the blue field in the upper corner . . . that's from me. A British artillery coat taken off the field at Peekskill."

Despite his failure to escape the fort and the increased ranks of the enemy without, as the women stood back from their work, and the flag— red, white, and blue—was hoisted, and *huzzahs* went up, and one of the guns was discharged in the direction of the British camp, falling short but making its point, Reginald wasn't insensible to the exhilaration and pride shimmering on the air like heat waves. His heart stirred with it but also with fear. Though he hadn't spotted him among the British ranks, William was surely on the other side of the fort's walls. And feeling just as trapped as he?

The Indians were back to sniping and making sport of it. They lay wager on every shot—particularly that of the warrior, Ki, who positioned himself in a tree to pick his targets on the ramparts.

William had moved his kit to the Royal Yorker's camp, positioned between Brant's Indian camp at the Lower Landing and St. Leger's to the east. Some of the Yorkers were still to the west, laboring to clear the water passage. Sergeant Campbell was, regrettably, not one of them. Detailed under Campbell to a nearby hay field, gathering bedding for the camp, he was bringing in his third load when he heard of St. Leger's intention to send an offer of surrender to the fort commander.

William had seen that flag hoisted over the ramparts. Heard the defiant boom of artillery. Surrender was unlikely. But if he could gain permission to accompany St. Leger's envoy, maybe he could find Reginald Aubrey and . . . what? Bring him back a prisoner to Sir John? Better a prisoner than dead.

He dumped the hay at the edge of camp and slipped off through the trees, headed for the army's main encampment, regretting he was out of proper uniform—they'd stripped to shirt-sleeves for the fatigue. Sweat-soaked, covered in bits of hay, he addressed the dubious sentry outside St. Leger's tent.

"Private William Aubrey of Johnson's Greens. I must speak to Captain Watts, if he's within. A matter of urgency." To himself alone, but the sentry needn't know that.

The guard was a private of St. Leger's 34th. Typical of army regulars, he peered down his nose at William's grubby disarray. "You've some intelligence to impart that could affect an offer of surrender?"

"What I've to say isn't for your ears. Permit me to—"

The tent flap moved aside. Captain Watts himself peered out, frowning as he took in William. "What is it, Aubrey?"

"A request, sir. I—"

Watts put a hand to his arm, glanced back into the tent, and said with thinly veiled irritation, "Come within—quietly."

Startled to have gained entry, however begrudging, William stepped inside the tent's interior, heart thudding as his eyes adjusted to the dimness. Assembled round a camp table were those of St. Leger's officers not back with the baggage at Wood Creek: the general himself, fleshy jowled and looking older than his forty years; Joseph Brant; Colonel John Butler, who led the rangers, and his son, Walter; Lieutenant Bird; others who turned at William's entry.

St. Leger, in the midst of speaking, paid the stir at the tent's entrance no mind. ". . . lack of ordinance confines our options at present, but we have nevertheless accomplished what ordinance alone could not. We have shown these rebels our resolve. And, gentlemen," the general added with a nod at Brant, "we have shown them our Indians. Captain Tice will proceed under flag of truce with my missive to Gansevoort, detailing terms. We'll have secured their surrender by nightfall."

The captain thus mentioned, Gilbert Tice, stepped forward to receive the letter still spread on the table, freshly inked, as yet unsealed.

"What was the urgency, Private?" Watts asked under his breath while the general instructed Tice. "Has it some bearing on these proceedings?"

"It does, sir. I request permission to accompany Captain Tice into the fort."

Watts's dark brows lowered. "To what purpose?"

William opened his mouth, seeking some excuse of substance to put behind the appeal—nearly all of Johnson's regiment had someone inside that fort they could lay claim to as kin or friend—when a familiar growl arose outside the tent: "Aye, he's in there, as he's no call to be." Campbell's pugnacious face poked through the tent flap. His searching gaze fastened upon William. "A word outside *if* ye please, Private."

Heads turned among the officers. The general paused, glancing up. Taking William by the arm, Captain Watts pushed him out of the tent into the bright heat of a sun now in the west. Campbell grasped William's other arm and started to speak, but the captain sent him a quelling look, whereupon they both released their hold. Watts addressed William. "Why should you wish to accompany Tice into the fort?"

"That's what he's about, is it?" Campbell interjected. "He wants inside the fort? Dinna let him, Captain."

Watts frowned in annoyance. "It shan't be my decision, but why should you object, Sergeant?"

"On account, sir, o' what our lad here is. He's Indian, a savage half-breed. Did ye no ken that?"

William blazed with heat as Captain Watts and even the sentry stared as though he'd sprouted horns.

"No' just any sort o' savage," the only man not rendered speechless hurried to add. "Oneida. For all we ken he's set to carry intelligence to his people in that fort. And ye ken, Captain, that's likely what his bosom friend, Reagan, has done—gone a traitor to the rebels."

Wanting nothing so much as to plow his fist into that smug Scotch face, William contained his rage and waited for the captain to speak. Watts continued to stare, desire to disbelieve Campbell's accusation clear in his gaze. "You're a Welshman, Aubrey. Your voice betrays you every time you open your mouth. Not only Welsh, but Oxford educated—and you've blue eyes!"

He'd have to tell the sorry tale. "I know, sir. You see—"

The captain waved a hand, silencing him. "I've no time for it. And it makes no matter for I shall not pass along your request. Rejoin your detail."

Forbearing to protest, William bowed and turned on his heel and stalked away through St. Leger's camp. By the time he reached the hay field, he could see in the distance the knot of riders advancing toward Stanwix's main gates, white flag fluttering.

Hours later, when word spread that Colonel Gansevoort had spurned St. Leger's offer, William wondered if Reginald Aubrey, whose face bore mute evidence of the outcome of Fort William Henry's surrender, had had anything do with it.

29

August 4, 1777
Kanowalohale

*T*he rising sun had chased away night's cool, but clad in a simple skirt and blouse gathered by a woven sash, Anna felt comfortable. Scandalously so. Lydia hadn't protested her adoption of Oneida garb, though Anna had caught her casting side-eyes at her uncovered hair and her calves bared above quilled moccasins.

Throughout the morning, Oneida women, with infants and children in tow, had stopped by Good Voice's lodge to see the white visitors, but now Lydia, Anna, and Good Voice were alone beneath the arbor, sorting through their collective stock of medicines—except for Strikes-The-Water, who sat a ways off oiling a musket. The brooding Tuscarora girl had spent much of the past two days at Good Voice's lodge, always with some task to busy her hands and command her attention. Always pretending she did not understand their talk, though Anna knew better now.

"You've a good supply of sassafras," Lydia remarked; Good Voice had unwrapped a bundle of the roots. "What of honey, for dressings?"

"Much honey," Good Voice said. "The bees your grandmothers brought across the water found us long ago and made homes in our trees too."

Talk of healing went on for a time before it returned, inevitably, to *why* they were taking stock of their collective pharmacopoeia. It was two days since the scouts brought news of Fort Stanwix's investment. Runners had come and gone since with nothing significant to report. No battle. No surrender. Apparently the British were delayed in bringing all but a few mortars up to the fort by the forward thinking of Stanwix's commander.

Their talk turned to another oft-visited topic, Papa and his conversation with Clear Day, and its results. Since news of the siege first reached them, they had feared for Papa's safety, having no way of knowing whether he'd reached Stanwix before the siege began and was now inside the fort, or if hearing of it he had turned back and was well out of harm's way. Or had found Stone Thrower. Or had been captured by the British. Lydia, Anna, and Good Voice had gone to their knees together many times and were bearing the uncertainty, the wrenching ache of hope, leaning into one another, opening their hearts to one another, deepening bonds they had begun a year ago to forge.

At last they had moved beyond their fear for the lives of their men and could venture to speak about their souls.

"With all my heart I pray that the need to find Stone Thrower was a step toward Reginald's healing," Lydia said. "It's only that I've waited so long, you see, and now . . ."

Lydia faltered, and Anna wondered if she feared she'd said too much. Anna darted a look at Good Voice, whose hands had stilled on the bundle of herbs she'd been retying.

Good Voice met Lydia's gaze, hers composed. "Now?"

Lydia blushed, recalling to Anna's mind how Papa had kissed her on the quay. "He's made no formal proposal, but I've reason to hope that, at last, Reginald and I might be wed once he returns. Once we *both* return."

Lydia closed her eyes briefly, and Anna knew she was praying again for Papa's safety. Anna clasped her hand, adding the same petition for Two Hawks, and whispered her "Amen."

Good Voice was studying them when they both looked up, a small frown between her brows. "And if this happens as you hope, this marrying, you will become this one's mother?" She bent her head toward Anna. "It is so among whites?"

Lydia gave Anna's hand a squeeze and with a blooming smile said, "In our case it certainly is."

Anna felt tears well at Lydia's tender look. "You've always been a mother to me."

Good Voice's frown smoothed away. Her features settled in decision. "*Iyo*. There is a thing I wish to do. A thing between mothers when the children have chosen."

With the aid of an arbor pole, Good Voice got to her feet, ungainly with her growing belly, and went into the lodge.

Anna's gaze flicked to Strikes-The-Water in time to see a quicksilver chase of thoughts cross her usually guarded face—startlement, comprehension, distress, anger—before the girl caught Anna's gaze, took up her gun, and stalked away around the lodge.

"What on earth is going on?" Lydia asked, staring after the girl.

Anna was as mystified.

Soon Good Voice came out of the lodge, looked to where Strikes-The-Water had been sitting, but made no mention of the girl's departure. Beneath the arbor she knelt in front of Lydia, placing between them a large basket woven of birch bark. She lifted the lid and began removing its contents.

"My son Two Hawks, called Jonathan," she said, her voice carrying a note of formality, "is not here to speak for himself, but it is the way of the People for mothers to speak first of these matters."

From the basket she withdrew a tunic of fine-woven calico scattered with tiny flowers, the hem and neckline worked in bands of ribbons. She laid the tunic to the side, then brought out a pair of leggings worked in a matching design and moccasins decorated in quills. Good Voice's eyes shone with pride, and not just in her workmanship.

"My son has not been called upon to fight, but he stands ready to do so and has proven himself a skilled hunter. Your daughter and her children will never go hungry or lack for protection as long as my son's hands have strength."

Halfway through this speech, Anna's breath had caught with comprehension. Good Voice was making a formal request to Lydia, as her mother, to accept Two Hawks as a husband for her.

Lydia turned to look at her, understanding dawning in her gaze as well.

There was more in the basket, gifts and tokens. One by one Good Voice placed them before Lydia. With each item she enumerated her son's merits.

A set of wooden spoons, carved and polished: "He has a good heart for those he calls his own and is even now doing his part to serve and protect them."

A china teapot with pink roses and gold edging, as lovely as one might find in the finest parlor in Schenectady: "He is a man of generous spirit. He will be such a man for whatever people he pledges his heart to."

A stunning belt made of blue and white beads: "He will be a good father to his children and will pass on to them much wisdom. He will tell them of Heavenly Father's Son Jesus and the good path made for men to walk. He will see that his children walk that path and know Creator's blessings."

Tears were coursing down Anna's cheeks, her heart swelling with love for the man Good Voice praised. Not until Good Voice had emptied the basket did Anna dare look at Lydia again, praying she would see acceptance in her face, approval, despite this custom strange to them. But Good Voice wasn't finished speaking.

"When I began to make or trade for these things, looking to this day, I did not expect my son to choose a wife not *Onyota'a:ka,* but your daughter-to-be is a worthy woman of her people. She will make a good wife to my son and mother to their children, even without a clan."

She paused at that, hands spread over her unborn child, and Anna felt a rush of regret—and understanding. *This* was the source of that sorrow she'd sometimes seen when Good Voice looked at her and Two Hawks. Their children, perhaps the only grandchildren Good Voice would live long enough to know, would have no clan. Would not be of the People.

"It is in my mind," Good Voice said, again addressing Lydia, "that Creator is in this joining of our children. He is doing this for our healing. He is taking what our enemy meant for evil and bringing good from it. I do not think we will soon see the end of the good He plans to give us, if you will accept my son as husband for your daughter."

Lydia opened her mouth, then closed it. Was she overwhelmed? Thinking about Papa and what he might say of her stepping into this role he would surely see as his?

Her speechlessness lasted only seconds before she took up the teapot and plunked it onto her lap. "I'm honored by your words, Good Voice, and I thank you for these beautiful gifts. I do accept Two Hawks as Anna's husband—with all my heart. He's an admirable young man, as I've come to know. Anna will be a good and faithful wife to him. And I promise to be their champion to Anna's father." Lydia leaned forward, earnest. "Not that I believe they'll need one, only . . . I want *you* to know I support them and will continue to do so."

Lydia set the teapot carefully aside. She held out her hands to Good Voice, who clasped them across the marriage gifts.

"I too support and . . . *champion.*" Good Voice smiled over the word. "It is sealed then. They will join as they wish."

Both women turned to Anna, who'd taken in every word and gesture with pounding heart. Rejoicing heart. "Thank you, both. Oh . . . thank you."

None of them had noticed Daniel Clear Day coming up the path to Good Voice's lodge until his shadow fell over Lydia's and Good Voice's clasped hands. They broke apart, blinking up at him, jarred out of the profound sense of linkage the little ceremony had created.

Clear Day stood in the sunlight, sweat running down his face. "That one called Herkimer is coming to the aid of Stanwix. He musters his farmer-soldiers at Fort Dayton. I go now to Oriska to see them pass, see if my nephew or your son is among them."

Anna was on her feet as if she'd springs beneath her. She looked down at Lydia, seated amid the marriage gifts. "Should we go with him?"

"To Oriska?" Lydia got to her feet, then reached to give Good Voice a hand in rising. "They're only passing through, the militia. Clear Day can bring our message to Two Hawks if he sees him. Would you?" she asked the old man. "Let Two Hawks know of Reginald's change of heart and . . ." She waved a hand over the gifts laid out beneath the arbor.

"It is settled," Good Voice explained. "My son must do as Creator leads in this fight, but tell him that he will have the wife he desires."

"I will tell him," Clear Day said. "If I see him."

Even Good Voice didn't seem compelled to go to Oriska. Anna couldn't bear it. "Lydia? What if Papa is with them?"

Lydia held firm. "It seems we may be needed after all. But I'm not letting you nearer either of those armies with a battle imminent, Anna. Yes, I know Reginald may among them." She paused, and even Anna could see how hard this was for her to say. "But we cannot go running off into danger even for him, and he wouldn't want us to. When the dust settles we'll go to wherever they bring our wounded. For now . . . we'll wait for further word."

Anna left the arbor, frustrated by fear and longing one moment, soaring with anticipation the next. She headed down through woods to the creek bottom, needing solitude to untangle her thoughts. Good Voice's lodge stood on the edge of the village near the creek; she passed no others on her way, but the sense of being a stranger in a place of customs and speech not her own intensified. She'd tried to endure the discomfiture with the same equanimity Two Hawks had shown while living in Schenectady. As he would need to do for years to come . . . if he survived long enough for them to marry.

He would survive. He must. And Papa . . .

Birds were noisy in the trees. Then the creek's rush swelled around her, chattering over stones at its edge. Sunlight reflected off the water, but in the west thunderclouds were building dark against the bleached linen sky. The riverine air smelled of sunbaked mud.

They'd hurt Two Hawks in Schenectady. She didn't want to think about that either, but she couldn't make herself blind to all he was prepared to endure for her. To pretend it wasn't so would be unworthy of him, of their love. With Lydia and Papa supporting them, in time it would be easier. But it would never be *easy*.

Was there a way to live in both worlds? What would those worlds even look like on the other side of this war? Would one or the other have been obliterated?

Let them all come through this alive. Then they would look ahead to what came next.

Oh, but waiting, enduring, was hard.

A dragonfly hovered before her face, then drifted off along the creek. She watched it, praying for wisdom, patience, the safety of the men she loved, those loved by Good Voice and—

The clatter of pebbles had her turning so swiftly she nearly lost her balance on the stones at the creek's edge. Strikes-The-Water was coming down the bank, face set, dark eyes aglitter in the light spangling off the water.

The girl halted a pace away. "I go Oriska."

Anna blinked at her. "You're going after Clear Day?"

"I look for that one you are to make husband."

Redness rimmed the girl's eyes. She'd been hiding near enough to overhear that marriage arrangement. Had it upset her so?

"Strikes-The-Water, are you—" Anna began, but the girl backed away, chin held proud.

"Do not say me go."

"But why are you going?" Anna asked, uncertain if the girl would understand the question.

Strikes-The-Water's face was like carved wood, polished and hard. "His mother much good to me. She worry. More eyes to look, I go."

She was doing this for Good Voice? Or was that what she wanted Anna to think?

"I'll keep your going a secret as long as I can, but I will not lie about it," Anna said, a pain in her throat preventing her swallowing. "But if there's fighting . . . take care. Please. I wouldn't see you hurt."

Strikes-The-Water's eyes flared with surprise, but she shook her head as if she hadn't understood. Putting her back to Anna, she sprang up the creek bank and into the trees.

30

Fort Stanwix

Hunkered behind a deadfall's twisted roots, Two Hawks and Stone Thrower watched the ramparts of Fort Stanwix as the day drew to a close. The British had brought up a few of their big guns. An artillery camp was set up northeast of the fort. They'd had to skirt this and come at the fort with far more care than when Two Hawks left it at the start of the siege.

Still lacking most of their cannon and the soldiers laboring to bring them forward, the British were building breastworks to protect their camps. Indians and green-coat marksmen crept around the forest fringe south of the fort, sniping at sentries. Those within were sniping back. Deeper in the woods, some Oneidas were shooting at the British when chance offered.

Two Hawks flinched at every crack of firearms. The Oneidas were trying not to shoot at Mohawks or Senecas, only white soldiers, but William would look to them like any other green-coat of Johnson's regiment.

When Two Hawks left the fort after seeing Reginald Aubrey chased inside it, he and Skenandoah and Two-Kettles-Together had met Stone Thrower coming up from Kanowalohale with a band of warriors. After he told his father what he'd seen at the fort, they hadn't gone with the others to Oriska but retraced Two Hawks's steps to their present position. Two Hawks wondered what was happening at Oriska. Would Herkimer's militia come before St. Leger's guns arrived to aid the siege? Would St. Leger decide he had enough warriors to leave a guard on the fort and set off down the valley to wreak destruction? His father believed St. Leger wouldn't be so foolish as to turn his back on a hornet's nest, leaving the hornets to come swarming after him. He must first destroy the nest.

"What do we do?" he asked, gaze trained on the fort while the sun hung low in the sky, shining between clouds that rumbled but hoarded their rain. "Do we seek for my brother or try to get into that fort to reach Aubrey?"

His father's profile appeared composed, save for the gathering of his bold brows. "I am praying about it now. Do you think that one now trapped in the fort meant to go in there?"

"He came with those bateaux and was still outside the fort when the warriors attacked. It may be he was trying to leave, to go back downriver, but it was too late." Two Hawks felt his gut clench at the memory of Anna Catherine's father running for his life, how near that life had come to being taken.

"I made him promise me a thing," Stone Thrower said, still looking at the shadowy fort. "The day I gave him the white beads. I made him promise not to go after your brother alone. I said we would do it together. At the time I thought only to keep him from going off and making matters worse, but now I see it has all been working toward this, our paths coming together again, here in this place, with your brother so near. I do not know why Aubrey has come here. Perhaps it was because of something my uncle said. Perhaps not. But I will go down to him and see what Creator wills to happen next. I will get into the fort—after nightfall I will do it."

"Then I will go into the enemy camp and find my brother." Two Hawks had been thinking of this as he and his father ran the distance back to the fort but hadn't spoken of it until now.

Stone Thrower looked at him sternly, alarm in his gaze. "No. That is too dangerous. I meant to send you back to Ahnyero and our warriors."

Two Hawks felt the familiar frustration rising. "They will be attached to the militia regiments, coming along to this place to keep these

British and their warriors from coming through our lands. That is not dangerous?"

Stone Thrower nudged him back behind the fallen tree. The smell of rotting leaves was strong, and the smell of their sweat and the earth. "There is no path going away from this place that does not lead through danger. But leave the finding of your brother to me and Aubrey, who are bound by the promise."

Two Hawks wanted to protest, but his father clutched his arm. The light in the forest was dimming, yet the regret in his father's face was plain.

"Listen to me," Stone Thrower said, the words thick with feeling. "I have not always been a good father. Many times I made you think you disappointed me, that my heart was fixed on your lost brother so that I could not see *you*. But that was not true in my heart. I would take back every one of those times if I could." Stone Thrower's fingers gripped fiercely, as if to drive the truth of his words into his son's very bones. "You make this warrior hold his head proud whenever he sees you, whenever he thinks of you. Remember that as you go. Be of good courage—and keep yourself whole."

It was the blessing of a warrior but also of a father. Strength and love. For a moment they stayed thus, Two Hawks awash in both, unable to speak. At last he said, "I will go back to Ahnyero and do my best to stay alive. But I will not shrink back from what Creator sets before me to do."

Stone Thrower's hand left his shoulder only to cup his neck.

"I would never think it of you." He pulled Two Hawks's head forward until their foreheads pressed together. "May Creator give you wisdom and keep you strong."

It was full dark before Stone Thrower left their place of hiding. In seconds he was gone among the trees, the rustle of his steps dying to silence. Two

Hawks fastened his gaze on the small side gate where already they had watched another Oneida scout make it through the enemy's thin line—and been shot at in so doing.

His heart beat hard as he waited, never taking his eyes off the cleared ground near the fort, until a figure, hardly more than a shadow, came out of a depression in the ground and seemed to crawl across the open space between that last cover and the fort, so low did he hunch himself to run. The shadow nearly made it to the gate before the first shot fired.

Two Hawks's belly clenched, but the figure did not fall. More shots cracked before his father reached the gate, but he never stumbled. The gate opened wide enough for a man to slip through. Then it shut.

Two Hawks stayed where he was, panting as if he'd been the one dodging and running. He bowed his head against his knees, reaching for the presence of the God whose wisdom and strength his father prayed he would receive and walk in, then rose to make his careful way back to Oriska.

31

August 5, 1777
Fort Stanwix

*T*hey'd set fire to an abandoned barracks outside the fort the previous evening. In the dark of predawn, smoke lingered on the air.
Such hadn't dampened the spirits of Joseph Brant's warriors. Along with
Watts's company and some of Butler's rangers, they'd positioned themselves around the fort, taking cover where they could. From behind a
breastwork of turf and logs hastily erected the previous day, William
peered into darkness just beginning to lift. He could make out the fort's
pickets, the bulk of the glacis and ramparts beyond. All was silent, until in
the wood behind him a cardinal loosed a string of short whistles that
ended on a low trill, not unlike the vibration of a plucked bowstring.

Though he'd done so twice already, William groped in the dark to
check his rifle's priming—his musket was in Sir John's camp, along with
the Welsh bow; the cardinal's song made him think of it and briefly wonder what the Indians would think if he brought *that* out—then settled
himself to await the light.

A moment later, down the line to westward, a sharp popping arose;
from the fort the cry of someone wounded.

William jerked, startled. Shouts and yelps of triumph left him reason-
ing his way through a morass of dread. Reginald Aubrey wouldn't be on
the wall. Wasn't part of any regiment, not with that bad hip. Like as not
he'd just been jarred awake in one of the barracks . . . yet William couldn't

know for certain. Thanks to Sergeant Campbell, he hadn't even spoken to Tice before the captain approached the fort under the white flag.

Not that it would have mattered, as it happened. Tice had been escorted blindfolded to Gansevoort's headquarters, where he'd remained for the time it took the rebel colonel to dismiss St. Leger's demands. The little Tice observed within the fort had flattened the general's crest. The garrison was strong, its commanding officers seemingly immune to intimidation. St. Leger would have to take Stanwix the hard way—once his artillery and supplies were brought forward.

Rather than spend the time necessary clearing the creek, the general had ordered a road cut along an old footpath. The bulk of Johnson's regiment was detailed to assist in that backbreaking work. William had volunteered to join those grabbing up axes and trudging off westward. Watts had refused him. "You're too good a marksman to waste on road building."

So might he have been, had his heart been in it.

Earlier, another Yorker had taken cover behind the breastwork. William had barely glanced aside, it being too dark to discern features, but when his start at the morning's first firing drew a snigger, he swiveled to face Archie MacKay, Robbie's elder brother.

"Lucky shot, that?" Archie asked, a hint of scorn in his tone.

"Aye," William said. "Who could see in this murk?"

"Indians, or so I hear. See like wolves in the dark." When William made no reply, Archie nudged him with his rifle barrel. "What say ye, Aubrey? Do they?"

William leaned against the breastwork, peering through a crack in the logs at nothing. Campbell or the guard outside St. Leger's tent—likely both—had been spreading rumor of him. "I've no notion what they see," he muttered.

"No?" Archie prodded. "If *ye* dinna, then who—look there!"

An arrow, bright with flame, streaked a blazing arc through the graying dawn toward the fort, disappearing behind the ramparts.

They watched. Waited. No fire sprang up within the fort.

Off to the east more fiery arrows flew, engendering derisive shouts from the fort's defenders. Someone on the rampart shot into the gloom. The ball thudded into turf paces from William's breastwork.

So dawned another day of siege.

Inside the militia barracks, on his straw pallet near the doorway, Reginald awakened to the crack of the day's first gunfire. He lay rigid in all his limbs, heart pounding, mind readjusting again to time and place. *Stanwix. Not Fort William Henry.*

One thing hadn't changed in the span of years since the last siege he'd endured. He was still groping in the dark to find his way . . . and missing the path completely. Redemption remained elusive. Because it didn't exist? Lydia believed nothing he could do would make right that terrible wrong he committed. Perhaps all along she'd seen it, and him, more clearly than anyone.

As he lay there beset by fleas and the deeper torments of fear, confusion, and dread, he ached for Lydia. He yearned to see her, touch her, hear whatever wisdom she might have to speak into his soul, wanted her by his side for the rest of his days. If he survived this siege and whatever followed, he would find the courage to make it happen. But he couldn't think of the kiss they'd shared on the quay, the hope and fear and love in her eyes as he told her he was bound upriver, without thinking of Clear Day and the words exchanged inside the office on the Binne Kill.

"I cannot wait for William," he'd told the old Indian. "Now you tell me he is part of Johnson's regiment at Oswego, I cannot wait for him to come marching to me at the head of an army. I must go to him. Convince him his course is a wrong one."

He still cringed to remember what Clear Day had said to that.

"The way you long for the return of that one you call son is the same way his parents have longed for him these many seasons of his life."

As those words hung in the air, Reginald had felt the decay of his sins like a desiccation in his bones. The Indian had drilled him with a steady gaze, unbearable—until Reginald had seen the gentleness behind it.

"Listen. I am telling you a thing you must understand and believe—that what you feel now is what your Father in Heaven feels for you, waiting and waiting for you to come back to Him, longing to run after you, to search you out. To show you a good path to walk."

Against thee, thee only, have I sinned . . .

Reginald had reared up his head, startled by the intrusion of scripture into his roiling thoughts. It had shaken him, hearing the voice of his Father in Heaven again after so long a silence. He'd flinched from it even as his parched soul yearned for it to wash over him. Cleanse him.

It wasn't so simple. He'd not sinned against the Almighty alone but against so many others. The evils laid to his account hadn't ceased their enumeration despite the mercy of the Oneidas he'd wounded. They went on in the void of his soul, stone piled on stone, a crushing culpability.

Then Clear Day had said, "But facing Creator without a breechclout to cover one's nakedness takes courage. My nephew found the courage to do it while he bled before you, on his knees with the white beads in his hands. Have you that courage now?"

Stone Thrower. In desperation he'd latched onto thought of William's father, an impulse for action, something he could *do,* crystallizing in an instant.

"Look you, I shall go upriver," he'd told Clear Day. "To Stone Thrower. There's a promise between him and me. I'll find him. Together we'll find William, restore him. Make it right . . ."

He'd dared to hope it was the Almighty's leading. But he hadn't found Stone Thrower, and now the pit of guilt and despair that had greeted him daily for two decades opened beneath his heart and he braced himself to keep from falling down into it again.

Around him men were beginning to stir, rustling straw, fouling the smoky, clammy air with their unwashed flesh and stale breath and night waste, groaning with weariness and dread for what they would face that day.

From outside the barracks rose a flurry of shouts and barked orders, voices tinged with alarm. It would be more flaming arrows, shot from Indian bowstrings. Thus far no fires had taken serious hold. No structures had been lost. Resigned to rising to help deal with the nuisance, Reginald opened his eyes—and sucked in a startled breath. Silhouetted in the gray of the open doorway stood a figure, tall and wide shouldered, long haired, the toes of his moccasins inches from Reginald's nose.

"You have seen my uncle?" Stone Thrower asked calmly.

Reginald managed to unfreeze his flesh enough to nod in affirmation.

"*Iyo.* Come, leave this stinking place. We will talk." The Indian turned and went out of the barracks.

He found Stone Thrower waiting outside the door. In the half light of a clouded predawn, soldiers scurried about, dousing fires engendered by the arrows still sailing over the fort walls every few moments. Reginald pressed close to the barracks wall, but Stone Thrower behaved as though all was calm around them, putting his back to the fort and facing Reginald. "My uncle is well? He is safe?"

Voice still hoarse from sleep, Reginald said, "He wouldn't come upriver with me no matter how I urged. He'd someone waiting for him near my farm. That is what he said."

Stone Thrower gazed at him, face unreadable in the barely lifted dark. "One went with him to that place."

"Two Hawks?" Reginald was thinking of Anna, who'd pleaded to come with him upriver to find that young man.

"My son is gone to Oriska to meet the warriors who will join with that general coming to help these ones here."

"General Herkimer. I met with him on my way upriver. He was preparing to come." Reginald paused, pinned to the barracks wall not by fear of arrows but by that dark gaze searching his face with unbearable scrutiny. He was at once overjoyed to see the man and ashamed to stand before him. "By now I expect Clear Day is back at Kanowalohale. He told me Wil . . ."

But his throat closed over William's name.

Silence lengthened, punctuated by shouts as arrows arced over the turf and timber walls.

"I know what he told you," Stone Thrower said.

Men were issuing from the barracks now, grumbling, cursing, staggering in weariness. It was as familiar as if Fort William Henry had happened yesterday. Only this time he was trapped with the father of the babe he'd stolen then.

The moment couldn't have felt more surreal.

Stone Thrower grasped his arm and led him away from the busy barracks to the cabin used as a trade store for the Oneidas. The air within was stale, smelling of ashes and the few skins lying stacked on largely empty tables. Stone Thrower left the door open for what light there was to see and pushed Reginald inside.

Unable to bear the tension, Reginald wrenched from the man's hold and faced him. "How are you come here? And when?"

"Our enemy's lines are thin. I made it through in the night."

"When you were safe out of this? Why did you not go to Oriska with Two Hawks?"

"My son was watching and saw you chased inside this fort. He told me of it, and so I have come for you."

"For me?"

Stone Thrower frowned. "Of course for you. There is a promise between us. But we must leave this fort to see it fulfilled."

Hearing nigh the very words he'd spoken to Clear Day, the blood rushed from Reginald's head so quickly he nearly swayed off his feet. He braced them wide. What he'd expected from the man he didn't know, but this matter-of-fact readiness, this willingness to unite, as though he'd known all along this was how it would all unfold, struck him like a blow to the senses.

Deeper still. To the marrow of his bones. Where once had been desiccation there surged now something fresh, vital, blood-red strong.

"William. You've come to help me find him?" Every syllable seared his throat, squeezing past the lump formed there. It was an emotion he'd denied himself so long it took him a stunned moment to identify it. *Hope.*

Had he heard the Almighty after all? Had he done a right thing in coming upriver? Not a wholly selfish thing, a foolishly desperate, groping-blind thing?

"It is what we agreed to do," Stone Thrower said simply. "Creator has brought our paths together again for His purpose. So let us be about the doing of it."

Reginald found his voice again, forced the words past his tightened throat, afraid hope would slip away as quickly as it had formed. "How? We're trapped now, the pair of us. Helpless to do anything for anyone, much less for William."

"Helpless?" The Oneida warrior stared at him as if it were a word he didn't know. "Do you still not understand? With Heavenly Father, that Great Warrior and God of all flesh, nothing is impossible. Even men trapped in forts He can set free if He wills to."

The words smote Reginald like a hatchet to his chest. He looked into the dark eyes waiting for his response and saw all that his own hand had wreaked in the man's soul, the suffering, the brokenness, the pain and grief. Healing now, but the wounds were there to see, would be for the rest of his days.

He'd known such was the case, but not until this moment had he truly comprehended the breadth and height and width of the pain that had lived behind the eyes of the warrior who'd chosen, in a clearing at the wood's edge, not to take revenge but to offer friendship. Was still offering it now.

And more. He'd risked his life to fulfill a promise made with the giving of those white beads Reginald had carried upriver tucked inside his coat—those beads, and nothing less than his yielded soul. Submitted, at rest, and victorious. *This* was what the Almighty could do with a man, if he would only submit his heart.

The blade in Reginald's chest twisted. He could deny it no longer. Not in the face of this obstinate grace, this unrelenting mercy, this encompassing peace. God had not abandoned him. Since Fort William Henry *he* had turned his back on the Almighty. *He* had closed his heart. He'd left his soul trapped and besieged in a fort that wouldn't surrender.

Oh, Lydia. She'd tried so often, by so many means, to tell him as much. Yet despite his miserable failings, despite his neglect and rejection, the Almighty had preserved in her a love for him that seemingly knew no bounds, could not be quenched. He'd seen it in her eyes on the quay at their parting.

Grace again, boundless, outrageous. He didn't deserve her. He didn't deserve a God still standing there waiting outside the fort of his soul, arms outstretched to receive him. The Almighty had taken him back to a place as near as could be to that in which Reginald had turned his back on him. Another besieged fort. And to this man whose son he carried away out of the first. Standing before Stone Thrower, he opened his heart, yielded it, and let it break.

For I acknowledge my transgressions: and my sin is ever before me . . .

He bowed his head and wept.

Make me to hear joy and gladness; that the bones which thou hast broken may rejoice. Deliver me from my guilt, O Lord, for it was against You I sinned.

The touch of a powerful hand on his shoulder was gentle.

Reginald raised his head. Stone Thrower's other hand was outstretched to him. He grasped it, full to bursting with words, unable to speak them. Not one.

William's father looked at him, eyes narrowed in scrutiny. Outside the light of morning had brightened, silhouetting the Indian, obscuring his expression.

"*Iyo,*" Stone Thrower said, the word warm with satisfaction. "At last we are ready to find our lost one."

32

August 5, 1777
Fort Stanwix

*T*he sun rose, but William never saw it. Dawn's gloom merely brightened, revealing the clouds that had obscured the stars. A haze hung over the fort, drifting down to the river with its abandoned bateaux. Once the light improved, Archie MacKay left their shared breastwork for other cover—or more desirable company. Morning passed, punctuated by rifle barks. William hoped no one noticed how often he fouled his aim or was looking elsewhere when someone made himself a target on the walls.

Late in the morning, an Indian came dodging out of the wood and took cover with him so abruptly, William thought himself under attack. Then he recognized Joseph Brant, who flashed him a grin made fierce by war paint and crested turkey feathers.

"They nearly had me," he said, deep chest heaving in breath beneath a calico shirt, the tails of which bore the ragged passage of a musket ball.

"Who?" With his rifle trained, William's gaze darted toward the tangle of grapevine-choked trees from which the Mohawk had appeared, expecting gray-clad militia to burst forth next.

Brant pushed aside the barrel of William's rifle, then winced at its heat, shaking scorched fingers. "Oneidas. I was ambushed coming from St. Leger's camp. But I fought my way free. They did not follow."

Even so, William felt his belly seize. Oneidas. Had the war chief heard the tales of him spreading through camp? He scrutinized the broad, striking face of the man crouched beside him but saw no knowledge of it in his gaze.

One of the fort guns fired. The ground before the breastwork erupted in flying clods. Earth and grass showered down. Along the British line, shouts and whoops and rifles answered. Brant rose in a crouch and loosed a scream of defiance that set William's scalp crawling. "You've come from St. Leger? Have you news?"

Settled back on his heels, Brant made a sound of derision. "That one will not let us go into the valley, even to raid. Now it is trenches he wants dug so he can drop his mortar shells into the fort."

A reasonable step, all things considered. Before William could say so, an explosion of rifle fire from high in a nearby tree was followed by an agonized cry from within the fort. From the leafy foliage came a drift of powder smoke and an exultant whoop.

The warrior, Ki, had made another kill.

Since dawn William had kept one eye on the Indian marksman fond of firing from treetops. Ki was patient, and he rarely missed. He fired no more than twice from a tree before quickly descending to choose another perch—laughing while the garrison sent a harmless rash of return fire at the vacated branches. Now he was climbing a tree some twenty yards from William, nearer the fort than any he'd yet chosen. Ki was growing brazen.

So was someone on the ramparts. A particular soldier appeared to be taunting Ki, pacing back and forth across an embrasure, pausing to gaze out briefly before disappearing. Laughter floated on the smoke-hazed air; Ki had seen the sentry. So had those gathered below his perch, eager for another kill.

William watched the rampart, certain the soldier wouldn't dare reappear in the opening . . . but he did. Leastwise his hat appeared.

Ki's rifle barked. The hat fell as a scream rang out. Soldiers and Indians on the field erupted in cries of triumph. Ki lowered his rifle for a reload.

William kept his gaze fixed on the rampart, his heart constricted. A cannon crew had moved a gun into a new position, aimed toward the cloud of powder smoke still drifting from Ki's tree.

A shout came from the wall. A spotter's shout.

Brant gave a warning cry, but the cannon's roar drowned it an instant before the upper branches of Ki's tree were torn to pieces by a blast of grapeshot. So was Ki, who tumbled from his perch to land in a bloody heap. Others wounded by flying metal writhed on the ground. A new roar filled the muggy air: cheers from what sounded like the entire fort garrison, celebrating Ki's demise.

Brant's face was set in fury. "They will die beneath our blades," he pronounced, nostrils flaring as he breathed his rage. "Every one of them."

The Mohawk rose to take Ki's remains from the field and see to those wounded from the blast. William held his position and didn't watch him go.

After Ki's death, some of the Indians quit the field to tend their wounded, but late in the afternoon William noticed a significant number of them abandoning the line, melting back toward the camps. Out of water and cartridges, William followed their lead.

Dashing between points of cover, he reached the Royal Yorker camp, where the explanation for the Indians' withdrawal met him. A message had arrived for Brant, sent from his sister, Sir William's widow, Molly. The Tryon County militia had mustered to relieve Fort Stanwix. They'd marched from Fort Dayton at German Flatts the previous day and had nearly reached Oriska, an Oneida town but a dozen miles eastward.

"St. Leger's sending the Indians to meet them—with an ambush!" was the word from the general's camp.

Unwilling to wait for an attack on his present position, to be joined by a sally from the fort, St. Leger had chosen to head off the Tryon militia at a distance. He'd ordered Colonel Butler to take his rangers and the Indians and prevent the rebel reinforcements getting through.

William watched them go, twenty rangers and upward of eight hundred Indians—two hundred Senecas, the rest Mohawks, other Iroquois, and Mississaugas from the Lakes. Though they'd left their colorful finery in camp, they'd painted themselves afresh and were fairly bristling with muskets, clubs, bows, and hatchets, weapons and scalp-locks bedecked with feathers of assorted hues. In the coming dusk they made a dazzling sight. William was both relieved he wouldn't be fighting them and filled with dread at thought of a father and brother who might well be about to do so.

As the last of Brant's warriors filed from camp into the shadowed wood, headed east toward the coming militia and their Oneida allies, he thought of Joseph Tames-His-Horse, who'd chosen not to fight this battle. Not for the first time he envied the freedom of an Indian to come and go as he saw fit, to change his mind if his heart was leading elsewhere . . .

He was turning reluctantly back toward that hateful breastwork— there was still light for shooting—when Captain Watts arrived in camp with word that Sir John had pressed his regiment's services to bolster the ambuscade and was now in command of the detachment. Watts handpicked the men who would go, William among them. They'd time to gather their gear—William trading rifle for musket and bayonet—replenish their cartridge boxes, powder, rations, and canteens, before filing out on the heels of Brant and Butler.

William trudged through the gathering dusk, wishing mightily he'd heeded Anna's pleading as night's coming leached color from the wood enfolding him now. At least she was far removed from this, away in Schenectady with Lydia. Safe.

Or were they safe? With Reginald Aubrey trapped in the fort, who was watching over them? And his mother . . . was she somewhere safe, guarded by his father and brother? Or were those two among the approaching militia, destined to meet him at last across the barrel of his musket?

"You turned your coat." Maybe it was within his scope to do so, he conceded now, but he mustn't. What was left to him now but his honor, his duty? Cold companions both, he clutched them near and followed Captain Watts into the wood.

Two Hawks had spent the night in Oriska after making his cautious way east. As dusk fell again, he came out with other warriors gathered in the town to find the militia of the American general, Herkimer, camped nearby in their passage to the fort.

Spotty rain had fallen during the day. It hadn't broken the heat that clung like a sopping blanket. Sunset brought fireflies lighting the brush through which they filed. From a distance that was what the small fires in a clearing off the road appeared to be—fireflies in the dusk. But when the warriors neared, they murmured over the small numbers they saw at the fires. Two Hawks heard a warrior talking, one who'd spoken to a militia colonel; over half the brigade was strung out miles down the rutted road that linked German Flatts to the Carrying Place.

While he made camp with Ahnyero and others—among whom he was pleased to find the Caughnawaga Louis Cook, whom he'd last seen at Oswego—Two Hawks learned the reason for this scattering. Many of Herkimer's Tryon brigade had come long distances from their farms to muster at Fort Dayton. Already worn from travel, unaccustomed to marching in the heat with heavy packs, many had fallen out and pitched camp where they halted. Only the head of the command and the main column had reached Oriska.

Uncertain if these farmer-soldiers would prove equal to the British he'd seen at the fort—not to mention Thayendanegea's warriors—Two Hawks left Ahnyero's fire and made his way toward the militia clearing, situated across a narrow ravine. On his way he spoke to Honyery Doxtater and his wife, Two-Kettles-Together, who had made it through with old Skenandoah. He shared word of Stone Thrower, how he'd gotten inside the fort. In turn he learned the militia officers had sent runners ahead to Stanwix requesting Gansevoort send out a sortie to them if the sound of battle was heard on the morrow, and to fire the fort cannons three times when the message was received.

It was full dark before he descended the ravine, picked his way across a runlet at its foot, then climbed up through trees to the other side. No sentries challenged him.

Across the clearing, a large tent stood. Two Hawks supposed it belonged to the general over them all, Nicholas Herkimer. A few more makeshift canvases had been raised, but most of these men would sleep on the open ground.

Passing along the edge of shadow, Two Hawks studied these men slung with powder horns and shot bags, sitting in the smoke from their small fires to discourage mosquitoes. Not one dressed exactly like another. Some wore tailed coats and waistcoats, their heads topped with fine cocked hats. Many were clad in fringed shirts of rough cloth or deerskin, floppy hats stuck through with feathers, moccasins on their feet. Most were armed with muskets, a few with rifles, their belts thrust through with bayonets, hatchets, knives, and pistols besides.

The camp was subdued. No music, no singing, no laughter rang out. There was only the clank of a pot, the chop of an ax, the hiss of water on embers, low voices conversing about food or gear. Already some slept, rolled in blankets or laid out in trampled ferns.

He wasn't the only Indian come over to the neighboring camp. Some Oneidas were friends with men here or had traded with them. A few were related through the marriages of sisters or daughters. As he would one day be, Heavenly Father willing.

Since leaving Kanowalohale, he'd tried not to think of Anna Catherine. Not too much. A warrior kept his head clear for battle. But he couldn't stop the upswell of longing to be with her, living in peace. Many branches still strewed the path to that place and time. Her father. His brother. This war. His life had become a blowdown of timber, something waiting to trip him up whichever way he turned.

He supposed that was true for all these here. Around him at the fires were men who called themselves Germans going off to fight Germans in the army of St. Leger. Men who once called themselves Englishmen going to fight other Englishmen. Oneidas going along to face Mohawks, Senecas, Cayugas.

Me going to face my brother.

Stopping short, Two Hawks reached for a nearby tree, its trunk smooth beneath his hand. Of course he'd had the thought before. He'd often hovered round it as he did these white men's fires, but until this moment he'd managed not to stare it straight on. Now all he could do was pray.

Let me find him—but not at the end of my gun barrel.

33

August 6, 1777
Oriskany Creek

*T*he sun was rising toward another sweltering day. In their camps, warriors and militia had risen and readied themselves . . . still no distant blast of cannon came rolling over wood and ridge. Across the ravine in the soldier camp, General Herkimer argued with his battalion colonels over what to do. Two Hawks knew it. So did everyone with ears.

Militia companies had straggled in since before dawn. Some waited on the road, ready to march. Others crowded into the clearing, within hearing of their commanding officers' rancorous words over whether to wait for the fort cannon's firing or push on regardless. Herkimer wanted to wait. Most of his colonels wanted to hurry forward.

They should send us to scout while they decide. Two Hawks was about to voice the thought to Ahnyero when a soldier arrived to say the scout was wanted by the general. Ahnyero hurried away.

Two Hawks settled by the fire's ashes and checked the powder, shot, and flints in the bag he wore at his side. Except for the bag and his weapons, he was stripped to breechclout and moccasins. Nearly all the warriors around him were painted red or black, the colors of strength and power. Two Hawks wasn't painted. He intended more than fighting this day, more than standing between this enemy and those they threatened. Despite his father's instruction, he meant to find William, if William could be found. Whether his brother would recognize his likeness in Two Hawks's face, now his head was shaved, was doubtful. If he painted himself, there was no hope of it.

He leapt to his feet at Ahnyero's swift return. On the road, dust was stirring. The militia column had started forward. Still he blurted in surprise, "They go ahead?"

Warriors and sachems gathered around to hear the answer to that question balanced on all their tongues.

"They called that one who leads them *coward,* those colonels," Ahnyero said, still catching his breath. "For wanting to await the signal, they all but called him traitor. Herkimer lost his temper. He bid them march."

"He sends no scouts?" Honyery said in disbelief.

"Too many of them do not trust us, brothers. I am sad to say it. But that doesn't mean we must hang back. You," Ahnyero said to one standing by, "come with me. And you." He chose several more warriors. "Thayendanegea knows these hills. There will be ambush waiting. Let us keep these ones from blundering into it if we can."

"Take me with you." Two Hawks grabbed Ahnyero's arm before he stepped away, but Ahnyero shook his head.

"It is a bad feeling I have about this day. You stay back with these soldiers, flank them if you will, but do not come ahead."

Two Hawks clenched his jaw, sick to his marrow of being pushed aside out of danger. Then he looked into Ahnyero's eyes and knew there would be danger for all today, no matter where they met it.

Ahnyero grasped his arm in farewell. "Listen for my voice. If there is ambush, I will not be silent about it."

The warrior-blacksmith took up his shot bag, slung his rifle at his shoulder, and ran to join the scouts hurrying to get ahead of the militia column led by the insulted General Herkimer astride a white horse.

William had passed half a mosquito-bitten night dozing in the position he'd taken up with the rest of the company. Morning brought light enough to see beyond the beech tree he'd leaned against and a climbing heat that already had him sweating through his coat. The uniform green of the Royal Yorkers made for decent woodland concealment, but the wool was stifling.

He washed down stale bread with a swig from his canteen, as did the rest of Watts's marksmen staggered out to either side of him along the ridgeline. On his left was young Robbie MacKay, with whom he'd been paired to fire since Sam's desertion. The lad was visibly trembling.

A corporal came by to inspect their readiness and collect knapsacks to convey to a site for safekeeping through the coming fight. William checked his flint, priming, cartridges, saw Robbie did likewise. They were perched some forty yards up a slope thickly wooded and choked with brush. Below and to the east ran a wide ravine with a shallow stream at its center. William couldn't see the road that climbed out of the ravine, ascending a ridge to the east, but knew what lay beyond that rise of land studded with hemlocks. Word had spread of the ambush conceived by Joseph Brant and the Seneca war chiefs, Cornplanter and Old Smoke. Yet another ravine lay beyond that ridge, a boggy creek at its bottom. The road from the east crossed the swampy ground on a causeway of corduroy logs, then climbed the dividing ridge, a passage no army traveling with cumbersome baggage wagons could negotiate with speed.

Before dawn, Cornplanter and Old Smoke had arrayed their Seneca warriors across both slopes of the western ravine, while Brant took his Mohawks east of the dividing ridge. Once Herkimer's regiments were over that ridge and down the other side, it was there in the western ravine, some six miles from the fort, the trap would be sprung. There the Royal Yorkers must halt the brigade's march, while Brant and his Mohawks cut off their retreat and the Senecas and rangers swarmed down upon them from both sides.

Most of the marksmen lay in wait on higher ground, while the Indians concealed themselves within the lower trees, ready to rush the rebels after the first volley of fire. William knew they were there but couldn't see them. He'd memorized the few square yards he could see. The mottled trunk of the beech. Trampled moss and ferns around its base. The debris of beechnut shells where some small animal had made a repast. Beyond that, he was as blind as the rebels coming up the road would be should they scan the slopes to either side.

He waited, sweated, anticipating the first sign of the rebel vanguard coming into sight, heat dulling his thinking despite the quickened current of his blood. Impressions of his surroundings penetrated in fragments . . . the rising tension of his fellow Yorkers, reddened faces glimpsed through summer foliage; a muffled cough; a curse; the whine of mosquitoes; the drone of flies.

At some point, he realized the morning, though warming, was no longer brightening. He gazed upward through spreading branches. The overcast had thickened, darkened, though he'd heard no thunder. A murmur reached him on the still air, a voice praying: "Our Father, who art in heaven, hallowed be Thy name . . ."

In that singular moment, knowing he might well be drawing his last peaceful breaths on earth, it came to William with clarity and a longing that wrenched his gut; he knew what it was he wanted. A father, one who would never betray him. Maybe that father existed only in Heaven, not on earth, but he wanted to survive this so he could find it out.

Help. Please. A pathetic prayer, but it was the best he had and *for all the love* what was taking this Herkimer so long? Had the ambuscade been detected? Were they being flanked by the rebel militia even now, about to be the ones taken unawares?

A few yards off, someone raised the very question, sharp with the unbearable stretching of nerves. Someone else told him to shut it. Then like a heralding breeze, word came rippling along their hidden ranks. A vanguard of scouts ranging ahead of the column, pausing to drink at the stream farther back along the ravine, had been taken out with silent arrows, their bodies dragged into the brush. Oneidas.

The air was heavy, still, as if the life had been sucked out of it. William gripped his musket as he strained to catch movement, some sign of Herkimer's advancing column. Eerie silence cloaked the ravine, save the faint chatter of the stream and the buzz of insects . . . which became the buzz of voices, swelling louder, and the tramp of feet, the clank of metal, the creak of leather.

William waited for Watts's signal.

At the popping of muskets, he nearly jumped straight into the air. Startlement erupted to his left and right, followed by bewildered questions. The rebel column wasn't yet in sight. Had the trap been sprung too soon?

Before the shots finished echoing, trilling screams filled the air. The Indians were rushing into battle. Shouts and the crack of firearms clashed. Then Captain Watts was shouting, "Forward and hold the road!" and William was out from behind the beech tree, skidding through the brush, hurtling down the slope, beside him the frightened blue of Robbie's eyes.

They burst from cover, running toward the smoke of battle where one resonant, commanding voice could be heard above the din.

Halfway down the ridge between the ravines, Two Hawks heard the bellowing voice of Nicholas Herkimer, saw the general on his white horse passing back along the lines of the first and second regiments pinned at the bottom of the western ravine, clustered in knots. The bodies of those struck down in the first volley of gunfire littered the road. The general's horse leapt them, dodging warriors who came rushing from the trees with tomahawks and clubs. The Americans were caught in a panic, many rushing to and fro, running into one another, but some had kept their heads and were returning fire in ragged spurts, shooting into the onrushing warriors.

Horsemen of the regiment behind Two Hawks came swift along the steep road, hooves drumming beneath his moccasins. Oneida warriors who had hung back near the center of the column loosed their war cries and rushed forward on the descending road, dropping down into the battle below.

Two Hawks went with them, rifle gripped, tomahawk thrust through his sash. Fear clotted his throat, for himself and for Ahnyero, who'd given no warning of this ambush as he'd promised to do.

Pushing that fear down, he leapt to the side, took aim with his rifle, and fired at a ranger rushing out of the woods to his left to attack two militiamen fumbling to reload their guns. He was up and running as the ranger dropped, reloading as he went, keeping near Honyery and Two-Kettles-Together. For a time he fought beside them. Always moving. Never making himself a clear target. The fighting ways of Senecas and Mohawks were their own ways—hit fast and run. Deflecting their blades was a matter of timing and anticipation. That these were brothers attacking them was a blade that could not be deflected. That blade pierced deep.

They were in among the second militia regiment now, a welter of bodies lurching and grappling and bleeding, half-obscured by choking smoke. Shouts of "Close up! Form up!" shrilled between the firing of muskets and the screams of men. Two Hawks couldn't tell if this ambush was becoming a slaughter or reforming into a proper battle. He'd heard his father say that to judge a battle when you are in the midst of it is hard to do. Mostly a battle is what happens an arm's length away.

Not far past the length of Two Hawks's arm, there was Herkimer again, his horse struck, the beast falling to the road, white legs thrashing, pinning its rider. Men of the general's command rushed forward to pull him free. A volley erupted from a company on the road. The smoke of it came between Two Hawks and the general being helped into the wood, wounded. Then the militia, grappling with powder horns and ramrods, were rushed at again by painted warriors hacking with clubs and blades.

Two Hawks got busy fending off attack, mostly from rangers crashing through the wood. He struck at their grim faces, parried thrusts of blade and bayonet, looking for soldiers in Johnson's green coats but not seeing them. Had William's regiment taken no part in this? Were they back at the fort?

He staggered under the passing blow of a Seneca's club, which he caught and thrust aside with his rifle before it did more than glancing damage to the head it had meant to crush. That smarting head was thinking furiously: should he fight through the ravine to the other side, get to the fort, find his brother while all these Indians and rangers were away?

A Mississauga rushed at him. Two Hawks ducked and lunged aside. The warrior swept past, but in lunging, Two Hawks's foot came down in a boggy patch. He stumbled, pushed up, and ran in a crouch for the trees north of the ravine. He took a moment in cover to catch his breath, tugging free his tomahawk. Amazingly he was still within sight of many of the Oneidas he'd come out with from Oriska. He saw Honyery kill a man attacking him, then take a wound in the wrist. Two-Kettles-Together snatched away his rifle and reloaded it for her husband while he wielded his tomahawk in his unwounded hand. Louis Cook, in cover not far from Two Hawks, leapt into the open and fired a killing shot at an enemy marksman lying in the fork of a downed tree.

At the high, piercing scream of a woman, Two Hawks turned back, thinking it would be Two-Kettles-Together, but he didn't spot her now. Were there more women in this fight?

One at least. Hair in a long braid whipping behind, she came vaulting over the end of a fallen tree where smoke hung thick, drifting through the dense wood. Only for an instant did he see her, then she vanished into the drifting haze. But her face in that moment of screaming flight was frozen in his mind.

It was Strikes-The-Water.

34

With their first forward push into battle, the Royal Yorkers had kept in formation where the terrain allowed, clambering over down wood and rocks to get into combat. Halting at Watts's command, they'd taken cover and fired in pairs into the gray wall of militiamen pressed shoulder to shoulder in the road ahead. With no notion whether he'd hit anyone, William snatched a fresh cartridge and reloaded, only to find it impossible to fire again without hitting their own Indians darting in to attack the rebels, their struggles obscured by dust and smoke—friend and foe indistinguishable in the surging mass and the din of screams, commands, and gunfire.

Clusters of militia began breaking from the melee. Men retreated across the creek, scrambling for the trees. William felt a hot surge of hope that this might be quickly over. Then Watts ordered bayonets out. They were going to charge the fleeing rebels.

Instinct screamed to escape this hell, not plunge into its heart. Steeling himself, William took cover behind another tree, a pine oozing tangy resin into the heated morn. He fumbled the triangular blade from its scabbard. Around him bayonets locked into place with a clatter of metal sockets. Robbie MacKay's hands shook so badly he dropped his. William snatched it up and affixed it for him. They formed ranks in the road, and, led by Captain Watts and his lieutenants, the company advanced.

The rebels at the column's head, those still ambulatory, had reached the trees. Many were still visible, dodging fallen timber, blundering through thickets, scrabbling, a few crawling, dragging wounded limbs.

The Yorkers entered the wood, loosed a volley after the rebels, and, on the tide of a raging shout, charged through the acrid billow of their firing.

The land rose under William's feet. Dense heat and dimness closed around him. Smoke clogged his throat. He blinked streaming eyes clear in time to leap a man's body before he sprawled across the tilted slope, joints jarring as he landed. He slid backward in leaf mold and ducked to steady himself with a hand to the ground.

A hatchet hurled from an unseen hand sliced the air where his neck had been, taking the hat off his head. A musket ball plowed into a nearby stump in an explosion of woody matter that peppered his face like hornet stings. To his right another ball struck a Yorker he didn't recognize in the confusion; the man's face contorted in a scream. William was set upon next by the shooter, bearing his discharged gun as a club. The man had a gash through one powder-blackened eyebrow, dripping blood down his cheek; his eyes were blue and ginger lashed, his front teeth missing.

By instinct more than calculation William got his bayonet raised and met the charge with a repelling thrust. He felt the blade puncture cloth and skin, jar on bone, then slide in deep.

With a rush of foul breath, the man slammed the butt of his musket at William, catching him square in the chest, a blow that seemed to stop his beating heart. He lunged back, withdrawing the bayonet as the man slumped to the ground. William finished him, caught in a contradictory grip of grief and relief that shook him like a rat in a terrier's teeth.

Rebels were falling under blades left and right, Yorkers under the assault of hatchets and knives wielded by those cunning enough to avoid the bayonets. His heart was going again now, savage and desperate, slamming against bruised flesh. Beside him one of Watts's lieutenants—Singleton—used his musket to club a rebel militiaman. Driven to his knees, the man scrabbled for his dropped gun, swept the weapon around, and fired upward.

Singleton crumpled.

Militia were retreating deeper into the wood, up to the high ground between the ravines, brown- and beige- and gray-clad forms vanishing in brush and smoke. Others took cover to reload and fire back. The charge had faltered.

Amid the clamor, William heard Watts's voice shouting but couldn't make out the order. Press on? Retreat?

Singleton had taken the ball through his leg and was lying at William's feet cursing, bleeding. William grabbed the green coat of another Yorker stumbling past. They got the lieutenant on his feet and half-dragged him down to the road.

In the open William saw the other Yorker was Robbie, and he laughed to see the lad alive, making Singleton curse the more as they maneuvered him past bodies already plundered and scalped. Around them, others of Watts's company staggered from the trees clutching wounds, some supporting bleeding comrades, streaming sweat or tears down blood-grimed faces.

For the first time William wondered whether he'd been wounded beyond the bruising thrust he'd taken in the chest. He felt on the verge of toppling. But that was due to heat and fatigue and Singleton's dragging weight. They deposited him at last near the head of the ravine, in a clearing serving as depot for the soldiers' belongings and the wounded brought off the field—a place for the officers to regroup. A dozen prisoners were bound to trees, eyeing the Indians present with dread.

Once William saw Singleton into the regimental surgeon's care, then drained his canteen to slake a raging thirst, he realized Sir John was in the clearing, talking animatedly to the Seneca chiefs, Cornplanter and Old Smoke, while Colonel Butler and half a dozen of his rangers looked on. William couldn't make out what Johnson was saying; his own ears were ringing.

Spying Captain Watts standing behind the colonel, he edged nearer.

Sir John, flushed with heat and fury, wasn't best pleased with the

Senecas. "Your young warriors sprung the trap prematurely! Now Herkimer is entrenched, his regiments regrouping, our momentum stalled."

The gleaming faces of Cornplanter and Old Smoke were a study of rigid pride and resentment. Only their eyes showed the shock they felt at the ferocity of the battle still underway back up the ravine. Or perhaps its cost. William had passed through a sea of bodies littering the creek and road. Indian losses were nearly as heavy as those of loyalist and rebel.

"Herkimer's boys took the worst of it," Butler interjected. "No chance in a thousand they can rally to advance now."

"They are not defeated," Sir John countered. "They hold the one defensive position in this terrain Brant chose. Now you wish to inform me," he said, turning again to the Senecas, "that you've had enough and will not command your warriors to assault them again?"

Old Smoke spoke for them. "Too many have died, when it was promised we would not even have to fight. We wish revenge, but not at the cost of more brave men. We will have our revenge on these prisoners." The war chief swept an arm, banded with tattoos, at the captured militiamen slumped against the trees. "If the warriors wish to fight on, they may do so. That is for each to decide."

Sir John's jaw bulged with its clenching, but he kept his composure as he ground out, "Where is Brant?"

"He and his warriors plundered the baggage," Cornplanter said. "Some have gone after soldiers who fled east. They are running them down like wolves after deer."

"I could better use them here." Sir John looked around, finding Watts behind him. "How stands your company? What are your losses?"

Watts glanced toward the wounded, his gaze fastening on Singleton. A group of green-coated Yorkers came into the clearing, bringing in more injured. "Unconfirmed, sir. I expect they will be heavy. What I can confirm is that another bayonet charge will be an exercise in futility while the rebels are entrenched on that height. Futility and wasted lives," he added, sharing a look with Cornplanter.

"So, then, what I have to hand is a parcel of rangers, a battered company of infantry, and several hundred Indians no more easily corralled than wildcats." Frustration rose off Johnson like heat waves. He huffed a breath and jerked his head in a nod. "Very well. I shall report to St. Leger that the column is halted and dispatch reinforcements back to finish what we've begun. Then St. Leger can sweep down the valley as he wills."

Johnson parceled out further orders to Butler and the Senecas, undoubtedly instructing them to keep the rebels pinned, batter them, wear down their resistance. William didn't hear the particulars. His mind had stalled. *"Sweep down the valley as he wills."*

A band of Mississaugas came out of the wood, loaded with plunder from the wagons in the eastern ravine. They untied one of the prisoners and hauled the dazed man away, following Sir John toward the fort. William watched as if through dusty glass.

Captain Watts stood before him, frowning. His commanding officer asked a question. William shook his head. He couldn't hear. The ringing . . .

Watts said something more, then left him. William barely noticed. His whole being was focused on one hope, one prayer—*Let General Herkimer not falter now but hold that height as a castle impregnable.*

That such a thing might well cost the lives of his regiment, and his own, spent like water dashed on stone, seemed for the moment inconsequential.

Ordered to help with the wounded, he moved in a daze, wondering vaguely why Watts left him behind when the captain rounded up what remained of the company and returned to the fight.

He was holding the hand of a dead man when he realized the day had darkened. Surely not toward evening. No more than a couple of hours could have passed since the battle began. He looked up.

Above the clearing, clouds hung low and black. Thunder rumbled, ominous, deep. He heard the pop of firearms. Smelled the smoke of battle, and blood. And a heavier, more elemental smell.

He let go the dead man's hand and pushed to his feet through the stultifying heat. The Senecas were gone. So were Butler and his rangers. There were fewer prisoners tied to the tree. The surgeon was busy with the wounded who had any hope of surviving, while the rest lay dead or bleeding out onto the ground.

Something like an electrical current shot through his veins, rousing him fully. He could do it. Now. No one would know. He could follow Sam's lead and slip away . . .

Thunder cracked, deafening as cannon fire. A raindrop struck his cheek, fat and cold. Another hit his shoulder. More battered leaf and earth around him. That was all the warning before the heavens tore wide and a deluge came down.

35

Fort Stanwix

*M*iles to the east, the Tryon militia had engaged the bulk of St. Leger's Indians. Perhaps some of Johnson's Greens. From the ramparts they'd heard the muffled noise of it, seen smoke and dust rising in the distance, before General Herkimer's messengers made it through British lines into the fort. Gansevoort had blasted the cannon thrice as requested, though Reginald doubted whether the general or his brigade heard the sound above the battle's din. Under glowering skies, Lieutenant Colonel Willett had mustered a sortie to march through the gate—two hundred fifty volunteers from the New York and Massachusetts troops—when a violent rain broke over their heads and they were dispersed to gloomy barracks to wait it out. *Wait.* While men were dying in the wood to the east. While *William* might be dying.

Too tense to remain within, Reginald filled the doorway, containing his frantic impatience as the rain pounded the parade ground to a bog. The temperature had fallen with the rain. Given the stupefying heat of the past days, it ought to have brought relief. Reginald felt none.

What the warrior seated on a bench against the outer log wall was feeling, Reginald could only guess. Blue shirt pulled taut across broad shoulders, Stone Thrower bent over his knees, hands clasped, gazing at the wall of falling rain, lips moving in silent prayer. It was almost a jarring thought to realize he could do the same. Ought to be doing the same. *God in heaven . . . please.*

For nigh on an hour the rain had pounded down, diffusing the acrid smell of smoke that had hovered over the fort. Yesterday British artillery had managed to land a few mortars on the parade. The craters they'd left were turning to mud holes in the downpour. Reginald strained to hear anything beyond the incessant drumming and occasional roll of thunder moving off eastward. Images of blood-soaked earth, rain diluted, sought to capture his thoughts no matter how he beat them back. A shiver ran through him. He crossed his arms tighter, fending off the chill driving into his bones.

"They will have stopped for this." Stone Thrower looked up, understanding in his eyes. "His brother is also in that fight. We will find them. I believe this." Despite his words, his brow furrowed as he added, "Do you have them still?"

Knowing what was meant, Reginald put a hand into his coat and withdrew the three strings of wampum, white in the gloom under the barracks eaves. Stone Thrower's mouth lifted in a faint smile. *"Iyo."*

Reginald met the Indian's gaze. "Did you wish them back?"

"Keep them. Let them speak to you of our covenant. One day, when you no longer need to be reminded, pass them on in the spirit in which they were given. You have Creator's Spirit in you now to tell you what to do with them when the time comes."

Taken aback, Reginald asked, "How can you know that?"

"You do not see the fire over your head."

"Fire?" Reginald looked up and was greeted with a splash of rainwater from the eaves. He swiped it away. "What mean you?"

"The Spirit of Jesus came as fire when His people prayed and waited. Fire leaping over their heads. I do not see it with my eyes when I look at you now, but I see it."

The man knew of Pentecost. Reginald returned the beads to his coat but couldn't tear his gaze from William's father, so fascinated was he by this man he'd spent half his life fearing.

"What our enemy means for evil, Creator uses for good," Stone Thrower said. "That is a thing always to keep in mind."

The words were still on his lips when the violence of the rain abated. Reginald could see across the parade now, make out the ramparts, the drooping makeshift flag left out in the soaking. Voices within the barracks ceased as men paused to listen.

Stone Thrower was already on his feet when a shout rose from a southern-facing rampart. They lurched into the still-falling rain. Reginald's boot slid in pudding-thick mud and he nearly went down, but William's father grabbed his arm, his grip steady. They crossed the parade toward the rampart in time to reach Willett coming out of the officers' barracks.

"What see you?" Willett called to the sentry who'd shouted.

"Soldiers in green, sir, being recalled from the wood line!"

Reginald caught a breath. Perhaps all this while William had been in camp, not in the battle.

"They're calling in reinforcements," Willett said, interpreting the news with a lightening of countenance. "Which means Herkimer's still in the fight—and St. Leger's guard will be all the thinner on this ground."

Beside Reginald, hair rain beaded, Stone Thrower was tense as a panther set to spring, ready as he to finally take action. If Willett would lead his sortie out on the heels of Johnson's troops . . .

As if he'd read Reginald's silent urging, Willett turned to one of his captains. "Order the men assembled."

They'd marched in eerie silence down to the Upper Landing. Not a shot was fired from the trees. No Indians rushed them. They passed unopposed straight into Johnson's camp, and what few guards were about fled into the trees or across a nearby creek. A few wounded were found in tents and taken prisoner. It was of little concern to Reginald, who'd left the fort without a by-your-leave from anyone, not intending to return.

Flankers and scouts reported no opposition. The Royal Yorkers seen leaving the siege line had gone to engage Herkimer's forces, but when this should have been apparent to Willett, when he should have reformed the detachment now swarming over the camp, ransacking tents, looting the Yorkers' belongings, no such orders came. Reginald couldn't spot Willett, even to offer protest. After shouting the question to half a dozen Continentals, he was finally told Willett and some of the troops had moved on to the Six Nations camp to raid it as well.

"What are they doing? There's no time for such as this." He turned to Stone Thrower, who was watching what had begun as a sortie to relieve Herkimer devolve into a looting party. As the rain tapered off, from the east came the distant sputter of musket fire. Battle was rejoined.

"Leave them to this," Stone Thrower said. "We are only two, you and I, but enough for what we mean to do."

William had had the sense to cover his firelock when the rain began, wrapping it in oiled canvas. The violence of the downpour had distracted him from the impulsive notion of desertion long enough for the regimental surgeon to notice him again and call him back into service. Since then he'd helped bring the wounded deeper under the trees, where shelters were erected. By the time they had everyone under them, William was soaked, but the rain's chill did him the service of clearing his head. How close he'd come to doing exactly as Joseph Tames-His-Horse had dreamed . . .

The bark of musket fire down the ravine had ceased during the worst of the downpour but had resumed as the deluge lifted to a light patter. Not fool enough to go blundering alone back into combat, he'd settled under cover to await Watts's return or Johnson's reinforcements.

At last came the clank of arms, the tramp of booted feet. Watts arrived with several of the original company, moments before some seventy Yorkers from the camps emerged from the dripping trees, a captain called McDonell at their head. Of Johnson there was no sign. Watts spotted William and called him over, giving him hard scrutiny as he came.

The captain's brow cleared. "Back with us then, Private?"

"Yes sir." Shock . . . fatigue . . . whatever had dulled his senses, it had passed. He was ready now to—

Find your brother. Your father.

His mouth dried at the jarring thought. Thought? It had been a command. But what in heaven's name was he meant to do? Go back to the fort for Reginald Aubrey? Search among the corpses in that hellish ravine for two Oneidas he'd never met? Return to the fight and hope he somehow recognized their faces at the end of his musket *before* he killed them?

"Good," Watts was saying. "Fall in with McDonell's men. Now," the captain went on, addressing the officers present, "the challenge will be getting in close to the rebels again. They hold the high ground between the ravines. Herkimer's corralled them into defensive circles, and not even the Indians are breaking through."

William kept his face set, revealing nothing of his desperate hope. He wanted St. Leger's forces halted, an outcome that still seemed a possibility until Colonel Butler came rushing in with a handful of his rangers, bloodied from battle, wet from the rain. Watts deferred to Butler as the highest ranking officer in Sir John's absence. Taking in the presence of seventy Royal Yorkers fresh for the fight, Butler's grim countenance lit with a wolfish grin. He turned to the nearest private of Watts's command, which happened to be William, and barked, "Remove your coat, soldier!"

William gaped at the man. "Sir?"

Butler glared. "Take off . . . your . . . coat."

"Aye sir." Hastily, William removed his gear to comply, lowering musket, cartridge box, and the rest to the ground. The coat was still wet and clung. At last he wrenched his arms free of the sleeves, in the process reversing them. The lining of the green coat was white, soiled with grime and sweat. Unsure what to do, he stood there holding the garment, torso assaulted by the cooler air.

All to Butler's apparent satisfaction. Turning to Watts and McDonell, he said, "We've interrogated the prisoners. Herkimer expects a sortie from the fort. I say let's give it to him. Have your Yorkers reverse their regimentals so the white's out-facing—they'll appear hunting frocks from a distance. Rebels'll think we're come from Gansevoort to reinforce them."

"Bayonets only," Watts added, approving of the plan. "Until we've broken through." He stared at Butler, then gave a decisive nod and raised his voice to carry: "Pass the word. Form up to advance—and every man reverse his regimentals!"

e'd turned his coat but hadn't betrayed his oath. A chill gripped William as memory of Joseph Tames-His-Horse, face painted by firelight, swam through his vision. Was *this* what the Mohawk had seen in his dream?

Watts, McDonell, and Butler granted no time to ponder it as the Yorkers advanced through the western ravine, picking their way through the morning's carnage. The creek ran red tinged, choked with bodies. Steam rose as they crossed the shallow water; the vapors, too, seemed tinged pink, as though the blood of the slain rose into the air, a crying unto heaven.

Find your brother. Your father.

William's heart galloped, bruising to his chest. He could sense the fear coming off the men to either side of him as, formed up in a triple column, they marched toward the rebels dug in on the wooded slopes ahead. The leaden sky was lightening by degrees, but the air remained thickly damp and clinging. The reversed coat and the shirt beneath chafed with abominable discomfort.

They were soon spotted, as they were meant to be. Shouts rose among the rebels in the high wood, faces visible here and there as necks craned. Cries of welcome issued forth. One man broke from cover and rushed down to the road with hand outstretched, shouting a name in recognition and relief. Another chased after the man, shouting, "Get back! It's the enemy!"

Others emerged from hiding, certain the opposite was true.

"Capt'n—they're friendlies!"

"It's Gansevoort. He's sent us reinforcements!"

"Fools—get back!" Ignoring his own command, the captain reached the man who'd rushed to greet a familiar face and yanked him backward, nearly off his feet. A scuffle commenced. Afraid the ruse would be prematurely exposed, McDonell hurried forward and attempted to slay the dubious officer but was himself felled in the clash after another of the rebels ran forward to his captain's defense.

From the skirmish ahead a shout arose: "Fire! Fire!"

Some of the militia obeyed. Gunfire erupted. Smoke billowed. One man in the column fell. Watts gave the order; shouting as one, the Royal Yorkers charged forward into the trees and up into the enemy's fire.

William's legs screamed with the effort to propel him up the ridge for the second time that day. A blowdown loomed, trunks snarled like latticework. From a gap, a gun muzzle protruded, aimed at him. He hurled himself behind a yew tree before the ball whirred past and struck someone coming up the slope behind him. An Indian. Friend or foe William couldn't tell as he whirled, gaze raking oiled features obscured by black paint and pain.

The Indian had taken the ball in the leg but wasn't down. Oneida? Must be, coming at him like this. Searching the features—nostrils distended, lips snarled back, head plucked nearly bald—he waited almost too late to fire. The Indian was a step away, hatchet raised, when William's shot took him through the chest and he fell, sprawled lifeless across the slope.

His brother? His father? He'd no idea. And no time to look more closely. Rain-soaked militiamen hurled themselves over fallen trees and rushed from cover to attack the Yorkers with knives, hatchets, rifle stocks, furious at the ruse. Indians were in the mix on both sides. Another warrior grappled William, knocking aside his musket. William clamped a hand to a corded forearm while he groped free his belt ax. The Indian butted heads with him. William's vision burst with bits of black and red. With a shout born of panic, he thrust the attacker away and swung his hatchet in a half-blind arc . . . at nothing.

He staggered, caught himself, shook his head clear. The Indian lay dead at his feet, shot through the head by Watts, already bounding away through smoke and writhing men. William hadn't heard the shot above the escalating clamor.

He heard the scream behind him, its pitch higher than other voices in the heaving fight. He jerked around. Another Indian was coming at him. Like most, this one clutched a rifle and tomahawk. Unlike most, this one had a full head of hair, half-straggled from a braid, flowing out wild and waist length. A woman's mane.

William stood transfixed as she rushed him, counting the crazed, pained beats of his heart. Her scream—and time—choked to a stop as their gazes locked, long enough for William to judge her young; beneath a layer of grime, her coppery skin stretched smooth over graceful bones. Her legs, bared as a warrior's, were muscled but slender. The blade in her hand flashed, raised to fall upon his neck.

She screamed again, a different sound than before—he'd have called it triumph if she'd made of him the easy kill he should have been, standing there too paralyzed by the sight of her to defend himself. But at the last instant she wrenched aside and sprang away with a panther's lithe grace, vanishing into a thicket, leaving him alive, if stunned.

Ahnyero was dead. Since the first guns' firing, Two Hawks had feared it was so. Not once had he seen his friend or heard his voice, or during the rain lull found anyone who could say with confidence he'd seen Ahnyero in the fight. Now he knew beyond doubt the scout and spy, the half-white blacksmith called Thomas Spencer, was gone out of the world. Out of both worlds he'd straddled in life. He'd fallen across Ahnyero's body, dragged off the road into the brush, shot through the neck with an arrow.

Two Hawks fought on, shoving grief to the corner of his heart to wait for space to blossom there. It was his brother, maybe still living, he must be concerned with now.

Living where? Among those Yorkers who had fooled the militia with their turned-out coats?

The Tryon regiments were mingled now, fighting side by side against friend and kin, as the Oneidas fought Senecas and Mohawks, Cayugas, Onondagas, and Indians from farther off. Some wept as they killed. He had killed a Mohawk warrior. Though he hadn't wept to do it, he'd found a moment during the rain to be sick over it.

He had killed two Yorkers, fighting close with his hunting knife and tomahawk. Both times he'd nearly waited too long to meet the white man attacking with bayonet, for fear it was his brother coming at him. But neither soldier had worn the face his father carried. The face from Two Hawks's dream.

General Herkimer had made good use of the terrain. He had his men fighting in pairs now, one firing while the second reloaded behind tree or stump. Even so, the enemy had penetrated far among them, nearly to Herkimer himself. That brave man was still propped against his saddle with his shattered leg outstretched, giving orders, rallying his men. A chief worthy of following. But Two Hawks wasn't heeding his wisdom. He wasn't using the tree cover to his best advantage, not fighting with another watching his back. He was moving alone through the skirmishers, twisting, lunging, fighting off attack as it came, searching . . . as someone, it turned out, had been searching this killing ground for him.

"Two Hawks!"

He heard the shout a second before she slammed into his side, dodging so hard through smoke and trees she'd no room to slow herself. Her rain-wet hair had straggled free of its braid. There was a gash on her brow. Another scored the knuckles that clenched her rifle. Otherwise she seemed whole. In body if not mind.

"Crazy woman!" He yanked Strikes-The-Water down behind two trees fallen together and shook her hard. "What foolishness brings you here?"

Glaring at him, she pulled free. Gunfire crackled around them, but even more shouting and thrashing as men fought hand to hand among the trees.

"I have seen him!" She panted for breath between the words, voice hoarse from screaming. "A white man with your face. A soldier with the turned-out coat who is your brother!"

The news left his anger hanging in shreds. "You saw him? Where? Alive?"

"Yes, alive—not a stone's throw from us now. I almost killed him!"

Two Hawks grasped her again, fingers closing over the sleeve of her shirt—she wore the breechclout of a warrior and nothing below but moccasins; her legs were bruised, scraped, smeared with earth and blood not her own. His mind spun with too many thoughts to sort out. He must get her out of this. He must find his brother. How could he do both?

"In which direction from this spot?" he demanded. When she pointed, he fixed what he saw in his mind, a gap beyond the end of a fallen tree where two small trees brushed the tips of leafy branches in an arch. "I see it. Now go. You should not—"

"I have more to tell you," she shouted back. "More from that one you want to make your wife. She and the black-haired one are at your mother's lodge. She looks for you to say her father no longer stands against you." Her face darkened as she shared this news. "You have his blessing—and that of your mother."

Anna Catherine was with his mother, in Kanowalohale . . . and there was no one now who stood against them marrying? It was hardly possible to take it in. Two Hawks had a second, maybe two, to exult in the words before a heavy body crashed over the felled tree behind which they hid. They started up, whirling to face an attack that didn't come. The soldier was dead, shot through the head.

Around them a pocket of stillness settled. The fight had passed over that spot and shifted down the slope. Two Hawks gulped acrid air through a raw throat to hiss, "This is no place for you. Go back to where it is safe."

A muscle in Strikes-The-Water's jaw flexed. "I have killed three. I have—"

Two Hawks turned her, planted a foot against her rump, and shoved her back toward the militia lines. "Go!"

She staggered, caught herself, gave him back a scathing glare, and went. Finding the place he'd marked, those two young trees growing close, he started out of hiding to find his brother.

They were deep into the western ravine, fighting through to the hottest part of a punishing battle that had raged since the morning.

Hampered by the pain in his hip, taxed from the effort to meet soldiers and warriors who rose from behind smoke-hazed stumps and hemlock trunks to engage them, Reginald doubted he could endure much longer. He'd lost count of the times Stone Thrower had blocked the blow of hatchet or bayonet meant to end him, even as the Oneida fought his own battles. In the confusion and desperation enveloping this fight, the lines between friend and enemy had blurred. They were taking violence from both.

It was some moments of glimpsing the white-coated figures dodging and rushing about before Reginald realized he was seeing men of Johnson's regiment—Royal Yorkers—wearing their coats turned inside out, not militia in hunting shirts. They'd been looking for *green* coats, first among the rain-washed dead where already the stench was gagging despite the cleansing downpour. Reginald had slowed their progress, insisting on looking into the face of every mutilated corpse in green. When the impossible scope of that grisly task grew apparent, he'd heeded Stone Thrower's urging to get in among the soldiers still fighting.

"My sons live," the warrior had insisted. "We will not find them here."

By stealth and force, they'd made their way toward the wooded height and the thickest fighting. Panting, scrabbling through brush, weaving through trees. Scored and grazed in sundry places but with no serious hurt. Thus far.

As the ground leveled beneath their feet and they sought their bearings for what confronted them, they sensed a shift in the surrounding chaos. Indian war cries had assaulted Reginald's ears for so many days on end, he hardly registered them. Now, though, their tenor was changing— the same word shouted, echoed back from throat to throat. Half-veiled in drifting smoke, lithe brown figures turned and leapt away, breaking off the fight, making for the ravine below.

Stone Thrower pushed him down, saving him from a musket ball that slammed into a hemlock trunk at head height. "They retreat to the camp. They know of Willett's sortie."

Reginald looked wildly about, relief and panic clashing. Would the Yorkers retreat as well? How could they possibly cover all this ground if—

Three warriors, faces painted, came crashing through a thicket yards away, headed straight for where they crouched at the base of the hemlock. Senecas. Stone Thrower hauled Reginald up again to meet the attack as a fourth figure, a soldier, stumbled into view and came between them and the onrushing Senecas.

The soldier's coat was smeared in leaf matter, but it had once been white. Whether a Yorker in turned coat or a militiaman in hunting frock there was no telling. Tall and hatless, tailed hair brown, he could have been anyone, but something about that span of shoulders, that set of head, the way he moved . . .

The Senecas met the soldier at the base of a stony ledge. One raised a club and knocked him to the ground with a blow to the head. While his companions turned back to protest, the Indian lifted the soldier by the hair, turning his face up.

A slack-mouthed face. William's face.

Beside him Stone Thrower loosed a cry of rage. The warrior grasping William's hair snarled something in defiance as his companions turned in alarm. Stone Thrower was already upon them, Reginald a step behind. While Reginald rushed at one of the Senecas, the butt of his rifle raised, Stone Thrower knocked the other's legs from under him with a powerful swipe of his gun, then raised his blade to the one fixing to scalp his son. The Seneca flung William to the ground.

Reginald broke off his attack on the third Seneca as the warrior went reeling from a blow then lunged through agony and panic to William's side. Staring blue from a mask of filth, William's eyes were dazed. He struggled to get his knees under him, gaping at Reginald, who felt a crushing of relief, a glorious agony in his chest.

"William!" He touched his son's head. His palm came away slick with blood.

William's eyes rushed full with recognition, before they sharpened, looking beyond him. "Father—take heed!"

Reginald turned instinctively, fearing he'd made a fatal mistake in abandoning that warrior without killing him, but it was Stone Thrower come to crouch beside him. William, perceiving an enemy, struggled to find a weapon, hand scrabbling, closing over a stone.

Reginald grabbed his hand. "Don't be afraid. We're going to get you away. This is your—"

But Stone Thrower had hurled himself away again.

What happened next was to Reginald a swift jumble of impressions. Stone Thrower's tomahawk arcing upward. Horror on William's face. Himself yanked bodily from the ground. Hands dragging him from

William's side. The scene at the base of the ledge opening up to him. Two Senecas lay dead. Stone Thrower drove his tomahawk into the neck of the third—which meant whoever had Reginald now wasn't one of those who'd attacked but another who had happened upon the chance to take a captive and leapt at it.

William shouted. Stone Thrower turned and saw him. More Indians flitted around them through the smoke. Two were rushing straight at William just above that lip of stone, on the verge of leaping down. Reginald twisted in his captors' hold, keeping Stone Thrower in view, and with all the strength left to him shouted, "Save him!"

He hadn't been attempting escape, but his captor couldn't know that. The last Reginald saw before pain exploded through his skull was Stone Thrower turning back, seeing the warriors bearing down from above. He reached William's side . . . then the pair were obscured by smoke and brush.

No one came after Reginald. On the ragged edge of consciousness, he embraced relief. Another face arose before him. *Lydia.*

Then darkness blotted out all.

As he came leaping down the slope, Two Hawks saw Stone Thrower's familiar shape below a stony ledge. And he'd seen—or thought he'd seen—a white man who looked alarmingly like Anna Catherine's father being dragged away through the wood by Senecas. Two more Senecas dropped off the ledge to attack his father and what appeared to be a turned-coat soldier slumped at his father's feet. Raising his tomahawk, Two Hawks leapt onto the back of the nearest Seneca. They landed hard together in a cracking of brush and fern. Two Hawks rolled free, his tomahawk bloodied. The Seneca didn't rise. He whirled to see his father grappling with the other, knocking him to the ground with his rifle, one powerful killing blow. There was only the soldier between them, still on hands and knees. Blood coursed down his face from a wound high on his head. Even so, Two Hawks knew him. He staggered, nearly dropped his weapon from trembling fingers, then hurried to his father, kneeling now.

"Here is your brother," Stone Thrower said, relief blazing from a face marked with exhaustion and strain. "Now you. Thank Creator for you!"

Two Hawks knew an instant of joy before the sight of so much blood on his brother's brow and face overshadowed it with worry. "Is he badly injured?"

They'd spoken in Oneida. His brother tried to rise but fell back into the leaves, groaning. Two Hawks might have groaned as well. All that study of English and in the moment it mattered the tongue had fled him! Impressions of the last moments swirled through his mind. One snagged, and a cold knot formed in his belly.

"Was it Aubrey? Did I see—"

"You saw," his father confirmed. "But we must save your brother now. Help me."

Two Hawks jammed his tomahawk through his sash. He got a shoulder beneath one of his brother's arms. His father did the same. They rose together with William's sagging weight between them. Two Hawks was touching his twin for the first time since the day of their birth and could not pause to wonder at it as they staggered over bodies clogging the wood, blocking their way.

"Where is our path out of this?" Two Hawks cried as they swerved aside from men still hacking each other, some so spent they fought on their knees, though half the British force and nearly all their warriors were turning back toward their camps at the fort, some dragging prisoners along, others wounded comrades.

"Run in their wake for now," his father gasped, chest heaving with effort. "We carry one of their wounded. Until we cross the ravine and can make our way out of this, we are Senecas."

William's head lolled between them, coming to rest against their father's neck.

"We must find help." Two Hawks didn't think the militia was pursuing the retreating British. He hoped that brave general, Herkimer, was still among the living. Many cried out as they passed, moaning for help, water, mercy to end their suffering. It tore at Two Hawks to pass them by unaided.

"Oriska," his father said. "We take him there."

There would be healers at Oriska. Women to tend the wounded. No doubt many would be brought there out of this battle today. But it was a long way to carry his brother. Miles.

Kanowalohale was much farther, still Two Hawks wished for Lydia and her healing skill, longed for Anna Catherine, his thoughts already reaching out in grief, though she didn't yet know there was reason to grieve. *Bear's Heart, we had to choose.*

Even if their brother survived, there would be hearts on the ground when he saw Anna Catherine again, instead of the joy they might have known. Would she forgive their choice?

37

August 6, 1777
Oriska Town

*W*illiam hovered on the edge of waking, aware of a fire's crackle, of voices speaking within range of his hearing. Men's voices, their tones uneasy. He couldn't make out their words. A louder voice was raised in an odd, broken rhythm. Chanting? Why could he not understand? Something about it all was wrong. The wrongness weighed like earth heaped over him, smothering and dark. An ache beat in the center of his chest. Worse was the throbbing in his head. Why did he hurt so abominably?

He'd seen battle, that was why. He'd been wounded. Struck down after hours of fighting. Memories flooded in, reeling like drunkards, until one steadied and caused his gut to clench. Reginald Aubrey. The man had found him and seconds later been captured.

Indians. He opened eyes, saw the face of a warrior looming over him, and flailed in panic. The pain in his head roared high and blinding. When his vision returned, the warrior still bent over him.

But it wasn't a warrior, he now saw. It was a woman. The one he'd seen in the heat of battle. That fierce, beautiful creature who'd started to slay him, then let him live. Only now her face was clean, save for a cut on her brow, her hair smoothed back in a braid, black as a raven's plumage. She studied him intensely, no longer fierce. Still beautiful.

"You—" He barely croaked the word, but her dark eyes widened, reflecting firelight. Her hand brushed his brow, her touch warm. When she smiled, William momentarily forgot both raging head and bewilderment.

"I am Strikes-The-Water, Deer Clan," she said in careful English. "You are He-Is-Taken, Turtle Clan."

He was what? Taken? Turtle ...? But she'd looked away and was speaking to someone else now. He made to push up onto his forearms. The pain raged up behind his eyes again, and blackness followed it.

Clear Day had tried to reach Oriska before Two Hawks left for the soldier camp but had hurt himself on the way. Just a twisted ankle but it slowed him. Strikes-The-Water had found him on the trail, helped him to Oriska by the morning of the battle, then slipped away and followed the warriors. Clear Day confirmed that Anna Catherine and Lydia were at Kanowalohale. Two Hawks longed to go to them, yet feared all the more to tell Anna Catherine he'd seen her father dragged away to what would surely be a brutal death. How could he go to her with such news?

That was what he and his father and his father's uncle were discussing when William woke. They broke off their talk and hurried to where Strikes-The-Water had taken root at his brother's side to clean the blood and powder soot from his face. Two Hawks moved to the other side of the pallet on which his brother lay in the lodge of one of Oriska's healers, where other warriors had been brought. These were not the worst injured and so were stoic in their suffering. Elsewhere in the town, many of Herkimer's men were being tended. They'd kept William away from them. They'd removed his coat—the telling green still turned inward—to check for injuries. What they found were scrapes, bruises, a bad one in the center of his chest. It was the blow to the head that had made his brother swoon over the four miles they'd carried him. They had gained help along

the way as others straggled out of the ravine, weaving dazed and exhausted through the bodies of horses and men slain on the road as they
fled, cut down by Thayendanegea and his warriors. It had been a gruesome
and worrisome march. Now at last his brother had uttered speech—and
Two Hawks hadn't been beside him to hear it.

"He spoke to you." He wrenched his gaze from that face so like his
own to frown at Strikes-The-Water. "What did he say?"

"He knew me."

The girl sounded pleased about it, but Two Hawks frowned. "After
seeing you once in the midst of battle?"

"And why not?" she challenged. "I do not think the sight of me in
battle is a thing a man might easily forget."

Two Hawks managed not to roll his eyes—or let her see he secretly
agreed with her. He would not forget the sight any time soon himself.

Stone Thrower knelt beside the girl and placed a hand on her shoulder. "You have done well, Daughter. You helped my uncle when he was in
need. You were first to find this lost son of mine. Now you tend him with
diligence. Since his mother is not here to do it, my heart is glad for you."

Strikes-The-Water's eyes glinted at his words. She looked away at the
women moving about the other wounded. "She will be so happy."

Two Hawks was abashed at his impatience—and for not thinking of
his mother. He was thinking of her now, wishing she could share this moment. He reached across his brother's chest and took Strikes-The-Water by
the arm. "My father speaks true. You have done much for us."

She nodded stiffly, accepting his words. He was withdrawing his hand
when William's shot up and grasped it.

Two Hawks stared into his brother's eyes, startled at how like their
mother's they were, though he'd known this to be so. But these were not
painted eyes, tiny soulless chips of blue, but living eyes looking at him,
looking through pain and fear and seeing him.

"Brother," Two Hawks said, glad to find his English hadn't deserted him. "Do you know me?"

For a stretching moment, their gazes locked, then William's flicked over Two Hawks's features, showing his thoughts clear to read. Doubt. Uncertainty. Recognition. "You. Anna called you . . . Two Hawks?"

Two Hawks let his breath out in a rush, unaware he'd been holding it. "That is my name. I am also called Jonathan. Did she tell you so?"

His brother's eyelids squeezed tight, but the strong chin with its scanty dark stubble—little more than Two Hawks's own—moved gingerly in the faintest of nods. "She tried to."

Was that regret in the strained and suffering voice? Did his brother want to know them now? Two Hawks wavered but a moment, then decided he didn't care what his brother wanted. *They* wanted it, his family.

"And here is our father, Caleb, also called Stone Thrower. Open your eyes, Brother, and look at him."

It came out a challenge. Perhaps his brother heard it so. His brows pulled tight as though he summoned courage, then he opened his eyes and looked at their father, who had tears running down his cheeks. William got his elbows under him and pushed himself up to sitting. He swayed as if he would fall back again.

Three sets of hands reached for him, but Stone Thrower's found him first. William slumped against their father, who started to wrap him in strong arms, then stopped himself, took him by the shoulders, and held him steady. Their father wore a look of vulnerability such as Two Hawks had never seen.

"My heart is full with praise to Creator for this moment. I have waited long to say a thing to you . . . my son." Stone Thrower's strong throat worked as he swallowed. "I ask you to forgive me."

William's brows tightened again. Confusion and wariness marked his features. "Forgive you?"

"For not being strong enough to fight off those redcoats who took your mother," Stone Thrower said, looking into the face of his firstborn, "and you and your brother unborn, into that fort and kept you there, so that I was not by to protect you when you needed me."

Looking rattled and pale, William glanced aside at Two Hawks. He looked again at their father but didn't give him the answer he sought. Instead he took in the lodge beyond their small circle. "You brought me out of the battle," he said. "To where?"

"Oriska," Stone Thrower said, voice still gruff with emotion. "Many wounded are here."

"Herkimer's men and our warriors," Two Hawks added, trying to deny the hard knot of impatience rising up. He lowered his voice, though he spoke in English, which not all in that lodge could understand. "They do not know what side you fought for."

William glanced at the turned coat lying in a grubby heap nearby. Distaste was in the look. "And my mother? Is she here?"

Two Hawks felt glad at this question, but before he could answer, Strikes-The-Water said in her broken English, "She at Kanowalohale. With others you know. That one, your sister. And other, black hair."

William blinked, clearly confused by this. Then understanding, and alarm, cleared his gaze. "Anna . . . Lydia. Here in the west? How come they to be?"

"Woman not always stay home when danger comes to her people," Strikes-The-Water replied and smiled again at his brother. She had captured William's attention fully now. Two Hawks felt impatience brewing again. He looked to his father.

"Will you do a thing for me?" Stone Thrower said to Strikes-The-Water before the girl could say anything more to William. "Will you go to Kanowalohale and bring my wife and her guests to Oriska?"

The swift thundercloud that moved across Strikes-The-Water's face portended a storm of protest.

"It is for my brother you would do this." Two Hawks had spoken in Oneida, so William couldn't know why Strikes-The-Water looked at him now as she did, but the softening in her face was telling. At least to Two Hawks.

"I will go for him." Strikes-The-Water rose gracefully and went to the door, pausing to look back once at William, who was looking after her. She smiled again, then was gone.

Two Hawks noticed how his brother's gaze lingered after her.

"My . . ." William put a hand to his eyes, pressing hard. "Reginald Aubrey. He was captured. Senecas, I think. Look you . . . was he saved? Is he here?"

Only the fire's popping and the murmurs of other voices in the lodge broke the heavy silence that followed. Two Hawks saw the moment his brother understood. If it was possible, he grew even whiter.

"It was a hard thing," Stone Thrower said, "choosing between. It was you he bid us save, not him."

His brother looked as though he would be sick. "They will show him no mercy."

Regret rippled over Stone Thrower's face. "There may be time. Now that my sons are whole and safe, I will go to find him."

William blinked at him, mouth agape. "Why?"

If their father was taken aback by the question, he hid it as he looked searchingly at William. "Is this not a thing you wish me to do?"

Two Hawks, who very much wished to find Aubrey, said, "We must try—"

Stone Thrower put a hand to his shoulder, silencing him, still addressing his brother. "I have forgiven Aubrey for taking you from us. He also has repented in his heart of this bad thing. He is making his peace with Creator over it—inside that fort he started on that good path. Since then we have fought side by side. I will not abandon him, though he bid me do so."

William absorbed this in stunned silence, then seemed to come to some conclusion; resolution gripped his features. "Why then do we linger? The Senecas who took him may still be at their siege camp, at the fort."

Two Hawks tensed, surprised by his brother's eagerness for action, ready himself to more than match it. But William had taken that blow, was clearly still in pain and weakened. Was he able to leap up and rush from the lodge? Two Hawks looked to their father, who didn't argue over whether William was fit for such a journey.

"I knew the face of one of those who took Aubrey captive," Stone Thrower said. "It may be he will remember me. You," he said to Two Hawks, "stay with your brother and wait for the women to come. I will go to the Senecas at the fort and find that one I—"

"I go with you!" Two Hawks said, and meant it. He would not be pushed aside again. Not this time.

"And I," William added as emphatically, surprising them by lurching to his feet and staying on them. "I'll not be left behind."

38

August 6, 1777
Kanowalohale

*N*ot until the violent rain that drove them inside the lodge, when Good Voice mentioned in passing that the girl's mother was worried, had Anna owned to knowing where Strikes-The-Water had gone—after Clear Day. With intention, Anna thought, of joining the battle if there was one. Hearing this, Good Voice had sat quiet in thought, then said, "If armies come together at that fort, wounded may be brought to Oriska. If not, we will get news there. We need not wait for it to find us here any more than that one has done."

With Lydia's consent, they'd gathered belongings and medicines, waited for the rain to taper off, then saddled the horses. They set out on the trail to the town near the Mohawk River where they hoped to find Clear Day and Strikes-The-Water. Perhaps even Two Hawks and Stone Thrower.

Evening was coming on when a rider on a lathered horse met them on the trail. Good Voice knew her: Two-Kettles-Together, wife of a warrior called Honyery. She brought word of ambuscade and battle, terrible and desperate. White men had killed one another. Red men had killed one another. Whether Two Hawks or Stone Thrower were among those killed she didn't know, though she'd seen Two Hawks in the fighting early on. Streaked with grime and blood, she was riding out to spread the news: the British and Senecas had retreated to the fort with their wounded;

Herkimer's militia and Oneida warriors limped eastward, bringing off their wounded to Oriska. The fort was still besieged by St. Leger's army.

Who had won the battle she couldn't say. "Maybe no one. So many dead." Two-Kettles-Together rode on to Kanowalohale, leaving them to press on toward Oriska with a mounting dread of what they would find there. Or fail to find.

Soon after, as fireflies were winking in thickets, Strikes-The-Water appeared around a bend in the trail, on foot and running. The moment she saw Good Voice, she called out in Oneida. Anna deciphered enough to grasp what was shouted: "He is safe! Your son—both your sons. They are together at Oriska with your husband and his uncle. They sent me to bring you to them!"

Their hearts lifted as if on eagles' wings, but they arrived at the village only to have those same hearts dashed to the ground. Stone Thrower, Two Hawks, and William were gone. As Clear Day explained why, Anna feared she would follow her heart to the ground with the shock and dismay.

"Reginald . . . ?" Hearing her father's name uttered on a devastated gasp, she turned to see that Lydia had beaten her to it.

Private William Aubrey brushed at his grubby regimental coat, turned green side out now. Realizing the pointlessness of such action given the general state of things, he desisted and stepped from the shadowed forest into what remained of Sir John Johnson's camp. A sea of ravaged tents lay in crumpled heaps, torn and burned. Battle-weary Yorkers sifted the wreckage. A few fires were lit despite the lack of provisions; much of the regimental baggage had been stolen. Around the fires clustered men nursing wounds and grievances, spent from battle, dispirited and brooding. Some wept openly while others stared with blank and haunted eyes. Few looked up to note William's passing. Making no attempt at concealment, he strode through camp catching snatches of complaints as he passed, confirming what his father and brother had told him as they made their way in dusk-fall from Oriska. Stanwix's second-in-command had led a sortie from the fort on the heels of that torrential rain. Lieutenant Singleton and the other wounded were now prisoners within its walls. The brigade's stolen flag and regimental colors hung beneath the fort's flag. An open taunt.

William dismissed a wrench of indignation at the disgrace. He was in the camp for two reasons, one of which lay before him now—his own mess tent, plundered and empty. He'd come for the Welsh bow, but other hands had been before him.

As he stood reconciling himself to the loss, the night erupted with a sound he hadn't heard since the blow that knocked him senseless. From the southwest, where their camp lay, the howls of enraged Indians lifted the hairs at his nape.

"Is that ye, Aubrey?"

He spun round. Robbie MacKay stood behind him, bundled canvas in his arms. In the flickered glow of the nearest fire, Robbie's face was haggard. He'd a gash across one cheek that would scar badly, but seemed otherwise whole.

"I'm glad to see ye made it, Aubrey. I lost sight o' ye and feared the worst."

"As did I, for a time." William gave the story they'd agreed upon should he be asked; left wounded on the field, he'd escaped the ravine and made his way back on his own—a reality doubtless unfolding a hundred times over as they spoke. "I've lost my musket, everything else it seems." He gestured at the tent's remains. He wouldn't speak of his second errand. Not to Robbie, whose gaze went to William's bared head, hair still crusted with blood.

"Come awa' then, we'll get ye looked after. I'm helping wi' the wounded."

Wounded William was, though he'd made light of it. They'd tried to leave him at Oriska with the old man, his father's uncle, but he'd refused. He heaved a breath through his nose. "I don't need tending, see. I'll be fine."

Robbie raised an appeasing hand, mistaking the exasperation as aimed at him. "Oh, aye. As ye wish. I'm just glad to see ye living."

It would likely be the last time, if William left that camp again. And he would leave it, whether or not he found Reginald Aubrey among Johnson's prisoners. Somewhere in the dark between Oriska and this moment he'd made his choice—never mind which side of his coat was facing out. *Father, brother, uncle. Mother.* And Anna nearby as well. He didn't know where he belonged as yet, but it wasn't in an army coming to annihilate them all.

"Robbie, bide a moment." The youngest MacKay turned back, swaying a little. "Did Captain Watts make it out of that ravine?"

Grief shadowed Robbie's beardless face. "They think he's dead. Maybe captured. We dinna ken."

William felt a churning in his gut. Watts was a good man. "Campbell?"

"Him? Dead sure. Saw wi' me own eyes." There was no sorrow for Campbell in his expression, but Robbie went a whiter shade of pale as he spoke; the shouting from the Indian camp had reached a crescendo. A furious sound, mixed with grief. "Whatever ye do, Aubrey, keep awa' from that lot. Pray they dinna turn on us next."

William's confusion must have shown.

"Right. Ye wouldna ken. Their camp was looted worse than ours—clothes, silver, wampum bundles, blankets. Their shelters are burned, their women and children chased awa'." Robbie's gaze went over him. "Find yourself a firearm if ye can, and mind it weel tonight."

William had a firearm. On the long trek back they'd stumbled upon corpses fallen in the wood. One had had a rifle by, half buried in leaves. It was in his brother's keeping, back in the thicket where his twin and their father awaited him. Likely with thinning patience. He must do the other thing for which he'd ventured back into this ravaged camp. Find where Johnson had put his prisoners and see whether, by some miracle, Reginald Aubrey was among them.

"I'll do that, Robbie," he said, and turned away.

Their father had waited until his brother headed for the Royal Yorker camp before revealing the rest of his plan—to go alone into the Seneca camp to look for Reginald Aubrey while William searched among Johnson's prisoners. Alarmed by the tumult issuing from that camp, Two Hawks had argued against it, but Stone Thrower was as stubbornly set as William had been at Oriska. Now they were each alone, Stone Thrower off to the howling Senecas, William to his regiment, Two Hawks awaiting their return, uncertain if his father would make it back alive or if his brother would choose to return.

Two Hawks recalled his brother lurching to his feet, determined they not leave him behind, his father's usually stoic face cracking like an eggshell, all his heart for his firstborn—pride, fear, hope—leaking through. He'd agreed to William's coming, though Two Hawks suspected he had a plan in mind should William prove too weakened by his injury to continue—sending him back to Oriska with Two Hawks's help. But his brother had seemed to gain in strength as they made their way back along forest trails in the falling night, skirting the terrible ravine.

Two Hawks would never forget those hours in the wood, knowing it was his twin moving near him in the dark, moving into danger with their hearts as one—for finding Aubrey, at least. They had him back. He-Is-Taken. William Aubrey. *If* he returned to them.

Stone Thrower hadn't shared his doubt but had gone into that uproar coming from the Senecas' camp as though all would be well, that he would bring back Reginald Aubrey and they would return to Oriska to find their women waiting to welcome them.

"They may be killing their prisoners, those warriors," Stone Thrower had said when the shouting escalated. "It may be the British cannot stop them. I must go now."

He'd taken bear grease and black powder from his bag and painted his face to help conceal him from familiar gazes. He had made Two Hawks wait for his brother, telling him that if he, Stone Thrower, hadn't returned by the time William found him again, to come close to the other camp but not into it.

"No matter what you hear or see. The two of you stay alive and return to your mother."

So Two Hawks was left to crouch in the dark, worrying, praying. He thought of Anna Catherine. She did indeed have a bear's heart, coming deep into Oneida lands to find him. It filled his heart with courage. Yet this meant the time of facing her would come sooner. Would it be with joy, restoring her father to her? Or in grief, telling her of his death?

He heard his brother coming, English boots tramping the brush like a buck in rutting season, heedless. *You have much to learn, Brother,* he thought, then remembered his brother was exhausted and wounded besides. The fatigue of the day was a weight in his own bones. William's footfalls halted.

"Brother." Two Hawks stood from the thicket several strides away. "I must teach you some bird call signals."

William's face emerged from the darkness. He ignored the jibe about bird calls. "Aubrey isn't in Johnson's camp." He paused, as if searching the darkness. "Where is . . . he?"

Suddenly angry, Two Hawks wanted to grasp his brother and tell him to call that man who had spent their lives suffering for his loss *Father,* but he restrained himself. None of this was his brother's fault. They were still strangers to him. He must be patient.

"Our father is gone to see if Aubrey is among the Seneca prisoners."

"He's *there*—in their camp?" Two Hawks heard William's alarm and hoped concern for their father was part of it. "Is he mad? Some of those warriors will have faced him in battle today."

"You think he does not know it? Our father will take care."

William fell silent, maybe feeling himself rebuked. Two Hawks started to say something softer but found he couldn't speak for the knot of worry in his throat. Silence grew, thick and tense, full of the voices of outraged Indians, the whine of mosquitoes, a hundred unasked questions. And the faces of the dead, foremost among them Ahnyero's. Other faces he'd seen in Oriska, living. Honyery and Louis Cook.

Beside him, his brother cleared his throat. "Stone Thrower . . . he's risking his life for my . . . for Aubrey." There was a question in those halting words. *Why?* It was a question he'd asked their father too. Two Hawks hadn't found the words he needed to give answer before a twig snapped and his father's voice spoke out of the dark.

"I have said this once, but I will say it again. Listen now. The man you called *father* is a man I now call *brother*. We have the same Heavenly Father, he and I, and the sins for which I have been forgiven by that Father are no better or worse than his. What I do for him I would do for any brother. For my sons. Even for one who is not sure he wishes to be my son."

Two Hawks heard William's intake of breath. He waited, but his brother didn't speak. "What is happening in that camp? Are they killing prisoners?"

"You do not wish to know what they are doing to their prisoners," his father said.

"Is he there?" William cut in. "Did you see him?"

"I went among them and spoke to one who did not know me. I asked after a certain warrior—one of those who took Aubrey. That one and others have started for their town far to the west. They took one prisoner with them. That prisoner was Aubrey."

Two Hawks stood close enough to his brother to feel the shudder that went through him. "Which town? Ganundasaga?"

"Yes, and that may be good for us."

"Good?" William asked. "How?"

"It is good," Two Hawks explained, "because our father once lived among the Senecas there. They take him to the women."

"What women?"

"The clan mothers."

"Clan mothers?"

So much his brother did not know! "All children born to an Oneida mother have a clan. We are Turtle Clan. *You* are Turtle Clan."

"I understand about clans," William said impatiently. "But why mothers—women—at all? What have they to do with it?"

"It is the women of a clan who decide the fate of captives," Stone Thrower said without the exasperation Two Hawks had not kept from his voice. "Whatever fallen warrior those Senecas mean to avenge, that warrior's women will decide Aubrey's fate. If he does not slow them too much and they kill him on the way."

Two Hawks didn't wait for William to react to that. "There is time to overtake them?"

"Yes," Stone Thrower said, but something in his tone gave warning of further evils.

William sensed it. "There is more, isn't there?"

Stone Thrower told them what it was and Two Hawks felt a quailing in his belly as he listened. A council of headmen made up of Mohawks, Senecas, Cayugas, and Onondagas had decided to send a bloody hatchet to the Oneidas. "We are now enemies to those who called us *brother*. The

Great Longhouse is torn down around us, and we are no longer a people bound together."

William said nothing. There was no knowing what he thought or felt, or if he understood the significance of this terrible thing. The Confederacy that had long held their nations together was in tatters. Perhaps even the Great Tree of Peace had been uprooted. Only time would tell about that.

Many had seen this day coming and feared it. Now it was here.

"What do we do?" William asked, and Two Hawks knew whatever was happening between the nations didn't alter the path before them this night.

"We do what I could not do for you the day you were taken—we follow those who took Aubrey," Stone Thrower told his firstborn. "And, Creator willing, we take him back."

39

August 7, 1777
Oriska

*I*t didn't need the fingers of one hand to count the loved ones Anna could name without attaching to them some dreadful anxiety. The rest stood in dire need of heavenly aid: Two Hawks, William, Stone Thrower. *Papa.* Even Lydia, who had roused by the time they'd carried her inside, only to stare unseeing at the fire in the center of the lodge they'd been given for shelter while Anna hovered and fretted, thoroughly ignored. It was Good Voice, with her refusal to despair, who brought Lydia back to herself.

"Clear Day says Senecas took him," she'd said, kneeling beside the pallet where Lydia sat ashen and mute. "For a time my husband lived with them. He has friends among them. That was a very bad time for us, but look now, Heavenly Father is using it for our good. And better even than friends among men, Creator is with my husband. And *my sons* are with him." She'd uttered that last in a tone of wonder, though of them all she alone had yet to see William.

Anna's eyes welled as Good Voice reached for her hand, sharing that wonder with her. When they'd wiped away their tears and looked at her again, Lydia's gaze, though still pain filled, had cleared.

"William is with them? I'm glad for that." She looked around at them all. "Pray with me?"

Strikes-The-Water held back, but Anna, Clear Day, and Good Voice joined in beseeching heaven for the men they loved to be strong, to be brave, to be kept safe, to yield to the will of the Almighty as He revealed it, as the fire sent its sparks flying upward. Then Lydia straightened and looked about them, as if remembering what lay beyond the bark walls of their borrowed shelter. "How many wounded are here?"

"Much wounded," Clear Day said. "Some will not see another sun. Some will, with help."

Lydia firmed her jaw with purpose. "Where is my medical case? Come, Anna. Let's go and see to them."

Everyone in Oriska who had strength to wipe a brow, change a dressing, hold a warrior steady while a broken bone was made straight did those things many times through the night, but none tended with more devotion than Anna Catherine and Lydia. Watching them, it came into Good Voice's mind that every soldier or warrior they touched might have been Two Hawks, or William, or Reginald, for all the care they showed. Good Voice was doing her part, though she tired easily. To be with child again at forty summers . . .

"Rest," Lydia told her often. In turn Good Voice kept a watchful eye on Lydia. She wasn't about to see her warriors bring Aubrey home to find this good woman had worked herself ill while they waited.

Of them all, Strikes-The-Water had the least patience with the injured. At some point during that first night, while no one was looking, she had left Oriska. Probably headed back to that fort still under siege. That one would go into danger with the boldness of a warrior, stubborn and reckless. Good Voice had sighed over her but thought, *She is as Creator made her.* Still it would be good to see her joined with a husband soon, though it wouldn't be with Two Hawks.

Some white soldiers had been put into bateaux, the morning after the battle, to be taken downriver to Fort Dayton to be nearer their people.

Anna Catherine oversaw their going. Many had taken comfort from her since the night hours when she came out of the lodge to see to their needs. She'd tended warriors too, those without people in Oriska to do for them. Anna Catherine was kind, gentle, steadfast, and brave. She would make a good wife and mother.

Good Voice stood on the riverbank where a stream came down to meet it, in the morning when the air was cool. Mist came off the water in tendrils. A doe with her fawn stepped out of the trees to drink. The bateaux for the wounded soldiers were filling up and departing. Watching Anna Catherine moving among the wounded, Good Voice could almost see the last shreds of disappointment over the choices of her second-born, what they would mean for his children down all the generations to come, rising off her like the mist lifting from the stream. Rising and drifting away.

Heavenly Father wove all things together for good, for those who followed His path. Did not the Book say it was so? That their families should be united now in love instead of hate . . . Was it not like a God of redemption to do such a thing?

May it be so with my firstborn. May my eyes see him at last. May his heart find joy in seeing me.

On the second day after the battle, the remainder of the injured militia departed Oriska. Lydia rose from the last of them, a young man whose badly wounded leg she'd managed to save, as he was lifted on a makeshift litter. He grasped her hand at parting, thanked her, then was carried to the waiting bateau, and Lydia found herself abruptly bereft of purpose. Most of the warriors still in need of care were those of Oriska; the Oneida healers had them well in hand. A few from Kanowalohale needing further time to heal would soon be making their way to that town.

Bloodstained and bedraggled, Lydia swayed as she watched the bateau carrying her last patient being poled away from the bank. As the vessel caught the river's current and was carried from sight, the fear she'd held at bay came crashing down with such force she nearly crumpled under it.

As if they had anticipated such a happening, beside her swiftly were Anna and Good Voice. "Now it is time for you to rest," Good Voice told her.

Rest. Lydia couldn't fathom the word. She closed her eyes but couldn't close her ears to Anna's plea.

"Don't lose hope, Lydia. They'll find Papa."

"Will they?" Lydia searched for the hope that had so long sustained her. Reginald was free in his spirit—Clear Day had learned that much from Stone Thrower. Something had happened between those two inside Fort Stanwix, before they joined the battle. And there was that kiss . . .

Or was that fleeting promise of love all she would ever embrace? A grasping at smoke.

She wept. They helped her to the lodge, where she must have slept. Voices spoke, words beyond her comprehension. Firelight flickered. Sometimes a gentle hand stroked her brow. Anna's, she thought. The next thing she truly remembered was hearing Clear Day speaking in Oneida, of which she understood nothing until the very recognizable name of General Benedict Arnold passed his lips.

She sat up, blinking and disheveled. Clear Day sat by the fire, Good Voice on a bench nearby. On another Anna slept.

"The messenger rode fast," Clear Day said, switching to English as a courtesy to her, "coming to find Herkimer with the news."

Lydia had seen General Herkimer after the battle, but only briefly. He'd conducted himself with level-headed courage after the devastating ambush had been sprung—she'd heard it from the lips of nearly every man of his she'd tended—and was the saving of many lives. But his leg was grievously wounded, already festering. He'd been taken swiftly downriver to his home at the Little Falls Carry.

"This war chief, Arnold," Clear Day was saying, "him who Aubrey fought with on the lake last autumn, he will be coming with more soldiers to relieve those at the fort. He will scatter the British back to the west. This is what the messenger had to say."

There would be no invasion of the valley. Not now. God willing.

Good Voice said, "I think, Uncle, we will return to Kanowalohale to await my husband and my sons, and the one they go to recover."

Almost Lydia spoke in protest of leaving Oriska, then reconsidered. "The warriors from Kanowalohale, the wounded ones, have they left yet?"

Good Voice met her gaze. "Soon they go. I thought we should go with them. Help them along."

"I should rather do that than sit waiting."

"That is my thought as well."

"I will remain," Clear Day said. "When they return I will tell my nephew and his sons where you may be found and come with them to you."

"*Iyo.*" Good Voice nodded toward Anna, lying with her hair fallen loose like a blanket, shining brown and gold in the firelight. "Let us wake this sleeping daughter of ours and make ready to return."

40

August 8, 1777

*B*y sunset of the second day pursuing the Senecas, William had stumbled often enough to prove he wasn't as recovered as he'd pretended. They were still a day's travel from the village where Stone Thrower thought the Senecas were taking their prisoner. Leaving Two Hawks to mind William, he'd gone ahead, hoping to overtake the Senecas and locate their camp.

William caught the flash of impatience on Two Hawks's face as Stone Thrower loped off through the trees, leaving them at a stream coursing through a wooded draw. Now his brother crouched at the stream, filling a canteen. Perched halfway up the draw where a lip of stone made a shelf, William watched him, still finding it unnerving that this lean, brown-skinned figure clad in moccasins and breechclout shared his blood.

Two Hawks ascended the slope and handed William the dripping canteen. He drank while his brother rummaged in a quilled bag, coming up with a pouch containing the parched corn he and their father seemed able to subsist upon. He offered it to William, who took a handful, chewed, then grabbed the canteen and drank again, feeling his belly churn and a cold sweat bead his brow.

"You are white as rendered lard, Brother. Let me look at that gash before the light is gone." Too slow to fend off the fingers parting his sweaty hair, William winced at the probing of the tender area. "It is nearly in the place of my scar," his brother observed. "Did you somehow know I had it and wanted us to match?"

Leaning away, he caught Two Hawks's half-amused gaze. Since leaving Fort Stanwix, William *had* tried to match his twin's woodland skills, all the while denying to himself that he cared how he fared in comparison. They weren't sure yet what to make of him, these warriors—no more than he them—but he wanted to move past this awkwardness of knowing them as close in blood as men could be yet still strangers. Move past it to what, exactly, he wasn't ready to decide.

"I ask you to forgive me."

To William's mind there was nothing to forgive. Not against Stone Thrower, who'd plainly stated his doubt over whether William was keen on being his son.

That wasn't true. Or he didn't think it was. He was more than a little in awe of the man. He respected him for his bravery, his dedication, and couldn't help but admire his astonishing selflessness toward Aubrey, who'd robbed him of so much. His son.

I am his son. It was a notion as slippery as eels, impossible to grasp and think on with his head throbbing, his gut churning. Not with the clarity it needed. And deserved.

"In this I'd have been content to let you best me."

He'd spoken wryly to his brother, acknowledging the rivalry, but Two Hawks didn't smile. They'd been stealing looks at each other for two days, measuring, curious, half-wary. Now that dark, steady gaze proved discomfiting.

"What?" William studied his twin in return, picking out subtle differences in their features beyond the shade of their skin. Did his own lips curve upward at the corners so? Not quite so much perhaps. Those prominent cheekbones were every bit his own, but did his eyes have that same slight tilt?

"I was thinking of a dream I had," his brother said. "Before the siege, while I was scouting. In this dream I sat on a slope like this, though the wood was not thick. You were beside me. Your painted face spoke to me."

"What? Was I got up in war paint like a . . . ?" *Like a savage,* he'd almost said.

Two Hawks's eyes flared. "I meant the little face our father carries. You left it behind. Aubrey gave it to our parents. Our father keeps it with him always."

"We do what I could not do for you the day you were taken." Stone Thrower's words, spoken in darkness, had never been far from William's mind. Like flint and steel they careened inside his injured head, sparking questions about them, his mother, their people. And Anna, their bridge.

"I don't know how long it's been since you've seen her—Anna." William hesitated. "She is well?"

The forest sounds were those of night now, with the stream gurgling below. Shadows were thickening, still he caught Two Hawks's sharpened look.

"Anna Catherine was well when last I saw her."

He'd spoken guardedly, though William couldn't fathom why. Anna had given the impression she and this brother of his were friends. "She never mentioned you all these years. Not once in all her letters to me. Did you ask her not to?"

"It was her choice first to say nothing of me in her words to you. My choice later." Before William could choose from among the questions *that* triggered, Two Hawks added, "Anna Catherine read your letters to me, until I learned to read them for myself."

"You read my letters?" A spurt of indignation rose, burning as bile.

Two Hawks studied him, seemingly untroubled by guilt. "Nearly all, I think. Have you still the Welsh bow?"

Surprise at the question held him silent for a heartbeat. His indignation simmered down, and he found himself, oddly, the tiniest bit pleased that his brother knew such a thing about him, that he had a bow. Or once had. "I looked for it, back at Johnson's camp. It was grabbed during the sortie. I suppose some rebel in the fort has it now."

Two Hawks's brows gathered in. "I would have liked to see that bow. It has much meaning for you."

William shrugged, unsure whether that was true now. Or was his brother merely testing him in saying so?

He'd questions of his own more pressing. "How came you to be friends with Anna and no one knew until after I'd returned? How did you find us—or her?"

His brother raised a brow. "She did not tell you this?"

"No," William said, irritated to be reminded again of his rash behavior the previous summer. "Not that I can remember."

"Then I will tell you of it," his brother said, sounding pleased to do so. "It was our father's uncle—him we left at Oriska—who found you."

As night deepened and they waited for Stone Thrower's return, Two Hawks told the story of how Clear Day found himself in the apothecary shop that had belonged to Lydia's father and overheard Lydia and Rowan Doyle speaking of Reginald Aubrey, all those years ago.

"That name was all our mother knew of him who took you, except that he was a redcoat officer. Knowing this, Clear Day followed the Irishman to your farm and saw you there. After some time he told our mother this, but our father was not walking a good path then. They feared to tell him where you might be found lest he go there and make worse trouble getting you back. Not until Clear Day and our mother began to walk the Jesus path did they tell our father. Then we came and there was Anna Catherine. But we were too late for you."

"I'd gone to Wales," William said, understanding more than his brother had put into words. His Oneida parents had survived the disappointment of losing him a second time, waited nine more years for his return, and what had he done when he learned the truth? Cost them another year. At last he asked the question he'd longed to ask.

"Will you tell me of her? Our mother?"

The noise of the stream swelled in the dark; Two Hawks's voice was soft, forcing William to lean close to hear. "What do you wish to know?"

Everything. Anything. He'd no idea where to start. Or . . . perhaps he did.

"Where did she come from? Was it anything like . . . with me? Was she stolen?"

"She was a captive once." Again William settled in to listen to his brother tell a story, this time of a tiny white girl taken in a frontier raid nearly forty years ago, adopted into the Turtle Clan. "She is *Onyota'a:ka* now, our mother, with no memory of that other life, as you have no memory of her. But now our families will be united. Soon, Creator willing, I will be with Aubrey again, working at the boatyard as I did in—"

"You worked on the Binne Kill?" William interjected. "With him—Aubrey? What made you want to do that?"

"You may well ask your brother that question." Stone Thrower stepped up onto the rock ledge, sending them both surging to their feet in startlement. They had neither of them heard his coming. "But there is no more time for stories this night."

The moon was risen. Enough light filtered through the trees to show the relief in his brother's posture, the same that was coursing through William now.

Stone Thrower must have found the Senecas.

Something shifted for William in that moment as he and Two Hawks faced their father, who was breathing hard from running, the sound audible above the stream's chatter. He felt drawn to the man, in a way that went deeper than respect or admiration, but he knew not what to say or do with the feeling.

"May I see it?" he blurted. "The portrait of me. I've seen that you carry it." It was too dark to tell whether the big warrior was surprised by the request as he fished inside the neck of his shirt and pulled out a corded pouch. He untied it, removed the small oval. Feeling foolish now—it was also too dark to see the painting—William reached for it.

Their fingers brushed. Stone Thrower's convulsed over his, gripping for an instant.

"I do forgive you." William had blurted again, as if his heart was bent on expressing what his mind had yet to untangle. "And I want to see my mother."

"You will see her," Stone Thrower said, with a fullness in his voice that fell upon William like an embrace. "Soon. And there will be much joy in your meeting. But we must also return Aubrey to those who wait for him."

"You have found him?" Two Hawks asked. "He lives?"

"I have seen him in the Senecas' camp. Alive still. Before this night is through we must take him back, though how it will be accomplished I do not yet know. Be praying about it as we go. Are you rested, my son?"

William realized the man was addressing him. "I am," he said and wanted to say *Father,* but the word clotted in his throat. He felt a strong hand grip his shoulder.

"Then take up your rifles, both of you, and follow me."

41

August 8, after nightfall
Seneca lands

*H*e couldn't be certain—they spoke no English in his presence—
but Reginald thought the Senecas were divided over what to
do with him. So enraged had they been over their battle casualties and their
possessions lost to Willett's sortie that Reginald had expected to be toma-
hawked—or worse, tortured first—the first night they'd stopped their
march westward. They'd given him water but no food. They'd taken his
coat, along with the strings of wampum hidden in its inner pocket. His
bloody scalp wound they'd ignored; he'd no idea of its severity save for the
throbbing pain and dizziness it caused. His wrists were bound. He wasn't
certain why they hadn't killed him.

Perhaps it had to do with one of their number—the oldest, by the
gray of his scalp-lock and the creases beneath the red paint adorning his
face—who'd taken an inexplicable interest in him, beyond a target upon
which to vent frustration and contempt. He was the one now wearing
Reginald's coat.

Lost in a focus of endurance, Reginald hadn't noticed the warrior
watching him during the first march from the fort. On the second day, the
gray-haired Indian had contrived to travel near him. More than once,
when Reginald would have stumbled, the man shot a rope-veined hand
out to steady him, grunting encouragement when he faltered. He'd
thanked the man, knowing he couldn't maintain this brutal pace much
longer. When he fell, they would club him where he lay. The thought

didn't unduly dismay him. He'd no wish to die—he'd left so much unfinished, unspoken; he yearned to see his Anna again. And Lydia; so much they might have shared, years and years at last entwined, heart and soul. But the most needful things were accomplished, and Reginald knew where he was bound beyond this life and in Whose presence he would stand redeemed. Because of that, death would be a celebration. A feast.

Thou preparest a table before me in the presence of mine enemies . . .

It was an amazement, the store of Scripture still residing in the recesses of his soul. He hadn't opened his Bible in years. Not since Heledd's leaving had he even tried to hear the voice of the Almighty in its pages, but there it was—grace unmerited, granted in his need as he followed the file of Indians on this trail that wound through wood and glade and gully, seemingly forever.

All the paths of the LORD are mercy and truth unto such as keep his covenant and his testimonies.

My foot standeth in an even place.

William was with his father, his brother, perhaps by now his mother as well. Where he ought to have been left twenty years ago. Reginald felt an assurance deeper than knowledge, beyond the little his eyes had seen, that Stone Thrower had gotten his firstborn out of that ravine, away from the battle, to safety. He mightn't wish to remain with his kin, but that would be for William to decide. And the Almighty.

Keep him. Guard him. Grant them all wisdom and patience . . .

Though hungry, bruised, and bleeding, nearly staggered with pain, with every breath left to him he meant to intercede for the souls once in his care. William. Two Hawks. His dear girl. Anna had his blessing to marry the man she loved, and for that he was thankful, but he might have done so much more—given her his name as well as his heart. Why hadn't he insisted upon it from the beginning? Might Heledd have softened in time had he stood stronger against her rejection?

There was no knowing. He confessed the failing to God and let it go,

marveling that atonement was made, that he need only accept it in gratitude, and rest. What freedom. What *joy*. It wasn't to be contained. And so
he smiled into the hard, painted faces of his captors, especially the old one
who showed him something more than loathing.

Not long before they'd halted that night, the man had made an attempt to communicate. Reginald discerned a word or two. Something
about women . . . or was it mothers? Surely the man was too old to have a
mother living. Maybe he'd meant *wife*. Did he fancy Reginald as a slave
for his womenfolk?

At last the old warrior had given up the attempt and vanished into the
wood with two others. The Senecas had been coming and going thus since
leaving the siege camp—with their provisions carted off to the fort, they
had no food for the journey home—hunting as they went. It made it difficult to know how many were in the party. At different times he'd counted
eight, ten, twelve. There could be more.

Soon after the old man's departure, the warrior leading the party had
signaled a stop. At a clearing's edge, Reginald had crashed to his knees,
feeling himself sliding into blackness, knowing they might kill him before
ever he woke again. Yet he had awakened—to the leaping of flames and
the discord of strident voices. Someone thrust the rim of a cup against his
teeth. He sat up and gulped the water before it choked him, his body
greedy for it.

The warrior set the cup on the ground beside Reginald and returned
to his fellows, lingering near enough to keep an eye on him. Reginald
reached for the cup with bound hands but succeeded only in tipping it.
They still hadn't fed him. He felt his strength ebbing, soaking into the
ground like the water, and didn't know come morning whether he could
rise again, much less walk.

How far had they to go?

He dozed sitting up, to be startled awake by a stream of words hot as
molten metal. The leader of the party, a tall, deep-chested warrior, bronzed

flesh gleaming and feathers bristling in his scalp-lock, was pacing before the fire and addressing the others—nine at present—throwing an occasional nod in Reginald's direction.

That one wanted to kill him. He'd started the process back at the siege camp. Along with other prisoners, Reginald had been made to run a gauntlet, though by the time his turn came, the twin lines of Indians waiting to thrash him with sticks and clubs had begun to dissolve in shouted dispute. Only a few had actually struck him, driving him to his knees but inflicting no serious injury. They'd fallen on someone else though, beyond Reginald's sight. Judging by the man's screams, what they'd done was appalling. That was when he'd been hauled up off the ground again and taken away into the night, as some of the Senecas abandoned their leaders and the disastrous campaign, and the march westward began.

Another warrior stood now and spoke. Among his words Reginald caught a name he recognized. *Niagara.* Did this one propose selling him to the British to be ransomed or traded back to the Continentals? If so, the suggestion was met without enthusiasm. These Senecas were returning home with less than they'd come with, in goods and men. There was nothing to satisfy them but a few scalps. And Reginald, his life, his blood.

He searched the clearing for the old warrior who wore his coat but didn't see him. What help would he have been in any case? Reginald only surmised the man had taken an interest in him—beyond what his death or suffering might serve. That mightn't be the case.

Out of the blue a thought struck him—that if he lived to see another sunrise, it would mark twenty years to the day since he walked out of Fort William Henry with a child he'd no right to claim, leaving his own dead son behind. *Twenty years You gave me to confess the truth, to make it right with You—and allow You to bring healing to those I wounded. I regret it took so very long. I regret . . .*

Lydia. Her smile that was light to him, her blue eyes imploring him. Her steadfast heart loving him, waiting for him. Believing the best. Hoping always for good things. *Grant her peace and wholeness after I am gone. Grant her life, and love, and, yes, children.*

They wouldn't be his children. It was a grief almost too great to bear, the only comfort that he needn't bear it much longer.

Over at the fire, the Senecas were shrieking in response to something one of their number had proclaimed. Another barked an order to the warrior who'd given him water. The young man approached him again.

"The LORD is my strength and my shield," Reginald said as hard fingers closed round his arm, dragging him to his feet. Pain seared the length of his lame leg, and in spite of his effort not to, he cried aloud, then through gritted teeth got out, "My heart trusted in him, and I am helped—"

A cuff across his mouth silenced him, bringing the taste of blood. He was thrust toward the fire at the clearing's edge. Did they mean to burn him?

Gunfire cracked in his ears, so close as to be deafening.

He didn't feel the shot.

"They're killing him!" William hissed through his teeth, though had he shouted the words, he'd not have been heard above the clamor the warriors were making across the clearing. They'd overtaken the Senecas but moments ago, drawn the last half mile at a run by the rising tide of angry voices. Now he'd lost sight of the man they'd come to rescue, obscured by drifting powder smoke and the bodies swarming round him. He started forward, ready to break from cover.

Hands clamped down on him, one to either shoulder, as a second musket barked.

"They shoot into the air," Stone Thrower said on his left.

On his right Two Hawks urged, "Brother—look!"

The warriors parted, revealing Reginald Aubrey on his knees in the firelight, wrists bound, half his face dark with dried blood. But alive. William got possession of himself, sensing through the hands gripping him the same need thrumming through his father and brother to rush into the clearing.

"They are not killing him," Stone Thrower said. "Not yet."

William strained in the dark to read the face of the warrior beside him. "You understand their words?"

"Yes. I lived among these warriors for a time. Some will know me."

Two Hawks shouldered between them, releasing William. "You are going among them?"

Stone Thrower drew himself erect. "I am. And I go alone."

"Thayendanegea has sent the bloody hatchet!"

Alarm was in his brother's voice. William could all but smell it on the damp night air as their father said, "These warriors left the camp before that thing was done, but whether they know of it is no matter. This is a thing I must do. Creator is with me and will see it through as He wills it."

Bereft of such faith, William asked, "What will you say to them?"

"I will know that when I say it." Stone Thrower took them each by a shoulder, grip and voice firm. "Listen, my sons. Stay in these woods and do not show yourselves—unless I call for you. Then come out together, straight to me, into the light."

William couldn't speak. Neither, it seemed, could his brother.

Stone Thrower's fingers pressed hard. "Do my sons hear my words?"

"I hear them," Two Hawks said with evident reluctance.

Satisfied, the big warrior turned the force of his attention on William, who knew he must say something. The words being shouted in that clearing were incomprehensible, but the roil of violent intent behind them needed no translation.

"Had I the choice to make again," he said in a rush, "I would stay. I would not go to Quebec."

A breath deepened Stone Thrower's chest, then William found himself engulfed in his father's embrace, the arms around him strong and sure, like the shielding of eagle's wings.

Stone Thrower uttered a word, muffled by the beating of William's own heart. It sounded like *iyo*. Then he was gone, striding out into the clearing, into the light of the Senecas' fire.

42

With every sinew strung taut, Two Hawks watched his father cross the clearing. The Senecas had yet to notice him, so focused were they on their prisoner. Beside him, William radiated a matching apprehension. "Will they kill him too, our father?"

"He goes with a shield of faith and a strong heart." Two Hawks's voice, dry as wood dust, betrayed the fear that lurked behind those words, and so he added, "Be praying, Brother."

Praying for words to turn aside the warriors' lust for vengeance and blood. Words like a dam skillfully laid across a raging stream. His father did not lack for courage, but the mood of these warriors was ugly. There was no telling which way their hearts would turn. Or their hands. Or what might be the word or deed to turn them.

Two Hawks gripped his rifle, felt the weight of the bow across his shoulder. Should he ready the bow? With it he could shoot in silence from the trees without revealing their position at once. Many arrows in the time it took to reload a rifle. He set by the rifle, slipped the bow from its case, strung it without taking his gaze from his father. Stone Thrower's back was lance straight, his stride unhesitating. Two Hawks's heart swelled with love and pride, pressing up into his throat. He remembered what his brother had said, his father's joy in hearing it. *Let it not be the last words they exchange.*

Stone Thrower was nearly among the Senecas before a warrior gave a shout of warning, alerting the rest. They swung to face him, seeming many in the firelight. Were others out ranging the wood? Two Hawks glanced into the tangled dark, then whipped his head around to scan the fire-lit clearing as sharp words of surprise fell away to silence. The Senecas had formed a wall, obstructing Two Hawks's view of Aubrey, on the ground behind them. A tall, powerful warrior strode out from their ranks and halted in Stone Thrower's path.

"Who are you, come thus among us? Do you follow from Thayenda-negea's camp with news?"

The tension of the warriors eased slightly at this. They had been look-ing beyond Stone Thrower to the clearing's edge, some with muskets raised, but here was only one man, unafraid in his approach as a friend would be. No threat against their numbers whatever his intentions.

Stone Thrower had wiped the war paint from his face, but thus far it didn't appear any of these Senecas recognized him. Where was the one he claimed to know?

Halted before the chief warrior, Stone Thrower spoke in the tongue of the Senecas. "I have come from that camp, though not with news to share." It was wisely spoken, Two Hawks thought, for his father did have news. Grim news for the Oneidas. Not news he meant to reveal if he could help it. "I come to speak on a matter of my own concern."

The words rang out with confidence but were met with silence, in which William hissed in urgent whisper, "What are they saying? Do you understand?"

Two Hawks didn't speak the Senecas' tongue as fluently as did his father, but he knew enough to follow what was said. "I will tell you what they say, only keep your voice down . . . and your rifle ready."

Staying hidden no matter what unfolded was a thing he didn't think he could do, now he saw his father alone among the Senecas. Not if they offered violence. Stand and do nothing while these warriors murdered his father and Anna Catherine's father? Already some menaced, edging nearer Stone Thrower. The blood of their fallen cried loudly in their ears. His father would need to balance his words on a knife's edge.

"What concern have you with us?" the chief warrior demanded. "I do not remember you from the camp at the fort."

"I am Stone Thrower," his father said. "Born to the Bear Clan of the *Onyota'a:ka,* and my concern with you is for that one you hold captive."

The warriors standing in front of Anna Catherine's father stepped aside, revealing their prisoner on his knees, hatless, coatless, tattered. His face in the firelight was tensed with pain, one side of it bloodied. Two Hawks could see his surprise at sight of Stone Thrower, but he didn't cry out or plead with his captors.

"What do they say?" William demanded to know.

"Our father makes claim on Aubrey."

"What mean you? What claim?"

Two Hawks grasped his brother's arm to silence him. "Let me listen, Brother."

His father's voice reached them. "I would speak for this prisoner before he is harmed. There is a thing I have to say of him."

As Two Hawks interpreted their father's words, a wave of disapproval swept across the clearing—the Senecas disputing such a claim. The chief warrior's voice rose above the murmurs. "What cause has one of the *Onyota'a:ka* to come among us speaking as a friend, a brother?"

Stone Thrower didn't hesitate. "I am both of those things to you, men of Ganundasaga. Some may remember that once I lived among you, hunted with you—or with your fathers, you younger men. I fought beside my Seneca brothers when you answered Pontiac's call to go against the British at their lake forts. I ask you to remember this and let me speak to you now as a man speaks to his friends. Will you hear me?"

Two Hawks tensed as the chief warrior stepped closer to peer into Stone Thrower's face in silence for a long moment before turning again to address his warriors.

"I do remember this one. I was young in that time of which he speaks, but I saw my first battle with Pontiac. What he says is true. He fought with us then. And fought well."

"But now?" Another came forward. "Did he fight for us in the ravine? Or for the Americans?"

The truth was Stone Thrower had fought for neither and against both in attempting to find William, but he was not given time to say so.

"That is a matter we will consider," the chief said, raising a hand. "He is one man alone, come to us in peace. We will hear him." He turned again to Stone Thrower, and despite his words, there was hardness in his tone. "Say what you have come to say about this captive, before we decide his fate this night."

At the edge of the wood, Two Hawks let out a breath and told William what was being said. "Now our father is telling our story. He is telling of our mother, and of us, and why he makes a claim on Aubrey."

"But why will they care? What difference can it make?" William asked, sounding as bewildered as any white man might be standing there beside him. Two Hawks's mind was a jumble. How could he explain in a few words the ways of a people his brother had never known?

"Our father has some right to vengeance against Aubrey for what he did, taking you from us."

William's voice held an edge of panic. "But he said he forgave!"

"He did that hard thing, yes. But *these* warriors do not know this."

While his father spoke of that long ago day at Fort William Henry, Two Hawks's gaze went again to Anna Catherine's father. While on the trail of the Senecas, his father had told them more of the change that had happened in Aubrey's soul. Two Hawks thought he was seeing evidence of that change. There was peace in Aubrey's face as he knelt among those who meant him torment and death. Though Two Hawks did not think Aubrey understood the words being said, he seemed to know he was listening to a tale of a shame no longer his to bear.

"This is the man?" the war chief questioned, gesturing at Aubrey when Stone Thrower finished speaking. "*He* is the one who stole your firstborn and kept him from you all these years?"

"He is," Stone Thrower said. "Now I ask you to give him over to me, that I may take him from this place to the mother of that lost son, who waits for me."

At this, a warrior who hadn't yet spoken stepped forward. "I also am one who remembers you and the tale of your sons, of the one twin stolen at his birth. Now you say this is the man who did this thing and you ask us to give him to you, but here is a thing *I* would ask. If we do this, what will heal the grief of *our* women when they hear of the sons and husbands who have died fighting the Americans? We were promised an easy victory and much spoil. Now you see even those things we had were taken by soldiers from the fort. Many warriors lie dead on the ground behind us. What is to cover our sorrow? We have but this one prisoner!"

More than one voice cried out in agreement at this. A warrior made a lunge for Aubrey, club raised to strike him. Two Hawks had an arrow to his bow but checked when the war chief shouted for his men to stop. He stared hard at Aubrey, then motioned to Stone Thrower, giving him the chance to answer the challenge.

Two Hawks lowered the arrow, trembling now, praying from the depths of his soul for his father's next words to be wise ones.

"I understand well your sorrow," Stone Thrower said. "Your hearts are on the ground, and your grief needs covering. But, my brothers!" he cried, his voice strengthening with conviction. "Do you think killing this one man, or bringing him back for your women to torment, will do this needful thing? I tell you it will be as a drop of rain to one dying of thirst. I know this, for no matter how many enemies I killed in the years I hunted for that man there, no matter how many scalps I took with Pontiac, it was never enough to fill the emptiness in my heart or heal the pain of the mother of my sons. I will tell you what, and who, will cover that grief. His messenger came to you once. Though many of you spurned his words of peace with Creator, a few began to walk the Jesus path. It is He who—"

"You speak of Kirkland!" one of the older warriors interjected. "We made that missionary flee Ganundasaga like a dog with its tail tucked."

"Your talk is like his," said another. "That of a weak man who flees his enemies in the night. I can hear no more of your words!"

The war chief stood with arms crossed and waited to see what Stone Thrower would say to that. Their father's back was to them, but Reginald Aubrey was looking straight at Stone Thrower. He gave the smallest of nods, encouragement to the man he must know was fighting for their lives, even if he could not understand his words.

"I was already a weak man when you first knew me," Stone Thrower replied. "So weak I forsook my wife and son, forgot how to be a man of the People. So weak all I could think of was killing that man you have bound as your prisoner. But Heavenly Father has made me strong—strong enough to forgive that man." He flung an arm toward Aubrey. "He was not in that ravine to fight you or those British who enticed you with their false promises. He was there to help me find the son he took. He wished only to restore my son to me. This hard thing he did, risking his life. We together found my firstborn in that battle. That son is with me, he and his brother, and now your eyes will see them, two-born-together united at last."

Ignoring the murmurs of startled protest rising around him, Stone Thrower turned his back on the Senecas and faced the place where his sons hid, the one furiously whispering to the other of all that had been uttered.

"My sons!" he called out. "Come out to me now. Let these warriors see you together under the eyes of Creator!"

43

*T*hey stepped from the trees in answer to the summons, sharing a glance as they passed into the firelight's edge. Mirrored in his brother's eyes were the conflicting emotions roiling in William's soul: fear and determination, uncertainty and wonder—at a Presence at work beyond that of flesh and blood.

That sense of flesh and blood alone was all but overwhelming. The brother beside him, the father who'd called them forth . . . they were his, and his heart was leaping like a crazed thing, swelling with a joy that had taken him unawares. Joy mingled with the dread of losing what he'd just found. Two Hawks had presumed their father meant to trick the Senecas into thinking he desired vengeance against Reginald Aubrey, that he had the higher claim on him as a prisoner. What was Stone Thrower doing now, talking of forgiveness and calling them forth?

The Senecas murmured as they watched them come into the fire's light. A few warriors strode forward as he and Two Hawks halted beside their father, but only the spokesman came near enough to look into their faces, frowning.

"These are your sons? Two-born-together?"

Two Hawks, shoulder pressed to William's, murmured what the man had said, but William could read that pull of brows, the indecision in the hard eyes darting between their faces. William's gaze shot past the Indian to see Reginald Aubrey looking back at him with longing, plain through his mask of blood.

Father. A buzzing erupted in William's head. The spot where he'd been struck throbbed, bone and bruised flesh echoing his heart's pounding.

"One son raised among the People, one raised white," Stone Thrower was saying, the unfettered pride in his voice crashing over William before Two Hawks translated the words. "These are my sons."

Father. If their fate teetered on a knife edge among these Senecas, another blade cleaved William's heart. He stood upon it, fixed to topple, but couldn't say upon which side he would fall. Only his brother's voice, providing clipped abridgement as the debate went on, kept him balanced on that edge.

"They are warriors," one of the Senecas who'd objected to Stone Thrower's presence from the beginning spat. He jerked his chin at Two Hawks. "That one I remember from the battle."

Stone Thrower moved a half step nearer Two Hawks. "This son of mine was in the battle also to find his brother. If he was forced to defend himself while doing so, it was not done gladly. Nor was it with joy that I went into that ravine. But to find my lost son, it was needful." Stone Thrower searched the faces of the Senecas, who gave him back his stare with varying levels of hostility. "Where is he who took the prisoner? Let him say what his eyes saw in that moment."

The warriors exchanged looks. None came forward to claim the taking of Reginald Aubrey.

"Some are hunting and may not return this night." The chief warrior waved the matter aside. "If we let this man go with you, what will you give in exchange?"

William blinked at the gazes leveled at them as his brother whispered the war chief's demand. They had nothing to trade for a man. Except another man. And Stone Thrower knew it. Two Hawks was staring at their father, who was looking between them with a gaze both tender and sorrowful. William felt the breath sucked from his chest as a horrific comprehension began to dawn.

Then a new voice shouted from the darkness.

Every face turned to see who now approached, a gray-haired warrior carrying the wrapped pieces of a butchered deer across wiry shoulders, wearing a coat William recognized as Aubrey's. Two Hawks leaned close to translate what the Indian was saying as he approached, but William only half took it in. He was frantically reading expressions, trying to discern the look of cautious relief on the face of Reginald Aubrey, that of recognition on Stone Thrower's as he held out a hand to the old man who slung the deer meat to the ground and clasped the proffered arm.

His name, Two Hawks told him, was Blue-Tailed Lizard. "He is the one who laid hands on Aubrey during battle," his brother added, voice stretched with hope now as well as apprehension. "Our father is telling him why we are here, what this is about."

William struggled to understand. Was this man their last chance of getting out of this, the four of them alive and whole?

Blue-Tailed Lizard listened patiently to Stone Thrower's words, then looked long at William, at Two Hawks, then at Reginald Aubrey. His puckered lips pursed tight, curving downward in displeasure. But a glint of something else showed in his hooded gaze. Curiosity? Speculation? Or was it calculation?

William's gaze snapped from warrior to warrior, watching eyes, hands, tensed for one of them to lose patience and reach for a blade. Amid the thickening tension, the chief warrior said something Two Hawks didn't translate.

Blue-Tailed Lizard shook his head. "What this warrior has told you about his sons is true. I know this to be so, for it was in my lodge he dwelled when he lived among us at Ganundasaga. At that time I followed the words of the missionary. I even helped persuade this warrior to follow Kirkland's Jesus. You know that after a time it became a hard path to follow, tangled and overgrown. I lost the path and did not try to find it again."

The old man put a ropey hand to Stone Thrower's shoulder, then turned to his Seneca companions. "Perhaps I was not clear sighted enough to stay on the path this man has walked. Look well on him. Here he stands with the son he lost twenty summers past, a son restored to him and to the one born with him." With his other hand he gestured toward the fire, where Reginald knelt. "And there is the one of which this man always spoke about in those days—the redcoat officer who took his son."

Turning again to Stone Thrower, he asked, "And it is your wish he not suffer for it?"

"He has suffered enough," Stone Thrower said, swallowing visibly over the words as though they came with an upwelling of grief. "I do not wish him to suffer more."

The old warrior searched Stone Thrower's resolute face, his own eyes narrowed to slits. William waited, sharing a glance with Two Hawks, gone ashen faced in the fire's ruddy light, as if he saw more clearly the direction this talk was headed, and it dismayed him.

William was completely at sea now. The old warrior's words of their father had seemed to offer hope, at least the way his brother translated them. What was causing Two Hawks such bleakness of expression?

"I was coming now to make my claim on the prisoner," Blue-Tailed Lizard went on. "I thought to keep him alive for my women to kill—or to let you here do it, if that is what seemed best." The old warrior's grip on Stone Thrower's shoulder tightened. "But I have heard this one's speech and it has changed my thinking. He has forgiven that one there for the taking of his son. This we all have heard. What is more, there is that son restored to him. What need has he now of vengeance? But *our* dead are still dead. Even so I will do as he wishes. I will give that one," he said, bending his chin again toward Reginald Aubrey, "to the mother of these young warriors of his to do with as she pleases."

Shouts of protest started up from all quarters before Two Hawks could finish translating. William, daring to hope, wrenched his gaze from that gnarled hand clasping his father's shoulder and turned to his brother, who finished in a barely comprehensible rush, his last words swallowed by a groan.

Stone Thrower, hearing it, caught his second-born's gaze, his own resolved, yet his eyes . . . such deep wells of sorrow and regret. The relief that had surged so briefly through William crumbled like dust. Something was wrong. He turned frantically to his brother for explanation. Before Two Hawks could say a word, the chief warrior held up his hand for silence.

"This warrior, our elder, has a voice in this matter. It is true he was first to lay hands on the prisoner. Let him finish speaking if he has more to say." He nodded to the old man to continue.

"I do have more to say, so listen." To the angry warriors, Blue-Tailed Lizard said, "A man is free to choose his path. The Jesus path this warrior has chosen may seem a strange one to you, even foolish, but for him it would seem it is good. Strong. There are words that go with this path, and some of them I have not forgotten. I will speak them to you, but first there is this I must do."

Blue-Tailed Lizard released Stone Thrower and crossed the firelight to Reginald Aubrey, shouldering younger warriors aside. No one raised a hand to stop him. Taking hold of their prisoner's arm, the old man hauled him to his feet. He waited for the prisoner to steady himself on legs that wobbled, then reached inside the coat he wore and took out three strings of white beads.

Wampum, William thought, mystified by their significance.

"These I found in the coat I took off this one," he said, turning in the firelight to address Stone Thrower. "You know them?"

Stone Thrower had taken an involuntary step toward them but was stopped by a motion from the chief warrior. "They belong to him," he said, nodding at Reginald. "They were given by my hand for a sign of the friendship that is between us. Between his blood and my blood."

Blue-Tailed Lizard put the wampum strings into Reginald's bound hands, then marched him to stand before Stone Thrower.

"Now I will say the words of the missionary that I have not forgotten. These are the words: 'Greater love hath no man than this, that a man lay down his life for his friends.'" The Indian made a show of looking at Reginald, straight into his face. Then he did the same to Stone Thrower. "You have called this man friend. Are you willing to trade your life for his, to show your heart for your Creator Jesus is true?"

Two Hawks stumbled in his speech as he interpreted for William, as if his lips had gone numb over the words. Their import—and compelling force—sank into William's heart. Two Hawks turned to him a devastated gaze, even as their father gave his answer.

Two Hawks didn't interpret it. There was no need.

A moment of utter silence followed, broken only by the fire's sputtering. Then around them rose the triumphant screams of warriors who wanted blood and were certain now that they would get it.

44

As eager yelps and screams rose around him, Reginald clenched the white shell beads until they bit into his palms, chilled to his marrow not for the terror of impending violence against himself—though he still expected it—but for the growing sense that he was no longer the only one in mortal jeopardy. He'd understood nothing of what had passed between Stone Thrower and these Senecas, save what could be interpreted through body language, but now all gazes were fixed on Stone Thrower; in most of them bloodlust welled. All save William's and Two Hawks's. In their eyes he read horror, denial, desperation.

That told him all he needed to know.

Reginald's next thoughts came in fragments, spiked with terror, shock, and dismay. Figures moved in the firelight, erratic, bewildering. He tried to keep Stone Thrower in his sights, and William, and Two Hawks, who'd shaken off his shock and was beseeching his father, arguing with the old warrior who'd thrust the beads into his hands and left him standing there, discarded and forgotten.

A fresh slick of cold sweat washed down Reginald's face. He had made his peace with his own death. He'd been ready to face whatever came. But not this.

Two Hawks and Stone Thrower spoke urgently to each other, but their words were in Oneida, beyond Reginald's understanding with such tumult surrounding them.

"You needn't have done this!" he rasped in a half shout, trying to make himself heard before this horde of angry Senecas descended upon them with more than screams. "I would have gone with them! Or died here!"

Though Two Hawks and William stood near, grasping at their father, Stone Thrower bent his full attention now to Reginald, features fierce with determination, his gaze filled with his unshielded heart. The force and fullness of it was unlike anything Reginald had ever seen—the acceptance, the urgency, the faith. The love. And not just for his sons.

"It is done," he said to Reginald, grasping his arm with a strength unyielding. "There is no undoing it."

Neither William nor Two Hawks had ceased their pleading for him to not do this thing. To find another way.

"My sons," Stone Thrower said, cutting off their pleas, "if you do not take this one away now, get him safe from here, what I am doing will be for nothing and we shall all be killed this night!"

Again Stone Thrower turned the force of that luminous gaze on Reginald, looking into his eyes, strong hand gripping hard enough to bruise. "Listen to me. You must be a father to both of my sons now. *Our* sons. You must do this for me. For their mother. Be to me as a brother and care for my family."

Blue-Tailed Lizard and the chief warrior were pressing close, pulling at them, wading in to separate them from their chosen captive.

"By Creator's grace and strength you will do this!" Stone Thrower shouted to make himself heard, and despite the declaration there was a note of question in the words.

"You have my promise!" Reginald knew his voice, broken with emotion, could never carry, but saw that Stone Thrower, gaze fixed on his lips, had read the words. There was time for nothing else. Nothing else Reginald might say could matter more. He'd have promised the man his life's blood had he asked for it, but that was a thing Stone Thrower was offering for him. For all of them. They must leave this terrible clearing, with all haste.

Two Hawks, not yet reconciled to that conclusion, reached for the blade at his belt. "Father! We will fight for you. We—"

"Do not fight!" Stone Thrower bellowed in English, perhaps for Reginald and William's sake, perhaps so the Senecas wouldn't know what they said, even as he was set upon by warriors with ropes to bind his wrists. "And do not seek me, my brave and faithful son! Only remember me. Remember our good God and—"

He was cuffed across the mouth and dragged backward, away from them, but they could not break the gaze that held him fast to his sons. To William he shouted, the words coming broken through bleeding lips, "I have loved you always, my bright arrow! Fly now to your mother's heart. She has waited long for you."

Reginald witnessed the instant Two Hawks yielded to Stone Thrower's last command, saw the young man's heart cleave in two as his gaze wrenched from his father's in submission and farewell, fixing on him and William.

What followed seemed more dream to Reginald than reality. The wounding during the battle, the wearing march, the hunger, the strain of these last moments, had finally done for him. A searing pain jarred from his hip down to his knee, turning his legs to sponges. He thought he must have fallen . . .

Next he knew, he was moving through the darkness of a wood, supported between two sturdy young frames. He swooned again and did not rouse until the screams and shouts of Indians had fallen too far behind them to be heard.

But he would never forget the sound.

He woke on his back with his bonds loosed. Blood still caked his face, his hair. Above him stars winked through leaf-heavy branches. He could hear them talking low together, a little distance off. Stone Thrower's sons. His sons. Grief crashed down on him, crushing as a mountain.

"William," he called, hoarse, feeble, urgent.

The voices stilled, but William didn't come. His brother did, touching him gently in the dark. "He is with us. Safe. We make a litter to carry you to Kanowalohale. Anna Catherine and Lydia are there, with my mother."

Lydia and his dear girl . . . so near? Another mystery to unravel.

Two Hawks was still speaking, shock and grief shredding his voice, but Reginald couldn't make out the words. His chest felt as though it would rupture, torn between sorrow and joy. Stone Thrower had gone to an unspeakable death, but the lad his Anna loved was safe and whole. And so, at long last, was William.

William couldn't bear the sight of those shadowed figures, his brother bending over Reginald Aubrey. He'd heard the man call to him weakly, but he couldn't answer. Not now with his father, so briefly restored to him, lost, before ever he could be truly known. He stepped away into the deeper darkness of the forest, too stunned yet to grieve or to rage—or to face Reginald Aubrey. He wasn't ready. He didn't know what he meant to say. He needed . . .

A stick cracked behind him. They were a mile at least from that dreadful clearing, a mile through dark woods, and he'd thought they hadn't been followed, that they'd been allowed to leave as the old warrior had decreed.

Whirling, William raised his hands in time to grasp a figure coming at him, eyes catching a swift glint of starlight. Instinctively he clutched at what his hands found in the dark, half fending off attack, half restraining escape: slim shoulders and a long silky braid that brushed his arm.

"It is me, Strikes-The-Water."

William felt a new shock sizzle through him. "It's *you*?"

"Ah." Her breath stirred against his throat. "He-Is-Taken."

He relaxed his hold but didn't let go. He'd held her only with his eyes—and that briefly—until now. "What are you doing here?"

"Finding you."

Small, strong hands gripped his waist. For one startling instant, William nearly yielded to the wild urge to clutch her tight against him—for need of something, someone, to cling to lest he spiral away on the tide of grief even now surging up against the thin barrier of shock.

Then his brother called to him, alarm in his voice.

"Where is Stone Thrower?" the girl asked, pulling away from him.

"He isn't coming—but I'm glad you have." Though his voice broke, William took Strikes-The-Water by the hand and led her into starlight.

45

August 14, 1777
Kanowalohale

*G*rief hung like a smoke pall over Kanowalohale, which was crowded now with refugees; Oriska lay in ashes, its people scattered—those who'd survived its destruction.

Since she housed guests already, Good Voice hadn't taken any of Oriska's homeless into her lodge, but under her arbor on that gray afternoon, Anna was helping Two Hawks's mother and Lydia sort through garments, blankets, and provisions collected from many to share with those who'd lost all but their lives and the clothes on their backs.

It was two days since the town from which the warriors had gone to fight with General Herkimer's militia had been attacked in retribution. Many of those warriors were still away to the west, harassing St. Leger's besieging forces at Fort Stanwix. When the attack came, it was old men, women, and children who bore its brunt. Some of the attackers had been rangers under Colonel Butler, but dozens more were Haudenosaunee— Mohawk warriors led by Joseph Brant. White or red, they'd shown the Oneida people no mercy.

It was almost too much to bear, so close on the heels of the battle and its aftermath. As many as five hundred militiamen and Oneidas had been slain in the ambuscade, their bodies scattered over miles of wooded ravines, scalped and horrifically despoiled. The sheer number of dead was staggering to Anna's soul, yet they'd been warriors, soldiers, men who'd chosen to fight. Oriska had been a slaughter of the helpless, perpetrated by those once counted brothers. She couldn't imagine the heaviness of heart Good Voice and the people around her were feeling now. Her prayers for them mingled with her constant petitions for Papa, Two Hawks, William, Stone Thrower, none of whom had yet returned. The days passed, grinding by in an agony of waiting, one eye on the trees for fear Brant would turn his vengeful gaze toward Kanowalohale next. Those warriors not away fighting ranged around the town, watching every approach.

Across a pile of garments, Lydia fingered a pair of tiny moccasins, staring at them as if unseeing. Thunder rumbled in the distance, snapping her head up. She met Anna's gaze, then glanced past her toward the village beyond Good Voice's arbor, blue eyes searching, hoping . . .

Hope faded, once again deferred.

Anna had stopped watching the lanes and paths, aching to see familiar figures rounding a lodge, striding toward them. It hurt too much. At first they'd spent hours talking of the men, but no more. Now there was only waiting.

Thunder again. They were too far away to hear the great guns at the fort, but the muffled noise made Anna think of those men still trapped inside it. Daniel Clear Day had made it safely out of Oriska just before the attack to bring them news of the ongoing siege. Of Strikes-The-Water, who'd gone after the men, there had come no word. The girl was another worry stretching Anna's nerves.

She placed a calico blouse on a pile designated for women and met Good Voice's gaze, noting she'd stopped sorting garments and simply sat, hands resting on the mound of her belly. She caught Anna's gaze. "I must go tend that stew." Maneuvering herself up off the ground, Good Voice rose and went inside to see to food for which none of them had appetite to eat.

"Anna?" Lydia was holding up a deerskin tunic heavy with smoked fringe. "A girl's dress? Or a shirt for a boy?"

"Girl, I think." Anna rummaged in the heap of clothing for another item.

"Anna?" Sighing, Anna looked up again, but this time Lydia didn't have a garment in hand. She was gazing past Anna, into the town, a furrow carved between her brows an instant before those brows shot high, the eyes beneath them springing wide. She reached across the clothing to grip Anna's arm. "Anna—look!"

She knew what Lydia had seen, yet she couldn't move. Her neck and limbs were locked tight. Her heart was banging, her blood rushing, commanding: *Get up*. Even when her body obeyed, it felt like pushing through deep water to rise to her feet. Lydia was already up and gone from the arbor. Anna heard her glad cry and knew that Papa, at least, was alive. It gave her strength to turn.

Then she was moving toward them, filling her eyes with the sight of them coming down the lane between the lodges. Papa led the way, clad in filthy shirt and breeches. Her heart soared, rejoiced, even as she saw he limped badly, moving with the aid of a stick crutch. But he was walking and whole, if battered. Lydia reached him and threw her arms around him, and so Anna looked beyond to . . .

"William!" Anna passed by Papa and Lydia locked in an embrace that permitted no other as yet and stopped in front of William. He gazed down at her, drinking her in with eyes so like his mother's. Eyes full of relief, pain, hope . . . and sorrow. She touched his face, which needed shaving. He grasped her hand and kissed it. She said words of forgiveness because the first that tumbled out of *his* mouth were words asking for the same— though forgiveness for what exactly she didn't catch and really did it matter now?

"Oh, William. You're here. You're safe." She embraced him. He kissed the top of her head. And then *he* was there, the one her heart longed for above all others. "Two Hawks."

She pulled out of William's embrace and stood before his brother, who'd been there all along watching her with his twin and smiling, dark eyes alight for her alone, a light of love and promise.

"Bear's Heart," he said. "Here you are."

She walked into his arms, not caring who saw or what they thought of it, and as those arms closed around her, all grief and fear were, for a few blissful moments, swallowed up in joy.

Thunder grumbled overhead, a feeble echo of the comprehension striking a current through William's frame, the first thing to cut through the veil of his grief in all the days it had taken them to reach this place his Oneida family called home. On one side of him, Lydia and Reginald embraced, in their faces a relief that for the moment banished the accumulated wounds of the past days. The surprise William felt at seeing them thus was eclipsed by sight of his sister wrapped in the arms of this brown-skinned, shaved-headed, bare-chested warrior twin of his. Anna's brow against his brother's chest, his brother's hand splayed across the back of her head, pressing her close, a look on his face as if he was breathing fully for the first time since William laid eyes on him.

William's mind swam and stuttered, floundering to deny what he was seeing, but there could be no misinterpreting. This was more than friendship, more than brotherly affection. They were in love—deeply, unassailably—and he'd had no notion of it.

That was no one's fault but his own. With Reginald Aubrey initially unable to walk, coupled with the necessity of avoiding bands of raiding Senecas and Mohawks ranging over the countryside, the return journey had been an agonizingly slow one, their every step weighted not only by one father's inert form but grief for the other father, left behind to the mercy of his enemies. Then they'd reached Oriska to find it smoldering in ruin. Bodies in the ashes. Strikes-The-Water had been the one to turn over every dead woman to see their ravaged faces. None, thank the Almighty, had been the ones they sought.

Strikes-The-Water. Her presence had made the past days bearable. She spoke English, but not well. As they journeyed, he'd spent an inordinate amount of time with her, teaching her more of it—she wanted to learn, she was bright, and lovely, and attentive, and as long as he was talking to her he needn't speak to Reginald Aubrey, or even overmuch to his brother.

But Strikes-The-Water wasn't there to distract him now. She'd gone to see her mother as soon as they'd arrived. That thought sent another jolt through William. *His* mother was here, somewhere. And she was going to have to learn what her husband had sacrificed for him, for Two Hawks, and for the man who had shattered all their lives.

Turning, he caught his brother watching him, still with an arm around Anna, whose face bore the stunned shock of comprehension and the welling up of sorrow. Two Hawks must have whispered to her of their great loss, but in his brother's eyes now he read compassion, a seeming understanding of his sense of dislocation.

And something else. Was it eagerness?

Two Hawks held out a hand, beckoning. "Look, Brother. One is coming now to greet you."

But William had looked past them already and seen her, a woman with fair hair braided, dressed in a simple skirt and tunic, coming down the path from a nearby lodge. She was staring at him as if, for the moment, none other existed. She had one fist pressed to her breastbone, against the hollow above a belly high and round with . . . pregnancy?

He looked again at Two Hawks, whose jaw was set so hard he knew his brother had anticipated this moment as intensely—maybe more so— than had he. Two Hawks's lips quivered over his words as he said, "Here is she who once carried us together as she now carries one she is certain will be our sister. She has waited long to see you—"

His voice cracked, and he swallowed to recover it. "Here is our mother, Good Voice of the Turtle Clan, also called Elizabeth."

William wasn't aware of taking the steps that closed the distance between them, only that when he began to move she halted, waiting for him to come to her. She wasn't young of course—up close he could see the fine lines that fanned from her eyes and bracketed her mouth, the strands of white woven like frost through her hair. But she was handsome, had no doubt been beautiful once. He had never seen her before, of that he was certain, yet she was disconcertingly familiar, for he was seeing in her features an echo of his own and his brother's—the curve of her lips, the shape of her chin, the set of her eyes and their hue, the arch of her brows. She was tall and would be slender if not for the expected child.

No one had seen fit to mention *that*. Until now. He was overcome.

So was she. Tears shimmered in her eyes, spilling down her cheeks. They reached for each other, hands clasping—fingers twining, squeezing hard as throats tightened. A moment thus, and the woman called Good Voice pulled one work-worn hand free and with it cupped William's face. Then she pulled his head down to rest upon her shoulder, her hand behind his head.

She was crooning under her breath.

William breathed in the scent of his mother and said that he was sorry, unable to articulate why he said it, that it was for her grief, her loss—the loss she'd borne for his lifetime, the loss she was about to begin bearing. He was weeping when, against his hair, she said, "I see your father is not returned with you, and I can think of only one reason that should be."

"I am sorry," he said yet again, still embracing her. "My father . . . He gave his life for us." He could say no more, nothing of that wrenching choice Stone Thrower made, speaking truth to those warriors when he might have lied and saved himself, or of the Senecas howling for his blood as they left him.

His mother groaned and sagged into his arms, only for a moment before she straightened and stood tall again. William raised his head as her hands found his face, and she did not take her sorrowing, loving gaze from him as she said, "Be not sorry, my beautiful son. For Creator does not leave us comfortless. We have each other now, and I will tell you everything there is to tell about that one who was your father. For all the rest of our days together, I will be telling you his story."

46

August 16, 1777
Kanowalohale

*B*ut I have no clan," Anna said, her thigh pressed close to Two Hawks's as they sat together on a log above the creek, dappled in the shade. The day had warmed, but a breeze came over the water, caressing her skin and lifting loose strands of her braided hair, ruffling the feathers in Two Hawks's scalp-lock. "Our children . . ."

"Will be ours," he told her, brushing a finger over her lips. "Will be treasured."

She searched his eyes, needing to be sure. In them was the sorrow they were all enduring—the grieving for Stone Thrower was still fresh and deep—but also the hope for their future, rekindled in each of their hearts because of Good Voice who, when told the story of Stone Thrower's sacrifice for Papa, had straightened her shoulders and through her tears said, "My husband is with his Heavenly Father. No man can touch him now. He made a good death, the best any warrior could hope to make, for by it he has saved both friend and sons and done for me the thing I asked of him so long ago. For look! Here is my firstborn taken from my side now returned to me—by the very one who took him."

Anna had wept when Good Voice crossed to Papa and put her hands to his face and spoke words of kindness and healing to him who most needed to hear it.

Had there ever been a woman of such courage and grace as Good Voice of the Turtle Clan?

"Bear's Heart," Two Hawks said to her now. "We have settled this thing between us, about our children."

"I know." She cupped his cheek, then traced the line of his healed wound across his bared scalp. Already the hair was coming in, soft bristles that soon would hide the evidence of the violence done him.

"*Kunolúhkwa,*" he said. *I love you.*

"And I love you." She thrilled to the sound of those words in his language. "I know it won't be easy . . ."

"For the joy set before me, I will face whatever lies across this path we will walk together." Even as Two Hawks spoke, sorrow passed afresh across his eyes; sorrow was never far from any of their hearts despite the moments of radiant joy that broke through again and again like rays of pure sunlight. "I have tried to be like one who lived his life in two worlds . . ."

It was another grief he was feeling now, Anna realized. He'd told her of his friend, the blacksmith and scout from Cherry Valley, Thomas Spencer, how he had lived, how he died.

So many deaths.

"Ahnyero," she said.

Two Hawks nodded. "His was the example I tried to follow. He is gone now too, but there is another who left us a better example. Another of two worlds—of earth and heaven. I will be looking to Him now."

She was going to cry again. She didn't want to cry, not when she was so happy in this moment, so she kissed him soundly. He kissed her back, until the peeling of giggles broke them apart and they looked up to see three—no *four*—dark-eyed children spying from the trees above. Seeing they'd been spotted, the little ones squealed and darted back through the woods to the village, their innocent laughter a balm to Anna's soul. Tomorrow might hold its new sorrows, for this war was far from over. She was learning to embrace whatever joy came *now*. With all her heart.

Already barefoot, she sprang off the log, hiked up her skirt, and waded into water and sunlight. Turning, calf deep, she saw Two Hawks watching her from the shade, the look in his eyes far from innocent. He came off the log like a panther rushing, feet splashing creek water in high sparkles. Grabbing her around the waist, he swung her in a circle, and now it was the two of them laughing, and the laughter was good medicine.

Down by the creek they walked, hand in hand along its bank of pebbled sand, escorted by dragonflies that darted over the water and hovered along its edge. Reginald had left his crutch propped against a tree where the path opened to the water's course. Lydia matched his limping pace, as she had nearly always done, through all the seasons of their lives.

It was settled; they would wed as soon as may be after their return to Schenectady, a journey to commence upon the morrow. Reginald, gifted thus with a second chance at life and love—at however staggering a cost— was, amid the grief for Stone Thrower, awash in a sense of grace unlike anything he'd known and yet . . . *William*.

The lad had barely spoken to him since their escape from the Senecas. Gone was the peace Reginald had found concerning William, thinking himself not long for this world. The Almighty had seen fit to leave him alive, still to reckon with the consequences of his past, which hadn't miraculously vanished with his acceptance of forgiveness—God's and Stone Thrower's.

William had spent most of the past two days with Good Voice, sometimes with the Tuscarora girl, Strikes-The-Water, sometimes with his brother—though Two Hawks and Anna were so absorbed in each other, they often had to be coaxed into a broader interaction. Reginald knew what the future held for those two. Two Hawks would remain for now in Kanowalohale, where all warriors and scouts were still needed for their people's protection, but, God willing, by the winter he would return to

Schenectady and resume his apprenticeship at the Binne Kill. And, in due time, he and Anna would marry. But no word had been said in Reginald's hearing of what William meant to do. Accompany them to Schenectady? Remain at Kanowalohale with his Oneida kin? Return to his regiment?

Mere thought of that last possibility tightened Reginald's brows, blinding him to cloudless sky, clear water rushing over sand and stone, but not to the treasure of his heart beside him, looking up at him with a decidedly knowing eye.

"Reginald." Lydia faced him, tethered by their clasped hands. "You're fretting again. Do try to desist. William is alive and reunited with his . . ." She hesitated, and he knew she'd almost said *family.* "With his mother, his brother. The rest will sort itself out. In time."

"A very long time is what I'm thinking." No doubt it would take until the end of his days, his final breath, the rooting up of the bitter fruit sown over many years, replacing it with better seed that would, in time, bear a sweeter harvest. He was thankful to have begun the sowing of it, but, oh, the grief he read in William's face . . .

The lad had found his rightful father, only to lose him before he could truly know him. Over the past two days, Good Voice had told him much. So had Two Hawks. And Clear Day, who had loved his nephew like a son. So would Reginald, if William could ever receive such words from him.

But stories could never replace the man.

"This path to healing will be a long one for us all." Lydia's eyes, unshaded by hat or bonnet, were bright and clear in the sunlight glinting off the water. "And none of us will come through it without some further hurt, I'm sure. But we will pray William, and each other, through it."

Her smile came, so full he knew it was over that *we.* It would be the two of them praying, husband and wife. Until death parted them.

"Always," he said, leaning down to kiss her.

Laughter from beyond a bend in the creek caught their attention mid-kiss. They continued along the bank to find Anna and Two Hawks wading the shallows, Anna with her hair simply braided, clothed indistinguishably from the Oneida women. His dear girl was radiantly in love, despite the heaviness that weighed them all.

"You've lost your crutch, Papa." Anna waded out of the creek and scooped up her discarded moccasins. Two Hawks followed, taking up his. "Does this mean we're heading home soon?"

"Tomorrow, my girl." Reginald shifted his gaze to Two Hawks, who came to stand beside Anna, their hands brushing just short of a clasp. "And you? You're still resolved upon a life with us, come winter?"

He could see the young man noted his choice of words. Two Hawks was choosing more than a wife. He was choosing a way of life. He'd come to Reginald the previous day to formally ask his blessing to marry Anna—a blessing now twice given. Then the lad had done him an honor he'd never expected, certainly could never deserve.

"I would ask another thing of you. In taking Anna Catherine as my wife, coming to live and work with you, I will need a name. I wish it to be yours. This is a thing Anna Catherine wishes also. She has always desired to share your name. Will you let us be called by it?"

It had needed a moment for Reginald to find his voice, though not his answer. "Yes," he'd croaked. "Anna Aubrey she'll be. And you . . . Jonathan Aubrey?"

"A good name, yes? I will make you proud that I wear it."

But Reginald had told him in no uncertain terms that there was no need to strive for a thing he already possessed.

Now the lad was returning his gaze, his fingers and Anna's entwining as if helpless to do otherwise. "I am resolved," he said, then cast a look at Anna that couldn't mask the yearning behind it. "And impatient."

"I completely sympathize," Lydia said and shared a blushing grin with Anna.

Behind them, above the noise of the creek, a throat's clearing stole their attention. They turned, the four of them. Surprise coursed through

Reginald as the ache in his chest expanded. He hadn't heard William's approach down through the trees from Good Voice's lodge.

"William," Anna said. "We were talking of heading home."

"I heard you. That's partly why . . ." Shifting his gaze to Reginald, he appeared to gather some measure of resolve himself. "I need to speak with you, sir."

Reginald felt the laboring of his heart, cramped and crowded as if the grief he carried over this young man was a physical thing taking up space in his chest. But alongside grief there now lived hope.

He was hardly aware of Anna and Two Hawks taking their leave. "William," he said, throat tightening over the name.

"Bright Arrow." William's tone was brusque, though full of emotion. Color crept into his face as he continued, "That is what I am to be called here."

"They called you He-Is-Taken," Lydia said.

William nodded once, acknowledging the name. "Yes, but my mother wishes me to have a different name now. Bright Arrow was the name of *his* father. My grandfather. Stone Thrower . . . he called me this as . . . as the Senecas took him away. Perhaps he meant for me to have the name."

They would never know whether Stone Thrower had gone into that clearing knowing all along that he would have to make the sacrifice he'd made, or whether his choice to speak truth to those warriors instead of the lie that might have delivered him had trapped him into making it, once it was revealed he no longer sought vengeance against Reginald—the only claim upon him the Senecas would have recognized. So many questions swirled in Reginald's heart, no doubt in William's as well.

He gripped Lydia's hand, seeking courage to face this, but William spoke again before he could find words. "There's to be a requickening ceremony. That's something they do—requicken the name of someone in the family who's passed. Although I think 'tis more usual for a name to come from the mother's clan than the father's."

Such pain in the blue eyes that would not quite meet Reginald's. Loss. Bitterness. Regret. Reginald's throat constricted as he said, "'Tis a good name, Bright Arrow."

But did it mean he would be staying in Kanowalohale, with Good Voice and his brother?

"I'd hoped to speak to you. I wanted to ask—"

Reginald broke off, feeling the pressure of Lydia's hand, reminding him to be patient.

"I know what you mean to ask." William's face was set now, controlled, betraying nothing. "And I mean to give you answer, but I would tell it once to everyone, so I'd best catch those two." He rolled his eyes in the direction in which his twin and Anna had vanished. "Before they disappear on us again. Will you both come now to my mother's lodge?"

*T*hey were gathered in Good Voice's lodge, her family and the family Two Hawks would soon join. Clear Day was there, and the girl, Strikes-The-Water, who had spent much time among them since her return with the men, though it was clear to all that Two Hawks's heart belonged to Anna Catherine. Good Voice knew it was no longer for her second-born that the girl was drawn to her lodge. Strikes-The-Water was careful never to be caught staring at William, but Good Voice had a mother's sense about it. She was cautiously pleased.

She was more pleased about the thing her blue-eyed son was standing up to announce now. Banished from her heart was the fear that her firstborn would look upon her and his Haudenosaunee people with disdain, or any of the bad feelings she once dreaded he might feel. He had felt them once, he had admitted, but no longer. There had been much talk with him these past days, many tears to bathe the memories of his father each had shared and the sorrow they shared as well. There had been discovery. Joy. The weaving together of hearts, seen and unseen.

"I wished to inform you of what I've decided to do," William began by saying. "I've thought long and talked to some of you . . ." He nodded to her, to Clear Day. "It's true I took an oath when I joined Sir John's regiment. It's also true I regret the taking of that oath and the decisions that led me to it." At this he glanced at Reginald Aubrey, not long enough to meet that man's gaze but long enough to see Lydia raise her hand to Reginald's arm in a comforting gesture. Good Voice saw something like contrition, then confusion, ripple over her son's face before he looked away.

Pain of different sorts lived in many hearts, but so did hope. And hope was growing.

"I tell you that it's possible I'm splitting hairs," William continued, sounding much in his speech like the man who had raised him in his early years, though already he had begun to pick up words of the people to whom he was born. "And that what I'm about to say reflects ill upon my honor. But look you, I'm no longer that person who fled into the arms of an army that has ravaged my . . . people. Whoever that man was."

Though it was clear to Good Voice he was finding this talk hard to hear, Reginald Aubrey nodded for him to continue. She didn't miss the brief softening of her son's face before it firmed again.

"I'm told I've had another name. He-Is-Taken, my parents called me all the years they waited for my return. Now I am to have a new name, and my mother has asked me to remain with her here. That is what I mean to do for now. Stay in Kanowalohale. 'Tis here, and only here, that I can come to know this person to be called Bright Arrow."

Murmurs erupted from those gathered in her lodge. Good Voice glanced around at all their faces. Strikes-The-Water looked surprised by William's words, but happy. Over Reginald Aubrey's face the feelings moved swiftly: resignation, regret, acceptance. Good Voice sighed for him in her spirit. The path his actions long ago had placed him on was not an easy one and never would be, but Creator had given him a good, strong woman to walk it with him now. A man could do much, become much, with such a woman beside him.

Good Voice caught Lydia's gaze and nodded, sending her encouragement without the need for words, thinking as Lydia nodded back, *It is not finished, this healing. This good that is coming of all the bad things. It will go on and be completed in time.*

Anna Catherine stepped forward. "I'll miss you, William, but I'm glad you'll stay, and I hope one day to better know this man, my brother, Bright Arrow—to know him very well."

William opened his arms to her, then looked across her head at Two Hawks. Good Voice felt a melting in her chest as her sons shared a grin that rose crooked at the same corner, making them look so alike, their mother could only stare from one to the other and marvel. And feel yet another sorrow. In a couple of moon's time, Two Hawks would be leaving her, going to live in that world where men were often unkind, even cruel, to such as he. But not all. Not Aubrey. And she would see him again. There would be much passing back and forth between their families now.

Beside her, her husband's uncle stepped forward and raised his hand, a gesture to draw attention and command silence. Clear Day did not often make speeches, but Good Voice sensed one coming now. Anna released William and returned to Two Hawks. He pulled her to his side, and she nestled beneath his arm as the old man, deep sadness etched into his face, cleared his throat and began.

"Listen, my family. I am going to speak to you, in the place and, I think, with the heart and words of that one who is no longer with us." The old man paused, a sheen gathering in his eyes, then continued, "We have in these days seen much of grief and the breaking of bonds. There was a thing called the Covenant Chain between the Haudenosaunee and the British. That is a thing that has been broken for us. And the Confederacy of the Six Nations is a chain that has been broken. But *Gayanashagowa*—The Great Binding Law—is a tree that has not been toppled. My heart hopes one day our peoples will be united again beneath its sheltering branches, though it be a long path coming to it."

Good Voice pressed her lips together, reminded of the terrible thing done at Oriska. As they'd trickled back to sift through charred remains, the anger of the People had grown, their need for vengeance sharpening. There would be retribution against Thayendanegea and the Mohawks. And not just from her people. All along the valley of the Mohawk River, white families were burying their dead and vowing revenge. How long would they be forced to travel round that dark and bloody circle?

Clear Day's voice, cracked with age but strong with confidence, cut through her worrisome thoughts.

"But it is another chain of which I mean to talk about now. One that is not broken. It is a chain of friendship between two families." He spread his arms wide, rope-veined hands extended. "I see it in the faces shining in the light of this fire. It is a chain forged through sorrow and pain, but it has come through that fire bright with hope and love. I think in time it will grow brighter as some hearts heal."

He looked steadily at her eldest son, then at Reginald.

"We have cause to mourn, but we also have cause to rejoice, for Creator has restored our lost one at last, and soon the family of Good Voice of the Turtle Clan and the family of Aubrey will be united in heart and in blood."

Anna Catherine, crying openly, and Two Hawks shared a lingering look. Good Voice felt the tears come to her own eyes, helpless to stop them, as she watched her son wipe away those from Anna Catherine's cheeks. She wrapped her hands around her swollen belly, feeling the child within kick and turn, and the heart above the unborn one burned with its aching. *Oh, my husband, that you should not be here to witness this, to hear these words, to see the child that is to come . . .*

Stone Thrower had seen his firstborn. Spoken to him. Touched him. Bright Arrow had told her everything, every word that passed between him and his father and brother at Oriska, during the journey to rescue Aubrey, and in that dreadful clearing. She would hold these words as treasures in her heart, as she once held the words Two Hawks shared about the boy called William Aubrey, told to him by Anna Catherine. And she would not rage against her husband's fate. She would not proclaim it unfair. She would believe, she would hope, that all things, even this, would weave together for good for her. For her sons. And for this new child to be born into a world that was changing so fast it threatened daily to throw her off her feet.

"The path Creator has laid for us to walk," Clear Day went on, as though he'd read her thoughts, "has not been an easy path. Not always straight. And it will not be easy in the coming days. But when Creator said He would make rough ways smooth, I believe He was not talking about moving us to an easy path. He meant He was going to make our stride long enough, our legs strong enough, to carry us through. And when we reach our limits, He puts us on His back and He carries us and shields our eyes and hearts from that which would destroy our souls."

Good Voice murmured her approval and wept a little more over these good, strong words of her husband's uncle.

They waited to be sure Clear Day was finished saying all he meant to say, then Reginald stepped forward. He held three strands of white beads, the wampum given in the greatest act of forgiveness Good Voice expected ever to witness. He raised them so all could see, a symbol of the covenant chain between them.

"Daniel Clear Day, your words are life and healing to me." Aubrey paused, struggled with emotion, and cleared his throat. "Look you, I know 'tis not your custom to name the dead, but I will name him now and give him the honor he is due, for it was Caleb Stone Thrower who forged this chain of friendship through his obedience to the Almighty, through his mercy, through many prayers for my soul, and through his sacrifice . . ."

Again he paused, and Good Voice was astounded at the softening in the man, the love he had come to feel for her husband.

"May the grace and forgiveness he offered me be the pattern by which we live our lives from this day forward. May that same spirit always shine in our hearts. And in the hearts of our children," Reginald Aubrey concluded.

Iyo. They were fitting words for this sacred moment, this moment of remembering and looking ahead. Good Voice of the Turtle Clan looked around her lodge at all the shining faces, but it was those of her sons, and the women who had chosen them—though her firstborn was likely unaware of it as yet—that pulled the strings of her heart with the surest strength. In them she could see the promise of children to come—a promise to which her soul clung.

And so she stepped forward, a hand resting on the child in her belly, and to all the good words already said added, "In the hearts of our children, and their children's children, like a fiery arrow may it shine and point the way."

EPILOGUE

June 1778
Aubrey farm

*T*he wedding was held on a clear summer day that promised to wax warm with morning's passing. Few friends had elected to be present— recent frontier raids by the war chief, Brant, had turned the hearts of many against all Indians, even those Oneidas loyal to the Americans—but they were surrounded by family, hers and his. Soon to be *theirs*. As Papa placed her hand in Two Hawks's, declaring to the attending minister he gave her willingly to be married, and she faced her husband-to-be, his strong brown hands clasping hers, Anna glanced round at those crowded into Papa's sitting room to witness their vows.

Good Voice wore her best and brightest garments, silver in her hair and on her arms and ears, beads around her neck. Her daughter, Autumn Moon, watched the proceedings nestled against her mother's shoulder, with eyes like polished brown pebbles beneath a cap of silky black hair. Beside them stood the Doyles, Lydia, and Strikes-The-Water, lovely and skittish—it was her first time inside a white man's house. Standing next to her was William, or Bright Arrow, as he preferred now to be called. This day marked his first visit to the farm since the night he learned of his true heritage and rode away in furious rejection of it. Rejection had transformed into acceptance, and, over the months, an embracing of his Oneida identity, an acceptance forged through joy and sorrow.

Stone Thrower's absence was keenly felt this day, though with nearly a year passed, the time of formal grieving had been set aside, freeing Two

Hawks at last to marry. His family had arrived yesterday, when Anna, Lydia, and Maura Doyle had been up to their ears in cooking, baking, and last-minute stitching to the embroidered cream gown Anna now wore. There had been insufficient time yet to talk to William or to coo over his baby sister, born in the Moon of Giving Thanks. Anna didn't know if William had yet spoken to Papa, beyond the courteous greeting she'd witnessed. Even now a prayer crossed the edges of her mind. *Let it be today* . . .

Papa left her to stand beside Lydia, who took his arm, smiling up at him. Anna thought the smile looked strained. Little wonder, vastly pregnant as she was with Papa's child who, by Lydia's calculation, was a week late in making its natal appearance. Beneath her gown Lydia went barefoot, her feet too swollen to fit her shoes.

Anna made a mental note to remind her stepmother to rest, once the ceremony was done. She would talk with them all, embrace them all, laugh and cry and remember with them all, but now her gaze settled on Two Hawks, who had never looked away from her, as the minister led them through the vows to love and cherish.

Lips speaking . . . hearts pledging . . . a part of Anna seemed to stand apart from it all, seeing the man before her in exquisite detail: brushed brown coat and matching breeches, the cloth at his neck white against the skin of his throat; hair grown long around his handsome face, raked back in a queue, glossy as wet ink; full lips curved with happiness, showing straight white teeth as he spoke; eyes clear beneath the strong line of his brows, seeing only her. Seeing her as only he had ever done. *Bear's Heart.*

She thought of how they used to look at one another, meeting as children at the wood's edge—unabashedly fascinated by the new, the strange. Now she saw all the ways they were the same, and the way he was looking at her, with a promise of long-awaited intimacy that tingled through her and found its echo deep within, a resounding yes, and yes, and *yes.*

Two Hawks slipped a ring onto her finger, the silver metal warm from his hand, and pledged to her all that ever would be his. Then the minister was praying, pronouncing them bound forever in the eyes of the Almighty and those witnessing: Jonathan and Anna Catherine Aubrey.

Voices then. Laughter. Her husband's dazzling smile . . .

Papa was the first to embrace her. "Anna Aubrey. My dear girl." She hugged him tight, whispering words she'd said many times in recent months. "Thank you, Papa."

Then Lydia stood before her, biting her lower lip and smiling.

Or was it a grimace? Anna hugged her tight from the side and was startled when Lydia didn't quite stifle a groan. The daze of happiness cleared like mist before a stiff wind. She placed a practiced hand on the swollen belly between them.

"Lydia? Are you . . . ?" She felt the telltale tension in her stepmother's flesh. "You *are*."

Papa, talking with Two Hawks, caught Anna's tone, looked their way, and blanched. "Lydia?"

Clearly mortified, Lydia admitted, "I was trying to hold on. I didn't want to spoil your—" The last words were bitten off between clenched teeth.

Anna didn't know whether to hug Lydia or shake her. "How close in time are the pains? Has your water broken? No, you couldn't have hidden that. You didn't, did you?"

Lydia shook her head. "It hasn't broken yet."

Two Hawks was at her shoulder. "Bear's Heart. What can I do?"

"Look after Papa?" She met his gaze with longing, hating to abandon him, but a baby didn't take the convenience of its midwife into account when deciding to be born. Anna kissed her husband's mouth, lingering briefly, then sought his understanding with her eyes.

He gave it. "You are the one she needs. Go."

She didn't go alone. As she propelled Lydia toward the bedroom,

Maura Doyle was on her heels, having seen what was afoot and run to the kitchen for water and kettles and towels.

Anna glanced back once at the scene of her wedding, at the guests and minister standing about the room, and saw Good Voice hand her daughter over to Strikes-The-Water, coming to join them.

He tried to be the attentive host, to encourage their guests to partake of the bride's cake and refreshments laid out on the table decorated with loops of tiny white paper chains, but Reginald was undone. He found himself gazing at the shut bedroom door, in agony for Lydia's agony, unable to prevent his thoughts winging back to a dim hospital casemate full of the dying . . .

God in heaven, have mercy.

He wasn't certain how he made it outside. Rowan and Two Hawks had to do with it; they stood one to either side of him in the yard while he drew gulps of air and his heartbeat settled, his mind cleared.

"Better?" Two Hawks asked.

"A bit."

"I thought you would go over into the cake."

Reginald smiled at the bridegroom, barely married before his bride abandoned him to her calling, but felt the effort sag. "'Tis not what either of us expected today, is it?"

Two Hawks gripped his arm. "Anna Catherine is with her. And my mother and Mrs. Doyle."

He didn't say all would be well. He'd merely named Lydia's allies in her battle. And formidable allies they were. Reginald was more reassured than he'd have been by empty promises.

They waited. Others came and went, talking to him in the yard. Ephraim Lang. A few of their crewman who had known them long. A few neighbors who took their leave with proffered prayers and words of encouragement. Two Hawks saw them away, performing the duties of a host, taking up the slack Reginald had let fall.

An hour passed. Then another. Reginald paced the yard, sat, paced again, refused to eat. Once he heard a babe's wailing and wrenched up off his seat on a fence rail with his hip protesting, only to realize it had been Good Voice's daughter.

Sometime after that, Two Hawks came out again and sat beside him, strong hands braced on his knees. He'd removed his coat and rolled the sleeves of his shirt off his forearms. "Mrs. Doyle says all is well thus far. It is a first baby for her, so it can take much time. We are praying."

Reginald grasped the young man's shoulder in a brief squeeze. Barely a month had passed since Two Hawks had returned from General Washington's camp at Valley Forge, where he'd gone in April with nearly two hundred Oneida warriors. They'd fought with the Continentals and acquitted themselves well at a place called Barren Hill. Again and again the Oneidas had amazed him with their sacrifice and dedication to their chosen allies in this seemingly unending war. Though conflicts had sprung up like wildfires all over the frontier, no further reprisals on the scale of Oriska had fallen from the hands of their fellow Iroquois since last summer's cruel destruction, but it had been a difficult winter for the Oneidas. Many warriors had scouted instead of hunting, and no one felt safe, not those who went out or those left vulnerable and hungry at home. And yet when the call came in spring of that year to join General Washington in the east, the Oneidas had answered.

Reginald hadn't expected Two Hawks to go, until William came through Schenectady and urged him to it. It had been the first Reginald had set eyes on him since their parting the previous August. Arriving by canoe with the warriors of Kanowalohale, he'd been distinguishable from them only by his lighter skin, his full head of hair. William hadn't wanted to see Reginald but had visited with the women and his twin at the house they still maintained in town.

It had been hard for Anna to see the pair go off to war together, but Reginald was surprised at the wrench to his own heart. He grieved after William, worried for his safety, yearned to fulfill his seemingly impossible promise to Stone Thrower to be a father to both the lads, yet he found his worry for Two Hawks just as deep. It was good to have him back, safe and whole. Good to see his Anna so happy on this day. Good, too, to see the bond that had formed between the brothers during that brief campaign, even as he was forced to watch from a distance, still waiting. Hoping.

Where was William, come to that? Reginald thought he'd seen him with Rowan, headed down toward the barn. That seemed hours ago.

"Sir," said Two Hawks, pushing off the fence rail to his feet.

Reginald looked up, blinded by the sun, high now in the west. Two Hawks was gazing past him. Reginald swiveled to look, and there was William standing in the lane, a stick in hand.

Not a stick. A bow.

It was a surreal moment, seeing the pair of them, Two Hawks in his wedding clothes, William in a calico shirt that would have stood out as garish on the streets of Schenectady even without the silver armbands constricting its billowy sleeves and an equally colorful sash belting his trim waist, a breechclout and leggings, beaded moccasins on his feet, hair tied back with feathers.

Bright Arrow.

Reginald stood, observing some silent communication pass between the brothers that had Two Hawks stepping away, going into the house, leaving him alone with William for the first time in nearly two years.

"I would speak with you, sir." William's tone was respectful, under-girded with a confidence Reginald didn't remember the last time he'd heard him speak, in his mother's lodge last August. "But first I need to give you this. I was waiting until after the wedding."

He held out the bow. Only then did Reginald see that it wasn't an

Oneida bow. It was Welsh. And old. "I thought it lost," he said, reaching for it. "Before General Arnold broke the siege at Stanwix."

"It was," William confirmed. "Taken in that sortie while the battle was underway. After the siege was lifted and St. Leger cleared out, I went to the fort and found Sam Reagan."

Reginald was glad to hear the name. "How is our rascal Sam?"

That made William smile wryly. "You know Sam. He's landed on his feet as always. But he helped me find the bow, still among some of the plunder taken out of Sir John's camp, stored away in a corner. No one had claimed it. I did."

Reginald hefted the bow, one he'd shot as a lad in Breconshire. In another lifetime. It must seem so for William as well. "Thank you," he said. He looked up to find William staring at him with that disconcerting blue gaze.

"That isn't all I wished to say."

Reginald nodded him on, heart thudding.

"I wanted to say I've made my decision. I'm going to stay with the People. My people." William looked aside. Reginald followed his gaze. The young Tuscarora woman he'd first seen in the woods near the Seneca camp last summer, Strikes-The-Water, had come out of the house, holding William's sister.

"I want you to know something else," William said. "Once all this fighting has passed and things begin to settle—and if it's still a thing a man can do in this country—I intend to finish what I began at Queens. I intend to read law. American law, perhaps."

Reginald felt his heart leap. "You mean to continue your studies?"

"I do," William said. "Whatever is coming, whatever this country will look like—under British rule or the states or Congress—it won't be easy for the Oneidas. Too much has changed, is changing, and I want to stand an advocate in whatever way I can. But this is what I want you to under-stand," he hurried on. "I see now that I could never have hoped to do such a thing without having been to Oxford, for having seen what I have of the world, and what my place in it could be."

"William," Reginald said, regret thick in his voice. "You know that if I had it to do over again—"

William held up a hand, a deliberate gesture that reminded him strikingly of Stone Thrower. "No more regret. That's what I'm trying to say to you, sir. That I'm thankful for all you provided for me, thankful to you and to Mother."

Heledd. The reminder of her jarred. Had she been better off never knowing? Was she happy, those last years in Wales? He prayed she'd found peace. And then all thought of his first wife was swept from his mind by the sight of William holding out his hand.

"Will you take my hand, sir?"

Still clutching the bow, too choked to speak, Reginald grasped William's outstretched hand and held it tightly.

"If I continue with the law, I would do so as William Aubrey, if you will permit still the use of the name."

Reginald's hand froze in that of his son's. He found his voice as quickly as he could, though it was but a croak, so gripping was his relief. "Yes. Yes, by all means. I would be pleased if you would."

Their gazes held, William's blue eyes vivid in his sun-browned face, and the moment stretched taut with fragile promise before a shout was heard, coming from across the fields of knee-high corn. Breaking clasp and gaze, they turned to see Daniel Clear Day coming down the track from the creek.

Over the past year, the wiry old warrior had made more than one journey to Fort Niagara as part of Oneida peace delegations, in the hope of convincing the Haudenosaunee nations to cease their warring. Such efforts had thus far come to nothing. He'd been late in returning from one such trip when the rest of Good Voice's family made the journey east for the wedding. They'd come with worry for him. Though he'd missed the wedding, Reginald felt relief to see him. But as the man drew near, he read something in the creased and leathery face that caused his heart to skip a beat.

"There is news out of Niagara?" he asked, striding toward Clear Day to meet him in the yard. But the man shook his head.

"I do not bring news about this war but about that one who gave his life for you." Clear Day looked from Reginald to William. "About that one who was your father."

Stone Thrower.

William lurched forward and took his father's uncle by the arm. "News? What news could there be?"

And could it be anything but evil? Reginald suddenly wanted to stop the old man's mouth. If he'd found out the gruesome details of Stone Thrower's death last autumn at the hands of those Seneca warriors, this was surely not the day for sharing it.

Clear Day caught the alarm in his gaze and again shook his head. "No. Of his dying I will not speak, only this. While in Niagara, I saw that one who took you captive in the battle. That one who chose my nephew over you and spared your life."

Blue-Tailed Lizard. The old Seneca warrior who had once professed himself a follower of Samuel Kirkland's God.

"The one who killed my father?" William asked, his voice tight with sudden pain. "You saw him? Spoke to him?"

"I did both of those things," Clear Day said. "And I have this from him. It is for you and for your mother."

From beneath his shirt, the old warrior pulled out a corded, bead-worked pouch and took it from around his neck. Reginald saw a light of recognition in William's blue eyes as he took it, then a rush of longing. He held the little pouch his mother had beaded and Stone Thrower had worn for months against his heart to his own chest a moment, then to his nose. He quickly opened it and removed the tiny oval portrait of himself.

None of them spoke for a time. Strikes-The-Water had crossed the yard to join them, Autumn Moon in her arms, and fetched up now beside William. She peered in silence at the miniature, then up at William's face, something of awe in her expression.

"I also have a story to tell, but where is my nephew's wife and your brother?" Clear Day asked William, for all his sober countenance a sense of anticipation thrumming through him, almost palpable. "They must hear it too."

All three started to explain in haste where everyone else was at present and what they were doing, but before they could finish, Anna came out of the house. Her hair was disheveled, her wedding gown changed for a workaday one. "Papa?"

Sight of her sent a jolt through Reginald like a dash of cold water. A hand took hold of his shoulder as if to steady him for whatever was to come. It was William's hand.

Seeing it, Anna broke into a tired smile. "We're all finished. Lydia's well, and so is your son. They're both very well."

Reginald felt his knees go out from under him, but William was there, supporting him until he found them again. He tried to speak. Couldn't.

Anna laughed. "Don't you want to come see him?"

He broke free of William's hold, limping toward his dear girl, who laughed again as he enveloped her in a hug. Then he was hurrying through the door, hearing her call out to those he'd left in the yard, "And you, Bright Arrow. And Strikes-The-Water. And Clear Day—you made it after all. Wonderful! Lydia is requesting everyone's attendance."

While they gave Reginald and Lydia a few moments to themselves, Clear Day, with lips that sometimes trembled thinly over the words, told them of his meeting with Blue-Tailed Lizard, who had seen him among the delegation of Oneidas at Niagara, approached him with caution, and taken him aside to tell him an astonishing thing.

"That one who chose my nephew as his prisoner, who stood by and allowed him to be killed, later had a thing happen to him that he did not foresee coming."

Good Voice drew a breath in deep, searching the face of her husband's uncle. She had seen the little portrait of Bright Arrow he had brought them, the one her husband had cherished and that her firstborn had hung around his neck. Now the old man's glance held hers, asking was she ready to hear what more he brought them.

Nodding, she braced herself.

"That one went back to his home at Ganundasaga, to his women there." Clear Day continued, "Instead of a captive, he brought them the story of my nephew, the things he said in that clearing, and how he died. And do you know what happened then? They began to weep, those women of his clan. They began to talk about what sort of man would do such a thing and why. They began to remember, not just things about my nephew when he lived among them, but about Kirkland and what he said to them, things they had once professed to believe—that they had opened their hearts to Creator through the blood of Jesus-on-the-cross. And now here is the thing about all of that: they have come back to believing. They walk the Jesus path again. Even that old lizard has found the path he once lost and is walking it again. This because of my nephew and what he said and did."

They were all in tears now, speechless, each grappling with thoughts and feelings. It was Two Hawks who gained possession of both first, and his face grew radiant as he slid his arm around Anna Catherine beside him. "Uncle, I am glad to know this about my father, that such good came of what he did. I am glad to have this news this day—though I would rather have him with us again."

"Amen," Good Voice whispered, standing there with the precious daughter her husband never had the chance to look upon held against her heart. Tears of joy and sorrow streamed onto her baby's head. "We will always wish him with us until we go to be with him. But here is a great good Heavenly Father has done through this thing that is still hard for us to bear. We will also remember our blessings. Both my sons are safe. Today one of those sons has a wife." She offered Anna Catherine a smile of welcome, thinking of her calm and steady presence in the room beyond, and all that had just happened. "Now a son is born to the family of that wife. Today we will have good thoughts, thoughts of peace, thoughts of hope for our future. So come, let us go and see this new son and tell his parents there is more good to be celebrated on this day."

They all filed into the room freshened now with clean linens and the window thrown wide to the warm June air. Sunlight streamed in, falling across Lydia, propped on pillows, hair streaming in dark banners around her face, a tiny swaddled infant asleep in her arms—and an ecstatic father sitting on the bedside near them, radiating pride and looking younger than any in the room had seen him look in a very long time.

Good Voice made room for Bright Arrow, Anna Catherine, Two Hawks, and Clear Day. Rowan and Maura Doyle squeezed in. Strikes-The-Water hung back at the doorway but came farther in at Bright Arrow's beckoning.

The full story of Stone Thrower's unexpected legacy among Blue-Tailed Lizard's family was told again at Lydia's request, then Reginald Aubrey, once he had gained mastery of his voice again, stood and with tears in his eyes said, "On this day that has been thrice blessed, by marriage . . ." He showered Anna Catherine and Two Hawks with a tender glance, then turned a similar one upon Bright Arrow. "By grace. And now by birth . . . I wanted all of you here to witness a thing."

"What will you call him, Papa?" Anna Catherine interjected. "Lydia wouldn't tell us."

"That's what we mean to tell you now." Reginald Aubrey's gaze traveled around the room, taking in each of them, but he couldn't keep his gaze long off the scrunched little face cradled in the crook of Lydia's arm. "We've decided to name him after the greatest man we know, a warrior both in body and in spirit."

Reginald bent to take up his newborn son from Lydia. He straightened, turned, and placed the baby into Clear Day's arms. As the old man raised startled eyes to him, Reginald said, "Will you stand in the place of one we wish was here with us?"

Beside her husband's uncle, Good Voice leaned close, looking eagerly at the baby's face, while Autumn Moon looked at the faces of the adults around her with wide, wondering eyes.

"His name is Caleb," Reginald told them in a voice gone husky.

Good Voice caught her breath. It was custom among the Haudenosaunee to requicken the name of a dead one, bestowing it upon another who would take his place in the clan—and his spirit. She knew that wasn't what was happening here, that her husband's spirit wasn't waiting to enter a new life but was safely worshiping in the presence of Jesus. Even so, the naming of this new child touched her more deeply than Aubrey could know.

"Caleb Aubrey," Anna Catherine said, smiling through gathering tears. "Papa, it's perfect."

"*Iyo,*" Good Voice said, and in her eyes joy and sorrow mingled. "It is a strong name."

"*Iyo,*" Two Hawks whispered and shared a look with his brother, who had been staring at the infant's tiny face, a lifetime of wondering in his gaze.

Eyes lowered to the baby in his arms, Clear Day said, "I speak for my nephew when I say that we will teach this little one, all our little ones, to walk a good path."

"We will point the way for them," Good Voice said. "And for their children, should we live to see them, then trust their way to Heavenly Father's guiding."

"For seven generations?" They turned to see Lydia watching from the bed, blue eyes ringed with the shadows of her labor but shining all the same.

Good Voice looked down at the newborn in Clear Day's embrace, and the sorrow fled her smile. "For as long as our names last on this earth," she said, then raised her gaze from her husband's namesake and fixed it on Reginald Aubrey, "your God shall be our God, and our blood shall be one."

AUTHOR'S NOTES AND ACKNOWLEDGMENTS

The Oneida Nation's contributions to American independence didn't end with the Battle of Oriskany. British and pro-British Indian raids continued on the New York frontier long after August 6, 1777. Settlements at Schoharie, Cherry Valley, German Flatts, and everywhere in between were devastated. Though by spring of 1780 the Oneida town of Kanowalohale still stood, its inhabitants knew its threatened destruction was inevitable. That summer the town was abandoned. Elders, children, women, and those warriors not busy scouting for the Continental army moved what could be carried and what livestock could be driven to Fort Stanwix, abandoning most of their possessions, homes, and crops. Soon after, Joseph Brant led a party of three hundred warriors to Kanowalohale, burned the town, then advanced to Fort Stanwix, where the Oneidas took refuge inside the fort. After briefly firing on the fort, Brant's warriors rounded up the livestock outside its walls and left. Still committed to the Patriot's cause, the Oneidas chose to relocate temporarily to Schenectady, farther from the troubled frontier. While warriors assisted the Continentals, or risked roaming the wilderness hunting for desperately needed meat, their women and children lived in an old barracks in town, lacking firewood, their clothing in tatters, traumatized by loss and destitution. Unable to face a harsh winter with no provisions, many Oneidas moved again to Saratoga for the winter of 1780–1781, where at least they could obtain food, shelter, and warmth.

General Philip Schuyler tried to help. Due to widespread raiding in the Mohawk Valley, food was in short supply, farms ruined, livestock slaughtered or stolen. The year 1781 saw Schuyler personally funding purchase of food and clothing for the people. Through all this hardship, most

Oneida warriors remained true to the Continentals, gaining exemplary reputations among Patriot soldiers. Here are just a few of their contributions post-Oriskany:

> **September–October 1777:** Oneida warriors joined the Continentals to fight Burgoyne's army at Saratoga and Freeman's Farm, culminating in Burgoyne's surrender on October 17.
>
> **Spring 1778:** At George Washington's invitation, Oneida and Tuscarora warriors joined his army at Valley Forge, near Philadelphia, as scouts and skirmishers, bringing a supply of corn to share with the starving American troops.
>
> **May 1778:** Under the command of the Marque de Lafayette, Oneida warriors fought in the Battle of Barren Hill, to great praise from their commander. Six warriors gave their lives.
>
> **September 1778:** Oneida and Tuscarora warriors raided the British/loyalist frontier stronghold of Unadilla while Joseph Brant and his raiders, who used Unadilla as a staging ground, were destroying homes along the Mohawk at Fort Dayton.

Despite devastating material losses and deep emotional scars sustained over breaking with their Iroquois brethren in their loyalties, Oneidas would continue to risk their lives and their families' safety to support the Continental army as soldiers, scouts, and guards until the war's ending. Notable individuals encountered in my research, like Skenandoah, Louis Cook, Two-Kettles-Together, and Ahnyero/Thomas Spencer, were far too many to list, much less to have worked into a novel of this limited scope. For readers interested in learning more about this pivotal time in history and the role the Oneidas played in it, I've provided a list of my most helpful resources at the end of this section.

Speaking of historical characters, the dialogue attributed to recognizable individuals in these pages was taken from many sources—journals or recorded words wherever possible. Where dialogue is of my own creation,

I've taken care to put words in the mouth of an individual I felt they would have said under the circumstances in which they appear. That being said, this story left the fate of some historical characters hanging post-Oriskany.

General Nicholas Herkimer, gravely wounded in the battle, reached his home at the Little Falls Carry on the Mohawk River, where his injured and infected leg was amputated. The operation was poorly done; Herkimer died of his injury on August 16, 1777.

Captain Stephen Watts was left for dead in the western ravine but survived, his wounds untreated, for three days before he was found by a patrol and brought to St. Leger's siege camp. He also lost a leg but recovered to serve in a limited capacity during the rest of the war. He died in 1810.

Kanowalohale was rebuilt and reoccupied, in conditions described as deplorable, in 1784, after the war had ended. Soon after, like the Haudenosaunee nations that supported the British, the Oneidas began to lose their homeland piecemeal to white settlement pressures and their own attempts to adapt to European ways of living. Beginning in 1823, Oneidas purchased land in and relocated to Wisconsin, until what once had been a near six-million-acre homeland in the new state of New York dwindled to thirty-two acres. In more recent decades, Oneidas have begun reclaiming portions of their ancient homeland through land purchases and court battles. The Oneidas now encompass three distinct groups, the Oneida Tribe of Wisconsin, the Oneida Nation of the Thames (Ontario, Canada), and the Oneida Indian Nation of New York.

The great rift in the Haudenosaunee was slow to mend, but mend it did. In the early 1800s the council fire was rekindled among the Six Nations survivors, and the Iroquois League was reformed. The Central Fire now burns among its traditional keepers, the Onondagas, and each nation sends their representative sachems to the council. The Haudenosaunee are sovereign nations and have fought as such in nearly every American war since the Revolution—as allies of the United States and warriors protecting their homeland and people.

An additional historical note: During the Revolutionary War, Fort Stanwix was renamed Fort Schuyler in honor of General Philip Schuyler, in command of the Northern Department of the Continental army during most of the period this novel covers. After the war the fort reverted to its original name. To avoid confusion, I chose to stick with its original name of Fort Stanwix.

As for that flag hoisted inside the fort during the siege, legend has it that it was the first time what became known as our national flag was flown. Maybe it was. Maybe it wasn't. I chose to portray it so.

For details of the Battle of Oriskany and the events of the months leading up to it, I drew upon many written sources, which sometimes disagreed on dates, times, participants, and other particulars. I chose to follow most closely the account found in *Rebellion in the Mohawk Valley* by Gavin K. Watt, because his prose most excited my imagination and helped me see the events of history from an emotional as well as historical perspective—important in the writing of a novel. But many other resources contributed to my vision of the New York frontier of 1776–77. Most helpful were:

> *Forgotten Allies: The Oneida Indians and the American Revolution* by Joseph T. Glatthaar and James Kirby Martin
>
> *With Musket & Tomahawk* by Michael O. Logusz
>
> *The Battle of Oriskany and General Nicholas Herkimer* by Paul A. Boehlert
>
> *Liberty March: The Battle of Oriskany* by Allan D. Foote
>
> *Fort Stanwix: Construction and Military History, Historic Furnishing Study, and Historic Structure Report* from the Office of Park Historic Preservation, National Park Service, U.S. Department of the Interior

Days of Siege: A Journal of the Siege of Fort Stanwix in 1777,
by William Colbrath and Larry Lowenthal

Along with my heartfelt thanks to the authors of the above works, and to the Oneida Nation, I'm grateful once again for the team I'm blessed to work with at WaterBrook Multnomah, the many people whose keen eyes and dedication to their craft helped make this novel what it is—Shannon Marchese, Nicci Jordan Hubert, and Laura Wright, my talented and hard-working editors.

Kristopher Orr, you created another gorgeous cover, bless you!

To Wendy Lawton, my agent—thank you for being a friend and prayer warrior as well as a cheerleader and shepherd of my writing career. I've lost count of the times you've done exceedingly abundantly above all I could ask or imagine.

Thanks, Jeane Wynn, for your encouragement and for helping me get the Pathfinders series into readers' hands.

Jodi Eleck, thanks for letting me borrow Autumn Moon's beautiful name.

Doree Ross, Nancy Jensen, and Capri Mulder, thank you for the blessing of your friendship and for doing the intense, demanding, and love-soaked work of raising up sons and daughters who desire to follow God's good path through life. My heart is full because you've let me come alongside you to pray for them through struggles and victories, and to watch them launch into their adult lives, bright arrows for Him.

And to a brave and faithful warrior I'm honored to know, Andrew Budek-Schmeisser, who inadvertently wrote some of the final words of this story—thank you for allowing me to put those words into the mouth of Daniel Clear Day: "He . . . make[s] our stride long enough, our legs strong enough, to carry us through. And when we reach our limits, He puts us on His back and He carries us." He does indeed, Andrew, and you are a shining example of that.

READERS GUIDE

Thus saith the LORD, Stand ye in the ways,
and see, and ask for the old paths, where is the
good way, and walk therein, and ye shall find
rest for your souls.

— Jeremiah 6:16

1. Scripture speaks of the paths we choose to walk. Read Psalm 16:11; 27:11; 119:35; 143:8; and Proverbs 2:9; 4:14–17. What are the promises God makes to those who seek to walk in His path of righteousness? Think about the characters in the Pathfinders series: Good Voice, Stone Thrower, Reginald, Lydia, Anna, Two Hawks, and William. Choose one word to describe each character's path through these books.

2. Good Voice's path encompassed long seasons of waiting, through which she clung to faith and hope in a heavenly Father who could, and would, bring healing and restoration to her shattered family. Has there been a season, perhaps when a dream was dashed, when you trusted that God is good and has good plans for you—no matter what? Encourage someone who may be struggling to trust by sharing your story!

3. For years Stone Thrower walked a path of bitterness, yet God enabled him to forgive Reginald Aubrey through an act of obedience. Have you forgiven someone who wronged you when it was the last thing you felt like doing? What happened in your heart when you did? Why do you think Scripture places such importance on our forgiving one another?

4. Just like our salvation is a work of grace, so is our sanctification. Why do you think it took so long for Reginald to understand he could

never atone for his sins, or to believe he was forgiven and welcomed by God to rest in the finished work of the Cross? Have you ever caught yourself thinking (or acting as if) your sanctification or atonement was based on your performance?

5. Lydia was a woman of conviction and faith, yet she wasn't immune to thinking God's will in the lives of her loved ones must be accomplished by her strength, on her timetable. If you've ever rushed ahead of God when you were certain of the path He'd set for you, what did you learn about patience and trust through that experience?

6. Anna's path in this book took an unexpectedly dark emotional turn when she failed to heed Two Hawks's exhortation to honor her father. Why do you think God instructs us in His Word to honor our parents? Have you struggled to honor a parent or grandparent, or someone else placed in authority over you? Have you experienced blessing or fruitfulness in a relationship through honor?

7. Two Hawks was concerned with finding a path to a life with Anna Catherine. Finding William to gain her father's favor seemed the answer, but he continually found the way forward blocked by circumstances or the choices of others. Have you had to be still and wait when the way forward was hidden or in question? What did you learn about trust, patience, and God's sovereignty during that season?

8. William came to regret his hasty choice to abandon his life and family. If you've made a rash decision you wished you could undo, know that God can take even what we sow in the flesh and use it for good. Has He done this in your life? In what way specifically?

9. "But when Creator said He would make rough ways smooth, I believe He was not talking about moving us to an easy path. He meant He was going to make our stride long enough, our legs strong enough, to carry us through." Do you agree with these words of Daniel Clear Day? Why or why not? If you agree, in what ways have they been lived out in your life?

Glossary

Oneida/Iroquois words

Satahuhsíyost—Listen

iyo—good

Onyota'a:ka—People of the Standing Stone, the Oneidas

Kanien'kehá:ka—People of the Flint, the Mohawk

Haudenosaunee—the Longhouse People, the Six Nations of the Iroquois

o-kee-wa'h—farewell

o'sluni'kéha'—white ways

a'no:wál—turtle; Turtle Clan

Náhte' yesa:yáts—What is your name?

shekoli—a greeting

kawʌniyó—a good word

a'sluni—white person

Kunolúhkwa—I love you

ONEIDA 13 MOON CALENDAR

Moon	Month
	approximate correspondence
Snow Moon	January
Midwinter Moon	February
Half-Day Moon	March
Thundering Moon	April
Planting Moon	May
Strawberry Moon	June
Green Bean Moon	July
Green (or New) Corn Moon	August
Harvest Moon	September
Storing Moon	October
Giving Thanks Moon	November
Hunting Moon	December
Long Night Moon	

ABOUT THE AUTHOR

LORI BENTON was raised east of the Appalachian Mountains, surrounded by early American history going back three hundred years. Her novels transport readers to the eighteenth century, where she brings to life the colonial and early federal periods of American history. These include *Burning Sky*, recipient of three Christy Awards; *The Pursuit of Tamsen Littlejohn*, an ECPA Christian Book Award finalist; and the first book in this series, *The Wood's Edge*. When Lori isn't writing, reading, or researching, she enjoys exploring the Oregon wilderness with her husband and learning to play the cello.

CULTURES COLLIDE.
CAN TWO FAMILIES
SURVIVE THE IMPACT?

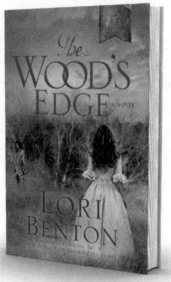

Book 1 of the Pathfinders series begins when British Major Reginald
Aubrey steals a baby from an Oneida woman. He cannot anticipate the
devastating consequences. He may never overcome his guilt. She may never
overcome her heartache. The people who love them long for redemption,
for reconciliation, for vengeance. Can a path forward be found?

WATERBROOK PRESS
www.waterbrookmultnomah.com